HARRY NAVINSKI

THE KEY TO MURDER

BOOK 3 IN THE DCI SUZANNA MCLEOD SERIES

Contents

The Key to Murder

DCI Suzanna McLeod Crime Series Book 3

Tuesday, 3rd March

Chapter 1

Mary trudged through the unexpected snow that had fallen the previous night, not realising the snap back to winter was prophetic. It crunched underfoot, crispy from the frost that came when the clouds had cleared and the moon shone through, casting its blue light on the deserted streets. It wasn't usual for this much snow to fall in March, but an Icelandic airflow had brought a dumping like they'd not seen in years. Her black flatties were unsuited to the conditions; were like ice skates on her feet. Very poor, uncontrollable skates. She stamped her chilled feet in a futile attempt to warm them. She shivered. But it was more than just the cold temperature. Her spirit sensed something was wrong. She walked on, cautiously.

A woollen, hand-knitted, tea-cosy-like hat covered Mary's head, protecting her ears from the icy air. Her overcoat flapped, her knees chilled by the freezing breeze, as she crossed the road and walked up to the Edwardian, bay-windowed, stone-built terraced house. With some effort, she prised off the combination-locked key safe cover, attached to the wall next to the front door. She extracted the Yale key and unlocked the maroon hardwood door, its paint now peeling and dirty. As the door opened, she breathed in familiar odours: pee, stale air, unwashed carpets and stair-lift gear grease.

She enjoyed visiting Mr White. Despite being unable to walk more than a few paces or do much for himself, he remained positive, replying to enquiries after his health with, "Not bad, dear, not bad. At least I'm still here, unlike most of my peers." She'd heard all his saucy jokes many times, but she still smiled or laughed at them. George's eyes shone when he smiled. It lightened her day to see his beaming face.

"Hello, Mr White. It's Mary," she called out as she entered. "I'll be with you in a minute." She pulled off her sheepskin gloves and slipped out of the woollen herringbone coat, leaving on her shoes, before clomping across the hard hall floor into the carpeted living room.

Mr White's chair faced away from the door towards the TV, where a chat-show host prattled on at an excessively high volume about mildly controversial matters. 'Was it important for children to have routine in their lives and consistency in standards expected of them? Of course it was,' Mary thought. 'Surely it's obvious?'

Noisy TVs were the norm in most of her clients' houses. Their hearing had diminished over the years and the volume turned up to compensate. Even those with hearing aids rarely wore them because they'd broken them or had dropped them somewhere and couldn't see them with their failing eyesight and immobility. "Mr White... George," Mary said, raising her voice as she approached him, expecting to see his smiling face.

"Oh, dear!" Mary exclaimed when she saw George, his face pallid, his chin on his chest. She touched his neck and found it to be cold and pulse-less. Mr White's winter had arrived, along with the Arctic weather. A tear trickled from the corner of her right eye.

She turned off the TV and withdrew her mobile phone from her bag to call the care coordinator. She'd miss George. As she turned back, she noticed a red splodge on George's chest – a horizontal slit in his sleeveless jumper and a bloodstain surrounding the area. George had *not* died naturally. Someone had pushed him from October into deep December.

Chapter 2

Mary didn't know what to do with herself. She worried about how George's death might affect her. Would they think she'd murdered him? She'd seen many a film and TV series where the person reporting the crime became the prime suspect.

A knock came at the door, relieving her mind of the stress. She opened it and saw a marked police car parked outside the house; its uniformed occupant standing on the pavement looking towards her. A plain-clothed officer stood in front of her, his eyes level with hers, despite being on a lower step. His bronze-brown wavy hair was short at the sides, longer on top. His trimmed beard matched the colour of his hair, masking his prominent chin.

"Mary Proctor?" the officer asked.

"Aye, that's me." The officer was muscular and lean and had a confident demeanour.

"Detective Sergeant Rab Sinclair, Edinburgh CID." He showed her his police identity card, then put it back in his pocket as she acknowledged him.

"You'd best come in, Sergeant. He's through there," she said, pointing to the open doorway to their left.

DS Sinclair instructed her to stay outside the room now as it was a crime scene and informed her the CSI team would be along shortly. They'd need to take evidence from her to match with what might be found – fingerprints and DNA. He donned plastic shoe covers before entering the living room. Rab wasn't feeling great, having drunk a few beers with his pals the night before. His stomach felt bloated. He squeezed his buttocks together to stop himself from passing wind. He didn't dare contaminate the crime scene that would soon be occupied by CSI officers.

***

Mary was restless. She couldn't enter any other rooms and wasn't allowed to leave, so she shuffled impatiently from one foot to the other like an Antarctic penguin. Her mind drifted to the weekend before, when little faces had brought light and laughter into her dreary life. Mary's children were now in their thirties and had children of their own. Her grandchildren. She loved it when they came to stay. Enjoyed their innocence and avid desire to learn by asking questions and exploring everything they came across. She wished her children had not moved away, so she could see them more often.

Her mind returned to the present. 'I hope they find others to call on my clients.' She imagined them watching the time pass too slowly, doing the wee-wee dance in their chairs, going hungry and thirsty. Although the stay-at-home care system was considered, for many, a better option than going into care homes – which were often impersonal, institutionalised and hugely expensive – It was times like these when it sometimes failed the people reliant on their care. Even without problems like this one, Mary knew some of the company's clients were put to bed at just after 6 pm and not visited until 10 am the next day – sixteen hours in bed, with no toilet. Some of them wet the bed because they couldn't hold it any longer. It was so degrading for them.

But at least they had the consistency of carers who called every day, rather than an ever-changing mix of strangers, called in from areas of high unemployment for brief periods, to fill the care home staffing

THE KEY TO MURDER

gaps. She knew one elderly lady – well had known her before she passed away last year – who had a different male attendant every week, hoisting her onto the toilet, pulling her knickers down and seeing her white pubic triangle and her muscle-less flabby bottom, all privacy taken away, all dignity stolen by the decay of age.

***

The victim's chin rested on his chest. Rab looked closer at White's jersey, where blood had coloured it. It must have been cut by a thin, razor-sharp blade, about one inch wide. It was neat and straight, with no pulls of fibre. Perhaps a kitchen knife? He looked repentantly sad. Apologetic. A dark brown and red checked picnic blanket covered his legs. Blood from the wound had run down the man's chest into his groin area, then soaked into the seat cushion. Rab bent and looked under the victim's chair, using the light from his smartphone, which confirmed his suspicions. Deep red blood had dripped through and soaked into the carpet beneath, congealing into a glutinous pool.

He turned, observing the surroundings. A large, flat-screen TV dominated the corner of the room where Mr White's chair faced. Its chunky bezel suggested it would be at least ten years old. The frilly piped sofa cushions and random pattern of the seat suggested 1970s. It was often the case with old folks. They spent their retirement lump sum on new furniture and perhaps a new car, then made it last the rest of their lives.

A small dark-wood table sat beside the victim's chair, sprinkled with cake crumbs and a plate holding two slices of jam on toast, with two bites taken from one slice. Other food debris laid on the carpet surrounding the table and chair legs. The carpet was earthy brown with olive swirls – their accidental camouflage pattern no doubt doing a great job of concealing most of the dirt. A display cabinet sat against the wall, its dusty glass panes obscuring two rows of flower-patterned plates and another shelf adorned with trophies of some sort.

Rab stepped closer, his jaw jutting forward as he peered within. Mr White's name was etched into the trophies' dull brass plates. Golfer figurines stood atop three plinths, with angler figures on the other two. Fly-fishermen. Mr White appeared to have been skilled at more than one pastime in his younger days. The right cabinet door hung slightly ajar and a vacant dust-free space on the trophy shelf suggested one had been removed recently.

Another chair stood against the opposite wall, matching the sofa. On its cushion sat a melamine tray, its daffodil design obscured by the objects arranged on it. The missing trophy was shattered, its pieces piled in the corner. A small plaque announced, 'Employee of the Year 1984'. Rab recognised the name of the company: Butler and Cargrove, a manufacturing company, famous for shortbread biscuits. They were sold around the world in tins adorned with tartan patterns, highlighting the Scottish connection. Rab continued around the room, careful not to disturb any potential evidence, then returned to the hall where the carer was shifting feet, left, right, left, right… "Ms Proctor"

"Yes." She welcomed the interruption of her boredom.

"We'll best leave the house undisturbed." Mary grabbed her coat and he led her away, ensuring the door remained unlocked.

Chapter 3

Rab opened the door to his Citroen Picasso, intending to use it as an interview room, but soon realised the car still stank like a toilet. He closed the door again and casually rested against it as if that had been his original intention. Mary responded to his questions, explaining the events of the day, her finding of Mr White and her subsequent actions. He noted her details and checked her work's identity, and got her to list her whereabouts during the day. When asked if she knew of anyone who might wish him harm, she offered no suggestion but told him Mr White had been a lovely old man.

"Did you notice anything different today?" Rab asked. "Not just Mr White being dead, obviously. I mean different about the house, the room, anything out of place or missing, any smells or sounds?"

Mary stamped her feet and shivered as she answered. "Now that you come to mention it, the TV was on a different channel. He normally watches *BBC Breakfast* but switches over to ITV to watch *Lorraine*. George said he met her once and that she's a lovely lady. On Tuesdays, he usually watches ITV for the rest of the day. But when I arrived, BBC1 was playing. Oh! And his breakfast still sat on his table. He doesn't like cold toast and jam, so normally eats it as soon as he's given it."

Rab looked at the list Mary had written for him. "I note that you were swimming from 7:30 am to 9 am. Is there anyone who can confirm that?"

"There are several regulars at the pool who'd recognise me but I don't know their names."

Rab checked the list. Mary had written down the name of the pool, so he could check on that later. "What about between 9 am and 11 am? Would anyone be able to corroborate what you've written here?"

"I dinna ken. Maybe they'll have CCTV at Tescos?"

"And the afternoon?"

"I was home from late morning until I had to leave for work, so no one will have seen me."

"Okay. Thanks, Ms Proctor. That's most helpful. That's all the details we need for the moment. You can go about your business now, but we may need to talk with you again, so please don't leave the city without notifying us."

"Oh! Don't you worry about that, officer. I've nowhere to go and no money to travel with, anyway."

Rab smiled sympathetically. "Oh! One last thing. Can you give me the number for your office? I'll need to find out who else visited Mr White today."

Mary gave him the details, turned and hurried away, calling someone on her phone as she went. He returned to the house and sauntered into the kitchen. Opening drawers with his gloved right hand, he checked for knives that might match the murder weapon. Beside the cooker stood a rubberwood knife block, with one empty slot about 1 inch tall. The missing knife could be the murder weapon. He extracted the other knives from the block and checked their condition. They were all fairly new, had dark, hardwood handles, were little worn and razor-sharp. He photographed a knife, then replaced them all into their block. He'd seen enough for the moment. As Rab opened the front door the CSI van turned up, followed by the pathologist in his car.

***

The CSI team weren't science geeks – there were plenty of them in the forensics team. Many of the CSIs were ex-coppers, keen to stay involved in solving crimes, and some were would-be forensic scientists but hadn't made it through their university science courses. They were all good at their job, methodically collecting evidence to pass on to the forensics guys. He greeted them, briefed them on the situation and left them to their work, asking them to let him know as soon as they were done.

Other uniformed officers arrived, so Rab tasked them with door-knocking around the neighbourhood to find out if anyone had seen something. He was impatient for the pathologist to give him a window for when death had occurred, as this was crucial for focussing on the right time period. Rab suspected – going by the pooled blood and temperature of the old man's cheek – that it would have been at least twelve hours ago, meaning the murderer had entered early that morning.

Rab let his mind picture the scene again and thought about the victim's position and dress. White must have been up for breakfast and dressed by the first carer of the day, prior to the murderer's visit. He phoned the care coordinator's number again, asked who'd visited Mr White that morning, and when that would have been.

DC Mairi Gordon arrived as he ended the call. She was wrapped up in a bright yellow quilted coat, masking her shapely figure. Its hood covered her dyed blonde shoulder-length hair. She was just two inches shorter than Rab's 5 foot 9 inches. "Hi, Sarge. What's the situation?"

"Hi, Mairi. Bloody chilly, isn't it?"

"Sure is, Sarge. I nearly came a cropper on the journey here – skidded on the bend when turning into the street and bumped the opposite kerb. Roads are like an ice rink. Just thankful no one was coming the other way. It's treacherous."

"Aye. I had similar problems. I passed a number of minor collisions on the way. Cars that had bumped into the one in front or slipped into a wall." He briefed her on what the carer had told him and what he had found, then informed her what he planned to do next. He asked her to coordinate the neighbour interviewing work and check for CCTV cameras – public or private ones.

Rab took out his phone. His boss, Inspector Una Wallace, was off work recovering from a knife attack, and the other DI, Angus Watson, had just broken his leg skiing. Detective Chief Inspector McLeod was away on holiday, so he called the superintendent.

"Yes, laddie," Alistair Milne responded when Rab had briefed him on what he'd found. "You did the right thing calling me. As you say, it's not a straightforward death. We'll need a senior officer assigned to the case. There's only one option open to us now, what with both DIs out of action. Unless we pull someone in from another station?" He thought for a moment. "No, she wouldn't want someone else interfering with her team. Leave it with me to sort, Rab. In the meantime, you're acting SIO."

Rab thanked the Super for having faith in him to stand in for the DCI. The case merited the involvement of a more experienced officer, so he'd gladly hand over when Suzanna McLeod arrived back in the city. She was a great person to work for. He'd come across numerous senior officers in the past who arrogantly thought they deserved to be revered by their staff. Others were incompetent bunglers and Rab wondered how on earth they'd reached their rank. Many of them were not interested in what their team had to offer; they merely saw them as pawns to do the legwork – pieces in a game, where they took all the glory and passed on no praise. But DCI McLeod broke that mould.

She was smart, extremely well educated, knowledgeable about forensics, had an analytical intellect and could see the wider picture. She seemed able to place herself in the victim's mind and picture what must have happened. In his time on her team, her direction to them had invariably been inspirational, motivating them to give their best and steering them down roads they'd not yet considered. He'd learned so much from her and had hopes of gaining promotion to DI in the not-too-distant future under her mentorship. Also, Suzanna McLeod was bloody good looking – fit, in more ways than one. He knew she worked out in the gym, ran and practised judo regularly. She'd earned her black belt third dan, and her skills had taken down many a criminal.

He'd seen some of his colleagues become overweight and unfit, leaving them incapable of pursuits or of tackling criminals, except with one or more colleagues' assistance. The uniformed guys now relied on their Tasers to overcome violent criminals because they didn't have the skills or fitness to deal with them. He suspected they also lacked the courage – feared for their own safety, so resorted by default to the electric-shock weapon.

***

"Hello," the woman answered.

"Good evening," Rab said. "Sergeant Sinclair, Edinburgh CID, here. Is this Gabriela Albescu?"

"Yes, I am Gabriela. Why you call me?"

"I guess you won't have heard yet, but Mr George White was found dead this evening. You were with him this morning, weren't you?"

Gabriela choked when she heard the news. "Yes, but why police involved? He old man. Old people die!"

"He didn't die of natural causes. That's all I can say for the moment. I need to speak to you in person. Can I come to meet with you straight away?"

Gabriela looked at her watch. It was getting late and she had to rise early for her duties. Then she realised that her first client wouldn't be needing her assistance tomorrow. Or ever. "Yes, Sergeant. Please come now."

***

Rab walked up two flights of stairs to reach the door. As usual,

12

with blocks of flats, he found the door paintwork to be chipped and scratched. Well overdue a repaint. The door opened and the face of a young woman appeared. Her looks matched her foreign name. She had olive skin and almost black hair which hung over her shoulders. A Roman nose perched above her wide mouth and full lips.

"Miss Albescu?" Rab asked, showing his ID card.

"Yes, yes. Please come in."

The furniture positioned around the living room looked like it had come from a second-hand shop. Each table was adorned with a white crocheted doily, some circular and others oval. Gabriela perched herself on a dining chair and Rab followed her lead, taking a chair on the other side of the drop-leaf table.

"I understand you called on George White this morning. Please tell me about that visit," Rab requested.

"Has someone killed George?"

"Gabriela, it will be quicker if you would answer my questions."

"I called on George this morning about seven."

"How did you get into the house?"

"I take the key from key safe near door."

"Go on."

"First thing I do is get George from his bed and help him wash at sink in bathroom. Then I help him dress. We go downstairs next. I walk down ahead of stair lift. Make sure he not fall off. Once, he go to hospital after falling from the seat."

Rab kept quiet but thought, surely the chair has a seat belt to hold him in, and waited for Gabriela to continue.

"George walked to his chair with Zimmer frame. I walk behind him, because sometimes he falls backwards. He is too heavy for me to lift from the floor. When he is seated, I make him toast with jam and a cup of tea. Then leave."

"This morning, was there anything out of the ordinary? Did George

THE KEY TO MURDER

seem different? Worried?" Rab asked.

"No. It was a normal day. Same as any morning."

"Did you see anything unusual in the house? Things out of normal position?"

Gabriela shook her head.

"When you left, did you notice anyone hanging around outside, nearby, or walking towards the house?"

"No. No one waiting nearby. People walk along road towards his house every morning. They pass, on way to somewhere," Gabriela replied. "Why you asking these questions? Has George been murdered?"

"Yes, Gabriela," Rab responded. "I can't share with you how he died but someone killed him and we must find out who did that. Can you think of anything at all that might help us catch the killer?"

Wednesday, 4th March

Chapter 4

Suzanna had just completed the most exciting ski run of the holiday and was looking forward to many more days of heady adrenaline rushes when her phone rang. The call from Superintendent Alistair Milne had not brightened her day. He had texted her the night before, but she'd not seen the message, so his call came out of the blue. She didn't want to cut her holiday short but knew that as the Chief Inspector and leader of Edinburgh's CID team, and with two DIs out of action, she must return to work to take over the latest murder enquiry.

She walked away from her disgruntled partner, skis over her shoulder, her own face now stern. It was bad enough to be recalled from the holiday, but James' attitude made the matter worse. Surely it was obvious that police detectives must sacrifice their own plans when the call to duty came. It annoyed her that some people, in low-pressure, non-operational day jobs, didn't understand.

The mountain café had only just opened its doors, so Suzanna was their first customer. She ordered a mug of hot chocolate then sat at a table near the bay window overlooking the lower ski slopes. There were magnificent views through the large window. Acres of pristine white slopes blanketed the mountains. A heavy mist hung in the valley, masking the village. Peaks poked through, like islands in a cotton wool sea.

She sipped her hot chocolate. A weak phone signal made it difficult to research possibilities for her early return, but she eventually connected to her cheap flights app and found flights to Edinburgh via London later that day. Suzanna booked the flights and the connecting bus. She finished her drink and stood, intending to return to the slopes, when James walked in with their friends. He seemed calm after his initial annoyance and appeared to have accepted that she'd be leaving early. But Suzanna hadn't yet cooled. She wondered if they were really suited.

"Suzanna, James tells me you have to cut short your holiday and return to Scotland. What a shame," Annabelle said, looking sympathetic. "You realise you're taking a big risk leaving James behind, don't you? I've been after him for years. I only married Roger because I couldn't have my first choice." She turned and looked at her husband with a cheeky grin on her face. Roger, however, looked like he was wondering if his wife had spoken the truth.

James looked at Suzanna, rolled his eyes and smiled as if to say, don't worry, she's just toying with you. Suzanna remembered noticing an instant bond between James and Annabelle when they'd first met in the ski lift queue. They had worked in the same company ten years before, when he was still married. Suzanna also wondered how near the truth Annabelle's joking had been. Could they have been lovers?

The friends sat drinking, eating pastries and chatting before heading back onto the slopes. The crowds had arrived. Suzanna could see a multitude of zig-zagging beginners and groups of tentative intermediate skiers following their instructors in packs. They were gradually descending the slope she'd earlier hurtled down, flat out, her heart pumping. She was glad to have made the effort to catch the morning's first cable car. She could fit in one more top-to-bottom run before needing to return to their holiday apartment to prepare for her return to Edinburgh.

Glorious sunshine illuminated the magnificent mountain-top views, with clear blue skies as their backdrop. They meandered down the slopes of the Italian snow-capped mountain, speeding along when safe but mostly spending their time avoiding everyone else. At the base of the ski slopes, Suzanna kissed James and they hugged before she gathered up her skis and headed back to their accommodation, leaving the other three to continue skiing. She had a phone call to make.

***

"Good morning, Rab," the Superintendent called out as Sergeant Sinclair passed his office. Rab spun around and returned to Alistair Milne's doorway. He respected the Superintendent and trusted his wise council. The Chief Super was another kettle of fish. He rarely had a good word to say about anyone, and didn't seem to understand the concept of encouragement and empowerment, to motivate his team to excellence – the method naturally employed by the DCI and endorsed by the Superintendent.

"Good morning, Sir. Any news on the DCI's return?"

"Aye, lad. That's why I called out. She'll get the earliest flight back to Edinburgh and be in the office late afternoon or early evening. Be prepared to brief her as soon as she arrives."

"Sure. No problem, Sir. Was there anything else?"

"No. Just that, Rab. I'll let you get on."

Rab had just sat at his desk when his phone rang. "Sergeant Sinclair, Edinburgh CID"

"Rab. It's DCI McLeod. I hear you're acting SIO."

"Aye. Until your return. Sorry you've been called back so early from your holiday. I could have held the fort a bit longer."

"I'm sure you could, Rab. But the hierarchy wouldn't allow a murder investigation to be led by a sergeant. And you've not done the SIO course."

"Very true."

"I have to travel via London as there were no direct flights available, so it's looking like an early evening arrival. I'd like to be brought up to speed as soon as I arrive, and we'll continue working well into the evening."

Rab had expected a long day.

"Look. I'll not tell you what to do now. You've been involved in enough murder cases to know the procedure, and you have the Super down the corridor and me on the end of the phone – well, when I'm not flying, of course – If you need advice. Do you have any questions for me now?"

"No. As you say, I know the drill. I'll be having a catch-up with the team in a few minutes. They're nearly all in now."

"Okay. I'll get ready for my return home and leave you to it. But call me anytime if you feel the need." Suzanna had faith in Rab. She was sure he'd do a fine job of following the necessary procedures to set things up and get the investigation going. What he'd not yet developed was what some would call gut feelings. Sure, he could tell when he was being lied to, and he had good analytical skills, but he had yet to cultivate that extra sixth sense. The sense that made all the difference. It would come, though. It would come.

***

Rab called the team together and informed them of the DCI's travel plans. "I spoke to the morning carer Gabriela Albescu last night. When she left George White yesterday morning just after 7:30 am he was alive, sitting in his chair, with fresh toast and jam by his side, watching BBC Breakfast TV. The evening carer, Mary Proctor, said that George would have changed the TV channel at 9 am, but it was still on BBC when she arrived. She also mentioned White's dislike of cold toast. So, that suggests he was disturbed immediately after Albescu had left. If that assumption is correct, the murderer would have entered his property around 7:35 am."

"That would be amazing if we already have a tight window for the murder. I hope you're right, Sarge," Mairi said. "And, if you are, the murderer must have been waiting around to enter as soon as the carer left."

"Yes." Rab agreed. "I asked Albescu whether she'd seen anyone hanging around, but she hadn't."

Owen joined in, "We'll need background checks on both those carers. I'll take that on."

Rab nodded. "Right... We'll need the incident board set up."

"I'll do that," Mairi volunteered.

"I'd prefer you to continue with the CCTV analysis, Mairi." She nodded acceptance of the tasking, but Rab could see the reluctance in her eyes. He also found CCTV scrutiny tedious. But it played a huge part in identifying suspects and locking up criminals. "Owen, you make up the board, please. Pictures of the victim and suspects, names, contact details and don't forget to draw in any links."

"Sure thing, Sarge."

"Zahir." Rab continued. "Update on the searches, please?"

"Uniform searched the area as best they could last night by torchlight but found nothing. I've requested they repeat the search this morning. I'll give the sergeant a call after this catch-up to see how it's going."

Rab pondered before speaking again, his mind searching for elements that might give them a direction to follow. "White's family rarely visit, suggesting a lack of fondness. They'd likely inherit his estate, so might welcome his demise. We'll need to get a copy of his will and testament, just to be sure, and find out if he has any life insurance policies due to pay out."

"I can do that, Sarge," Murray offered. Rab nodded acceptance.

"Right, I think that's all for now. I'll follow up on Mary Proctor's swimming alibi."

Caitlin spoke. "As you guys are all involved in this murder, someone needs to progress the other cases. I'll look after them and leave Rab to direct the murder enquiry?"

"Sounds good to me, Caitlin," Rab replied. He admired Caitlin. Not just in the male-female attraction sense, although he couldn't deny she was a cracker. But her insight, her willingness to volunteer for the right jobs at the right time, and her excellent interviewing skills – particularly vulnerable victims and witnesses. He felt privileged to work with a great team of colleagues, all pulling in the same direction, instead of competing with each other as he'd witnessed in other police departments.

Chapter 5

On the road to Milan's Bergamo Airport, Suzanna's mind drifted around her recent life, like eddies along a riverbank. She recalled her meeting with James when she had come clean about the night she'd slept with her ex-husband. Callum had won her over on an evening in which they should have been discussing divorce but instead made passionate, urgent love, rekindling her feelings for him. But the renewed emotions soon faded once she realised it was mere lust. She had to admit that Callum still knew how to press her buttons – to thrill her. Damn him!

James had been incredibly understanding. Extremely upset, of course, but once he'd got over the shock of her revelation and calmed, said he didn't want the incident to end their relationship. Suzanna had reassured him it was a one-off event. She'd never again give Callum an opportunity to seduce her. They'd made love that night, re-bonding, then booked the ski holiday. And here she was on the way back to Edinburgh, having already retested the strength of their relationship. Only time would tell whether the calls of her work would be too much for him – as it was for many police officers' partners.

Her breakup with Callum hadn't been caused by the demands of her job, though. It had been his infidelity – his willingness to screw a younger woman in their matrimonial bed. She'd seen the intimate act from the bedroom door when she'd arrived home unexpectedly early from a trip. Naked bodies writhing in pleasure. Until Callum had seen her in the doorway, his face transformed instantly like that of a free-fall sky-diver who's just found his parachute won't open. The young marriage-breaker had rolled off him, gathering the bedclothes to hide her nakedness. Suzanna had gone bright red with anger but had said nothing. She'd turned and walked away, suitcase still in hand, as Callum leapt from the bed and called to her, "Suzanna. Sorry. I love you, Suzanna," as she walked out the door. "It was just sex!"

If there had been water in her head, it would have been spewing from her ears like steam from a boiling kettle. "Fuck you, Callum McLeod," she'd yelled. "You'll not be having sex with me again," Suzanna had muttered to herself as she descended the stairs, heading out with no destination in mind. She'd dumped her bag in the boot of her car and driven away. Away from her errant husband, out of the city and its 20-mph speed limits, onto the open roads. Her car accelerated, driven by her foot pressing the pedal to the floorboard. She was angry, frustrated, hurt. Hurt so badly. Tears had flooded her eyes as she drove, obscuring her vision. She wiped the tears away as the speed hit 90 mph. Her dash soon ended when she caught up with a stream of traffic doing fifty. She flipped the auto gearbox into sports mode, ready to accelerate past, but there were too many cars in the queue behind a large truck to make overtaking viable.

She'd settled into a zombie driving mode, following the vehicle in front. Her mind washed around in her skull. Why had he betrayed her? Was it her fault? Had sex become mundane? Had she lost her good looks? Had she become boring? She just wanted to be happy, to share her life harmoniously with someone, to laugh and cry together, to hold hands and cuddle, to share common goals. But now he'd wrecked that. Why? Why? Why?

After a while, Suzanna realised she was heading towards Cumbria. She'd stay with her sister until she figured out what to do. It was a Friday and she wasn't due in at work until Monday. Her eyes had remained red and stinging, but her mind swung from self-doubt to cold analysis of the split's practicalities. It was her home. She'd bought it cash with her inheritance, so Callum had contributed nothing towards the asset. He'd have to go, so she could move back in. The break-up was his fault. He'd just have to live with the consequences. Her love for Callum had instantly flipped to hate. She'd told herself she would never share her bed with the traitor. Would never trust him again. The miles had swept by – the hours dissolving as she drove. She'd felt like she'd swum the English Channel of emotions on her journey. Her eyes, still red and moist, would soon give away her broken heart.

As she'd turned into the housing estate where her sister lived, she'd thought 'I hope Charlotte is home!' How could she have driven nearly three hours and not thought to call ahead? She'd parked on the street, taken her bag from the boot and wandered up the path, holding back, not looking forward to the next roller coaster ride of sharing with her sister.

The door opened shortly after she'd rung the bell and a chest-high face exploded with glee as Athena spied her aunt. "*Suzanna!* Mummy, Aunty Suzie's here." She'd leapt forward, grabbing Suzanna around her waist, gripping her like a baby brown bear.

"Suzanna. What a surprise. What brought you here?" Then Charlotte had spotted her sister's eyes. "No matter. Come in. Come in. Athena, let go of your aunt." Her daughter had loosened her grip and the three of them walked into the 3-bed semi, the door closing behind them as Charlotte's husband, Pete, emerged from the kitchen.

"Suzanna! What an unexpected pleasure." He'd walked towards her, wrapped his arms around her shoulders and kissed her cheek before letting go. "Leave your bag there. Come on into the lounge." Pete went ahead and Suzanna lowered her bag to the floor, freeing her hands. As Charlotte lovingly hugged her, she returned the affection, enjoying the comfort of the cosy embrace.

"Would you like a cuppa, sis? Or something stronger?" It was only 5 pm, but it *was* a Friday, so she agreed to a glass of white wine – she could do with a drink to soften the blow to her ego and calm her emotions.

Athena settled herself on her aunt's lap after she'd sunk onto the sofa, collapsing into its comforting embrace. "Don't hug your aunt so hard, Athena. She won't be able to breathe," Pete said, smiling. Obediently, Athena loosened her grasp, then looked up at Suzanna. "You've been crying!" The young were never tactful. But it saved her parents from raising the subject.

"I've left Callum. I can't live with him anymore. Not after what just happened."

"But Aunty Suzie. I like Callum."

"Yes. I know. And so did I. But now I don't like him anymore. I can't tell you why yet. Maybe when you're older." The tears returned to Suzanna's eyes. Athena hugged her aunt again as she sobbed, her own tears flowing, distressed to see her aunt so upset.

Charlotte and Pete looked at her, heads tilted, sympathetic looks on their faces, waiting for her tears to subside, keen to hear more, but knowing she couldn't share any details while their daughter was in the room. After they'd eaten and Athena retired to her bed, Charlotte took her sister out for a walk around the town. "So, what happened, Suzie?"

"I caught him in bed with another woman. In *our* bed! The bastard!" Tears rolled from Suzanna's eyes again. "I arrived back from the police conference much earlier than planned and he was lying there naked, with a young woman straddling him, riding the shit out of him. I saw every intimate detail of the betrayal."

"Oh my Gosh! What did he say?"

"It was only sex! As if that made any difference."

"Men are so weak-minded, aren't they? Ruled by their penises."

Suzanna didn't fully agree with her sister's statement but clearly Callum was under penile control. "Your Pete hasn't betrayed *you* though, has he." It was a statement, not a question.

"Not as far as I know. And I don't have any suspicions. But sex does seem to be more important to men than to us girls. If they've not just had an orgasm, they're thinking about how they might get the next one." They walked in silence for a while, their minds wandering. "What will you do, sis?"

"I'm not sure yet."

"I'd tell him to get out of your flat and find somewhere else to live. You'll need to be back at work on Monday, won't you?"

"Yes. If I don't get a call earlier, of course. I hope there are no major crimes over the weekend. As you say, Charlie, it *is* my apartment. But I don't want to speak to him. I'll go home Sunday morning, provided he's gone. I couldn't look into his face, with the image of his girlfriend's backside still in my mind. I couldn't trust myself not to deck him."

"Would you like me or Pete to call him instead?" Charlotte offered.

Suzanna walked as she thought about her sister's suggestion. "Maybe? I'll text him first and see what he says. If he's not cooperative, perhaps Pete would speak to him, man-to-man?"

Men and women stood outside some of the pubs, smoking, supping their drinks and chatting loudly. At the end of Main Street, Wordsworth House – the childhood home of the poet William Wordsworth – stood dusky-orange-faced behind its high walls. They turned left up the hill, then doubled back on the road parallel to Main Street, passing Victorian terraced houses, business premises and the back of the town's main supermarket.

"If you decide to take a complete break from Edinburgh, you'd always be welcome here, Suzie."

"Thanks. I doubt it will come to that and, in any case, I'd have to leave my job if I left Edinburgh."

"Could you transfer to a role in Cumbria?" Charlotte asked, hopefully.

Suzanna thought about the suggestion. It would be great to live and work near her sister, niece, and the Lake District. "If there was a suitable role, it might be possible. But there aren't many DCIs in the county, so the chances of a vacancy are low." She thought more about the idea before continuing. "Besides, I'm not ready to leave my team. I've not been there that long and they're still developing."

"Surely you won't let that stop you from moving on if you need to. They'd find another DCI to take over from you."

"Yeah. But I'd feel I was abandoning them. They're a young team and they're learning fast. I'd feel guilty if I left with only half a job done. Possibly leaving them to the mercy of a crap detective, like Ferguson."

"Fair enough."

Suzanna had told Charlotte about DI Ferguson and his management style. It had led to her taking a break from the police.

On returning to Charlotte's home, they finished the bottle of white wine and opened a red. Pete diplomatically didn't pry, knowing Charlotte would share her sister's troubles with him when they retired for the night. Eventually, Suzanna laughed at something Pete said, her morbid spirit washed away by conversation with people she loved, helped by the alcohol.

Suzanna had checked her phone before bed, ignoring the multiple texts from Callum. In the morning, she had texted Callum and told him to get out before she returned on Sunday. If he was still there, she'd throw him out. There would be no conversation, no listening to his pleas. It was over. She had been determined he would never get a second chance to break her heart.

Chapter 6

Mairi slipped her arms into her grey woollen overcoat, tied the belt around her waist, grabbed her bag and walked away. Rab watched her shapely figure as she exited the room. Although his wife was as classy and solid as a Mercedes saloon, there was no harm in admiring a Porsche, even though he had no intention of driving it. Mairi had just told him that she'd requested footage for yesterday morning from the CCTV control room but she still needed to get her hands on private CCTV from the street. That's where she was heading now.

He dragged his attention back to business. "Owen, any progress with the background checks on Proctor and Albescu?"

"Neither of them has a criminal record. I've requested financial background checks, but, as you know, that could take a while to come in."

"Aye. Hopefully tomorrow," Rab concurred. "Where's Zahir?"

"He left when you were making a coffee. He's gone to speak with the uniform guys doing the search around Coates."

"Good. Nice to know he's on it." Rab swivelled his head, then spoke again. "Murray –"

"I've put in a request to White's solicitor for a copy of his will and testament."

"Great. Give me a hand with the incident board then, please. We need to get it finished off."

* * *

Suzanna's flight to London Stanstead had been uneventful. There was a short wait for her connecting flight to Edinburgh, so she found a seat in departures and pulled a paperback book from her bag. But before she started reading, her mind slipped back to when Callum had obediently moved out. She had returned to her apartment and resumed her life, throwing herself with gusto into her work and meeting with friends instead of hiding away. Unencumbered by a partner, she'd become more active, resuming judo training once a week, running and going to the gym more regularly. Although the break-up had been painful, she was glad of the no-compromise freedom she now had.

She had many books on her iPad but still liked to read real books when it was possible. The paperback she had with her was a fast-paced spy novel, with ex-SAS men employed on black ops by MI6. It was exciting. Gripping. As she started to read, a man sat opposite spoke to her, his public-school English accent at once grabbing her attention. "It's not really like those stories would have you believe, of course."

She looked up at him. Despite his accent and implied knowledge of such matters, he looked nothing like James Bond. He was probably in his forties, lean and fit looking, but not the handsome, debonair character in the movies. His hair had departed from the centre of his head but still hovered above his large ears, which protruded from his head like a double-handled coffee cup. Of course, if he had been an MI6 officer, he'd hardly announce it in a public space. Perhaps he was a Walter Mitty type. "And how would you know?" Suzanna asked.

He tapped the side of his nose and Suzanna returned to her book. "Can I buy you a coffee?" the man asked. "A cappuccino?" he said, standing. She couldn't think of any reason to refuse the offer. "There's a spare table in Costa. Would you like to join me?" He walked away as if expecting her to follow, going straight to the coffee shop's counter.

'Why not,' she thought. The book could wait. Suzanna would have been shocked and concerned if a female friend had done what she was now about to do. But she felt at peace with the situation. Her gut was not telling her to beware. She took a seat at the empty table, taking the opportunity to recharge her phone in the socket provided. She breathed in the coffee aroma emanating from behind the counter while the machines hissed like a bag of snakes and she awaited the intriguing man's return.

He placed their drinks on the table and sat opposite her. "Lansdowne, Greg Lansdowne." Suzanna smiled at the 007-style introduction. He offered his hand across the table, but before she took it, he continued. "I'm glad you agreed to pass the time with me, Suzanna."

She froze, her hand retracting. Had he been behind in the queue when she checked in? Was he a stalker? She kept her calm as she tried to penetrate his mind with her eyes then replied, "How do you know my name?"

"We've been observing you for a while, Detective Chief Inspector McLeod." He couldn't have known that from being in the same queue. "I'm not with the government department we were just talking about. I'm an officer in the internally focussed one."

So, MI5, not MI6, Suzanna thought. "And why would your department be interested in a detective, and why would you approach her in an airport on her unplanned journey home after a shortened holiday?"

"Good questions, Suzanna. You see, my role is to seek out new talent. I've seen your police records. I've heard of your reputation. You're special, Suzanna. And we like special people – gifted people. We're aware of your great-great-uncle's test and your inheritance. We've observed your career and, you might not like to hear it, but also your private life. I'd been planning on talking to you soon, so when I was notified you would be travelling through Stanstead today, I took the opportunity to pop up here and meet with you, rather than take time out for an Edinburgh trip." His thin lips parted as he took a sip of his black Americano.

Suzanna wasn't pleased. The idea of the state spying on her reminded her of George Orwell's 1984 prophetic novel. "Surely your department would look out for young talent, rather than people over halfway through their working lives."

"Mostly, yes. We like to get them young. But there are exceptions to the rule, for those extraordinarily talented." Suzanna's mind churned as he continued, trying to assess whether he was the real deal or someone to worry about. "My purpose in approaching you today isn't to recruit you for my department but to sound you out for a role where you would lead a team in the police organisation that works alongside us. Some might say we're joined at the hip."

"Special Branch?" Suzanna whispered.

Greg tilted his head, his steel-grey eyes remaining locked with Suzanna's. "The risk of terrorism remains high, especially from the Middle Eastern and South Asian sectors. We're aware of your recent mission to Bangladesh and West Bengal and your fearless pursuit of justice there. By taking terrorists off the street, you can help us stop terrorist acts before they're committed."

The proposal was flattering and a complete surprise to her. Apart from the persistent annoyance of the soon-to-retire Chief Superintendent, she loved where she lived and worked. She sipped her cappuccino. "You've piqued my interest, but I have no wish to move to London."

"There'd be no need for that. You could remain in Scotland and lead the Counter-Terrorism section, based at Tulliallan Castle, just north of Kincardine. You wouldn't even have to move home." Greg paused, allowing Suzanna time to absorb what he'd said, then resumed. "You'll be aware that since the formation of Police Scotland two years ago, there's been a move for Major Investigation Teams to take over all murder enquiries and large-scale complex criminal investigations.

You may not yet be aware that your team in Edinburgh will probably be split up and downgraded, with the big stuff allocated to an MIT. Your post will go and your team will be left investigating burglaries and muggings." Suzanna understood there were changes afoot, but no one had informed her this was the future for her team.

"I know this is a lot to take in. You may soon be approached by someone from Police Scotland about a move to an MIT. That's why I wanted to get in first, to tell you we think you'd make more of an impact in counter-terrorism."

An announcement informed Suzanna her flight was about to board. She sipped the rest of her coffee, then spooned up the remaining froth, as she considered the MI5 officer's suggestion. "Here's my card," Greg said. "I believe your team has until the year's end, at the latest, before it's restructured and you'll be forced to move on. Bear in mind what I've just said. Call me if you feel counter-terrorism is the worthiest cause to put your skills towards. We'd love to have you working alongside us. The team needs a superintendent, so it would mean promotion."

Suzanna gave nothing away in her face. She took the card, placed it in her handbag, then extended her hand. "Good to have had this chat, Greg. I'll give some time to considering my future and get in contact when I've made my decision." She stood and walked away, her mind already analysing the options.

Chapter 7

Superintendent Milne leant against the door frame of his office and crossed his feet as he spoke. "Thanks again for cutting short your holiday, Suzanna. How did your man react to you abandoning him halfway through your holiday?"

Suzanna had just arrived at the office late afternoon. "Not well, Alistair, but he'll get over it." She'd never thought of James as *her man*, as Alistair put it, but she supposed he was right. "I'll have to ban Angus from skiing in Scotland when I'm next due to go on holiday. The Scottish ski resorts are too dangerous."

"Och! Don't be daft, Suzanna," he replied, his face showing surprise at her description of Scottish skiing. "Our ski centres might not be as refined as the Alpine resorts, but there's good skiing to be had on those mountains. It's *meant* to be a challenging sport."

"Yes. Well. I guess you're right if your meaning of challenge is to have thousands of pieces of wood sticking out of the ground at the edge of ski runs, and T-bars that swing around and try to knock your head off as you're getting off them."

"Och! That's the trouble with you Sassenachs. You like everything easy."

The flash of a frown crossed Suzanna's face before it brightened again. "It's just as well we're friends, Alistair. Or you might have been called on by Internal Affairs to answer a formal complaint for that racial slur," she countered with a smile.

"Whoops! Good point." Alistair straightened, ready to move. "Anyway, enough of skiing. You'll need to get brought up to speed on the case. Rab's in the office, so best you catch up with him first. And again, thanks for returning early."

Suzanna smiled, then left Alistair to get on with his work. She stopped off at her office and discarded her coat, gloves and handbag before switching on her computer and grabbing her coffee mug. The gold framed, smiling face of her cute niece, Athena, caught her attention. The glass looked a little dusty – a sign that she needed to clear aside her excuses for not visiting her sister lately.

She found Rab in the main office, munching on a sandwich. "Do they still make corned beef, Rab?"

"Oh! Hi, ma'am," he said, trying not to spray white bread and beef over the desk. "Can you give me a minute?"

"Of course." Suzanna continued through the office to get herself a coffee. Rab was on his last mouthful when she returned. After swallowing, he welcomed her back. Suzanna had respect for her sergeant. He was a fast learner, had a positive attitude, mostly stuck to the rules, was hardworking and dedicated to the cause of catching criminals. Suzanna knew he was as passionate about seeing justice done as she was. Seeing criminals getting away with their crimes because of a skilled barrister infuriated him. She wondered if that passion might one day see him bend the rules to get a conviction, if utterly convinced of a criminal's guilt and was worried he might get off. Whilst tempting, Suzanna had resisted the call to plant evidence or give false witness, believing that once an officer steps over that line, it would make them a criminal and could lead to their downfall.

Hailing from the Scottish borders town of Jedburgh, Rab's accent was softer than some of her colleagues, especially those from Glasgow and Dundee. She remembered hearing that he'd spent two years working in an estate agent's office after leaving school, then realised that he wanted a career that would make a difference. He'd had three years on the beat before becoming a DC. And it was five years later when he earned a promotion to sergeant. He'd definitely get promoted again. Perhaps make it to Superintendent rank before retiring, if he tried.

"Okay. Give me the lowdown, Rab."

Typically, Rab ran his fingers through his wavy brown hair before he spoke. He briefed her on his interviews with the carers, then talked her through the incident board. The carer who'd found White, Mary Proctor, had an alibi for the time of his death, so that was one less person to consider a suspect. Mairi had obtained CCTV footage from official systems in the area, plus some private systems on houses in adjacent streets. She was going through the footage as they spoke.

"Anything of note?" Suzanna asked.

"Not yet."

"What else have you done so far?"

"Background checks are underway on all the carers who've supported Mr White in the last year, to see if any have a history of interest."

"What about the coordinators and managers?"

Rab paused. "I'll get onto that right away."

"Did the door-knocking show up anything?"

"Not really. No one had seen anyone visit his house, except the carers."

"Okay. Give me a shout when Mairi's finished scrutinising the CCTV or finds anything relevant. I'd like us to get together and combine our brainpower."

***

Suzanna had caught up with her email backlog by the time Rab informed her the team was ready to brainstorm.

"Hi, ma'am. How was the skiing?" Mairi asked.

"Fantastic but too brief, thanks to the murder and our two DIs being off work."

Apart from Una and Angus – both off work recovering from injuries – Suzanna's entire team was there. PC Zahir Usmani seemed to have become more self-assured over the last few months, having grown in confidence during their time investigating the washed-up woman case in Bangladesh and West Bengal. His knowledge of the Bengali language had proven to be useful, as was his ability to fit in with South Asian colleagues. His combat skills were also proven.

Caitlin Findlay normally worked with Angus and was supported by PCs Murray Docherty and Owen Crawford. She'd shown herself to be a talented sergeant with much potential but still had a way to go before she'd be ready for promotion. Suzanna liked that she managed her weight and kept fit. Her dark-chocolate-coloured bob-cut hair was always neat and tidy. Today she wore a white sculptured blouse that accentuated her light brown skin. Suzanna envied Caitlin's natural suntan. She'd not yet asked her how she'd inherited such a gorgeous skin tone – maybe Mediterranean descent or an Indian grandparent?

Murray, by contrast, was a white, freckle-faced, ginger-haired Scot. There was little doubt of his heritage. His wide nose might have stood out on any other head, but Murray's face was broad and his neck thick, matching his stocky build. She had heard he'd applied to become a detective after a uniformed colleague had been stabbed to death by a gang of youths, but his assailants never brought to justice.

Rab had risen to the challenge of running the investigation during Suzanna's absence and had progressed the investigation well, but they now needed to move things along with more pace. At Suzanna's request, he talked through what they'd done so far and highlighted any suspects or lines of investigation that yet needed to be followed. They'd not identified any specific suspects yet. The house hadn't been ransacked, so burglary seemed unlikely. But they couldn't be sure nothing had been stolen as there was no one to make an inventory of

White's possessions. And there was the broken trophy to consider.

Any of the carers, their supervisors or the managers could have entered the house, as they had the key safe code. But none seemed to have a motive and, in any case, they'd all been busy working, off sick or away on holiday.

Mairi's review of CCTV had uncovered nothing obvious yet. In the time window they'd been looking at, there had been dozens of people moving around the area but they had no way of telling who these pedestrians were. They had focussed on people and cars that had been seen at the beginning of the time window because the victim would have been dead a while by the time his evening carer, Mary Proctor, had discovered him.

Rab's plan was to visit the neighbours again and show them pictures of the people seen in the area in case they might identify them. And, of course, speak to the car owners. Background checks on the victim had not given them anything to follow up. George White had been a nondescript manager most of his life. What piqued Rab's interest was that the award won by the victim whilst employed by the biscuit manufacturer had been broken and left out on display. This suggested the murderer thought he didn't deserve it.

"Have you spoken with Butler and Cargrove?" Suzanna asked

"Not yet."

"Right. You concentrate on the neighbours and car owners, and I'll contact the company. Has there been a search conducted for the missing kitchen knife?"

"Aye. Zahir coordinated that," Rab said, looking at his constable.

"I had uniform search the streets and drains within 500 yards walk from the house, including front gardens of houses bordering the street. But nothing was found."

"I'd like to see the search area on a map, please, Zahir."

Zahir rose and went to his desk, returning with an Edinburgh street map, and showed her all the streets included. "Okay, you seem to have covered the area well. But the murderer could have disposed of the weapon outside that zone, so we may have to widen the search area. Before we do that, though, I'd like to know whether there was a refuse collection along any of those streets that day, or since? And whether any of the bins have been searched?"

"There wasn't a collection on the day of the crime. I'm not sure whether there's been one since. We searched the communal bins along Coates Gardens – that's the street the victim lived on – and adjacent streets but didn't find a knife. The murderer could have taken it home with them?"

"I doubt it, Zahir. Most knife murderers ditch the weapon as soon as they can, so they're not caught with it – except arrogant gang members, who have a special favoured weapon they like to show off. The murderer will probably have washed it in the house before leaving. But if we can find it, it's possible we'll obtain some evidence. I'd like you to expand the search but first check the bin collection days. There might have been a collection in the expanded area, which would mean a search of the landfill site. Let's hope that's not necessary as it's a horrible task. Coates Gardens is not far from my home. The bins around there are normally emptied on Mondays, so we may be in luck."

"Okay, ma'am. Will do."

Suzanna turned to Rab. "What's the feedback from forensics and the pathologist?"

"Forensics are still processing the crime scene and the pathologist has not yet reported his findings. Obviously, the cause of death appears to be the knife plunged directly into the victim's heart."

"Right. Before I do anything else, I need to see the crime scene. Rab. You're with me." She stood and strode to her office, collected her coat and bag, then headed out with Rab at her heels.

Chapter 8

Suzanna and Rab entered the house with plastic shoe covers on their feet and purple silicone gloves on their hands, passing through a small white gazebo guarded by a uniformed constable. Just one CSI officer was in the house. Suzanna recognised him behind his PPE. "Hello, Neil. How's it going?"

Neil was amazed the DCI had remembered his name. He'd only met her once and only briefly. "Good, thanks, chief inspector." He briefed them on the evidence gathered by his team. They were now free to roam the house and touch things with their gloved hands, as the CSIs had completed their evidence gathering. Neil packed his bag as he spoke to them, seemingly preparing to leave, so Suzanna asked him to stay on for a while until she'd looked around and could then ask questions. He checked his watch before confirming.

Suzanna stepped through the living room door and paused, Rab almost walking into her. He halted sharply, just avoiding placing his hands on her back, then stepped away to give her space. He should have known she would stop just inside the room, as he'd seen her do so many times. It was the way she assessed the scene.

The dingy room measured about fifteen by ten feet. It reeked of old man. Walls papered twenty years ago, dark carpets, grubby flower-patterned curtains framing the small windows. It was devoid of brightness. No sunlight, no bright colours - apart from the yellow flowers on the tray, now dusty from where the CSIs had taken fingerprints. The TV dominated the room's corner, towards which the brown recliner chair faced. The dark lacquered wooden furniture further added to the gloom.

Suzanna took it all in, noting the pictures hanging on the walls. The sort of pictures that languish in cardboard boxes on the floor of charity shops. The dining table, with its off-white crocheted runner, looked unused. DVDs were scattered on the TV cabinet's shelves next to the player, its door protruding. A three-lamp ceiling light with dirty glass shades dimly lit the room. It was uncared for. Family members, if they ever visited, evidently took no interest in their relative's surroundings.

Suzanna walked forward and examined the chair. Despite the blood-stained seat cushion, she could still see a broad grimy line running along the centre, where food scraps had slipped between the occupant's thighs and been ground into the fabric. The arms were worn thin on their edges and the recliner's control buttons had lost their chrome coating from years of wear. As she turned away, something caught her eye. Suzanna extracted a bag that had been stuffed down the side of the chair, noting its contents: Foxes Glacier Mints. She placed the sweets into an evidence bag and passed it to Rab, surprised the CSIs hadn't seen it and worried about the thoroughness of their work. He silently acknowledged the object and the need for it to be checked.

The DVDs called out to her. She picked each one up from the cabinet and checked their titles: The Railway Children (she loved that old story), The Sound of Music and Mary Poppins (more great classics), Rambo (that was a huge leap), Rambo II and III, Dirty Dancing (unexpected) – a rather eclectic mix, she thought. The next unlabelled DVD case felt tacky. She inserted the disc into the player, switched on the power and pressed play before turning on the television. She looked for the controller but didn't find it, so fiddled with buttons on the edge of the TV, until DVD showed on the screen and it switched to the already playing video. A woman laid over a man's lap, naked. The man, also naked, was slapping her backside with his hand and the woman responded with poorly scripted words, asking him to forgive her for some misdemeanour. She watched for another minute, then switched it off and ejected the DVD. There were several more similar discs, so she checked each one and found the theme to be the same. Clearly, the old man liked S&M pornography. Interesting!

Rab had mentioned the trophies, so she stepped closer to their glass-fronted cabinet and peered inside. The golf and fishing trophies were all dated in the 1960s and 70s; nothing more recent. She wondered if he'd lost interest in the sports or lost his touch? The broken award that Rab mentioned before was nowhere to be seen. "I take it the CSIs have removed the smashed award?"

"Aye. There were prints on it, so it's been bagged and taken away," Rab responded from the doorway. She hoped the prints might provide clues. Nothing else caught her attention. Rab stood aside as she re-entered the hallway. Before climbing the stairs, she examined the stairlift, testing its function with the controls. It whirred slowly, the motor emitting a groan as the seat began its snail-like climb. She'd hate to need one of these. The journey would be so long, the occupant might be asleep by the time it reached the upper floor. She made a mental note to get a bungalow or ground-floor flat if she survived her life and job long enough to lose her mobility through old age.

Suzanna walked sideways up the stairs, staying away from the fluff-clinging greasy chairlift runner, to get to the first floor. She checked out the bathroom and bedrooms, lingering in the largest of these. The divan bed with dusky pink, velvet-covered headboard, was unmade. The sheets were crumpled and stained. She noticed a stiffness to stains in the centre of the sheets and guessed what would have caused them. She turned and called over her shoulder. "Rab!"

"Ma'am." He must have been on the landing anticipating questions. "Have these sheets been examined by the CSIs?"

"I'll check." He called down the stairs. "Neil. You still there?"

"Aye. Do you want me to come up?"

"No, I'll come down." On reaching the bottom, he asked, "My boss wants to know if the stains on the victim's bed sheets have been swabbed?"

Neil's face turned red. "Aye of course they have. What does she take me for? That question's an insult to my professionalism."

Rab would have had sympathy for Neil but under the circumstances the CSI's outburst was unjustified. He handed Neil the bagged sweets and explained where the DCI had found them. Neil's face remained flushed, as embarrassment took over from annoyance – his tongue stilled, his resentment washed away.

Suzanna opened the bedside locker and removed its contents: porno mags, a book of erotic BDSM short stores, a box of tissues and some sort of lubricant. She was not surprised. Nothing else caught her eye, so she withdrew. Rab confirmed that swabs of the sheet's stains had been taken. Forensics would check for a DNA match with the victim.

She descended the stairs and looked around the hall. Neil had slipped outside again. A telephone sat on a small table and beside it a phone book. She flipped through the book. "We'll need to find out who these people are and check the phone records for calls made over the last few months." She slipped the book into a polythene bag and gave it to Rab before entering the kitchen.

The units were probably fitted in the 1970s. The entire house would need modernising. Mustard-coloured, well-worn Formica covered all the door surfaces and end panels. The brown wood-effect worktop was chipboard with a laminate covering. It had bloated around the sink, where water had seeped into it from a bad seal, and there were two circles on either side of the free-standing cooker, burnt by carelessly placed hot pans. Greasy Venetian blinds obscured the view from the window. She leaned forward and pulled the cord to open them, then peered across the street. A CCTV camera mounted at an angle that would have captured visitors to the victim's house, was mounted on the home directly opposite. "Rab!" He appeared beside her and peered through the window.

"CCTV from the house opposite?"

"I'll check." He called Mairi but her phone went unanswered. He texted her, then returned to the kitchen. "Mairi's not answering her phone. I'll find out about the CCTV and let you know."

Although she had heard Rab's update, Suzanna didn't respond. Her mind focused on the kitchen's contents. The pans in the cupboard didn't appear to have been used for a long time, being covered in dust. The microwave, however, was splattered with sauce from baked beans and other food items. She opened the fridge. On the shelves, dotted with dried up milk products, there was a milk carton, some mild red cheddar cheese and some individual yoghurt pots – no fruit pieces, just artificial flavouring and colouring. White sliced bread but no fresh vegetables. The freezer held numerous ready meals, some ice-cream tubs and, bizarrely, packs of Mars and Snicker bars but nothing else.

The knife block stood beside the cooker. She extracted each of the knives and noted their condition. They'd hardly been used, and as Rab mentioned earlier, were still sharp and spotlessly clean, unlike the rest of the kitchen – indeed, house! She agreed with what Rab had told her; the missing knife was probably the murder weapon. "I've seen enough, Rab. Let's go."

Chapter 9

Keen to get home, the woman rushed along the street. Despite the haste, her mind returned to Tuesday. She smirked as the memories returned. She'd paid back the old bastard. Took the lecherous grin off his face. It had been the first real pleasure she'd encountered in years – orgasmic in its intensity. She wondered whether she might do it again? She'd sensed a new strength; powerful, having taken his life. Had watched the blood drain from his chest, his face whitening and his stature shrivelling.

She'd stayed until his head slumped and his breathing ceased. Afterwards, she'd washed the knife clean and taken it with her to dispose of, knowing the police would check the bins on the street straight away. They always did in the TV police series. So, she'd found a better place to get rid of the knife – smiled again at her cleverness.

Over the years, she'd become frumpy. Mumsy, some people would say. She couldn't remember the last time she'd been to a hairdresser for a cut and blow-dry. And she'd never paid for anyone to do her nails or massage her aching body. God knew she could have done with a massage after slaving away six days a week. Her back ached most evenings.

She hadn't chosen her profession. A spell in prison put an end to any hope of a normal life, a white-collar job, a three-bed semi in the suburbs. And it started with George *sodding* White. Life had been hard.

She'd lost her husband, turned to drink and lost her children. The depression took her into drugs, first prescribed by her doctor, then illegal highs. It was the drugs that turned her into a criminal. She'd been lonely, living in crap housing most of her life, with few friends. She had no real best friend, either. Sometimes she wished for death as a relief from her predicament, but she didn't have the resolve to commit suicide, so soldiered on with the drudgery of mundane living.

But now, finally, she felt free. Free of the memory of Mr White. She could rebuild her life. Change her name? Find a better job? Possibly find a man if she could love again? She almost skipped as she imagined how it might be. Then she slipped and fell, her hands reaching out to stop her fall. She squealed as her palms slid along the ice-coated rough concrete pavement – the skin torn away, then laid on the dirty wet pavement, the smile wiped off her face by the pain.

A passer-by helped her to her feet and offered an anti-septic wipe she had in her handbag to help clean up the grazes. There was some kindness in the world, after all. As she waited at the bus stop, she returned to her earlier thought. Killing the old man had been an emotional rush. Perhaps she would render a service to society by disposing of other shitty men like George White. She would listen out for stories of people who'd abused others, then plan revenge for them. A smile came to her face as the idea germinated. How she would achieve this wasn't clear, but she sensed a new purpose in life – seeking retribution for others who weren't able to take it themselves. A seeker of justice for those denied it by circumstance. A sort of superhero.

The bus arrived and she boarded, paying her fare to the driver before finding a seat. She positioned herself on one of the side-mounted inward-facing seats near the front of the bus, watching as each person entered, assessing them. Did they look to be hiding an evil side? Might they be abusers of vulnerable people? Should she follow one when they got off the bus and find out where they lived? During the ride, she pondered her idea and the people she'd seen get onto the bus. No one stood out to her. Thinking about it, she supposed such a shallow, momentary assessment would never highlight someone who deserved to die. She would park the idea and wait for inspiration.

The bus dropped her on the main road a short distance from her flat. As usual, the stairwell was grubby. Empty crisp bags and cigarette packets huddled in the corners, where they'd been kicked by occupants clearing their way as they walked. She climbed the two flights of steps, then turned the corner onto the concrete-floored hallway, its bland white walls grimy from neglect. The doors of neighbour's flats, all originally glossy dark blue, were scratched and dull, their coating having long lost its lustre. Paint was missing in straight broad lines on some doors, where tape once attached notes – saying, 'popped out for an hour,' 'please deliver packages to number 58', and other directions to callers – had stripped away the dull blue, to expose the grey primer.

Her own door was no better, but she excused herself of any responsibility, knowing the door had been like that when she'd moved into the flat. Besides, the council was responsible for maintaining its housing, not her. She passed no neighbours on the way to her flat. The place seemed deserted.

The woman dumped her bag on the sofa and put the kettle on before taking a jar of coffee from the wall cupboard. She'd never tried a 'real' coffee in a coffee shop (a fancy name for a café), as they charged over £2 for the smallest cup! A small jar of instant only cost that! Besides, it probably didn't taste any better than her supermarket's own brand granules. And she didn't need to wait for ages listening to hissing from a machine to get her cuppa. As she added milk to her mug, stirring the coffee granules into the milk, she heard the kettle click and the boiling noise fade. She poured the now-boiled hot water, added sugar, stirred again, then sat at the age-yellowed pine kitchen table, its varnish peeling, scuffed and marked by white rings.

CHAPTER 9

Whilst sipping her sweet coffee, she pondered how she might find the next man deserving her justice.

Chapter 10

Suzanna emerged from the house onto Coates Gardens, followed by Rab, stopped on the pavement and looked up and down the street. "What time of day did you say the murder probably occurred?"

"Early morning. Can't be precise, I'm afraid."

"Hmm…" She imagined the street at 8 am on a Tuesday morning. It was a through road, so traffic from adjacent streets would likely travel along it to take their drivers and passengers to places of work or education. The communal bins would have been emptied the day before, so no overflowing rubbish on the street. Many of the cars would still have been parked outside homes, their owners munching their Weetabix, chewing on muesli, or biting into toast. But some cars would already have been driven away, leaving gaps in the row.

She strode along the street, looking around her, putting herself into the murderer's mind. A person who had the murder weapon in their bag or pocket. She stopped and turned. Rab was a couple of paces behind her. "Would you put a large, sharp, probably wet, kitchen knife into your pocket and walk away?"

"Certainly not. Too risky. It might slice through the pocket fabric and cut my leg."

"Precisely. So, it would need to be in a bag. That suggests a woman or a man with a rucksack. Make sure more scrutiny is given to anyone on CCTV carrying a bag."

As his boss turned away, Rab typed the task into his phone's notes app. He caught up. "Ma'am, if it's okay with you, I'll knock on a few doors and see if anyone recognises the people we've caught on CCTV."

"Good idea, Rab." Suzanna continued along the street, imagining she was the murderer. On reaching the end, she stopped. Where would they have gone from here? Which way would they have turned? Where would he or she have been heading? A bus stop stood fifty metres away to her right. If they'd not driven, they might have caught a bus. She marched along the road to the stop and noted the bus routes that passed along Haymarket Terrace. As she headed back the way she'd come, a double-decker bus passed, its unique engine note announcing its approach before she saw it. As it accelerated away, its exhaust spewed black particles, like a swarm of Lilliputian bees; the smell of burnt diesel distressed her senses. It wasn't just the stench; she could virtually taste the fumes. She wondered how long it would take for buses to be switched to electric or hydrogen-powered motors.

She returned to the junction, deep in thought, then doubled back to the crime scene at pace, continuing onto the next junction, where she repeated what she'd just done. There were no bus stops in sight, but an eye-shaped park was sandwiched between Glencairn and Eglinton Crescents. She continued along Glencairn to the junction with Palmerston Place. To her left, she saw another bus stop with more routes to check. She crossed the road and noted the route numbers that stopped there, then set off back to White's house.

Rab was about to walk away, thinking no one was at home, when the door creaked open. He turned back. "Good morning. Sergeant Sinclair, Edinburgh CID. I'm investigating the death of Mr George White, a few doors down from you." The elderly woman looked puzzled. "I have a few pictures of people captured on CCTV around the time of his death and wondered if you would take a look at them." He started holding each one up so the woman could see. "We need to talk to these people.

They may have seen something that could help with our enquiries. If you recognise any, please do say."

She watched as he flipped through the pictures, her face indicating no recognition. As she saw the last picture, her face changed. "You recognise this man?" Rab prompted.

"Aye. That's Mr Melrose, from number 23. He'll likely be in if you call now. He's retired. Always goes to the corner shop for his newspaper first thing in the morning. I rarely see him outside his house after that until the afternoon. His wife died last year; bowel cancer, don't you know? She was in hospital for months, on morphine for the pain."

"Thanks, Mrs?" Rab said, cutting short her gossiping.

"Mrs Rathbone, Maggie."

"Thanks, Maggie. Most helpful. Do you know much about Mr White, by the way?"

"Aye. He's lived on this street for the last fifty years, I reckon. Here before me, anyroad."

"You're not a native of Scotland, Mrs Rathbone?"

"Nay, lad. Moved up here forty years ago, from Yorkshire. My husband's a Scot... Rumour has it that George White was a perve. I never heard anything specific but that's what Robert, my husband, told me his drinking pals had said. He did seem a bit creepy."

"Anything else you can tell me?"

She pouted her lips as she pondered. "Nay, lad. Nothing else to say about the man. He didn't socialise with his neighbours, nor did his wife." She paused, thinking again. "I do recall his daughter – Shirley, I believe. Often being in tears, when leaving the house. She avoided going home until she had to. My Norah – that's my eldest – told me Shirley was scared of her dad. Said he was an ogre."

"Thanks, Mrs Rathbone. That's exceptionally helpful. I'll let you get back to whatever you were doing." He stepped back and she watched him leave before closing the door. The DCI was approaching, so he walked back to White's house to meet her and report what Mrs Rathbone had said.

Suzanna told Rab about the buses that stopped nearby and instructed him to obtain any CCTV from those buses. He was also to arrange for questioning of all the drivers. One might have noticed a passenger that could provide a clue. She continued, "I don't recall Zahir mentioning a search of the parks, only front gardens, drains and bins. Has the park between Eglinton and Glencairn Crescents been searched?"

"I'm not sure. I'll check with Zahir and get him to organise it if it hasn't been done."

"Rab, the houses across the junction have commanding views of Glencairn Crescent and might have seen people walking towards them. The same goes for houses opposite the ends of Coates Gardens."

"I'll get Mairi onto it."

Suzanna switched on her phone mapping app and studied it. "There's also a park on West Coates. Get that searched. We need to find that knife." She returned to the map on her phone. "Rab. Haymarket station is a short walk away."

"Got it, ma'am. CCTV at the station."

Suzanna nodded in agreement. "Okay. At the junction of Douglas Crescent and Magdala Crescent, there's a footpath heading off towards a river – the Water of Leith. We'll need divers in that river. Start with the section between Belford Bridge and the AIDS Memorial Park. The murderer might have gone either way."

Rab acknowledged the tasking. "If there's nothing else, ma'am, it might be worth knocking on a few more doors. I'll start with Mr Melrose in Number 23."

***

After they'd knocked on a few more doors, Suzanna instructed Rab to go home, then returned to the station for one last job. She'd received a message from Alistair that a press briefing was required. She fired up her computer and drafted the communication.

Press Briefing Wednesday 4th March 2015. An 84-year-old man, George White, was found dead in his own home in the Coates area of Edinburgh yesterday. The death was not due to natural causes, and a murder investigation is underway. The motive for the attack is as yet unknown.

If any member of the public was in the Coates Gardens area between 7 am and 10 am on March 4th, we ask that they contact Edinburgh CID, in case they may have seen something important to the investigation.

There wasn't much Suzanna could say, but the newspapers would push for information and a press conference would probably be necessary within the next day or so. She read it one more time, then sent it to Steve Gibson in the communications department. After hitting send, she shut down her computer and headed home. She had a lot to catch up on.

Chapter 11

Suzanna entered the main door of the five-storey Edwardian town-house on Drumsheugh Gardens, then climbed the stairs to her first-floor apartment. The apartment benefited from high ceilings, large rooms and a bay window that overlooked a triangular grassed park, peppered with trees and shrubs and surrounded by black-painted wrought-iron railings. Daffodils had broken out in, so far, small splashes of summery yellow. Normally, their appearance indicated the arrival of spring, but the usual green backdrop was instead white and fluffy.

Suzanna slipped A-ha's latest album, Cast in Steel, into her CD player and hit play. She'd loved all their earlier work: the *Lifeline* album and *Hunting High and Low*. She wasn't so sure this latest album made the grade. As she prepared dinner, she listened to the lyrics of the title track.

'Don't you hate how everything falls, just falls away? I'll never get over what we said. It lingers in my head. I'll always remember what we knew, One hundred percent to be true.

To be right. To be real. Set in stone. And cast in steel.

We made a pact, eye to eye. Cross your heart. And hope to die

It lingers in my head. I'll always remember what we knew. One hundred percent to be true.'

It sent her back to thinking again about her failed marriage to Callum.

53

They'd sworn to be true to each other, through thick and thin, until death... But he'd betrayed her. Slept with a colleague. In the bed she'd shared with him. The bed just a few paces away, behind the door that she could see from where she stood. She'd washed the bedding and given the set to a charity shop. She couldn't bear to sleep on those same sheets where their fluids had mingled. Suzanna had eventually disposed of all the bedding they'd shared, buying replacement sheets and duvet sets, to symbolise a new beginning – a new phase of her life as a single woman.

She finished preparing the veg, dribbled oil into the wok and put it on the stove. In a separate pan, she heated oil then added gnocchi as the onions sizzled in the wok. When the veg was al dente, she stirred in pesto sauce and yoghurt then placed the pan-fried gnocchi into a bowl, followed by the now-coated veg. Suzanna loved the crunch and taste of roasted nuts, so added a sprinkling of cashews and crumbled on feta to top off her dinner.

She savoured every gorgeous mouthful as A-ha continued to play, and updated herself on the current affairs on her iPad news app. A-ha now sang *Objects in the Mirror*.

'*Looking back is bittersweet. All the world was at your feet. Love could make your life complete. Yeah, love could make your life complete.*

Teach your heart to skip a beat. Lift your eyes above the street. This is where you once belonged.'

The lyrics spoke to her. Life *could* be bittersweet. She had loved Callum. Loved him with an intensity she thought would never wane. And he'd loved her too. She truly believed that. Even when he'd betrayed her, he'd still loved her. He said it had been a stupid, sex-only thing. Love had made her feel complete, but it turned sour when they split. It was an emotion she didn't want to repeat. She'd been reluctant to get that close to another man in case he hurt her, like her first love. But now she was with James. Not married. Not even living together yet. But it was moving that way. Hopefully, he would want to see her at the weekend when he arrived back from Italy.

She would welcome feeling loved again. It would fill the emotional hole that being single brought. She could hide behind the convenience of a no-compromise solitude if she wished but in her heart, Suzanna wanted to share her life with another person. With someone who would reflect her love for him, where a bond would grow and hold them forever in its adoring grip. She longed to sense that warmth, not just the heat of sex. It was more than short-lived excitement that she craved. She wanted longevity, assuredness, cosiness, companionship – to grow old with a person she could rely on and trust.

Her stomach was now heavy with food. There would be no gym session tonight, no run around the streets. Instead, she donned her grippy-soled boots and went for a brisk walk, switching off A-ha, *'nothing is keeping you here, nothing is keeping you here....'*

As Suzanna strode along the pavement, watching out for icy patches, she pondered the lyrics, 'nothing is keeping you here.' It could be taken in a number of ways. Perhaps a hint that it was time to move. To seek a new appointment in a new place, far from Callum – in Cumbria, possibly. Maybe the song suggested a new role, like that proposed by the secretive Greg Lansdowne. Or the lyrics perhaps implied it was time to move on emotionally? To commit to a new relationship; not stay in the past; not worry about betrayal. It occurred to her she'd never asked James why his marriage had ended.

A few minutes later, she realised she was walking along Glencairn Crescent. The next road off to the left was Coates Gardens. She took the turn and marched along the street. Outside the house where George White's life had been taken from him, she paused. Across the street, a camera mounted on the wall by a first-floor window pointed directly towards her. She'd mentioned it to Rab but not heard anything since. It might be the key to the identity of the murderer. Logged in her mind to follow up tomorrow, she continued her walk.

She arrived back at Drumsheugh Gardens forty-five minutes after leaving, having covered two miles. Not bad, considering the conditions. She put away her boots and winter coat, then settled herself on the sofa, with a coffee and a book. She needed to switch off from the case, to let her mind relax and her subconscious do its work.

Thursday 5th March

Chapter 12

Murray pushed open the outer door and walked into the single unin-habited workspace, holding it open for his boss. He called out. "Hello there. Anyone in?"

Suzanna had left Rab in charge of coordinating the searches and CCTV work, taking Murray with her to visit *Cairngorm Community Care*. It was a glass-fronted unit squashed between convenience stores.

They heard a toilet flush, then a woman – legs and arms as thin as a birch sapling and bordering pensionable age – emerged, drying her hands on a paper towel. She had black hair with grey roots and wrinkled, sallow skin. She reeked of cigarette smoke, reminding Murray of Dot Cotton in the London-based soap East Enders. It was not a show he watched nowadays, but he had seen it a few times last year when his wife had it on. Murray disliked continuous conflict and the hatred shown by the characters towards each other. Anyone watching it regularly was bound to be indoctrinated by its characters' attitudes, he thought.

"Yes?"

Suzanna stepped forward and held up her card. "DCI McLeod, Edinburgh CID. This is DC Docherty. We'd like to ask you a few questions about Mr White, who was found dead on Tuesday."

"Och. Aye! Mary called it in. Terrible business. She telt me he was a lovely old man. Who on earth would have wanted to murder him?"

"That's what we're hoping to find out. For the record, your name, please?"

"Barbara Long." She said, elongating the second name as if to emphasise its meaning.

"Well, Barbara, what I need to know is where and how you keep your records for each client?"

Barbara shuffled to the nearby filing cabinet, opened the bottom drawer and extracted Mr White's details. She placed the folder on her table. "We keep a file on all the clients. No electronic stuff here. I don't trust it. And in any case, haven't a scooby how to use it." Suzanna had been in Scotland long enough to understand Barbara. In England, people would often say 'haven't a clue,' or 'no idea.'

No computer could be seen. She wondered how they managed their business without one. She put on silicone gloves before picking up the folder. On opening it, she leafed through the documents within, noting White's key safe code was logged, as expected. "We'll need to take this with us for evidence. How many people can access this folder?"

Barbara was surprised by the confiscation of the folder, which Suzanna slipped into a large poly bag Murray held open. "You dinna think one of us killed the man, surely?"

"We investigate all possibilities. Anyone who had access to these documents could have gained entry to the house, so we'll interview them all to eliminate them from our enquiries. We'll start with you."

Barbara sat in her chair behind the desk and indicated the officers should sit. The chairs were moulded plastic with steel legs, similar to those used in school canteens. Murray opened his notepad and took out his pen, poised to write.

"So, Barbara," Suzanna said, "were you in this office when Mary called in the death?"

"Aye, I was. I start at 3 pm and stay 'til ten unless there's a need to stay later. Sometimes I get away a little earlier."

"Is there any way that can be corroborated?"

"What do you mean? Can I prove I were here?"

"Yes. Exactly."

"We've no CCTV or anything. I canna think how to prove it."

"Did you speak to anyone else before Mary called?"

"Aye. I took a few calls. Mostly they were from clients whose carers hadn't arrived at the expected time. And Jennine Bottomly called to ask if I could get someone to take on her next client because the fella she was with had messed himself and she needed more time to sort him out."

"And did you arrange that?"

"Och, no! We did'nae have spare carers to send, so I telt her she'd need to make up the time somehow."

"Okay. I'll need a list of all your staff, with their address and contact details. Oh! And details of their shift patterns and client schedules for the next week or so."

Barbara pulled a folder from the top drawer and laid it on the table. "You will'nae take that with you, I hope?"

"No. That won't be necessary. Murray, take a picture of the staff list and schedules with your phone, please." As Murray followed instructions, Suzanna continued. "Would Mary have been working on the morning that George White was killed?"

"Nae. She's on the late shift."

"So, you won't know where she will have been, then?"

Barbara shook her head.

"Who else works in this office?"

"There's just the two of us. Davina and me. Davina Perkins. We take turns doing early or late shifts and covering the weekends. Sometimes we end up having to double shift, 'cause Mr Higgins – he's the owner – won't take on any more coordinators. It's a nightmare if one of us takes a holiday."

"Who sits in on those occasions?"

"Mr Higgins, sometimes. We also use one of the carers to fill in if we have to and if we can spare one."

"I'll need a list of the carers who've been used as temporary coordinators."

Barbara picked up the document that Murray had finished copying. She ran through the list and called out names, which Murray noted in his pad.

"Barbara. Are you aware of any reason someone might want to murder Mr White?"

"As I said before, not a scooby, dear."

"Are there any members of staff or management who are odd, in any way? Someone that you might consider strange, out of the ordinary?"

"There's plenty of strange folk walking past this office every day," she said flippantly, before pausing. "There's one or two odd ones amongst the ladies, plus Mr Higgins. Maja Basinski is rather uptight. She's Polish (as if that explained it). She can be bolshie. I seen her once in the office when Davina was still in the chair. She got real angry and went red in the face. She raised her hand as if to strike Davina but stopped and stormed out."

"What was that about?"

"She'd wanted to take time out to go home to her mother in Krakow but Davina said we couldn't cover her absence at such short notice. Maja said she had to go; Davina must find another carer to do her rounds. Davina telt her if she went without our permission, she would'nae have a job to come back to.

"I see. Who else do you consider suspicious?"

"Well. Not suspicious but certainly odd. Georgina Elliot is a quiet one. She only speaks when she has to. I don't know how she manages the clients when she's so reluctant to talk. She doesn't seem to be the carer type. She's a cold fish. It's just a job for her. Most of the women care about the old people they help."

Suzanna didn't think Georgina sounded suspicious. She was probably doing the job because she needed the money and had few skills for other work. "What about the owner?"

"Mr Higgins. We call him Huggy. Not to has face of course. Huggy Higgins. His real name is Marcus. He likes to cuddle the women if they let him. He's not tried it on with me, but he's handled Davina a few times. She just shrugs him off and gets on with her work. She doesn't want to make a fuss in case she loses her job. If he touched me, I'd tell him to piss off and keep his hands to himself. But I guess I'm past it now. Who'd want to touch me?"

Suzanna ignored the women's self-deprecation – but noted Murray's expressions, suggesting he agreed with Barbara – and continued. "Does the list provide details of all your past employees?"

"No. I'll dig out previous years' lists. Just a minute." Barbara returned to the filing cabinet and pulled out the old records, passing them to Murray to photograph.

Once Murray had done the job, Suzanna rose. "Thanks for your time, Barbara. we have all we need for the time being. We'll leave you to get on with your work." As if there were something magic about those words, releasing a hold over calls, the phone on Barbara's desk rang.

Chapter 13

On returning to the station, Suzanna went directly to the superintendent's office. Alistair looked up as she stopped in the open doorway. "Ah! Suzanna. What news?"

She stepped into his office and took the chair opposite him, warmed by his positive body language. "The searches and video checking carried out so far resulted in nothing useful. So, I visited the scene and walked the nearby streets. Rab now has some additional work to follow up on, searches, buses and CCTV. Our focus has to be on finding the weapon and identifying potential victims of White. I think I might have uncovered our motive."

"Revenge, I suppose," Alistair said, "going by the broken award. There seems to have been some sort of grudge held by the murderer."

"Agreed. I believe the motive has sexual connotations. The old guy had S&M porno DVDs next to his TV, and magazines and books with a similar theme in his bedside locker. My thinking is he's abused a woman in his past – as far back as the 1980s when he won the award for best employee."

"You need to remember, Suzanna, that he's a lonely old man. Porn films and mags may well be his way of bringing some spice into his tedious life. There might not be any connection to the crime. Male masturbation is common even into old age."

"I get that, but equally they might be connected. It's certainly a line worth following."

"I can't disagree. Nothing was taken from White's house as far as we know, was there? And no other motive has presented itself." He paused, obviously in thought. Suzanna patiently awaited his next question. She had great respect for Alistair. He always treated her and the rest of the team well, never humiliated them, was encouraging, thoughtful and willing to offer advice but didn't force his views on them. "Anything else worth mentioning?"

"No. Not yet."

***

Suzanna's team were all at their desks, staring at computer screens, immersed in lists, or on the phone, when she entered the main office. "Five minutes, guys. Team meeting," she said, passing through to the kitchenette. Like a herd of sheep noticing a passing walker, they all turned their heads towards her, then acknowledged her announcement in their own way. Some raised their hands; others nodded or caught her eye to confirm they'd heard.

When Suzanna returned, they were all ready to talk, having finished their calls and paused their computer searches. She placed her steaming mug on the corner of a desk. "The way I see it – and I assume most of you will have already started – we need to focus today's work on background checks for the past and present employees of *Cairngorm Community Care*. And, on following up any leads from neighbours and CCTV."

"We've completed the CCTV reviews, ma'am," Mairi said. "I've printed off faces of people caught on camera in that area and put them on the board, starting with those spotted closest to the crime scene at the top, then spreading down the further away they were from Coates Gardens."

Suzanna liked Mairi. She was a good officer. Respectful, courageous, determined and possessed a sharp mind. She'd come up with some

64

excellent lines of enquiry during the last murder case and grown in Suzanna's estimation.

"Thanks, Mairi. Did any faces ring bells? Anyone..?"

There were head shakes all around. Then Murray piped up, "There was one chap who was dressed like a town crier. He'd have had a bell."

The team looked at Murray in disbelief at his rubbish joke. Suzanna ignored the flippant comment and turned to Mairi. "Opposite the crime scene, I noticed a camera on a house, pointing towards our victim's door. What did you get from that one?"

"Nothing, ma'am. When I asked for data from their camera, the lady said it had been inoperative."

Suzanna frowned, silently cursing their bad luck. "Cars?"

"It was a busy time of day, so hundreds of cars passed the city's CCTV cameras. It was a mammoth task to identify any worthy of following up. We used footage from private CCTV in Coates Gardens to match with cars that had been seen on the official cameras. My next job is to run them through the system and identify drivers and their addresses."

"Fine. That all makes sense." Suzanna paused. "Zahir. Searches for the murder weapon?"

"I've had the search area expanded as you suggested, ma'am. They've yet to report back."

"How come you're not out there coordinating the searches?" Suzanna was surprised and a little disappointed that Zahir had not assumed direct oversight of these crucial searches.

"Sergeant Duffy from the Haymarket station offered to do it. Most of the guys are from his station, anyway."

"Okay." She knew Sergeant Duffy, having worked with him previously. She changed her view about Zahir's judgement, as she would also trust Duffy to supervise the search. "When do you expect them to have completed the searches?"

"By early afternoon, today, ma'am."

"What about the river search, by the divers?"

"The dive team is *submerged* in a search at Glasgow." Zahir grinned at his clever choice of adjective. Mairi rolled her eyes. He was as funny as a Christmas cracker joke writer. "They should have some of them back tonight and they'll start the Water of Leith search tomorrow."

"Fair enough... Employees, Rab?"

"Half of them have been contacted to find out where they'll be today. After calling the rest of the current employees, I will start interviewing them. Haven't started the ex-employee list yet."

"Murray and Owen can deal with the ex-employees," Suzanna said. "They can split it and start making contact." The two DCs nodded. "Has anyone contacted the relatives yet?"

Rab responded. "I arranged for the Inverness police to break the news to Edmond White, the victim's son. They reported back that he didn't seem too bothered about it. Hadn't seen his father for over a year. The daughter, Miss Sheila White," he said, checking his notes, "is on the island of Iona – living and working in the religious community there. So, the Highlands and Islands division was asked to do the same. I haven't heard back from them yet."

"Any other family?" Suzanna asked.

Rab replied, "Parents died over twenty years ago. He has a brother, Albert White, living in Peebles. His sister passed away in 2013."

"I guess the son will have contacted his uncle... We should call on the son and daughter. The uncle might also be worth talking with. And check to see who will benefit financially from his death – his children, presumably. I'd like background checks run on them both, as well." Suzanna hesitated.

"Already underway," Rab reported, feeling good that he was ahead of his boss.

"We haven't yet established a motive," Suzanna continued, "although the broken award suggests someone who worked for George

White during his time with Butler and Cargrove. I'll follow that one up today. Any other lines of enquiry?"

She could see them pondering, but they all soon returned their attention to Suzanna. "Okay. Let's get stuck into the work then. Zahir. I want feedback from the searches as soon as they're complete." She left them to their work, returned to her office and searched for the contact details of Butler and Cargrove. They were headquartered in Glasgow but had a factory in Edinburgh. She headed out via the main office to let the team know where she was going.

***

The Butler & Cargrove factory had evidently been around for many years. Its stone walls had darkened from decades of soot from passing diesel engines and 20th-century coal fires. A gateway, broad enough for trucks to pass each other, broke the wall's flow. Electric operated red and white striped barriers stood across the gap. Suzanna found a place to park on the street and went through the pedestrian entrance next to the road gateway. A security office window overlooked the pathway. She approached, showed her card and asked to speak with the head of HR.

It took ten minutes before someone from HR arrived and escorted her into their offices. Mrs Milligan, the HR Manager, greeted Suzanna and invited her into her office, having instructed her assistant to bring coffee and biscuits. "How can we help you, Chief Inspector?"

Suzanna explained she needed to see the records of Mr George White, who'd worked in the company's accounts department during the 1970s and 80s. She'd also require the details of anyone who worked with or for Mr White.

"Oh dear! I was hoping we could help you. But thirty years ago, you say? There'll not be any records available for that time period. They might have been destroyed by now. There's a possibility the records could be in the archive facility but that's in Glasgow. It would take a

67

day or two to have that checked."

Suzanna was disappointed. She should have thought of that and not wasted her time driving to the factory. "Might there be anyone still working here who'd been around during that period?"

"I'd need to ask around. I've only been here seven years, but there might be some long in the tooth staff who were employees in that era. Just a minute." She moved into the HR main office and instructed a member of her team to do some digging. As she returned, the coffee and some oaty biscuits arrived. Suzanna politely accepted a biscuit and nibbled at it between sips of filter coffee.

"May I ask what this is about, Chief Inspector?"

"You'll get to hear soon enough, so I may as well tell you. It's in connection with the murder of Mr White."

Mrs Milligan's sat up at the news, like a meerkat starting guard duty. "Was this related to the incident reported in the papers the other day about a crime committed in the Coates area?"

"That's the one. White's house is on that street. His name wasn't released to the press because the next of kin hadn't been informed at that time. One line of enquiry we're pursuing is that he was murdered by someone who worked with him during his time here. I can't tell you why yet as the information hasn't been formally released. And it is just one possibility we're investigating. Please keep this to yourself for the moment, because if the press gets hold of this information before we're ready to release it, it could hamper the investigation and delay justice."

"So, this former employee would have held a grudge against him and taken revenge? That seems doubtful. Why would anyone wait thirty years for vengeance?"

"It might appear to be unlikely. It *would* be strange to wait that long, but we have to investigate that possibility, just in case."

The door opened and another lady entered. She placed a piece of paper on the desk and retreated. Mrs Milligan picked it up and studied the list before passing it to Suzanna. There were eleven names. All men. "Apart from Mr Carmichael, the rest are all factory workers, nearing the end of their time. I shouldn't think any of them will know what went on in the accounts department. But Mr Carmichael will have been a lowly HR clerk at that time. He's now my boss – Head of Administration and Communication for the whole company. I understand they let him remain at this factory, because that's where his home is and he had no wish to transfer to the Glasgow HQ. He's a stickler for procedures and protocol but good at his job. Never seen him make a mistake."

"Is he in at work today?"

"Yes. Would you like to talk to him?" Suzanna nodded. "I'll see if he's free." Mrs Milligan replaced the phone after speaking with Carmichael's PA. "He's coming here to meet you."

"Wonderful!"

Two minutes later, Carmichael marched into the office. "Chief Inspector." He held out his hand, almost snapping his heels as he did, his posture straight as a soldier on parade. "Welcome to Butler and Cargrove. Brian Carmichael. How can I help you?" His eyes swayed to the biscuit plate and the empty coffee cup. "I see Mrs Milligan has offered you refreshments. Excellent!"

Mrs Milligan rose and walked towards the door. "Take my chair, Mr Carmichael. I'll leave you to it."

Carmichael took up the offer. "So, what is it I can do for you?"

"I understand you worked here at the same time as George White. He managed accounts at the time. This would have been around 1980, plus or minus a few years."

Carmichael looked perplexed but nodded.

"He's recently been murdered and we believe there may be a connection to his time with this company. What can you tell me about the man?"

69

"Not a lot. I was in my early twenties. At the bottom of the ladder and he was a senior manager – in his fifties. I never came in contact with the man, except for passing him in the corridor. "

"Did you pick up on any character traits in those brief encounters?"

"He never said so much as good morning or afternoon. He always seemed focussed on his destination, like a blinkered horse. I doubt I existed to him. He'd talk to other senior people in the company but not erks, like me."

"That's an interesting term to describe yourself. Did you ever spend time in the Royal Air Force?"

"No, but my brother did. He said that's what they called those in the lowest ranks. It sort of stuck with me."

"Yes. I've heard it used, as well, because my father was in the RAF... Was there any talk around the company about George White? Gossip?"

Carmichael thought back to those days. "Nothing specific. There were rumours he was a bit hands-on, in managing his ladies," he said, waving both hands. "But other than that, I couldn't say. He left to take up another accounts management job elsewhere in the city. He wasn't fired as far as I know. The records will give us more detail. I understand Moira is arranging for the archives to be searched."

Suzanna looked at the nameplate that sat on Mrs Milligan's desk. It confirmed her first name as Moira. "Yes. She said it might take a couple of days. If there's any way that could be achieved earlier, that would be most helpful."

Chapter 14

Suzanna parked behind a twenty-year-old, tatty, white Ford Fiesta, with rusting sills and a delaminating tailgate, having stopped off on her way back from the Butler and Cargrove factory. She checked the car's details to confirm it belonged to the carer she had come to interview. The car desperately needed a wash, but she guessed anyone with a car that old loses pride in it. Suzanna reflected on how cars in their teens and twenties were considered to be old bangers, but when they became over thirty years old, they became classics – collectors' cars – and started increasing in value again. Not surprising though, given that most cars didn't last that long – only those tucked away in garages and polished at weekends.

A few minutes passed before a squirrel-faced woman emerged from the house. She had puffy cheeks and her hairline sat less than an inch above her eyebrows. Suzanna closed on the woman as she approached her car. "Margaret Lightfoot?"

The woman looked up, surprised, then likely remembered that she'd been asked to speak with the police. "Aye. That's me."

"Detective Chief Inspector McLeod. I'd like a quick word."

"It'll have to be quick. I'm due at my next client's in five minutes and there's no slack in the timings."

Margaret's record showed she was the same age as Suzanna. But the woman looked a lot older. Her greying hair had probably been cut in a bob a few months ago but had now grown out and hung messily on her shoulders. Suzanna hoped she'd not been dishing out food for an elderly client or they may have had some unwanted extra ingredients.

"I'll make it as quick as I can but this a murder enquiry! Have you ever provided care for Mr George White in Coates Gardens?"

"No. I normally stick to this area of the city. It would take me too long to get there and back in the busy traffic."

"You have run the office in the city centre once or twice, though, haven't you?"

"Only because they persuaded me. They were desperate and they said I was the only person they could trust. "

"But you've never been to Mr White's?"

"I said so, didn't I. Now stop wasting my time. I need to get to my next appointment."

"On Tuesday, this week, you were off work. Where were you?"

"I visited my sister in Coatbridge."

"All day?"

"Aye, all day. Now can I go?"

"If you'll give me her name, address and phone number, I'll hold you up no longer." Suzanna passed her a pen and notepad. Margaret huffed but took the offered pen and scribbled on the pad, before unlocking her car door.

"Thanks for your cooperation, Mrs Lightfoot," Suzanna said ironically. Margaret turned over the car's engine for a full minute before it started, then drove away, the car's exhaust burbling and smoking. It probably needed a service as well as a wash, Suzanna thought. She called Mrs Lightfoot's sister, Nadine Pritchard, who confirmed the visit timings: arrived about 9 am and left at 3 pm. She returned to her car and looked up the next carer before heading to Longstone, the engine of her BMW starting without fuss. Suzanna was thankful she earned enough to afford a decent car.

***

Rab completed his work on background checks of current care company employees and found Murray and Owen had also finished their work on previous employees' records. A couple of CCC's previous employees had died since leaving the company. One with breast cancer, another due to a heart attack. They delved deeper into their results. Some had criminal records but for minor crimes, like shoplifting, drunk and disorderly, and assault (when drunk). But nothing that raised their hackles. They checked the employment histories of the women – they were *all* women.

"We need to speak to these women," Rab said, "and find out where they were on the morning White met his end, then verify any alibis. The chief is checking out two of them already, as she's in the west of the city and they're working out that way. Murray, correlate them all geographically and then split them into three groups, please. Then we'll get stuck into tracking them down and interviewing them." Fifteen minutes later, their phones were hot with use.

***

Mrs Leslie McPeters didn't own a car. Instead, she rode between clients on her bicycle, which Suzanna assumed was the one leaning against the hedge surrounding the five-storey block of flats across the road. Ten minutes later, a woman dressed in the CCC blue carers' uniform emerged from the flats and walked to the bike. Like most of the carers she'd come across, she was middle-aged and overweight, but not severely obese. "Mrs McPeters?"

"Aye. Are you that polis lady they said would be coming to see me?"

"Yes. Detective Chief Inspector McLeod. I need a few minutes of your time." Now nearer to the woman, Suzanna noticed a small beard – just a few long straggly chin hairs – and a faint moustache, below her aquiline nose.

Leslie checked her watch before speaking. "Okay. Fire away."

"Have you ever looked after Mr George White, on Coates Gardens?"

"Not a chance. I canna travel far on my push-bike. I've only ever worked this part of the city."

"And you've never worked as a care coordinator?"

"They did ask me once but it would have been too difficult. When I told them they said not to worry, they'd find someone else."

Suzanna peered into her eyes, looking for signs of deception, surprised the office staff had let her off so easily. There are numerous buses into the city, so not having a car wouldn't have prevented the woman from working in the office.

"Look, I'd best get on or I'll not get around all my clients." She turned her back on Suzanna, secured her bag on the bike's rear rack, then cycled away, standing on her peddles initially to accelerate. Suzanna wondered whether the urgency to get away was genuine, or an excuse to avoid further questioning?

Chapter 15

Suzanna's phone pinged like a bicycle bell and she glanced at the new WhatsApp message. 'Enjoying Livigno's slopes. Missing you. Hope you're not working too hard. Love James.' She messaged back. 'Missing you too. Wish I was there.' She placed her phone back in its tray and drove off along the wet road, the snow having dissolved.

On reaching the station, Suzanna found the guys had spoken with many of the CCC employees by phone, but they still had about twenty remaining. Of those they'd talked to, five admitted to having served Mr White at some time. This correlated with the office's records. She tasked them with speaking to clients once the staff interviews had been completed. They needed to hear about the character of each CCC employee, from the people they served. Had any carer given them cause for concern? Did any of the women have significant character defects? Could any be mentally unstable? Suzanna asked Mairi for an update on the CCTV and cars research.

"I have the names and addresses of all registered car drivers. And I've visited the two closest to the station. Nothing to report on those. We need to get out and talk with the others. I planned to do that next."

"Before you do, did any of those vehicles stop in Coates Gardens for more than a minute that morning?"

"There were only three, recorded on a CCTV camera entering the area, seen on a private CCTV moving along the street, then logged again at another."

"All drivers must be interviewed in case they saw anything. The three that stopped need more scrutiny. Why did they stop? Where did they park? Did they get out of their cars?"

"Got it."

"Great." Suzanna rose and strode to the crime board, then studied the pictures of the pedestrians who'd been captured on CCTV. She didn't recognise any of them.

"Zahir?"

He turned and spoke without further prompt, guessing what she intended to ask. "The park, road, garden and bin searches have all been completed, ma'am, including the expanded area, as instructed. The dive search team confirmed they'll start their search first thing in the morning. I'll head along to the Water of Leith before coming into the office and ensure they're looking in the right place and know what they're looking for."

"Thanks, Zahir. Please work with Mairi for the rest of the day on tracking down the drivers and interviewing them." Suzanna rose and returned to her sanctuary, needing some thinking time. She closed the door and reclined her chair, staring at the ceiling, before closing her eyes and letting her mind drift.

Updates from forensics and the pathologist were due. She'd need to chase them. She also realised she'd not been updated on White's children and not yet seen his will, so returned to the main office. Rab had already left. "Mairi. Zahir. Has Rab mentioned anything about the son and daughter or the will?"

"He said the son is coming down from Inverness for the formal identification. Should be here tomorrow. Rab also has details of Mr White's solicitor and has asked for a copy of the will," Mairi said.

"Anything from the pathologist or forensics, yet?"

"Not seen anything, ma'am," they chorused.

****

The journey to the mortuary frustrated Suzanna and she found it difficult to find a parking space, but as soon as she saw Mark, her spirits brightened. A fellow Englishman, Mark had been educated at Woodbridge School in Suffolk before training as a doctor. His upbringing had instilled in him a healthy self-confidence, unlike some graduates of independent schools Suzanna knew, who'd become arrogant. Muscularly built, he stood an inch taller than Suzanna, his wavy light brown hair long on top but short at the sides.

The mortuary was as ever clinically clean, the floors squeaky under her feet as they walked together through to the examination room where White's body still lay. Smells of bleach and blood made Suzanna's nose twitch.

"A knife to the heart was the obvious cause of death," Mark said, peering over the top of his tortoiseshell framed reading glasses. "I confirmed this during my examination of his body. I didn't find any contributory factors. No poisons or drugs – apart from the drugs you'd expect a man in his late eighties to be taking. I checked his records and matched the drugs in his blood with those prescribed by his doctor. There were no scrapes and bruises. The only other wounds were on his hands. The injuries – here, have a look – would have been caused by attempting to deflect the knife. But he was evidently unsuccessful because the knife thrust went directly into his heart between the fourth and fifth ribs, adjacent to the breastbone. Whoever killed the man was precise with the placing of the blade. It was no casual stabbing. The knife was evidently held horizontally because the one-inch blade could not have gone cleanly between the ribs at any other angle."

"So, this was well planned. Premeditated murder, not some crime of passion or lashing out in anger?"

"Agreed. An assassination or execution."

She wandered around the body, observing him from all angles. What

77

type of man was George White? She knew he watched porno films and masturbated but Alistair said that didn't make him a pervert. She couldn't disagree. The award had been smashed to pieces, pointing towards a grudge, but they'd yet to uncover a definite motive or find out what he'd done to earn the wrath of his killer. He didn't look evil but then some of the most wicked people she'd met and locked up, had not given away their vile nature by their looks.

"Any other observations, Mark?" Suzanna asked, returning her attention to the pathologist standing beside her. "Whether or not you consider it related to his death?" Mark noticed her looking at his crooked nose.

"Nothing. Sorry. It was a straightforward stabbing... Before you ask, my nose was broken during a rugby game at school. It never set straight."

"Oh! Sorry. I didn't realise I was staring." She said, turning back to the body. She imagined George White clothed and sitting in the dirty brown chair in his gloomy living room. Had he seen the knife before it was thrust between his ribs and into his beating heart? Had he known the reason for his assassination? She pondered as she stared into his soul. He must have known. If this were a revenge killing, the perpetrator would have ensured he knew why he was about to die. It wouldn't be an act of retribution without him knowing the reason. She wondered how he had reacted to being confronted by an old adversary from perhaps three decades ago. Would he have been afraid? Would he have understood? Would he have repented?

"Thanks, Mark. I'll let you get on."

"Any time." He looked at her admiringly, his eyes fixed on her shapely figure as she walked away.

Chapter 16

"I'm concerned, Alistair," Suzanna said. "The murder was precisely planned. In the words of the pathologist, an assassination or execution. My worry is that White's death could be the start of a new serial killer's career – a person who sees themselves as doing society a service by removing old burdensome people. Like Colin Norris and Kenneth Erskine," Suzanna said.

The superintendent pondered for a minute before answering. "If I recall correctly, Colin Norris was the nurse who killed four patients in Leeds Hospital in 2002 by injecting them with insulin. And Kenneth Erskine, aka the Stockwell Strangler, sexually assaulted, then strangled seven elderly people back in the 1980s."

"Exactly right, Alistair. Even if White's death was planned as a one-off revenge murder, the person who killed White might acquire a taste for killing. It's possible they'll strike again."

"Agreed. Best you catch them before they do, then!"

"By the way, I'm conscious that Police Scotland is forming MITs and that they will pick up major crimes, including all murders. Are you aware of any planned restructuring of my team?"

"There are talks going on at the upper levels and I'm aware of the plan to form these specialist units. But I've not seen any details or heard anything specific about your team. Why do you ask?"

"It might lead to the breakup of my team. I'd like to know about it in

THE KEY TO MURDER

advance, to prepare. It would be a waste of their talents if they were to investigate only minor crimes. We have an excellent record of solving murders and tackling organised crime within the city."

"Aye. True. Look, I'll keep my ear to the ground. In fact, I'll ask a few questions upstairs and let you know what I find out."

Suzanna left Alistair to get on with his work. She sometimes wondered what he did. He attended meetings, contributed to policy-making and managed his team, but she'd believed he was also involved in strategic decisions. From what he'd just said, that didn't seem to be the case. And he rarely involved himself in investigations. If getting promoted meant leaving behind the detective role, she'd prefer to stay in her current rank. The challenge of tracking down criminals got her out of bed every morning – gave her a reason to live. The thrill of the chase made her feel alive. But she thought back to what Greg Lansdowne had said. She wouldn't be satisfied investigating burglaries and muggings. Would she want to move to an MIT?

***

Suzanna looked through the vast glass window into the forensic laboratory. A spotless stainless-steel sink, similar to those used in professional kitchens, sat in the room's centre atop a bench, with multiple drawers and cupboards. White-coated men and women sat staring into microscopes, at clinically clean Formica topped benches, plastic shower-hat-like head coverings containing their hair. The lab seemed to be silent, everyone concentrating on their work, rather than chatting, as was common in other workplaces. She had been to the Scottish Police Authority's Forensics Services offices, in the south of the city, many times. But being so far out, she normally only visited occasionally when in the area anyway, or needed to be shown something of importance.

Suzanna couldn't shut herself away in this environment. She needed to interact with people, breathe fresh air – when she got out of the office – and explore the streets and countryside. Seeing the same walls every working day of her life, as these scientists must, would drive her mad. She was thankful these specialists were intrigued by their work and provided the evidence she and her team needed for identifying criminals and gaining convictions.

"So, what do you have for me in the George White case?"

The Head of Forensic Services, Jonathon Trimble, spoke. "We had a number of full and partial prints from various locations around the house, none of which match with known criminals. But once you gather prints from suspects, they'll certainly help prove their presence in the house. We also analysed the contents of the doormat and living room carpets. Most of the debris matched with that on the path leading to the front door and on the street in front of the house. But traces of unexpected cleaning products were found. One particular chemical was specifically for wooden floors. There are no exposed wooden floors in the house and, as expected, the cleaning chemical in question was not present in the property. We even have a brand for the product – it's listed in our report. That might help you link a person to the crime scene."

"Yes. That might prove helpful. I just hope we can find the murder weapon and get that to you. Chances are it will have been wiped clean, but I know you can pick up tiny traces," Suzanna responded. She paused before speaking again, wondering what other evidence might help them trace the culprit and link them to the scene of the crime. "Do you believe the victim's blood might be on the murderer's clothes?"

"We found the victim's blood on the chair and in the carpet in front of it, as well as under the chair, of course. The pool under the chair was caused by his blood draining, running down his body, into the seat cushion, then dripping onto the floor. The other blood traces were not from dripping but from spraying. When the knife had been pressed into the man's pumping heart, the blood would have sprayed from the

81

wound under pressure. It's been suggested that blood can squirt up to thirty feet. In my experience, however, blood has never been found that far from a body."

"Interesting. In this case, how far had blood travelled?"

"We found blood in the carpet up to one metre away from the body. There was a pattern to it, which would indicate where the murderer stood in relation to the victim. This confirmed they would have been directly in front of the man, with the knife in their right hand. The wound is in the left side of the victim's chest. The murderer will most definitely have been sprayed by the blood, although they might not have realised it because a fine spray may not be obvious. Given the height of the chair and the victim's wound, the spray will have emanated from the body at 39-40 inches above floor level. That's roughly waist height in the average man. So, I'd look at the murderer's trousers and whatever they'd worn on their upper body. "

"Or skirt, if a woman."

"Indeed. Any blood on a dark fabric would likely go unnoticed."

"That might be useful. As soon as we arrest a suspect, we'll get their clothing to the lab. Is there anything else of note, Jonathon?"

"Yes. We took prints off the key safe cover that might belong to the murderer. The cover can be difficult to grip and often difficult to take off. So, the prints on there are well defined. We also got partial prints from the safe and the key."

"Okay. Good to know. Obviously, taking the suspects' prints will be one of the first things we do."

"Yes, yes. Of course."

"Any prints on the broken trophy?"

"Some faint prints. Probably from when the trophy had been handled some time ago but nothing fresh. What we did find, though, was the print of a rubber glove. Not a clinician's glove but a domestic rubber glove. The sort worn when cleaning. Again, we've identified the brand, but it won't be possible to link the murderer directly to the victim by that print, although it may well provide further circumstantial evidence."

"I'm surprised you got a print from the rubber gloves. I thought the reason fingerprints showed up was the owner's sweat and amino acids created a pattern shaped by their prints?"

"Yes. You're right. That's how prints are created. And that's why people with very dry hands don't always leave useful prints for us to detect. But a cleaning chemical on the gloves had the same effect as bodily fluids, creating a print in the glove's fingerprint grip pattern."

"Hmm... Anything else?"

"No. That about covers it."

"Thanks, Jonathon. I'm glad I called in."

"By the way. You'll recall the Shirley McKie case?"

"Yes. It called into question the accuracy and reliability of Scotland's fingerprinting services and led to the establishment of The Fingerprint Inquiry."

"Exactly! Well, we've made significant changes across the board, with improved training, upgraded equipment and procedures. I've just signed off on implementing all the inquiry's recommendations and we're expecting UKAS to visit and confirm we now meet the required standards."

"What's UKAS?" Suzanna asked.

"Sorry. The United Kingdom Accreditation Service."

"That's good to know. If there's any doubt about the evidence provided, it's more difficult to gain convictions."

"Precisely why I thought you'd be keen to know."

News of the forthcoming accreditation pleased Suzanna, but it didn't excite her as it appeared to the Head of Forensics. Jonathon was a typical scientist. Not the frizzy-haired, mad scientist type, like the *Back to the Future* movie character, but a bespectacled, serious person, interested in minute details.

"Listen. Are you doing anything at the weekend? It's just that Julia and I are celebrating our 10th wedding anniversary with a party at our house on Saturday. If you've nothing else on, we'd love you to join us – and bring a partner if you have one."

For the first time since they'd started conversing, Suzanna looked properly at Jonathon, seeing him as a person rather than a white-coated head of department. Their heights matched but his eyes were lower than her own, his bullet-shaped head and high forehead squashing his features into the bottom half of his face. Susanna's build was more robust, probably because he spent much of his time operating microscopes and writing reports, rather than being active. "That's kind of you to invite me, Jonathon. I'm not sure if I'll be able to come. Depends on how the case is going. But I'll take your address, just in case."

***

Suzanna grabbed the woman's collar and pulled her close, her hand snatching her sleeve. Dropping and spinning, she extended her right leg, trapping her opponent's shins. A downward pull on the neck and arm saw the woman falling forward, tripped by Suzanna's foot. She tumbled. A twist of Suzanna's arms and rotation of her shoulder sent her opponent squarely onto her back, with power and control. "Ipon," called the referee.

Suzanna stood and helped the other woman to rise from the matting. They stood facing each other, bowed, then walk away – contest over. She smiled to herself. After the session finished, Suzanna and her opponent met in the changing rooms. It stank of perspiration and perfumed soap. They both needed to shower after working up a sweat in the ninety-minute session. Hair still damp, they walked out of the judo club together. "You might be old for a judoka," the other woman said, "but you can still pull off the moves."

"Hey, not so much of the old, young lady," Suzanna smiled as she responded.

Angela, who was in her early thirties, smiled back at her. They walked to the car park side by side, the air crisp cold. "Are you up for a drink tonight, Suzanna?"

Suzanna checked her watch and contemplated the suggestion. "Yeah, why not." They dumped their sports bags in their cars and walked across the road to the local pub. Angela was a little shorter than Suzanna. Despite being ten years younger, Suzanna noticed flecks of grey in her auburn hair.

The bar was busy and noisy, despite being a mid-week evening. The odour of spilled beer permeated the air. But thankfully the room wasn't smoke-filled, like pubs used to be before smoking restrictions came into law. Her mother had been a smoker when she was young but stopped shortly after an event. She'd asked her daughter for a good night kiss but Suzanna had refused, saying she didn't want to kiss her because she stank of smoke. That had thrown a switch. Her mother stopped smoking almost immediately.

They found a table in the corner and Angela went to the bar. She returned carrying a white wine spritzer for herself and (without asking) a J2O for Suzanna. Suzanna always ordered the same after a judo session.

"Thanks, Ange. Cheers." They clinked glasses and took sips from their drinks. The orange and passion-fruit flavours refreshed her dry mouth and the chilled glass helped cool her from the earlier exertions.

Angela spoke. "I heard in the news about an old guy stabbed in his home yesterday. I guess you'll be leading the investigation?"

"You got it. I'll be heading home straight after this drink to get my mind back into thinking it through, ready for tomorrow."

"I could never do your job – dealing with murders and the criminals who commit them. You must come across some awful people."

85

"Yeah. That comes with the job. Fortunately, a lot of those awful people end up behind bars. That's what keeps me going. The satisfaction of seeing justice done."

"Surely most crimes go unpunished, though?"

"I hate to admit you're right. It pains me to think that those who commit violence and steal from others often get away with it. We need sufficient evidence before the Procurator Fiscal's office will sanction a charge and subsequent court case. It's the frustrating part of the job. My team has a good record of catching criminals, though. Higher than the UK average."

"Good to hear it." Angela sat quietly for a minute and Suzanna took another sip of her drink. "Did I ever tell you my ex-husband knocked me around?" She murmured, not looking at Suzanna.

"No. I'm sorry to hear that. Tell me more."

"I married young – just nineteen. My husband was twenty-three. It was great to start with but after a while, he started getting possessive. He didn't want me going out with my friends, or anywhere, without him. He first punched me about a year into the marriage. Split my lip and made my nose bleed. He blamed it on me for antagonising him. I'd only told him I needed some space, some time to myself. After that it became more regular. I ended up in hospital after one beating. The staff called the police, but I refused to press charges. I believed he still loved me and, despite his violence, I still thought I loved him."

"So, what changed?"

"My best friend persuaded me to leave him. I moved in with her. It was such a relief to get out from under his control and away from the fear of violence. Definitely the right move." She paused. "He came after me a few days later, after he realised where I'd gone. But when he tried to get into her house, Chantelle decked him. It was Chantelle who introduced me to Judo. He stopped coming round after the humiliation of being beaten by a girl. But he accosted me in the street a few months later. I put him on his back with an Osoto-Gari throw. I probably overdid it as he bashed his head on the concrete. He wandered off, dazed. He's not been near me since."

"Sorry to hear that Angela but glad that you solved the issue by yourself. Did you ever get counselling about the abuse?"

"No. I probably should have done but no one offered it and I just got on with life."

"If you feel it would help to talk it through with a domestic abuse counsellor, let me know. I can put you in touch with an excellent charitable organisation, whose role is to help women who've suffered from domestic abuse and other forms of abuse. They're called *Shakti Women's Aid*."

"Thanks, Suzanna. I'll bear that in mind. How's your love life, by the way?"

"I've just returned from a skiing holiday with my boyfriend, James. Had to cut the holiday short because of the murder case."

"Bet he wasn't happy about that."

"Not initially. But he got over it quickly. If he's going to stay with me long-term – and I hope he does – he'll have to get used to my job interfering with our social life." Suzanna finished her drink. "I'd best get going, Angela. Thanks for the drink. And don't forget, if you want to talk to someone about the abuse – it's Shakti Women's Aid."

"Got it. Thanks, Suzanna. Take care."

"You too, Angela. See you next week, hopefully."

***

As Suzanna approached her car, it seemed like someone had turned on a floodlight. She looked up into the night sky. A bright globe dominated the heavens, illuminating the landscape but beyond the moon, the stars twinkled – light that had left them years ago. It set her thinking. Some galaxies are millions of light-years away, so by now may no longer exist. Each of those stars sat at the centre of a solar system, a sun with planets orbiting. And some of those planets could have life on them. Animals, fish, perhaps intelligent creatures like humans. It was incredible to think that one day humans may find life elsewhere in the Universe – like in *Star Trek*.

She opened her car door and sat behind the wheel but didn't start the engine. The Earth had to have been perfectly distanced from the sun for life to exist. Any further away and the whole planet would be covered in ice. Any closer, it would be too hot, the Earth scorched. Perhaps God *had* created the Universe and placed the Earth exactly where it was. She'd never know. Never be able to prove it, one way or the other.

Friday 6th March

Chapter 17

Rab left his home looking harassed. His wife, Ainslie, had moaned again about him calling his son Hamilton, *Hammy*. He'd been trying to stop using this disliked nickname but occasionally let the name slip out. He'd wondered why Ainslie was so annoyed with him again. This morning she'd revealed that the kids at nursery school had heard from Hamilton that his dad called him Hammy. They'd made fun of him, calling him Hammy the Hamster. He'd returned from nursery school in tears and said he didn't want to go back tomorrow. This morning, Hamilton had refused to get dressed and thrown a tantrum. It was all Rab's fault, of course!

Rab was surprised the kids at nursery school had heard of Hammy the Hamster. The Tales of the Riverbank series had been on TV in the 1990s when he was a child, but he'd not seen it in recent years. His mind was dragged back to the present when his boss arrived at the office. "Morning Rab. Get everyone together for a catch-up, please." She walked off towards the kitchenette, returning to the office a couple of minutes later with her coffee.

"I'll give you a shout as soon as the whole team is in."

Ten minutes later, they gathered to hear reports of how the enquiries had gone the previous day. Suzanna briefed them on the pathologist's findings and the evidence gathered by the CSIs that the forensics scientists had since analysed. There was some useful evidence ready to be matched once they had a firm suspect. Her interviews of CCC employees had shown up nothing, except confirming that one of them could have accessed White's records when standing in as a coordinator. The rest of the team's findings were similar.

"Has anyone yet started talking with clients of this group?" Suzanna asked. "We need to know if any of them demonstrated unusual behaviour, bad attitudes, or anger issues." There were no responses. "Rab, get uniform to ask for the fingerprints and DNA, as discussed, then work with Owen and Murray on speaking with the clients. I want more information about these people by the end of the day." Rab acknowledged the tasking with a nod.

"And what news on CCTV from buses?" Suzanna asked, still looking at her sergeant.

"The video files came in late yesterday. They're waiting to be viewed when we can find the time."

"Fair enough... Mairi, an update on the car drivers, please. Have they all been interviewed yet?"

"I got uniform to assist. They've all reported back with results of owners' addresses, their places of work and their destinations that morning. I also spoke to owners who live nearer the city centre. There are still three we've not yet contacted. And I need to follow up on those we have spoken with, to make sure what they said about their destinations is true and find out when they arrived. Of those who we know stopped in the Coates area, they all had good reasons to be there."

"Okay. You crack on with checking on the remaining drivers. When you've completed that work, tell me."

Mairi nodded. Suzanna's phone rang. "Excuse me. I'd better take this. Morning, Zahir. How's it going?"

"I'm by Bell's Mills, beside the Waters of Leith, where the dive team leader said they would be setting up, but no one's here yet. I've tried calling their leader, but his phone keeps going directly to voicemail.

91

Guess wherever he is, he's out of phone signal. I'll take a walk along the river up to Belford Bridge and see if they've set up somewhere near there, without informing me of the change. There's no easy road access to the stretch of river we want searching from anywhere else around here."

"Right. Call me immediately if you find them. If you haven't made contact within the next half an hour, call me anyway." She hung up and returned to her office, noticing her team had already started work on their tasks.

***

"Ma'am," Zahir said as Suzanna lifted her phone forty minutes after she'd spoken to him. "I finally tracked down the dive team. Part of the team left Glasgow yesterday and returned home. But when they turned up at their HQ, they found that some essential equipment was still in Glasgow with the other divers. They had to send someone back this morning. They've just arrived where we'd agreed to meet and only an hour later than planned, so not bad."

"Fair enough. Good to know they're there. Have you briefed them yet?"

"They know what they're looking for and I've shown them on a map which section of river needs trawling. The team will be in the water soon to start their Jackstay search pattern. They use a guide rope, then move the rope once they get to the end, to make sure they cover the whole search area."

"Thanks for the explanation, Zahir. Now they're briefed, you may as well assist Mairi with her work. Get her to assign you some interviews."

"Will do."

Suzanna returned to her scribblings – a mind map of what they understood so far. Who were the suspects? She asked herself a series of questions. Why was he killed? Why stabbed with a knife from his own kitchen? Why through the heart, bringing instant death? Why on that day? Why wait thirty years? What could White have done to the person to justify such late but final revenge? A picture started forming in her mind of George White's victim, turned avenger.

***

Rab knocked on the door of the 3-bed, semi-detached house, its pebble-dashed wall as dull as the low cloud that had swept in during the night. The door must have been replaced in the 1970s when aluminium windows and doors provided an expensive double-glazed upgrade to older houses. Its hardwood frame hadn't seen a coat of varnish in many years, the wood having paled to grey. There was no answer to his knocking and he couldn't find a bell.

Rather than waste his journey, he called the care company's office and obtained Mr Fitzgerald's phone number. But when he called, the old chap just kept asking, "Who's this?" but he never seemed to hear Rab's response. He called the office again and they gave him the code for the external key safe, so he let himself in, calling out as he opened the door.

Mr Fitzgerald jumped when Rab entered the living room, having finally heard his shouts. "Who are you? How'd you get into my house? I'll call the police," he said, picking up his mobile phone.

"No need to call the police, Mr Fitzgerald. I am the police," he said, showing his police ID card. "I called earlier but it seemed you couldn't hear what I was saying."

Fitzgerald settled after seeing Rab's identification but still seemed perplexed. "What did you say, lad?"

"Do you wear hearing aids, Mr Fitzgerald?"

"What's that?"

Rab pointed to his ears and acted speaking into a microphone, then mouthed slowly and clearly, "hearing aids?"

"Oh! Aye. Just a tick, young man." Fitzgerald fumbled around on his side table, then lifted an aid to each ear. The hearing aids whistled,

93

but soon quietened when the volume controls were adjusted.

"The batteries are nearly flat. I was conserving them for later, so I can listen to my radio programme."

"Can you hear me now, Mr Fitzgerald?"

"Aye, lad. No need to shout."

"Do you have spare batteries? Can I help you sort them out?"

"That'd be grand, lad. The batteries are on my bedside locker. Forgot to bring them down this morning and can't get back up there without assistance."

Rab turned and walked towards the stairs. The old man called out. "It's the front double bedroom."

"Okay. No problem. Back in a sec." Rab retrieved the batteries and speedily returned to the living room.

"Thanks, lad. Just put them down here," he indicated his side table. "I can change them later when these ones finally give up the ghost. Now, why is it you've called? It's not that kiss I forced on Margot Fisher behind the bike sheds in 1944, is it?" he said, looking like a cheeky young boy again.

Rab grinned back but didn't respond to the question. In those days, that sort of behaviour had been acceptable, but nowadays a forced kiss might be seen as a sexual assault. How times change. "I just wanted to speak to you about your carers. I need some background on them, because there's been a crime and we need to eliminate them as suspects."

"Well, you've come to the right place to get a bit of dirt on the young ladies. They tell me everything."

***

"DCI McLeod." A call came as Suzanna passed by an open doorway. She turned and strode back to his office. "Yes, sir."

"What progress on the murder of the old man?" Chief Superintendent Ewan Robertson asked.

"Still early days yet, sir. Our main focus is on employees of the care company because the murderer let themselves in with a key. We're interviewing, taking forensic evidence, confirming their whereabouts at the time of the murder and doing background checks on them all."

"What's the pathologist said about the murder?"

"Between us, we've agreed the attack was planned. Premeditated. The murder weapon looks likely to be a kitchen knife and we've already checked all the bins, gardens and parks around the area. A river search is underway now."

"That's over the top. It's not like we're looking for a body. Looking for such a small object in murky waters is like searching for a needle in a haystack." Nearing retirement, the grey-haired Chief Super seemed to treat his office like a bear cave, roaring from within and snapping at those who dared enter. "You do realise the cost of the search comes out of my budget? Have you ever dived in water with low visibility, McLeod?" he said condescendingly.

"Actually, sir. I *have* dived in dirty waters. I'm a BSAC Dive Leader. The waters around the UK were where I trained. Not in some warm holiday destination with crystal clear seas. So, I do understand how difficult the task will be. Much of the search – the shallower sections – will be conducted using bathyscopes, which means just wading, not diving."

"Well, I just hope it's worth it." He said in a schoolmasterly tone before dropping his eyes to the work on his desk, signalling that the grilling had finished. Suzanna turned away, rolled her eyes and walked away; her lips pursed.

Chapter 18

Suzanna returned to her office fuming; her face flushed, talking to herself. "How dare the man talk down to me like a headmaster to a student-teacher? I've served over twenty years and deserve respect. He knows I always get results, so why the hell does he have to criticise all the time? Every time the man opens his mouth it's to chastise me. Christ, I could punch him." She paced the office. "The man got paid a fortune for sitting around in meetings, chatting to colleagues whilst drinking coffee and eating sandwiches provided by the Force. He did nothing to steer investigations, to coach or motivate his staff; to inspire the best from them. He just criticised." Suzanna felt like just kicking it into touch and finding another career.

She dropped into her chair, which moved backwards under the force. "What could I do if I left the police? ... Property development, maybe? ... I enjoyed managing the remodelling of my apartment. I could do it for a living." She'd seen many of the TV programmes that featured buying a doer-upper and turning the property into a desirable home. She usually thought she could have done it just as well or better. "James would appreciate me not being called away from social occasions or from our bed during the night, because some low life had committed murder. But I'd miss the camaraderie of the police. I'd miss my team. I'd miss the satisfaction of seeing criminals punished for their crimes; being taken off the streets.... Sod it! I'll not let the man drive me out."

She was restless; felt the need to get out, to stretch her legs and breathe some fresh air. She left the building and walked away from Chief Superintendent Robertson, across the asphalt beneath the grey cloud onto Fettes Avenue, then wandered up the road alongside the fenced-off school playing fields. The snow had almost disappeared now, so the vista was green again. She increased her pace, confident the path wouldn't be slippery, raising her heart rate, feeling alive and alert. This was another way that Suzanna freed her mind to work, out of the confines of office walls, the constraints of rules and regulations.

As she watched the cars travelling up and down the avenue, like ants following a trail, she realised that the murderer could have driven into the Coates area but walked into the street where George White lived. So far, they'd assumed the person drove in or walked in having used public transport. But this murder had been well planned, so they needed to widen the CCTV search. She turned and strode back to the HQ to find Mairi. As she entered the Police Scotland grounds, her mobile rang. "DCI McLeod," she said into the phone.

"Ah! Chief Inspector. It's Moira Milligan here, from Butler and Cargrove. I've some good news for you. My boss pulled a few strings. We already have the archived records for George White and those who worked for him, here in my office if you'd like to peruse them or borrow them?"

"Excellent. We'll collect them," Suzanna replied, then ended the call and marched into the offices. She found the main office to be devoid of detectives, except Sergeant Findlay, who was working on other cases. She returned to her office and texted DC Gordon. 'Mairi. When interviews are finished, expand the CCTV search. Look for people parking within ten minutes' walk of Coates Gardens and walking towards the crime scene.' Before she grabbed her car keys and headed out, she posted a message on the team WhatsApp group. 'Off to Butler and Cargrove'.

***

As Suzanna arrived at Butler & Cargrove, the usual aroma of baking made her stomach rumble. The area surrounding the factory, for a mile or more, permanently smelled of baking biscuits. She wondered how the locals coped with that enticingly sweet aroma every day.

"Chief Inspector. I didn't expect to see you here again," Moira Milligan said.

"The rest of my team were busy with other tasks, so I came myself."

Moira passed her the document folders and Suzanna flicked through them. George White's records were on top. There were nine folders with a wrapper around them saying *Accts Dept.* A further seven annotated *HR Dept.* Then another pile marked *Others.* "Does the 'Others' category include factory workers?"

"I don't think so. The factory is rather separate from the offices, so Mr White, being the accounts head, would have had little contact with them – all men."

"Hmm! I don't recall saying I didn't want to see the records of male factory workers."

Moira frowned, considered what Suzanna had said, then answered. "I suspect Mr Carmichael made a judgement call."

"I wish he hadn't. He's not a detective. It's important that we see the whole picture. I'd be grateful if you would arrange for the rest of the files to be provided."

"Yes. Sorry about that. I'll get on to it. And as we've messed you about, I'll get them delivered to you as soon as they arrive. You're in the headquarters off Fettes Avenue, aren't you?"

"Yes. Please call me when they are on their way."

"Certainly."

"By the way, is it still mostly male workers in the factory today?" Suzanna asked.

"Yes. Several women work there nowadays but it's still largely men.

Most girls prefer working in an office than a factory, I find. The ones who work in the factory now are almost all involved in the technology side. Engineering, or programming manufacturing systems, rather than on the production line. It's not like baking biscuits at home. They're moving tons of product around, not ounces."

"Yes. I understand."

"Oh! And there are a couple of women in the logistics department."

Moira escorted Suzanna off the premises before returning to her office to call the archives department. Before starting her car, a passing truck distracted Suzanna. On its side was an Alpine scene, with the name of a well-known muesli brand blazoned across it. She thought of James and wondered how the holiday was going. She messaged him on WhatsApp. 'How's it going on the slopes? Hope you're getting lots of sunshine and great skiing. It's dull, damp and cold here. Missing you. Suz xxx.' She hit send, then drove out of the factory car park. Two minutes later, as she was heading along the A71 into the city, her phone pinged, indicating a message had arrived. She didn't stop to check what it said.

When Suzanna checked her messages in the station car park, she wished she'd read the one that had come in on her journey. It hadn't been from James, after all. But from Mairi. There had been two addresses on her route that she could have visited while passing. She chastised herself for letting her personal relationship interfere with work. As she opened the car door, a message arrived from James. She thought about leaving it unopened to avoid further distraction but that would have been rude, as she'd messaged him.

A photo of a fantastic snow-capped mountain scene was accompanied by a message. 'Hi from Livigno. It's glorious here. Wall to wall sunshine. Perfect skiing. Having a great time with Annabelle and Roger. You should have stayed. Missing you too. Love, James.'

At least he's signing off with *love*. She hit the 'like' emoji, then left her car. When she arrived at the main office, Caitlin was still there and Mairi had returned. Both turned and acknowledged their boss. Caitlin returned to her work. Mairi spoke. "Ma'am. Did you get my message?"

"Sorry, Mairi. I was driving when it came through. Only just read it after I'd parked up outside."

"Not to worry. I'll head out again once I've finished writing up the results so far."

"Anything of note?" Suzanna laid her coat over the back of a chair, dropped her bag on its seat and took another chair nearer Mairi, expectant. "What have you got?"

"We've covered half the cars so far. Nothing suspicious. I've requested more CCTV footage from cameras in the expanded area, as you suggested."

"Looks like we'll be working most of the weekend on this one, as we haven't any substantial leads." Mairi's face dropped at the statement. "What had you got planned, Mairi?"

"Oh. It was just that Brodie and I were intending to visit his parents this weekend. He hasn't seen them for months."

"I see. Sorry. Do you get on well with the in-laws?"

"They're not exactly in-laws. We're not married. But yes, they're alright. I haven't fallen out with them yet. Though I wonder whether his mother, Pam, will interfere if we start a family. She has strong views about how to bring up children."

"Are you thinking about starting a family?" Suzanna asked, concerned she might lose a key member of her team for a while or possibly forever if Mairi became a mother.

"No. We discussed it a few months back, but neither of us is keen to go down that route yet. We're enjoying our lifestyle. Sufficient money for foreign holidays, eating out regularly, dressing well and having the freedom to do what we want without having to worry about a child all the time."

"I'm in my forties now and have no children," Suzanna responded. "My reasoning was similar to yours. It's a lifestyle choice. Glad to hear I won't be losing you to maternity leave anytime soon."

Chapter 19

Suzanna opened the first HR folder – George White. She scanned the top-level data, then dived deeper into areas of interest. His time with the company started in 1977 and he left in 1986. The previous employer had been a medium-sized construction company. It was noted in his CV, presented back when he'd joined Butler and Cargrove, that he'd been with that company for seven years and prior employments periods had varied from two to eight years. Starting as an accounts assistant, he'd worked his way up to accounts manager. His employment with Butler and Cargrove had been a promotion to Head of Accounts. Later in the folder, she came across details of his leaving. He'd accepted a new position as Accounts Director for a large retailer with outlets all over Scotland and northern England.

The last letter on file was the Managing Director wishing George well in his new position. Clearly, if he had been abusing his staff, he'd done a good job of keeping his behaviour a secret from the management. All his annual appraisals were good. 'Solid performance, again; external audit of company accounts yet again highly praiseworthy of accuracy and clarity.' The only minor comment that could provide some clue was that the Director of HR had noted that the accounts department's staff turnover was above average.

She closed his folder and picked up the first from the accounts department pile – Susan Williamson. Susan had been employed throughout the time White had been in charge and she'd consistently done well, moving up into White's role, when he'd left. Her file held nothing to hint at any departmental issues. She opened another file: Sally Henderson.

Sally had joined the department in 1983 when she was twenty-two. Her annual reports suggested she'd been a steady worker in her first year, but she'd become slack in her second year with growing mistakes in her work. There was one note on file from HR saying she didn't get on with Mr White and she'd asked if there were any other jobs available in the company that she could transfer into. There hadn't been.

Lyndsey Lewis had joined the company in 1979, then left in 1984, aged thirty-two. Her performance had been fine throughout her period of employment, with no detrimental comments. When asked why she was leaving, she had reported a job offer with higher wages and closer to home. So, nothing there.

Next up was Maureen Stevens. She'd started work with the company when only nineteen. Stevens lasted two years, leaving in 1985. Her report in year one stated she was on a steep learning curve, but she finished the year with fewer errors in her work. She didn't have a second annual report, because she left before it was scheduled. She said she'd found another job but didn't elaborate on the reason for leaving.

Frances Greenwood came up next. She'd been twenty-one when she joined Butler and Cargrove and, like Lyndsey Lewis, left in 1984, having only worked there for nine months. No reason was given for her departure. She had been off work sick numerous times during the second half of her time with them. One day, she just didn't come to work. Refused to say why. Suspicious! Certainly the behaviour one might assume from an abused woman. Like a bullied child pretending they're ill so they don't have to go to school. One to note.

It was 1978 when Elizabeth Jenkins joined the company, aged twenty-eight. She'd left in 1982. Good performance throughout. No issues. Left because of pregnancy. Planned to be a stay-at-home mum. No maternity leave for most women in those days, Suzanna remembered. It was 1993 before it finally came into being because of a European Commission directive.

Moving on, Suzanna flipped through another three folders, none of which recorded anything noteworthy. The final accounts section folder caught her eye at once. Yvette Lancashire was shown to have worked from March 1984 to April 1985. The flag was that when pushed during her leaving interview, she'd indicated that a male manager had made inappropriate suggestions and touched her. She refused to give the man's name because she didn't want any fuss made.

Suzanna checked her priority list for interviews: Yvette Lancashire, Frances Greenwood, Sally Henderson, Maureen Stevens, followed by Susan Williamson, then the remainder. There was nothing in the HR department records to indicate any concerns, but Suzanna made a note to speak to the man who led the department through that period — Mr Stephen Masterton. And his deputy, Mrs Martha Fotheringham.

The *Others* batch included post room staff, cleaners, engineers, receptionists and security personnel. Again, nothing of note in their folders, but it would be worth talking to these eleven former employees because they may have observed the goings-on of all departments.

***

White's killer sat listening, transfixed by the early evening news, her face red, angered by the announcement. A man who'd been charged with sexual abuse against seven women had been released. Acquitted by the jury. Not guilty. The journalist spoke to the tearful women who'd given evidence against him. They had not reported the abuse when it occurred, thinking they would not be listened to, that they would not be believed, that there was no proof of the offence. They'd been encouraged by the 'Me Too' movement and thought they would finally see justice. But justice had failed them. Each case was assessed on its own merits – the jury not allowed to consider all the offences together in reaching their verdict.

She'd heard about the case as it built up to the hearing. His name was already etched in her mind. Another predator – a fox of a man. Cunning. Clever. And now that he'd been released, perhaps her second target. If the system refused to deal with these men, to protect women like her, to bring them justice, then she would be the one that did. She'd already taken her first. Now she would begin planning her second. She felt alive, fired up, with a new purpose to keep her from stagnating into oblivious, powerless old age. The woman couldn't afford a computer but owned a second-hand smartphone, handed down to her as a cast-off by one of her clients. She Googled the man's name. Found where he lived. Alone now, his family having abandoned him when he was charged with rape. They, at least, had realised his true nature.

***

One by one, the team returned to the headquarters as the afternoon came to a close. Mairi arrived last and stuck her head around her boss' door. "We're all back now if you want a catch-up?" Suzanna joined the team in the main office. It hadn't been redecorated in several years and showed signs of wear. At the far end, strips of paint were missing from the off-white walls where previous team members had taped pictures and documents onto them, having run out of space on the incident board. A row of square single-glazed windows ran along one wall, their original steel frames having warped and corroded, letting in draughts.

"Right. Let's get this over with so we can head home," Suzanna said. "The personnel files for all Butler and Cargrove employees who worked there at the time George White headed up accounts have now been provided. Except for the factory workers. They'll come later. I've shortlisted twenty-two of the employees to be interviewed and given them a priority order, as well as noting where any emphasis should be placed when questioning them." She paused. "Rab. Over to you."

"White's son, Edmond, has formally identified the body. He's overnighting in the city before returning to Inverness tomorrow. I've arranged to interview him first thing tomorrow morning before he leaves." Rab paused. "We now have a copy of the will and testament. As expected, White's children are sole heirs of his estate, estimated to be around half a million. Definitely a worthwhile reason to commit murder. I've requested financial background checks on the son and daughter. It will probably be Monday before we get that info, though. The Highlands and Islands police h spoken with the daughter, Miss Sheila White. They say she hasn't seen her father in years but was shocked to hear of his murder. Unfortunately, they didn't confirm where she was on the morning of her father's murder, so we need to follow up on that. The Inverness police have confirmed Edmond White was at home on Tuesday morning. His wife was away visiting her sister, but his next-door neighbour said he'd seen him about 9 o'clock, heading out on a walk and returning about an hour later.

Rab referred to his notes before continuing. "We've followed through on confirming the whereabouts of the carers. Almost all of them were with clients. Haven't yet confirmed alibis for the managers – another job for tomorrow. And we've made a start on interviewing CCC clients. I visited a Mr Fitzgerald earlier. He reckoned all the girls shared with him about what was going on, but it turned out he knew nothing of use to us. We'll continue with client interviews tomorrow."

"Thanks, Rab," Suzanna said. "Zahir?"

"The dive search team has finished for the day. They've covered two-thirds of the requested search area and have so far found three shopping trolleys, two bicycles–"

"Okay. We get the picture, Zahir. No knife yet," Suzanna interrupted.

"Correct, ma'am," Zahir confirmed. "They'll recommence search–

ing at first light tomorrow. Should have a result by mid-day."

Mairi spoke before being asked. "I've interviewed the last three car owners. They all had good reason to be in the area. Nothing suspicious at all. I've also followed up on almost all car owner statements, confirming their destinations and timings. No holes in their stories. There's only one that I've left open. A Mr Philip Musgrave, driving a Citroen C5, was noted passing a bell-push camera at one end of Coates Gardens at 07:58, then passing a house security camera at the other end of the street five minutes later. There was sufficient time for him to stop, enter the property, commit the crime, then leave. Although, if you take into consideration driving time, parking and exiting the car, retrieving the key and entering the house, there'd be little time left to knife the old man, let alone smash the trophy."

"Yes but not impossible," Rab said.

"I'll interview Musgrave in person," Mairi continued, "rather than over the phone, so I can see his face while asking him why it took so long to transit the street."

"What about the expanded CCTV analysis?" Suzanna asked.

"The footage has arrived. I'll start its scrutiny in the morning."

"Fine," Suzanna responded. "Okay. Let's get off home. We'll need to put in a full day again tomorrow." Working weekends were the norm in these circumstances, so no one commented.

Suzanna returned to her office. Before doing anything else, she emailed Police Scotland's facilities management team, reporting the office windows and asking when they would get replaced. She pondered what she'd do with herself this Friday evening when she'd normally be with James. She missed his company, his intelligent conversation and his hugs.

***

At home and having eaten, Suzanna settled down with her book again, but couldn't focus on the story, because it immediately sent her mind into the realms of MI5 and counter-terrorism. It would seem that doing nothing was not an option, as her CID team would be discontinued. She had a choice, MIT leader or combatting terrorism. She considered what motivated her most: investigating crimes and locking up the perpetrators, or intelligence work and leading undercover operations – arresting those who were about to commit atrocities.

The first role would be more of what she had been doing. She loved the challenge of following clues, interviewing suspects and finding the evidence to enable the perpetrators of crimes to be punished, but – apart from while the criminals were locked up in prison – it didn't stop crimes from being committed. The work was reactive, seeking justice for those wronged by the crime. Counter-terrorism, however, would be mostly proactive, aiming to prevent the crime, rather than responding once it had been carried out. If her team could prevent innocent people – potentially hundreds – from being killed, maybe that would be more satisfying than just seeking justice after the event?

Saturday 7th March

Chapter 20

The hotel stood on the corner of Magdala Crescent and Haymarket Terrace, just around the corner from Coates Gardens and close to Haymarket Station. Rab entered the foyer and headed to the reception area, a grey and yellow corridor of a room. It gleamed and smelled of fresh polish. Before looking for White, he introduced himself to the receptionist and asked whether Mr White, their current guest, had previously stayed at the hotel. She confirmed he had. The last time had been thirteen months ago. Satisfied, Rab went through to the dining room, where Edmond White said he'd be. They were still serving breakfast and Rab wondered whether a coffee might be available. He found him sitting at a table for two, in the far corner of the room. "Good morning, Mr White. Sergeant Sinclair, Edinburgh CID. Thanks for agreeing to meet me before travelling home."

White responded cordially and indicated Rab should take the empty chair. "How can I help you, Sergeant? Would you like a coffee? There's spare in my pot." If Rab remembered correctly, Edmond White was sixty, but he looked much younger – slim and fit. His Greek nose emphasised his narrow, tall head, topped by short, straight, salt & pepper hair. He looked nothing like his father.

Rab smiled. "Yes please," he hadn't even had to ask. He poured himself a cup and took a sip. It had already cooled and tasted weak, but it provided a caffeine fix to sharpen his thinking. "I'm sure you'll want us to find the killer of your father." Edmond nodded confirmation. "To help us do so, we need some background information about your father. One motive for the murder could be a burglary gone wrong, but we have no way of knowing if anything of value might have been taken. Can you help us with that?"

"I doubt it, Sergeant. I've never seen anything of value. He sold his car several years ago when he could no longer drive it. My mother's jewellery was passed on to Sheila. I wouldn't think my father had any items of high value."

"What about his relationships with colleagues, friends and family? What can you tell me?"

"Sorry. I've no idea what friends he might have had and I've never met any of his work colleagues. I left home at eighteen to join the Army and I've not lived with him since. Or even in the same city!"

"What about relationships with family? Did you get on with him alright?"

"Dad was a disciplinarian. He set hard rules and would use corporal punishment on me and Sheila if we transgressed. Even for fairly minor rule-breaking. I couldn't wait to get away from him. Not sure I ever loved him. I only visited occasionally because of Mum. How she stuck it out for all those years I'll never know. He had to be in control all the time. Had to get his way. Mother passed away... seven years ago, now."

"Was he ever violent towards you?"

"Not uncontrolled violence but he loved to dish out punishment in the form of spankings. He would use his belt if he judged the offence to be significant."

Rab judged from White's body language that he probably spoke the truth. He certainly showed no sign of sorrow. More relief than grief. "Did he ever strike your mother?"

"Not in our presence. He talked down to her as if she were a child and she obeyed him without challenge. I'm sure over the years, though, he will have taken his belt to her in a closed room."

"Why do you say that?"

"I heard her cry out on multiple occasions."

"I see. What about your sister?"

"When young, he would spank her in front of me and Mum, but later, when she became a teenager, he'd take her into his study to do it. I heard her squealing then whimpering but didn't possess the courage to enter the room. And nor did my mother. It was out of bounds to all unless invited or ordered in. I remember the few times I was ordered into the room. It felt like entering a lion's cage. I shook with fear because I knew what would happen. He was more violent when he didn't have any witnesses.

"Is there anything else you can recall that might help us find his murderer?"

"Not that I can think of. When will I be able to get into my father's house?" White asked.

"I can't say precisely. It's still a closed crime scene. Typically, it could be shut off for another week yet," Rab responded.

"Look, I'm due to catch the 09:13 from Haymarket, so I must make a move soon."

"Just one last question, Mr White. Do you have children? If so, I'll need their names and contact details. We'll have to interview them to eliminate them from our enquiries."

"Oh! I never thought they'd be considered suspects."

"We know you weren't in the city on the day your father died but we're required to confirm that for all close family members."

White wrote his son and daughter's details in Rab's notebook, then stood. "If that's all?"

"Yes, thank you. I'll keep you no longer, Mr White. We'll be in touch when we have news and to let you know when the house is free for you to sort out. Safe journey home, sir." Rab stayed behind in the restaurant to finish his coffee and make phone calls to the police stations nearest to Edmond White's children, to seek their help.

***

A pattern of spots on the ceiling looked like the Plough star constellation. The dots distracted Suzanna as she reclined her chair, intending to review the case with her eyes closed. Probably just flyblow. She made a mental note to clean it off. She could do without the distraction when wishing to meditate on cases.

Eyes now closed, she let her mind drift around the facts. Their focus had been on scrutinising those with access to the house by using the key held in the external key safe. Are there any other ways someone could have accessed the house without breaking a lock or window? Was the front door secure? Could there be other keys to the property? Who might possess those keys? Might the morning carer have left the door unlocked – open even? What about a burglar with skills to get past a Yale lock or someone with a thin piece of flexible plastic? A locksmith? Might there be someone with a grudge against him? They had yet to finish interviewing current employees and her team hadn't spoken with people at other companies that White worked for since leaving Butler and Cargrove, or before them. Plus, they still had the company's ex-employees to interview. Some planning was required.

Twenty minutes later, Suzanna left her office with a prioritised list of actions. Rab was still out. Murray and Owen were also away, interviewing the CCC employees and clients. Mairi was stuck into more CCTV scrutiny, but Zahir wasn't fully employed. "Zahir. I have some work for you."

He spun his chair 180 degrees and nearly fell off it as it wobbled like a drunkard. He chuckled at his near-miss. "Yes ma'am. What would you like me to do?"

"Here's the list of twenty-two ex-Butler and Cargrove employees that I mentioned yesterday. I need you to call them all, find out where

113

they are and when and where we can catch up with them. I'd like us to get around as many as we can today, then complete tomorrow." Zahir took the offered list.

"Right-o. I'll get onto it straight away."

"Mairi." Suzanna waited until she had Mairi's attention. "How's the CCTV scrutiny going? Have you looked through the footage from the buses yet?"

"Yes, ma'am. I've printed out pictures from bus footage of people alighting or boarding in the Coates area. I've noted on the printouts which way they were travelling. This should help us correlate with other images of people seen in the area."

"Good work." Suzanna returned to her office. The Superintendent and Chief Super weren't in today. One advantage of higher rank. Working weekends usually ceased above DCI level except for major crises. The HR departments of companies that George White had worked for wouldn't be operating today either, so that would be a job for Monday. Forensics only worked a standard week, unless processing urgent matters, so they wouldn't be around to query about locks. She pondered what would be the best use of her time; the answer soon dropped into her mind.

Chapter 21

Suzanna had White's house to herself this time – no hovering sergeant waiting to take notes and tasks. She stepped in and caught sight of the opposite house before closing the door. Why had their CCTV been inoperative that morning? Had it been a coincidence or related to the crime?

She turned back from the door and stepped across to the telephone table. Rab hadn't yet mentioned anything about White's phone book, which he'd taken away to check out. Had he or anyone else called the numbers in the book yet? If so, what resulted from that research? She opened the drawer of the table and checked its contents. There were three pencils of various lengths, two with broken leads and the other worn down to the wood. Not much use having pencils without a means to sharpen them, she thought, not seeing a sharpener. Odd scraps of paper and some business cards lay scattered around the drawer. She picked them up and read each one.

The business cards must be many years old, as they were dirty and the writing faded. A local electrician, a plumber and a chimney sweep. She doubted they'd been used in a long time. Particularly the chimney sweep because George White's fireplace had been boarded up and an electric fire stood on the hearth. The scrappy pieces of paper held nothing of relevance. One was an old shopping list: bananas, apples, margarine (disgusting), mild cheddar (yuk – has to be mature to make it worth the calories), baked beans, tinned soup (no way; it had to be fresh for Suzanna), tinned carrots and peas (never) and twenty JPS cigarettes. Suzanna remembered the brand. John Player Special used to adorn Formula 1 racing cars, but the UK had long ago outlawed the glorification of smoking in this way. The list must be ancient. There was no evidence of anyone smoking in the house. She would have noticed as soon as the front door opened, because smokers' houses reek of burnt tobacco, the stink hanging in the furnishing, and the walls were usually stained dirty yellow.

She replaced the items in the drawer and closed it before moving into the lounge. On the dining table, a bunch of orange *chrysanthemums* drooped outward, their shrinking bedraggled blooms kissing the table as if saying a last goodbye. The chocolate brown recliner chair still stood sadly where George White had died, facing the TV, its blank screen sending out some secret message to its missing occupant. It seemed to cry out for its black silence to be washed away by colour, light and voices. Suzanna hid her TV away in a cabinet to avoid the siren's call, only to be utilised when *she* chose.

George had a small bookcase stacked with books. Her eyes were drawn to the only book not neatly lined up in the dark-wood bookcase. It laid face down on White's chair-side table. She picked it up and read the cover. Shadow Hunter, by Jeffrey Archer. If nothing else, George had good taste in books. She'd read the book recently, about a rogue submarine captain who tried to take Britain to war with Russia. George had not finished the story before his death. A bookmark protruded halfway through the book.

Suzanna opened the book where the card poked out. It wasn't a bookmark after all but another business card. This one was fresh, the card still white and letters clear. Special Massage Service, the words read. A website and phone number were listed. When she turned it over, she was greeted by a picture of a scantily clad young woman with pouting lips, her tongue protruding, in contact with her vertical finger. It was clear what services were actually on offer.

George didn't own a mobile phone, so she would have to wait for Rab to provide the list of calls made once he'd received it from the telephone company. She paused, thinking, before taking out her mobile, then called the number on the card. An Eastern European woman's voice answered, stating the name of the service. "Hello. I'm calling on behalf of my father. He would like someone to visit and provide his usual service. He's not been well lately and still cannot use the phone."

"Yes. Surely we will help him. What is his name and address, please?" Suzanna gave her the details and asked when someone could come, as he was keen to receive a visit.

"The earliest we could send his usual masseuse would be Monday at 2 pm. Would that be good for Georgie?"

They appeared to know him intimately. She'd not heard anyone call him by that name. "Just a minute. Let me check." She paused as if she'd gone to consult him before speaking again. "Yes. 2 pm on Monday will be good. He seemed excited by the idea. I guess at his age, and spending most of his time sitting in a chair, a massage would be welcome."

Suzanna heard the woman on the other end of the line almost choke, presumably as she held back a chuckle at the suggestion that Georgie was looking forward to a massage. She probably thought his daughter must be naïve, to think that. "Oh yes. Georgie always likes his massage. He tells Zena her visit is the highlight of his month. Monday 2 pm, then." The phone went dead.

Alistair had said the porno films and mags were probably White's way of spicing up his boring, lonely life. If the magazines and videos were the peppers in his life, Zena's visit must be the chilli. The masseuse would likely need the key safe code to gain entry, so others within Special Massage Services may also possess the code. Another line to follow.

The home's windows and doors all seemed to be secure. The front door remained the murderer's most likely route into the house. It was an original, made from hardwood but the lock was merely a round-rimmed cylinder latch. Easy to defeat with the right tools. There were internal deadbolts at the top and bottom but as these were only operable from the inside, they would not have been used since George started needing care.

She checked for signs on the frame – surely the CSI team would have already done this – but she'd not seen their report yet. She couldn't see any marks that suggested force had been used, or even that thin, bendy plastic had been slipped between frame and door. A key was still the answer; either the one stored in the key safe or another. There were so many people with access to the key, any of them could have had a copy made and used it even after the key safe code change. She wondered when it had last been changed. She WhatsApped Rab and asked him to find out.

Suzanna continued wandering, looking in drawers and cupboards, uncovering more aspects of White's life and character from what she found. He'd probably played tennis when younger; an old wooden tennis racket, trussed up in its frame, hid in the under-stairs cupboard. She wondered if he'd been a member of a tennis club in the 1980s. Might there be someone in that club who knew him?

She found some bank statements in the sideboard's drawer and scanned through them. There were regular payments by direct debit to utility companies and the council, and numerous cash withdrawals from ATMs. As he was housebound and had been for some time, she speculated on who might have made these withdrawals and who shopped for him? His son and daughter lived nowhere near and she wasn't aware of any other relatives nearby. Perhaps a neighbour helped him? Another person with access to the house?

Back in the hall, Suzanna found fresh mail had arrived since the murder – still unopened. She slit the one that caught her interest. As she expected, it was from his bank and contained his latest statement. A cash machine withdrawal of £30 had been made *after* George's death. They'd need to check the ATM where the money had been withdrawn and access the inbuilt CCTV to identify the person.

George evidently couldn't walk far as he needed help with washing and dressing, and the carers provided some of his meals. He used a stairlift to get to his bedroom and the bathroom. She'd noticed a Zimmer frame on the landing but hadn't spotted one downstairs. She returned to the living room. Next to the recliner chair, there were faint indentations in the carpet but no frame in sight.

She wandered around the room, looking in every corner, under furniture and inside drawers and cupboards, hoping something would jump out at her. She peered through the French windows and noticed an out-of-place item in the garden! She tried the door handle. It moved freely.

Opening the door, Suzanna stepped into the garden to retrieve the missing Zimmer frame. It was sound, although wet from languishing outside, and the rubber feet were in good condition. George could not have thrown the frame into the garden. He needed it to move around and, in any case, why would he discard it? It was inconceivable that the CSIs would miss the frame laying outside. They'd have checked for fingerprints on the door and for footwear prints in the garden.

She placed the frame on the carpet, just inside the French window and locked it. As she turned to leave, she heard the front door open and voices. She stopped where she was and stared at the living room entrance door. As Neil Tendering entered the room and saw the DCI, his jaw dropped. He came to an abrupt halt and his colleague, Susan, walked into his back. A discussion broke out about his emergency stop and her failure to notice before his attention returned to Suzanna.

"Chief Inspector. What brings you here again?"

"I could ask you the same question, Neil. Who's this with you?"

"My colleague Susan Pickering."

"Hello," Susan said. "Pleased to meet you, Chief Inspector?"

Neil responded to Suzanna's query. "We wouldn't normally return without your knowledge. But I didn't think we needed to confer, because we're just completing the work, not doing anything extra."

"How come the work wasn't completed before?"

"When reviewing the notes and evidence, I realised the garden wasn't mentioned. Can't think why that would have happened. I can only guess I must have been distracted."

"That would account for it, then!"

"Account for what?"

"For Mr White's Zimmer frame, having been in the garden these past few days. I just noticed it laying outside and retrieved it – gloves on, she said, showing her hands."

"Oh! I see. Yes, well, we'll need to dust it for prints and check the yard and any rear entrance ways. The French windows were closed and locked, though, weren't they?"

"No." Neil's mouth dropped in surprise. Suzanna continued. "So, it's possible the murderer came in through these windows and left the same way. The French windows could have been left unlocked on a recent visit. You'd best have a good look around. But before I leave, please brief me on your analysis of the front door, its lock and the murderer's likely means of entry through it, if that is indeed the way they entered?"

Twice now, Neil had been embarrassed by the Chief Inspector finding things he should not have missed. "Of course... We found no sign of forced entry and concluded the murderer must have used a key."

Suzanna nodded, pleased they had confirmed her belief about the front door. "Thanks, Neil. I'll get out of your way and let you get on."

She left the crime scene to walk the streets again. Before setting off, she called at the house across the street to enquire about the CCTV but no one answered her bell-ringing and door-knocking. She took the footpath that led to the Water of Leith. The riverside track brought her to the AIDS Memorial Park, then across the footbridge. She looked up the river. The dive search team was at work, but they were too far off to engage.

The Gallery of Modern Art's green-painted cast-iron archway faced her as she stepped off the bridge. Passing through the arch, the path swept off right and upwards on steps through the trees. Eventually, she emerged through a hole in a high stone wall into the gallery's grounds. Suzanna followed the road around the imposing three-storey building and beyond it to sculptured gardens with a pond at the gallery's front, then beyond to Belford Road.

She scanned the area and noticed another bus stop, noting the route that passed through. She would get the guys to look for CCTV around the area. There would probably be cameras at the Art Gallery and on the buses.

Chapter 22

Rab appeared at Suzanna's office doorway, looking like he'd just won a lottery. He held a piece of paper with a picture of a kitchen knife. "They've found this knife. It's now with the forensics team."

"That looks remarkably like the other knives in White's kitchen," Suzanna replied.

"It does, doesn't it? Let's hope forensics can pick up some evidence from it. The dive team is continuing their search, just in case. They should be complete within the hour. I suspect they'll not find anything else, and that this is the murder weapon," Rab surmised.

"That's great news. As you say, let's hope there's something forensics can glean from the knife. How are the client interviews going, by the way?"

"So far, there's been nothing of concern. No one has highlighted any worrying carer personality traits but we've still plenty more to talk to."

As Rab sat, his phone rang. He picked up. "Sarge. It's Murray. I've just spoken with a Mr Condon. He said that one of his carers had once threatened that she'd purposely miss him off her rounds and leave him in bed all morning if he didn't behave. I thought you'd want to know."

"Aye. Thanks, Murray. Who's the carer?"

"Gabriela Albescu."

"That's the Romanian woman who assisted George White on the morning of his death. The last known person to have seen him alive! We'll need to speak to her again. But first, dig into her background. Contact Romanian authorities to see if she's noted in any police files. She could have a history in her home country that might be relevant... I tell you what. As I'm in the office and you're out and about, you carry on as planned. I'll contact the Romanians."

"Right-o, Sarge. Good luck with getting the Romanians to help."

***

"I thought you'd want to be told straight away, Sarge," Owen said after Rab answered his phone. "One of the CCC clients, Anthony Heathcote, had been visited by two cats and one dog before the mid-day carer arrived."

Rab smiled. "Tell me more."

"His morning carer, Maja Basinski, had stormed out of the house that morning without completing her duties, leaving the door open," Owen continued. "Heathcote said that Maja had not been back since that event two months ago. I'm surprised the company didn't sack her."

Rab agreed and said they would need to interview Maja Basinski and delve deeper into her background. He thanked Owen and hung up. Rab turned his attention to reading through the CCC staff background checks, starting with Basinski. The reports highlighted nothing of concern, but many workers were not UK nationals. So, as he'd done with Gabriela Albescu, Rab initiated checks on all foreign workers. He'd have to wait and see whether the information returned would shed any further light on their characters.

***

"Ah! Ma'am." Rab called as Suzanna entered the main office. She paused, questioning him with her eyes.

"You remember you asked me to check into the numbers in George

White's phone book?" She nodded, thinking he'd beaten her to it. "There were dozens of numbers in the book, so rather than calling everyone, I matched them with his phone records. I went back over the last two years as there were few calls made or received. It doesn't appear he had many friends."

"Okay, and?"

"The only calls made that matched his phone book entries were with his son in Inverness, to the centre where his daughter lives on Iona and the care company. There were also calls to a number not recorded in the book..."

"Don't keep me hanging, Rab. Where were the calls made to?"

"A company called Special Massage Services."

"I was going to ask you about calls to that number. It's doubtless a front for sexual services."

"That was my assumption," Rab said.

"I want to know how often it was called and when it was last dialled. I phoned the number earlier and arranged for George's favourite masseuse to visit on Monday at 2 pm. So, we can find out what she did for him and follow up by ascertaining who else might have had access to the house. In fact, while we're waiting for the Monday meeting, start digging into Special Massage Services. Hunt for any links to people of interest: criminals, gang connections, etc. Most of these service companies have links to crime – trafficking, for example."

***

Mairi handed Suzanna a list of cars that had been spotted on CCTV and sat back on the edge of her desk, while her boss scanned it. The paper identified all registered owners and noted their addresses, ready for the team to check with them.

"Interesting," Suzanna exclaimed. "One of the registered keepers is Mrs Margaret Lightfoot, an employee of CCC. I spoke to her on Thursday and she said she went to visit her sister in Coatbridge. She said nothing about visiting this area of the city. What time did this car show up on CCTV?"

"Far right column of the table, ma'am."

"Oh, yes! I see. 7:40 am. That's a perfect fit. She could have driven to Coates Gardens, entered the property after the early morning carer had left, killed George White, then travelled straight to her sisters. It would need to have been a slick operation though because, at that time of the morning, it would take an hour at least, possibly ninety minutes for the journey. And her sister said she arrived at 9 am." Suzanna paused. "Right. Pull Lightfoot in for questioning. She has some explaining to do."

***

When Suzanna opened the door to Interview Room 1, Margaret Lightfoot immediately stood and ranted at her. "You've no right bringing me here for questioning. I still have clients to visit. I've not done anything wrong. There's no reason to question me again. I told you where I was the other day – at my sister's. I want a solicitor."

"Margaret. Please sit. I'll keep you no longer than necessary. If you wish us to call the duty solicitor, however, there will probably be a delay of 2-3 hours." Margaret sat, then crossed her arms, her face set like a scolded child.

"Margaret, the reason I requested your presence here today is that we now know you were in the area of George White's home around the time he was killed, when you said you were at your sister's."

"I never said I was at my sister's at that time of day. I got there just after nine."

"You previously said you didn't know Mr White and that you never went to that part of the city. But you were captured on CCTV parking your car just up the road from his house and leaving a few minutes later. How do you explain your presence near the man's house around the time of his murder?"

"I *did'nae ken* what time the man was murdered, or even that I was near his street. My sister asked me to collect a package from her friend, who lives in Coates."

"We'll need the friend's details," Suzanna said, passing her a pen and paper. Margaret reluctantly took them and wrote the address of her sister's friend, then passed it back. "If you're happy to wait here while we visit the house, that's fine, but it might be easier all around if you also gave us her name and phone number."

Margaret looked annoyed. "I don't know her name. My sister just asked me to call there and pick up the package. She never even told me what was in it. Perhaps books. I'll need to call my sister to get the details."

Suzanna turned her head to Mairi and gave her a nod, which was intuitively interpreted. Mairi left the room. "My colleague has left to call your sister. Let's hope she answers her phone, so we don't have to keep you longer. Is there anything else you'd like to tell me?"

Margaret sat in thought for a minute before answering. "Like I *telt* you, I *dinna ken* the man that was murdered. And I *did'nae ken* I had been anywhere near his *hoose*." She sat for another few minutes as Suzanna stared at her, letting the silence do its work. "Thinking about it, I suppose I should've mentioned I'd been into the city before driving to my sister's house but it *did'nae* seem relevant."

Mairi re-entered the room. "I've just spoken with your sister and her friend. Luckily, they were both able to speak with me. They confirmed your story, Mrs Lightfoot."

"Thank you for your cooperation, Margaret," Suzanna said. "Sorry, we had to take you away from your duties. As you said, if you'd told us about your trip into Coates, it wouldn't have been necessary to question you again. Mairi, please escort Mrs Lightfoot out of the building." She turned and walked away.

Chapter 23

"Somewhere to go, Owen?" Suzanna quipped, having noticed him checking his watch as the team gathered, late afternoon.

"I'm supposed to be off to the cinema this evening, with Ailsa. We're booked to see Chappie," he said, as if they'd all know the film.

Most of them were blank-faced but Rab spoke, "That's the movie about a police robot with artificial intelligence, isn't it?"

"Aye, that's right. Looks exciting from what I saw in the trailer."

Murray jumped into the conversation. "We should get one of those robots, ma'am. It wouldn't be difficult to replace Owen with just a tiny bit of artificial intelligence. Owen punched his comrade on the arm.

"Right. Best we get on with this so Owen can get home in time to take his wife out on the town. First off, I just wanted to be clear that half the team will need to be in tomorrow. We've not made enough progress to take the day off entirely, as much as I'd like to. Any volunteers? Or do any of you have commitments tomorrow that would prove difficult to get out of?"

"I'm okay to work tomorrow," Rab offered. "I've nothing on. Don't suppose Ainslie will be happy, but she knows working weekends is par for the course."

"Thanks, Rab."

"I'd rather not," Murray said. "Inverkeithing is playing Edinburgh University tomorrow."

"You'd be better off coming to work. At least you won't have to watch them lose again," Owen joked.

"I reckon they'll win," Murray retorted. "Mark my words, they'll be moving out of the Fife Amateur League and up into the Lowland League before long."

"I thought you were keen to get away, Owen," Suzanna interjected. Owen at once clammed up.

"I can do tomorrow, ma'am," Zahir said. "But could I get next Friday off in lieu? There's an event at our mosque that day and my parents want me to attend."

"I'm sure that can be arranged."

Mairi spoke. "I'll volunteer as well. I can't have my sergeant and colleague at work and me skive off. Let the Comic Duo take the day off."

Owen and Murray looked peeved initially, but then pleased when it registered that they would not need to be at work the next day. The two DCs were often referred to as the Comic Duo, the Two Comedians and, once or twice, the Terrible Twins. They worked well together, were highly competitive and the banter flowed between them. Two years younger than his colleague, Owen matched his compadre's height but that's where the similarities stopped. Owen had silky, mid-brown, receding hair, wavy on top and short at the side, framing his high forehead, bulbous nose and thin lips. Like Murray, he wasn't expected to make high rank in the police. He was diligent and hard-working but not as mentally astute as others in the team. Suzanna heard that joining the police was Owen's way of securing a reasonably paid secure job with the promise of a good pension, rather than a passion for justice. Nonetheless, he was a good copper.

"Sounds like a plan. Right, let's debrief as quickly as we can," Suzanna prompted. "I revisited the victim's home and found some anomalies and potential leads." She briefed them on the further CSI checks in the rear yard and the masseuse appointment, along with her assessment of other lines to follow – others with keys, perhaps?

Rab was next to speak. "We may have the murder weapon. The knife is with forensics and I've asked them to prioritise work on it. Background checks on all CCC's carers have not flagged up anything of concern, but we've now requested police checks on all foreign workers from the home countries' police forces. The request has gone through Police Scotland HQ, so we need to wait for the responses. There are two women in particular that we're interested in, because of their behaviour and personality: Gabriela Albescu and Maja Basinski. Oh! By the way, calls to SMS from George White's phone were monthly, always around the same time. Last call was just over three weeks ago."

"Any connection between SMS and known organised crime gangs?"

"I couldn't find any connections, ma'am."

Mairi jumped in after a short pause. "Of all the CCTV checks, we've only made one connection between a car seen near White's and CCC. The carer in question, though, had a legitimate reason to be there and alibis that place her elsewhere when George White was murdered."

"I met with the victim's son, Edmond White," Rab came back in, "and it seems his father had been a controlling and abusive man. Edmond's sister, Sheila, is living on the island of Iona and has been for several years."

"If she's hiding away from society, perhaps it's because of what her father did to her," Suzanna said. "We need to speak to her sensitively – a woman's touch – to ascertain whether there's any truth behind our suspicions. If so, White's abuse of other women might be the motive for his murder. Revenge."

"Why does it need to be a woman? I'd love to visit Iona." Owen whined.

Suzanna turned to Owen, surprised that he engaged mouth before brain, again. "Let me ask you one question. If a young woman had been beaten and raped throughout her teenage years, by her own father, do you think she'd be open about that with another man — a complete stranger?"

"Fair point, ma'am. Sorry. I wasn't thinking."

Suzanna tore her eyes from Owen, fighting her instinct to roll her eyes or shake her head whilst giving him the mother-naughty child look. "Caitlin is holding the fort on the minor crimes, so that leaves me or Mairi."

"I'll go, ma'am. You'll need to be here to lead the team." Mairi volunteered.

"Agreed. Set it up for Monday, Mairi. It's too late to go tomorrow. I'd like you to go there and back on the same day, if possible." Mairi nodded.

There was another pause, so Zahir filled the silence. "I've been through the ex-Butler and Cargrove employees, found out where they live and arranged appointments with half of them tomorrow and the rest for Monday. The only way that can be achieved is if all four of us split the list."

"Or we call in help from nearby stations," Suzanna added. "Let me see the list again please, Zahir." She perused the names, positions once held, their locations and the interview timings. "I'd say we request local stations to take on these interviews," she said, showing Zahir which ones she'd marked on his sheet, "and we'll take the rest. I've appended names against each, to share out the burden as evenly as possible."

Zahir nodded, agreeing with his boss' allocations. "I'll call the stations straight away, before knocking off, and put the names, addresses and interview timings for the rest onto our WhatsApp group."

Another thought popped into Suzanna's head. "We'll need the B&C ex-employee list cross-checked against current and ex-employees of the care company."

"Good point," Rab agreed. He grabbed both lists and passed them to Zahir to scan.

"Did you speak with CCC about the key safe code change?"

"Aye. They said it had never changed in all the time they've been providing care. That's three years. They reckon it's the family's responsibility to change it and inform them. But it rarely happens. All CCC management staff's alibis checked out. There's no way any of them were in Coates Gardens on the morning White was murdered."

"Mairi. Did you speak to that car owner you mentioned yesterday?"

"Not yet. He's away on holiday, so I wasn't able to speak to him in person."

"Hmm. When's he returning to Edinburgh?"

"Not until next Friday."

"Right. We'll have to outsource his questioning. Find out where he's staying and get the local police to speak to him."

"Err... He's in Portugal, ma'am!"

"In that case, we'll forgo the face to face. Call him and ask the question. If you're not satisfied with the answer, and if we still don't have a suspect, we'll need to talk to him again when he gets back." Mairi nodded to acknowledge the tasking, as Suzanna turned back to the group.. "Has anyone spoken with George White's brother – Albert, isn't it?"

"Edmond White confirmed he had informed his uncle of his brother's death," Rab said.

"Hmm... Is there anything we've missed?" No one spoke but all eyes remained on the DCI. "Let's wrap things up then and head home. Have a good evening, but not *too* good, of course." Suzanna looked at her team like a mother speaking to a teenager before they headed off to a party. She returned to her office to wrap up and head out. Before leaving, she texted Jonathon.

Chapter 24

On Spylaw Road, the homes were mostly substantial four or five bedroomed detached houses, with bay windows and large gardens. As Suzanna walked up the driveway, she looked up beyond the house's roof and multiple chimney pots, to the sky. When the sun had set about 6 pm it had been overcast, but it had since cleared and, despite the city's glare, she could make out stars in the distant sky. It would be chilly when she left the house later.

Jonathon opened the door to her knock. The aroma of freshly cooked sausage rolls wafted out with the warmth of the house and the hubbub of many voices conversing over background music. She'd liked to have brought James to the party, but his plane had only landed an hour ago and he just wanted to get home and rest.

"*Suzanna*. Welcome. So glad you could make it. Come on in. Let me take your coat." She gave Jonathon a box of chocolates and a bottle of red wine, then slipped off her red quilted coat. Jonathon hung it over the stair banister. "I'll put your coat in the cloakroom later. Let me get you a drink and introduce you to some people."

"Before we go through, Jonathon, I'd like a quick word about your CSI man, Neil Tendering." Jonathon paused and waited for her to continue. "Sorry to bring up work tonight, but I thought you should know that Neil has made some basic omissions lately. I'm not complaining. There was no harm done. But I'm concerned his mind might not be on the job because of personal matters. Relationship issues at work or home, perhaps?"

"Thanks for letting me know, Suzanna. I'll have a quiet chat with him. He's a good man. Now let's get back to having a fun evening." She nodded and smiled agreement. Jonathon led the way into an expansive lounge/dining room. Heavy drapes framed the windows at front and rear, matching pelmets hiding the curtain tracks. Two bespoke rugs covered most of the floor at each end of the room, with parquet flooring showing around the edges. The dining table had been moved into a corner. Bottles of wine, spirits, beers, ciders and soft drinks covered the entire surface. "What would you like to drink?"

"I'll take a glass of red, please. A small one. I have to drive home."

"There's a wide choice. Would you like French, Italian, Australian, Merlot, Shiraz, Cab-Sav?"

"Do you have a South Australian Shiraz or Chilean Merlot?"

"No problem. There's a Barossa Valley Shiraz open already." He poured her a glass and handed it to her. Suzanna took a sip of the wine. It was rich and smooth, full-bodied and she sensed a hint of ripe plum and blackberry. The dark fruity liquid slid down perfectly and she wished she had come by taxi so she could drink more.

Jonathon led her to a small group standing around the fireplace. "Excuse me, folks. Let me introduce Suzanna McLeod. She's a colleague. A Detective Chief Inspector, here in Edinburgh." The doorbell rang and Jonathon excused himself.

A dark-haired woman smiled at Suzanna. "I suppose we'll all need to be on our best behaviour tonight."

The man next to her responded. "We certainly will. You'll need to keep the illegal drugs in your handbag until later, darling."

Suzanna smiled. She was used to such comments.

Each person in the group introduced themselves, including their profession: Penny Flaherty – the first woman to have spoken – a part-time homemaker, part-time art gallery owner/manager; Michael Flaherty, Penny's husband, a consultant surgeon; Olivia Tallentire, clothes designer; Erika Lindholm, Head of Finance for a large Scottish company; and Art Fisher, author. She couldn't imagine the same happening in another situation: 'Hi I'm Jeff, plumber by trade; I'm Billy, postman; Susan, nurse; Charmaine, hairdresser...'

Penny spoke again. "Is being a detective anything like it's portrayed on the TV, Suzanna?"

This was a common question when Suzanna met people for the first time. "There's some procedural and cultural truth in TV series and crime novels but also many inaccuracies. I doubt anyone writing those stories has ever been a police detective. They're making it up. It *is* fiction, after all."

"The DCI is almost always depicted as a bossy, non-consultative, prima-donna, with significant personality defects. Is there any truth in that characterization?" Erika asked with a smile.

"If it were true, I'd hardly confirm it, so anything I tell you should be doubted." She let that hang. As they absorbed what she'd said, she continued. "From my experience, there *are* a few inspectors who are full of self-importance and assumed infallibility, but they are rare. I can't speak for everyone in the police, but *I* believe in teamwork, where everyone's views and ideas are valued and encouraged, where the investigative route is mutually agreed, rather than directed by a single person." Suzanna paused, then turned to the author in the group. "What genre of books do you write, Art?"

"I'm a crime writer," he said sheepishly. They all looked at him, probably wondering how true to reality his books would be. "And, no, I haven't been a police officer, so Suzanna's correct in her assumption."

"What I find in most crime novels," Suzanna continued, "and I'm sure Jonathon will confirm, is they get the autopsy wrong," Suzanna commented. "They use incorrect terminology and processes, and some findings are pure fantasy. There'd be no way, for instance, that the autopsy could conclude which restaurant the victim had last eaten at." They all smiled at the silliness of the suggestion, but Art said nothing.

Michael jumped in. "How many crime writers does it take to change a light bulb," he asked, with a grin on his face and his eyes flitting to Art. Penny scowled at her husband, and the rest of the group waited in unexcited anticipation of the answer. "Two. One to plug it in and the other to give it a subtle twist at the end."

Penny sighed, Art groaned, but Olivia chuckled and the rest raised their eyebrows.

***

Jonathon greeted his new neighbour. "Come on in, old chap. There's a lovely unattached lady I'd like you to meet." He took his neighbour into the lounge, poured him a drink, then took him to the fireplace group. "Ladies and gents, I'd like to introduce my new neighbour Callum. I didn't get your surname?"

"It's McLeod," Callum said, looking at the group and at Suzanna apologetically.

"You two aren't related, *are you?*" Jonathon said, but he walked away without waiting for an answer.

"Sorry, Suzanna. I had no idea you'd be here." Callum said.

Suzanna tried to not show any emotion, but her body language gave away the connection. Olivia said, "You *are* related, aren't you?"

Callum spoke first. "Yes. We're married... but separated."

"Oh my God!" Erika exclaimed. "How awkward for you."

"Yes. Exceptionally awkward," Suzanna responded. "Please excuse me. It was lovely to make your acquaintance, but I'd better leave." She turned and strode away, placing her now empty wine glass on the mantelpiece.

Callum followed her across the room. "Please don't go yet, Suzanna. I need to speak with you, anyway."

Suzanna turned to him; her lips pursed. "I don't think now's the time to be discussing our past relationship. We don't want to cause a scene, do we?" She strode off into the hall in search of her host and her coat. Jonathon was understanding and apologetic when she explained why she needed to leave. Apart from the music and voices from Jonathon's house, the street was quiet and mist had created halos around the streetlamps as Suzanna marched back to her car. She couldn't understand why he wouldn't accept it was over.

***

The taxi pulled up where Brodie instructed the driver to stop. They stepped out of the car. "Come on, Mairi, this way. We'll soon be there." Mairi had dressed up for her evening out, with multiple layers of eclectic clothes she had picked up in charity shops and re-purposed. She'd taken trouble over her appearance and was eagerly anticipating the surprise dinner venue that Brodie had arranged when their trip to his parents was postponed.

She took his offered hand and he led her around the corner and along the street. Mairi knew there were several intimate restaurants further up the street, so was shocked when he swung right and dragged her through the double doors of a place she never dreamed he'd be taking her, the whiff of frying food enveloping her. "Double Mac and Fries?" Brodie asked.

Mairi froze to the spot and pulled her hand from his. "You must be joking," she shouted above the crowd of children's voices, excitingly asking for fish burgers, McFlurry ice creams and fried apple pies. She turned and stormed out, letting the doors swing back in Brodie's face. He just avoided having his nose flattened.

"Got you," he said with a huge grin on his face as he emerged. "Come on. The restaurant's this way," he said, holding out his hand. Mairi took it, her lips still puckered. But then she laughed. "You bastard, Brodie Buchan. You had me there." They marched off along the street laughing.

Chapter 25

As Suzanna took the car keys from her bag, she heard running feet, then a hand grabbed her shoulder. She spun, dropped and thrust her fist into her assailant's abdomen, knocking him backwards, her eyes looking for any glint of steel, her body ready to take further evasive action. The man stumbled and fell to the ground. Winded.

"Bloody hell, Suzanna. There was no need for that," Callum said as he struggled for breath.

Suzanna stepped forward and held out her hand towards him. "Sorry, Callum. I didn't know it was you. My reaction was instinctive." She helped him stand. "I had a rough time on my last case. I had to fight off attackers several times when I was in Bangladesh and West Bengal. You should have spoken, not run up and grabbed me!"

Callum had tears in his eyes. Partly the pain of her punch, partly upset that *she* had struck him. They'd never physically fought during their marriage or afterwards. "Why have you ignored all my calls and texts, Suzanna?" he said, still gasping. "I thought after that night out and sleeping together, we were destined to reunite – to become a couple again. But you've cut me off. I don't understand. I love you, Suzanna. Don't you feel anything for me?" A tear trickled from the corner of one eye.

"That evening and night we spent together was wonderful and I thought I'd fallen for you again. But it made me feel I'd betrayed James like you betrayed me. It took me back to that day when I walked in on you having sex with that young woman. I could see every intimate detail in my mind." She paused and Callum opened his mouth to speak, but she held up her hand for him to be silent. "Because of the guilt I felt, I almost finished my relationship with James, but I admitted my duplicity and asked him what he wanted to do. I'm still with James, now. There's no future for you and me, Callum. Let's leave it there. Get divorced and move on." Her face was stern, her eyes drilling into his.

He blinked before responding. "That's easier said than done. I'm still madly in love with you. I've never stopped loving you. For the last two years, I've continued to love you. After our night together, I thought we could rebuild our relationship and share the rest of our lives. If James can forgive you for having sex with someone else while in a relationship with him, can't you forgive me for doing the same while we were married?"

"There's no comparison, Callum. I admitted what I'd done, asked for forgiveness and gave him the opportunity to decide whether he wished to stay with me. You would never have told me about your extra-marital sexual relationship and you may well have carried on having an affair if I'd not come home early that day. You knew you were being unfaithful to your wife – to the person you had sworn to be loyal to 'until death do us part.' That's the point I could never get over. I would never trust you again, Callum. No matter what you say. It's like the difference between first-degree murder and manslaughter. One is planned and the other accidental. Our night of passion wasn't planned – certainly not by me, anyway. But you and your colleague must have pretended to be somewhere else on business, lying to your firm as well as betraying me. That's premeditated."

Callum looked defeated. "I'm so sorry, Suzanna. I never meant to hurt you. You're right. The sex had been planned. We *were* deceiving both you and our firm. But it *was* a one-off. It was a midlife crisis for me. The younger woman coming onto me was too much temptation when I was feeling uncertain of my desirability. I've not been with anyone else since our night together. I wanted to be faithful this time. Had hoped there would be a future for us again." He started crying but, seeing her firmly set features, realised he wouldn't win her over with tears and couldn't return to the party red-eyed, so turned and wandered up the street towards his home, like a chastised dog, its tail between its legs.

* * *

Raised voices exploded from behind Owen and Ailsa, just after they'd cleared their ice cream tubs - Belgium chocolate for Owen and Ailsa a mango sorbet.

Neither of them appreciated fine dining; the food was always overpriced and portions too small. They enjoyed the chain restaurants serving pizzas, pasta and Mexican. Tonight, they'd eaten at Nando's before going into the close-by Cineworld. Owen didn't want any popcorn, having devoured a heap of spicy chicken wings. Ailsa was also replete, but they'd both found room for ice cream.

Owen turned to find out what was happening. In the aisle, two men shouted into each other's faces, pushing and shoving. Their girlfriends also exchanged foul words but kept their distance. Owen thought it best to leave them to it, provided it didn't escalate. But the two men fell against a woman seated behind him, knocking her drink from her hands. Owen jumped to his feet. He wouldn't stand by and allow these idiots to hurt other people and spoil their evenings out. "You two. Get out of here. Take your disagreement onto the street. This is no place to be fighting."

Surprisingly, the men turned and walked out of the cinema, their girlfriends following them. "I'll be back in two minutes, luv," Owen said to Ailsa, before walking away.

The adverts had concluded and the film had been running for ten minutes by the time Owen returned to his seat. Ailsa turned to him, her face showing her disappointment. She reluctantly allowed him to take her hand.

* * *

The grey painted restaurant, with bike racks out front, looked nothing special and Mairi looked at Brodie as if to say, 'why all this way out of the centre?' They had walked for a few minutes north from New Town, down the gently sloping hill of Dundas Street, through residential streets away from the commercial areas and the roads lined with shops and restaurants, before turning right onto a side road.

Brodie could see the question in her eyes. "Friends recommended it. Come on. Let's go in." As they approached the entrance door, it opened and a smiling maître d' welcomed them to his restaurant. Intimate conversations merged with easy-listening music. The smells of frying onions and garlic, and the sound of sizzling steaks greeted her. She couldn't believe the transformation.

Sanded oak floors contrasted with magnificent chandeliers, their light sparkling around the room. Smooth plastered, painted walls with an eclectic mix of framed pictures, juxtaposed with exposed brick walls. A bar, illuminated by purple lights, stood at the room's end, behind which a vast array of drink bottles sat on shelves.

The maître d' invited them to sit at a table for two, with red roses at its centre. Wine glasses and polished silver cutlery sparkled, reflecting the overhead lights. Deep red napkins were unfolded and laid on their laps. Mairi hadn't eaten anywhere so opulent and classy as this restaurant. She wondered what the cost would be but put the thought aside. Brodie was paying. She'd simply enjoy it.

They chatted, sipped quality wine, nibbled at their starters, luxuriated over the mains – fillet steak for Brodie, lamb for Mairi – then savoured their sweet desserts. Brodie looked across the table at his partner. They'd been together now for three years, two of them sharing a home. He looked into her green eyes, framed by her shoulder-length, dyed blonde hair, hanging free this evening instead of being tied back. He loved her high cheekbones, her dimple chin and full lips. In fact, he loved everything about her, even when she was grumpy in the morning. He told her so: "You do know I love you, Mairi Gordon."

"And I love you too, Brodie Buchan," she replied, grinning. "Thanks so much for treating me to dinner in this wonderful restaurant. It's been fabulous."

Brodie didn't reply; instead, he slipped off his chair, went down on one knee and pulled a diamond ring from his pocket. "Mairi Gordon, love of my life, will you marry me?"

Mairi's face illuminated as if backlit. She glowed. Tears came to her eyes, overcome with being asked. "Yes, yes, yes," she cried. Brodie grinned up at her, took her hand and slipped on the ring. The restaurant erupted with cheers and clapping, and the maître d' arrived with a bottle of champagne, which he opened with a delicate pop, before filling the two flutes. They toasted their future life together, kissed and hugged before sitting again, both grinning like kids at Christmas.

* * *

As the lights switched on at the end of the movie, Ailsa noticed Owen's face – his cheek bruised and his lips swollen. "What happened?"

I tried to get them to leave but they started throwing punches in the foyer. I got caught by a stray fist. Had to call 999. The uniform guys have arrested them and taken them away.

142

"Why did you have to interfere? You should have left those men to sort themselves out. Now you've got yourself hurt and spoiled our night out. Why do you have to get involved all the time? How can we ever have a good night out if you're always on duty?"

"I'm a copper, luv. I don't stop being one, because the hands of the clock have passed a certain point on its face. You're a nurse. If you saw an old lady collapse onto the pavement, would you walk on by and leave it to someone else to deal with?"

Ailsa saw his point. Smiled sheepishly and placed a peck on his cheek, avoiding the swelling. "Come on, take me home, Mr Crawford. I'm in the mood for baby-making."

He grinned, then grimaced as the tensing of his face caused him pain. He grasped her hand and squeezed gently as they meandered up the aisle in the crowd of exiting cinema-goers, heading home for what he hoped would be a passionate night.

Sunday 8th March

Chapter 26

In the morning, Mairi was keen to share her news with the team. But when she arrived at the station, she found she had the office to herself. They were all out interviewing ex-Butler and Cargrove employees. She searched for train times to Oban – a journey of about four and a half hours – before checking ferry times for the crossings to Iona, via Mull. She returned to the train bookings to get a seat on the train that would get her there in time. It would mean leaving Edinburgh shortly after 9 am on Monday. She should be on Mull by 3 pm and arrive on Iona about half four or five o'clock. She'd need to overnight on Iona because the ferries would have stopped by the time she'd interviewed Miss White. The return would be a dawn ferry from Iona to Mull, then out of Craignure, about 7 am across to Oban. A train from the town around 9 am would see her arriving back in Edinburgh at about 1:30 pm. It was the best she could do. Next step: find accommodation for the night. The admin office didn't work at weekends, so she booked all her tickets and accommodation online using her credit card. She'd claim it back before the bills arrived.

Trip sorted, Mairi grabbed her coat and headed out into the crisp cold morning for her first appointment, dropping a note on the group WhatsApp before leaving. She saw messages from the DCI and Rab saying they had completed their first interviews but they had zilch to report. Nothing from Zahir yet. She felt frivolous and still excited by what had happened last night, so took a photograph of her ring and posted it on WhatsApp, with the words, 'The lady said yes!'

**

Suzanna strode up the concrete path towards the basic white UPVC front door. Either side of the path were unkempt patches of grass – you'd be hard-pushed to call them lawns. The spartan blades were straggly and multiple dandelions dominated. An old Volvo 340 hatchback stood on the drive. Its red paintwork had long ago dulled, its colour hidden behind a fog of oxidisation. Rust spread along the sills and wheel arches, like fungus growing on a rotting tree. Grime shrouded the windscreen and the tyres were almost flat.

Suzanna's phone pinged. She glanced down and noted WhatsApp had some messages. She smiled at Mairi's picture, immediately typing a response. 'Great news, Mairi. Congrats.' She hit send. The door key was in the latch and when she rang the bell, an old man's voice called out. "Let yourself in. I'm in the front room."

Suzanna opened the door and called out. "Hello, Mr Gregory. It's DCI McLeod from Edinburgh CID."

"Yes, yes. Come on in. I've been expecting you."

She closed the front door and opened the next one, entering the old man's living room. It stank of stale urine, sweat and unwashed clothes. He sat in an upright chair with wooden arms, a tea table nearby, sprinkled with biscuit crumbs and wet from tea spillages. A Zimmer frame sat by his side and the TV was on in the room's corner. A Scottie dog rose from its slumber and greeted Suzanna, its tail wagging ferociously. "Sailor. Get down," the old man said, as it placed its front paws on Suzanna's legs.

"That's an unusual name for a dog. Why did you call him Sailor?" Suzanna asked.

"So I could say *'Hello Sailor'* whenever I came home," he smiled mischievously. Suzanna smiled back. Ronny Gregory was probably the same age as George White and of similar physical condition (although still alive, of course). "Turn off the TV, lass," he instructed.

Suzanna hit the red button on his controller, silencing the television, then replaced the device on the table. "Mr Ronny Gregory?"

"Aye, that's me. Haven't changed my name in all my eighty-odd years," he chuckled. "Now, why's a pretty young woman like you coming to visit an old fella like me?

It was good to be called pretty, but the chances were Ronny would have called any woman under 50 young and pretty. It was all relative. "You might not have heard, but George White died a few days ago. We're trying to find out more about him to help piece together the events that would have led to his demise."

"He died under suspicious circumstances, then? That's how you say it, isn't it?"

"Yes. He'd been murdered. So, we need to understand George White, the type of man he was, his history and any enemies he might have made along the way. That will help us establish a motive and identify suspects."

"I see. So, you want me to tell you about George White, warts and all?" He paused and thought for a minute, his bottom set of teeth wandering around his mouth as he considered his response. "Well, I was in the engineering department, responsible for maintaining the manufacturing machinery and carrying out upgrades and new installations. My office was in the factory but I saw George quite often as we both attended weekly management meetings. I also shared an occasional drink with him, but only at company functions. We were never pals."

Suzanna kept her eyes locked on his and nodded as he explained his relationship. "Did you ever notice anything about George, perhaps being inappropriate with other members of staff?"

"You mean flirting with the women?" He said with a wink.

"A bit more than that, I wondered?" Suzanna's expression remained steady, not giving into Gregory's flippancy. White's attitude towards women was an important matter.

Ronny noticed her seriousness. "Well... he had a reputation for trying it on with the ladies in his department, but I never heard anything specific. Rumour had it, though, that one or two of the women left the company to avoid his attention." Ronny lifted one buttock off his chair and noisily passed wind before settling himself in the chair again without a word.

Suzanna was shocked but tried not to let it show. Sailor jumped up and ran out of the room, perhaps predicting an unpleasant stench. "Is there anything else you can recall that might help us paint a picture of George White?" Fortunately, Suzanna's nasal senses were not attacked. What was it she'd heard on Radio 2's Factoids the other day? Humans typically expel enough methane each day to fill a party balloon.

Ronny's eyes stared straight ahead as he thought back to those days, thirty years ago. "There were two lasses left within a few months of each other. I think one was called Sally and the other Maureen. Both youngsters. Around twenty, I'd say. I remember one day – I'd stayed late to change the maintenance schedule for the following day – I saw George White leave, then ten minutes later Maureen left work. It was unusual for the girls in accounts to stay late. She looked dishevelled and flushed, and her eyes were red and wet. Perhaps it had something to do with her boss?"

"Perhaps? That's most helpful. Do you recall when that occurred? Approximate would do?"

"I can do better than estimate the date. The following day, despite me publishing a revised schedule of work, some of my team carried out work that would normally have been done that day. At the same time, other team members did the work I'd freshly scheduled. The combination of the two actions, which should never have coincided, shut down the whole production line. I took the blame for it, of course, because they were my engineers. The date is etched in my memory. April the 1st, 1985. So, the night before would have been 31st March."

Chapter 27

Her third interview completed, Suzanna checked the WhatsApp messages and noted that Rab and Zahir had caught up with her. Mairi's first interviewee had not been at home. Now on her second. She typed into her phone. 'Back at station in 30 mins. Let's catch up.' Her phone pinged twice, shortly afterwards. There were thumbs up icons from Rab and Zahir.

Suzanna parked near the building and walked in, noting Zahir's Honda now filled a certain senior officer's designated parking place. She dumped her bag and coat, then took her mug to get a coffee, passing through the main office on the way. "Hi, guys." They both greeted her back. "Zahir, I see you've parked in the Chief Superintendent's slot."

"Yes, ma'am. He'll not be using it today, will he?" Zahir responded.

"You're *probably* right. But if he does come into the office and finds your car parked there, he'll hit the roof. He's precious about his allocated slot."

Zahir stood up, took his large bunch of keys and headed for the door. "I'll move it just in case." Suzanna smiled as she watched him leave, glad that he had taken the hint, before turning to Rab.

"You're right about the Chief Super's attitude to his slot," Rab said. "Angus told me he'd received a right bollocking last month for using it late in the day when he thought the Chief Super had already finished work.

"Oh! I hadn't heard about that one. Useful to know. So, did you get anywhere with your three interviews?"

"Yes. One of mine was Sally Scott (nee Henderson)." Suzanna's ears pricked up. "When asked about George White, her face reddened and said we'd best go into the front room. Her husband stayed in the kitchen. She'd heard about his death on the news but didn't realise the interview was connected to his death. I asked her to tell me about the man who'd been her boss for two years."

Rab continued, "She said he was a dirty old man. He'd touched her bottom and brushed against her breasts a number of times – some obviously on purpose and others supposedly accidentally. But they weren't accidents. He'd also asked her to stay back after work to help him with a project, then tried to have sex with her. But she pushed him off and went home, then kept her distance from him until she left. I mentioned her record showing her worsening performance at work in her second year. Her response was that if you had to keep looking over your shoulder to avoid a predator, you'd make more mistakes. And she confirmed she'd requested a transfer to get away from him, but she had to look for work outside the company as nothing had been available."

"The second interesting one was Yvette Lancashire." Rab picked up his notebook, turning to the relevant page. "I asked her why she left the Butler and Cargrove after such a short time with the company. She said she didn't want to dig up thirty-year-old dirt. But when I pushed her, she admitted that Mr White had been trying to get into her knickers. There's little doubt that he *was* a sexual predator, using the power of his position at work to influence female staff. But neither of these women admit to having been subjected to serious sexual assaults, so I doubt they have a motive to murder him three decades later. They both seem to have good lives and happy families, now – well, as much as anyone does."

Just then Zahir returned and Suzanna asked for a briefing on his interviews. All three of the people allocated to him were at home. One, a security man, said there were rumours Mr White was a pest to the women in his department, but he'd not seen anything himself. His second was Frances Greenwood. "I questioned Greenwood about her reason for being off work frequently in the latter part of her time with the company. She said she often felt sick, but when I pressed on the reason, she admitted she was anxious about going in to work. Mr White incessantly pressured her to assist him in his office. In the privacy of that office, he would touch her inappropriately. One day, she decided she'd had enough and didn't return. When asked if he'd sexually assaulted her, she clammed up. She wouldn't say what he'd done. So, he might have committed an offence or might not have."

Zahir paused. "Miss Greenwood is a rather anxious woman. Insisted on her sister sitting in on the interview. When I asked for her location on the morning George White was murdered, she said at home, sick. Her sister corroborated what she'd said – they live together – but she'd left for work at 7 am. In reality, Greenwood has no alibi for the time of the killing and possibly has a motive."

Suzanna thought for a minute. "Zahir, have a look at the CCTV images of people captured in the Coates area that morning. Could Greenwood have been there?"

Zahir studied the pictures, many of which were of poor quality. "This one's a possibility," he said, pointing to an image. "It's difficult to be sure, though, because of the grainy image and the angle of the camera."

"Okay. Draw a dotted line on the board from the image to her name, to remind us to consider it again, and run some background checks on Greenwood, in case there's anything relevant. Find out whether there's any CCTV near her home. If she went out, that would blow her alibi."

Next, Suzanna briefed them on her talk with Ronny Gregory and her meeting with the head of the HR department when the rate of staff turnover increased. "Mr Masterton knew of the rumours about George. But despite encouraging the women to explain why they were leaving, none named him, so he could do nothing. He was glad when George moved on."

"I also spoke with the deputy HR manager, Mrs Martha Fothering-ham. She concurred with her boss' recollection. She said White was a slimy man. The sort you'd expect to be a flasher in the park. She kept her distance from him. She felt sorry for the young women who'd left. There must have been something going on, but with no one willing to name him, they couldn't take any action."

They took a break to refill their coffee mugs. Mairi joined the gathering and reported that Maureen Stevens was not in when she called, so that would need to be followed up. Her second interviewee, Mrs Susan Williamson, said that George White had never acted inappropriately with her. However, she harboured suspicions about his dealings with the younger ladies in their department. She'd tried her best to get them to share with her their reason for leaving. Although no one said Mr White's behaviour was the cause, their body language suggested differently. She'd shared her concerns with HR, but this changed nothing. When George White left, the whole department breathed a huge sigh of relief. The atmosphere brightened and it became a happy workplace.

"Thanks, Mairi. That reinforces all we've heard so far. Rab, have reports come in from the stations yet on the other eleven staff?"

"Aye. Ten interviews proved to be fruitless but a cleaner, Sheena McDermott, recalled something of relevance. She remembered a couple of occasions when emptying the litter bins in accounts after the departure of most staff. There were noises from the manager's office that sounded unusual for a workplace. She'd not mentioned it

THE KEY TO MURDER

to anyone."

"Did she elaborate on the sounds?"

"Yes. On the first occasion, she'd heard a man talking, his voice excited. She didn't pick up any words, but she guessed he was engaged in sex with someone. The second time it happened, she also heard a woman squealing. She was embarrassed and didn't hang around in the department and avoided emptying the manager's bin."

"More evidence of something going on between George White and one or more of his staff," Suzanna concluded. "But we mustn't be blinkered. There may well be another reason someone could have wanted him dead that we've yet to uncover."

Suzanna picked up some papers from the desk. "I received an update from the CSI team's additional work yesterday. They completed checks in the rear yard of White's house, finding the gate to be bolted and locked. The padlock was rusty and they believe it hadn't been opened in a long time. The fence didn't show any signs of having been climbed, so they concluded the murderer could not have arrived or left by that route. They also confirmed there were no signs of forced entry through the front door. This establishes that the killer *must* have obtained a key or knew how to open the key safe."

"Our focus," she continued, "obviously, has been on the care company. But we need to look wider, because we've yet to find a motive for any CCC staff to want White dead. I'd like us to go through the neighbour interview records. See if we can spot anything. We may need to go back and interview them ourselves because our uniform colleagues might have missed something. We have time to do that now, so let's get onto it."

Another thought popped into Suzanna's mind. "Mairi, what travel arrangements have you made?" Mairi shared with her boss the times of trains and ferries and that she'd booked a room within the Iona community. "Okay. Sounds like you made the trip as short as possible.

Well done. Let's hope Sheila White has something worth hearing."

***

The team completed scrutiny of neighbour interviews after two hours of solid work. Zahir replaced the phone handset just as the DCI entered the office. "Ma'am. Forensics say they have DNA evidence linking the knife found in the river to George White, but no one else."

Suzanna stopped, coffee in hand. "At least we know it's the murder weapon, but without a link to the murderer, we're still not much further forward." As she walked to her office, Suzanna cursed silently. She'd been hoping the knife would be the key to identifying White's killer.

No sooner had Suzanna sat at her desk than Mairi appeared in the doorway. "Ma'am. I spoke with Musgrave. He's on the Algarve."

Suzanna looked intrigued as Mairi continued. "I asked him why he'd been in Coates Gardens that morning and why he'd taken five minutes to transit the short street. He said he'd picked up a colleague from number 23. They travelled together to a meeting in Dundee that started at 9 am. I spoke to his colleague, who confirmed his story and checked with a person in the company they'd been meeting with, who corroborated what he'd said. So, that's another person eliminated."

"Did you ask him if he'd noticed anyone walking past or acting suspiciously while he was waiting?"

"Yes. But he said no. After parking, he called his colleague to inform him he was outside, then read messages on his phone until his colleague arrived."

"Okay. Good work. Thanks, Mairi."

Mairi grinned as she walked away. It was always good to be told you were doing well, provided it was genuine and not said like check-out assistants she'd come across in other countries when they wished you insincerely – almost robotically – to "have a nice day."

Rab and Mairi headed off to Coates Gardens to re-interview White's neighbours. Their last task of the day before heading home.

Chapter 28

"Took your time. Lift out of action?" James called out. His apartment was on the fifth floor, the building being on Old Tolbooth Wynd, a cobbled lane ending in an arched pedestrian throughway. Suzanna had walked up the stairs – an advocate of *use it or lose it* when it came to fitness. Her heart and lungs had a little workout on the way up to James' floor. He'd left the door ajar after buzzing her in through the outer door. She removed her coat and shoes in the small hallway.

"Hi James," she said, raising her voice. Suzanna walked into the open-plan living room, the sound of sizzling food and the aroma of frying onions coming from the kitchen end. When she explained the reason for her delayed arrival at his door, he looked impressed.

Although spacious, James' penthouse felt more enclosed than her high-ceilinged Georgian home, with its bay window overlooking a park. She always thought it odd that the top floor of an apartment building had a special name and normally a special price. Some justified the extra cost, because they enjoyed private roof terraces and views across the city, but many didn't.

The room was characterless, a bland rectangle, lights built into the ceiling and no architraves. James had a view of roof-tops, scattered with TV aerials and satellite dishes, although when she looked off to the right she could see Canongate Kirk and its high-walled, terraced graveyard. Beyond the kirk, the steep banks of Salisbury Crags rose tall in Holyrood Park above the tiny buildings at its feet. She couldn't see the magnificence of the mount because the sun had already set and the sky was only just hanging on to its fading light.

James had furnished the apartment stylishly, although a bit too masculine for her tastes, with chestnut brown leather sofas facing each other across a light oak coffee table. Behind the sofas, more light oak furniture – a boxy extending dining table that could take six chairs around it, for when he had guests. Today, it was closed and the spare chairs were placed in the room's corners. Two chairs faced the table, looking in at the placemats, surrounded by cutlery and glasses for water and wine. Cloth napkins lay neatly folded and a candle burned in the single glass candlestick, beside a vase, with one red rose.

Suzanna approached the kitchen counter. James turned from the cooker and leaned across. Their lips met and lingered for a few seconds before he pulled away to return to his cooking. "Plenty of time for more of that later," he said, smiling. He started adding ingredients to the pan, stirring them vigorously. After a minute, he slowed the fan on the cooker hood, the onions having now lost their watering eyes potency.

"How's your Sunday been?" James asked.

"Busy," she responded. "Interviewing people, reading reports, analysing findings and figuring where to go next with the enquiry."

"I reckon it was Colonel Mustard in the kitchen with a knife," James quipped.

Suzanna smiled indulgently. "You guessed correctly on one count. It was a knife. But in the living room. And I doubt the murderer was a colonel."

"Oh well! One out of three isn't bad. Is it the old fella that was found dead in his home in the Coates area?"

"Yes. That's the one. Most murders are straightforward and often involve drugs, alcohol or close relatives, but this man's relatives live miles away and haven't been near him in ages. And he certainly wasn't involved with a drugs gang, being home bound and in his mid-eighties!"

More veg went into the wok, causing fresh sizzling and steam. "How did the skiing go, James?"

"Fabulous. The cloud remained in the valley and the slopes were flooded with sunshine. Had some snow overnight on the Wednesday, so conditions remained good all week. Can't remember a better week's skiing in my life. Would have been better still if I'd had you to cosy up to each evening, of course." Suzanna didn't respond. "Annabelle and Roger were great company, so I didn't get lonely. Every evening, except one, we spent drinking, playing cards and having a laugh."

"What happened on the one exception?"

"Their wedding anniversary. They had a night for just the two of them. I stayed in the flat and drowned my sorrows."

"Ah! Poor you. Were you lonely?"

"Of course, but we're both used to being alone, aren't we – living separately as we do?"

"True."

James added a tomato sauce that he'd been simmering with herbs in a separate pan, to the wok and tossed all the ingredients, then drained the penne pasta through a colander over the sink. Separating the veg mixture into two, he added diced chicken to one, heating it for a minute before serving the meals into two large bowls. To Suzanna's bowl, he added a handful of lightly grilled, chopped Halloumi cheese.

Suzanna took their bowls to the dining table and James pulled garlic bread from the oven before joining her. He poured Chianti into their wineglasses, which they immediately lifted and chinked together, James saying *salute* and Suzanna responding *cin cin*, before taking their first sips. "Here's to a lovely evening," Suzanna said.

"And to a wonderful night," James replied with a wink. Suzanna hoped her car would be safe on the street overnight; this wasn't the best area of the city, she knew – too many drunks wandering the streets after a night out.

The food was wonderful. As the first course came to its end, Suzanna asked, "James, you know how my marriage ended, but what happened to yours?"

James placed the last forkful of his pasta into his mouth, then held up a finger to say excuse me a minute. After swallowing, he laid his fork in his bowl and began to share. "Millie and I married in our mid-twenties. We'd met at university in Sheffield and in our final year started dating. We stayed on in the city after graduation, both found employment there and moved in together. Life was great. Money was tight to start with, but more than we'd had as students. We partied, holidayed; met each other's parents. One day, I asked her to marry me and she said yes."

"How long were you married?"

"Fourteen years."

"You mentioned before about having two children. How often do you see them?"

"About once a month. I miss them so much. Aimee's twelve now and already a teenager! Josh is eight. He started rugby training last year and is loving it. I'd like to spend more with them, but Millie stayed on after our breakup and I moved back to my home city. It's not practicable to see them more frequently. I travel to Sheffield and stay in a hotel over a weekend, except in the holidays. I try to take them away somewhere or bring them to Edinburgh. That's going to get more difficult before long, with Aimee beginning to turn into a woman. She certainly wouldn't want to continue sharing my spare bedroom with Josh once she hits puberty."

"Why did you end up separating after fourteen years of marriage and two children?"

"We just fell out of love. We were both busy with our jobs and looking after the kids. Millie wasn't happy in her chosen career and had started studying with the Open University to gain relevant qualifications – Psychology. We hardly had any time for each other and when we did, we were too tired to enjoy it. Life became tedious, a chore. I confronted her about our lack of quality time together and she just said, *you can leave if you like.* I was shocked by her reaction. She obviously didn't want to make the relationship work. After that, we started arguing frequently and in the end, I moved out. The kids were devastated but they've forgiven us and settled into having their dad part-time and their step-dad full time. Only three months after I left, he moved in with them. I suspect they were seeing each other while I was with Millie but I've no evidence of that."

Suzanna looked at him empathetically. "Thanks for sharing that with me." She reached out and took his hand. "How do you see your future, James? If you could magic up an ideal life – and I don't mean a post-lottery-win utopia – what would it look like?"

He stared through her for a moment, conjuring up an image in his mind. "Well, if I ignore the desire to live in a luxury bungalow with an infinity swimming pool and an airstrip for my jet on a Caribbean island…" He pondered again. "I guess it would be to have a gorgeous, loving wife, a house just outside a city with views of rolling hills or mountains, private but not isolated. Perhaps on the edge of a village with a good pub, serving excellent food, a roaring fire in winter and friendly locals. I'd be running my own business, earning enough money to live a good life but not enough to own a super-yacht or a plane. A nearly new car on the drive – perhaps a Jaguar or Mercedes. Not a new car – they lose too much value in their first couple of years. I can't help being pragmatic, even in this ideal life. I'd like to holiday abroad two-three times a year. To visit places only seen in TV documentaries. To experience different cultures. And I'd want to be philanthropic, helping good causes, lifting people out of poverty and rescuing the oppressed. Later, I'd want grandchildren to bring me joy from time to time – to watch them grow into adults." He paused. "And what about you?"

Despite having asked James the question, she didn't have a ready answer. Suzanna wondered why? She should give the future more thought. Without a destination, how would she ever get there? If you let life decide which road to take, she thought, instead of choosing, who knows where you'd end up. But when she started describing her ideal, it came easy. "We have a lot in common, actually. My home's location, like yours, would be outside the hustle and bustle of a city but close enough to access its facilities easily. I'd want views as well – to have the luxury of looking across a valley to distant hills or lofty mountains when opening my bedroom curtains in the morning. My ideal climate would be temperate but it should be sunny every day, with fluffy white clouds dancing across the sky. It would rain each night when I was in bed to provide lush gardens, forests, and fields that I could walk through. The daytime temperatures would span the high teens up to high twenties." She paused, thoughtful. James waited patiently for her to continue. "I realise that bit is a fantasy. I'm sure there's no such place in the world with a climate like that."

James jumped in. "But it would be fun trying to find it." He smiled and squeezed her hand.

"Being realistic, children are out of the question – it's too late for that – and therefore no grandchildren, but I'd like to see more of my niece. Oh! By the way. I just found out Charlotte's pregnant again, so I'll have another niece or nephew before long."

"Great news." James hesitated. "Is Charlotte happy about it?"

"Yes. She's over the moon. They've been trying for the last few months and were beginning to wonder if it would ever happen." Suzanna paused, bringing her mind back to their visionary speculation. "Like you, I want to travel, to experience new things, new places, new people. I want ample money to have no worries about paying the bills, but not so much that I could travel first class on every flight, although it would be good to travel business class on long-haul flights. I'd like to spend time overseas again – making a difference in people's lives. Perhaps it would be Freeset again, the social enterprise I worked for in India. Depends on what grabs me. My partner must be someone who's caring, loving and trustworthy. Being pleasing to the eye would be a bonus."

"Not sure whether I'm pleasing to your eye, Suzanna, but there's a good match in our desires, wouldn't you say?"

Suzanna nodded, her eyes still locked with his, her mind wondering whether she should make a suggestion. Was it too early?

James broke the mood by standing and taking away their dinner dishes. Suzanna watched him as he cleared away, wiping the surfaces clean, loading the dishwasher and pouring water into the wok to let it soak. He pulled two desserts from his fridge and returned to the table. Indulgent chocolate mousses, topped with toasted almond flakes and dried cranberries. She luxuriated in the flavour of the chilled, smooth dark chocolate, the crunch of the nuts and the chewy tang of the berries. Heaven on her tongue. "Divine," she exclaimed.

They savoured each tea-spoonful of the mousse, not speaking until they'd both scraped up the last of the dessert. "Good, eh?" James stated.

"Oh yes!" Suzanna responded. "Did you make the mousse, or was it from a posh shop?"

"You insult me, Ms McLeod. I'm hurt." He pretended indignation, then smiled again. "I'd like to say I made it, but I just embellished it."

"Well, I have to say, the topping made all the difference."

"Shall we move to a comfy seat?" James offered, standing before Suzanna answered.

They sat side by side on a sofa. Relaxing, contemporary instrumental music still played in the background. They chatted for a while, sipping their wine, then drew together until their lips touched. They kissed slowly at first, then passionately. James tasted of red wine and chocolate. Suzanna wanted to devour him. The kiss became urgent. All thoughts of futures faded as their senses magnified. She felt the tingle of excitement, the rising desire to make love.

James stood, took her hand and led her to the bedroom. He undressed her slowly, kissing her skin as he exposed it, nibbled her earlobes and kissed her neck. They fell onto the bed and tangled their bodies in a loving embrace, connecting intimately, excitedly, fervently...

Monday 9th March

Chapter 29

Mairi sat with her takeaway coffee admiring the magnificent ceiling of Edinburgh Waverley's booking hall, with its intricately painted panels, with swirling wrought iron patterns, framing acres of glass. A beautiful cupola, its glass rim made up of eight-petalled floral shapes, sat at the ceiling's centre. The grandeur impressed her. If she recalled correctly, James Bell had designed it in the late 1800s. They didn't make buildings like this anymore.

Mairi looked up at the electronic boards listing train arrivals and departures. The top-listed train on the board disappeared and the listings moved upwards. Her train to Oban now showed its departure time and platform. Dozens of travellers started walking towards the platforms and she joined the throng of passengers in their pursuit of a comfortable seat in the warmth of a carriage.

She extracted a Kindle from her handbag and opened it to her current book. Ten minutes later, the train jolted as it pulled away. A slight whiff of electric motors entered the carriage. She paused reading, to look outside as the train left the platform behind and clattered over the multiple track points, returning quickly to her book – a steamy romance.

She changed trains at Glasgow, boarding a ScotRail train to take her north and west. The journey took them alongside lochs and mountains, her eyes switching between reading and sightseeing. After the Arrochar and Tarbet station, the train swung in to run parallel with the northern shores of Loch Lomond. There were views across the water to the peak of Cruinn a'Bheinn and beyond it to the 3000 ft high Ben Lomond. Occasionally she glimpsed its sunlit rocky peak, the clouds teasing her as they swarmed around the mountain – now you see me, now you don't.

***

Rab walked from his car to the police station entrance, noting the change from calm, cool and damp weather the previous day. Today fluffy clouds, driven by the breeze, danced in front of the rising sun. His mood reflected the improved weather and he felt more confident that they would make further progress today.

They gathered in the main office, steaming drinks in hand, to recap on the previous day's work. Rab briefed them on his and Mairi's re-interviewing of the neighbours. One neighbour said when she opened her lounge curtains that morning, she'd noticed a woman approaching Mr White's house. "The woman had been dressed in jogging bottoms and an old, padded jacket, in a nondescript pale colour." Rab expanded. "She had paid little attention to the woman and couldn't be sure she called at the victim's house, but she was certainly heading that way when the neighbour noticed her. When urged to think back, she remembered she had glimpsed the right side of her face. The woman wore spectacles and a crocheted hat. It was also pale. The neighbour couldn't define the colour. She thought the glasses were dark coloured plastic because they had chunky temples." The others looked at him curiously. "The temple is the sidebar of the specs, going to the ear. I Googled it."

"Hmm. That doesn't give us much to go on. Do any of the Butler and Cargrove employees who've been interviewed wear thick, dark plastic glasses?" No one responded to Suzanna's question.

"Right. Next job this morning is to contact the other companies

George White worked for and find out if they have anything to say about his reputation or behaviour. Let me know as soon as that work has been completed, so we can review the case again."

"One other thing," Rab spoke before his boss walked away. "The financial background checks on Sheila and Edmond White have turned up. Sheila has little money but no debts. Based on where she's living and the lifestyle she's chosen, that's not surprising. Edmond, on the other hand, is living off his Army pension but still has a large mortgage, debts in the thousands on two credit cards and is overdrawn every month."

"Hmm. A potential motive then, given his forthcoming inheritance – a half share of £500,000! We'll need to keep him open as a suspect. See what else you can find out about him. Why is an ex-Army commissioned officer so financially unsound?" Suzanna went to leave but remembered an outstanding query. "Rab, did you visit the house opposite White's?"

"Aye, I did. I asked Mrs Knowles why her CCTV wasn't working that morning. Apparently, the power lead had become disconnected – it was just in its socket but not making contact. She thought perhaps it had become loose during dusting."

Suzanna's face screwed up at this unwelcome news. Another unsuccessful line of investigation! She had to remind herself that every dead end got them back onto the right road. It brought back a memory. Her sister had said that was how God guided her. By closing some doors but leaving others open. Suzanna had discounted the idea at the time but now saw the logic of it.

***

As the train pulled into Oban station, the sun caught the finger on her left hand and the diamond sparkled again. She had loved the journey northwest. The often-rugged landscapes had been beautiful to see, and the romance story she'd been reading had churned her emotions.

Mairi smiled as she stood, picked up her bag and joined the queue to exit the train.

Outside the station, taxis waited to transport passengers to their homes. Across the street, modern buildings housed shops and restaurants. Signs pointed to Tourist Information and Bus Station. Over the water, more shops and cafés were visible, as well as the grand Caledonian Hotel, in buildings whose architecture gave away its 19th-century heritage. It looked enticing, but her destination was in the opposite direction.

She turned left and walked along the coast for three minutes to the ferry terminal. After showing her ticket, they ushered her on board. She wondered whether the vessel should be called a boat or a ship. She would check the definition later to satisfy her curiosity.

Mairi wasn't looking forward to the ride across to Mull. The wind had strengthened and although the harbour wasn't choppy, she could see out through its mouth that the sea had become rough. She moved inside to escape the blustery conditions and found a chair fixed to the deck's centre. Mairi heard there would be less motion at that point. She wasn't normally seasick, but she'd never travelled on rough seas. As she waited for the ferry to leave, her mind returned to the question of ship versus boat. The ferry must surely be a boat, not a ship. Who'd ever heard of a ferry ship! A song popped into her mind – Chris de Burgh's *Don't pay the ferryman*. The lyrics came to her: ... *don't pay the ferryman. Don't even fix a price. Don't pay the ferryman until he gets you to the other side.* A bit late for that, she thought, looking at her ticket. Twenty minutes later, a resounding heavy clang indicated the boat's doors had closed. Crew shouted orders to each other as they performed their duties, then the ferry pulled away from the jetty and set sail for Mull.

As they exited the calm of the harbour, white foam blew off the breaking waves and the ferry started to pitch and roll. She didn't dare read her book, remembering it was best to look towards the horizon. Her eyes would be in sync with her other senses and motion sickness less likely. Some passengers wandered around, holding onto railings and chairbacks while the boat bucked in the waves. Many people laughed as they fought to stay on their feet.

After a while, passengers settled, but some started looking pasty. A child – probably about eight years old – was the first to throw up, losing her lunch across the floor. Others, in sight of this eruption, put down their food and looked away. But the stench of vomit drifted into everyone's nostrils. This first event became the catalyst for more sickness. Another child vomited. An adult ran towards the toilets. Within minutes, two queues had formed – everyone looking pale. Some with hands over their mouths. Mairi tried to ignore them – gazing out across the sea.

A robust-looking man stood near the boat's stern, clutching a railing with both hands, his knees bent and a smile on his face. As the boat leaned and bucked, his softened knees absorbed the motion, allowing his abdomen to stay upright and fairly stable. He was enjoying himself. Mairi rose, stood behind her seat and held its back, copying the man. Within a few minutes, she felt much better. She looked back at the man. He removed one hand from the railing and gave her a thumbs-up sign. She smiled back, not daring to ride single-handedly.

As the travellers departed the ferry onto the stable ground of Mull, colour flowed back into their cheeks. Many passengers voiced their relief at being on solid ground. The man from the back of the boat spoke to Mairi as they queued to leave. "I see you learn quickly."

She turned and looked up at his rugged, ruddy face and smiled. "Yes. Thank you for the demonstration. I'll always remember the transformation from holding back the contents of my stomach to enjoying the ride."

"Are you staying on Mull?" He asked.

169

"No. I'm going to Iona. Stopping there tonight."

"Shame. If you'd been heading for Tobermory, I'd have offered you a lift and a meal in the bar of my hotel."

"If I'd been staying and not recently engaged," she said, flashing her new ring, "I'd have accepted." She smiled and he smiled back. As they exited the terminal, he waved to her. "Safe journey, lass. Enjoy your trip to Iona." She waved back as he strode away.

***

As Suzanna passed through the main office, Rab updated his boss on progress. "One of George White's previous employers said he left before he was pushed because an employee complained about him. No action was taken."

She waited for Rab to turn the next page in White's story. Intrigued. "Also, the company he worked for after Butler and Cargrove said a complaint was made against him for sexual harassment. Just her word against his, so nothing proven. The police weren't notified. There hadn't been a high staff turnover or further indications that might suggest he'd been up to no good. Maybe he'd had less opportunity because his higher position separated him from the more vulnerable younger women?"

"Perhaps? Okay! Thanks for that. There's definitely a picture building of George White being at least a sexual pest." Suzanna concluded, before continuing on her way.

Chapter 30

Owen and Suzanna listened as the lock turned and the door creaked open. The woman shut the door, took off her coat and hung it on a cloak hook, calling out as she did. "Hello, Georgie, its Zena."

Suzanna had entered George White's house at 1 pm, ensuring all evidence of crime scene tape and fingerprint dusting had been removed from the entrance and hallway. She'd made sure the living room looked normal again, not wanting the masseuse to turn tail and scarper before they spoke to her. Owen sat in George's chair, having first covered the still blood-stained seat with a cloth. Suzanna waited in the kitchen for the woman to enter the living room. Rab sat in his car up the street and Zahir observed from a neighbour's window.

Zena entered the room where the TV blared, walking directly to Georgie's chair. Under the coat that she'd discarded, the young woman wore a basque and thong, her pert buttocks jiggling as she walked. Owen sensed her overpowering cheap scent as she approached. Zena placed her hands around from behind and covered Owen's eyes. "Guess who?" she said demurely.

Suzanna emerged from the kitchen and Owen took hold of Zena's soft hands. He stood and she jumped back, pulling her hands free – prepared to run. But on seeing Suzanna, she instead dug into her bag and, unseen by the two officers, pressed a button before pulling out a can of pepper spray to defend herself.

Rab's attention was focussed on White's house. He didn't see a figure approaching fast in his wing mirror. A man sprinted past his car and rushed straight to the house. Rab hastily exited his car and ran in pursuit. "Man entering front door. *Now!*"

Suzanna was talking to Zena when she received Rab's message and heard the front door open. She turned and hastened to the door, arriving as the man burst through. She held up her card and shouted, "Police! Stop where you are."

He spun on his heels, rushing out the way he'd come like a springbok that had sensed a leopard, crashing into Rab, knocking him backwards onto the pavement. The man jumped over Rab and sprinted off along the street. Zahir gave chase. The man's legs were muscular and his arms bulging, but his strength had been built at the cost of speed and agility. Zahir soon closed the gap and rugby-tackled him, taking him to the ground. Rab recovered instantly and went to Zahir's assistance. Between them, they held the man down and handcuffed him before frogmarching him back to White's house, the man spitting and cursing. Suzanna had returned to the masseuse and asked for her name. Her response: "Piss off, policewoman." Suzanna confiscated Zena's pepper spray before she could slip it back into her bag.

Noise from the front door told Suzanna that Rab and Zahir had returned with their quarry. The man struggled, despite the cuffs, his face covered in sweat from the exertion. Suzanna looked him in the eye and spoke authoritatively. "Calm down. You're not going anywhere." She continued to look at him as she spoke. "Rab."

Rab understood without further words being spoken. He called for uniformed officers to take them into custody.

***

A large, red, single-decker bus stood close to the ferry terminal, emblazoned with the words *West Coast Motors*. Mairi asked the driver if this was the bus for the Iona ferry. "Aye, lass. We're bound for *Finn-*

a-fort" (she'd wondered how to pronounce Fionnphort). "Hop on."
Mairi paid the driver for the journey, then found a seat, before placing
her small bag on the luggage rack. The bus was three-quarters full
when they departed. A middle-aged woman with a headscarf covering
her dark, messy hair spoke to her. "Off to Iona?"

"Yes. Visiting someone at the Abbey. Only staying one night. I have
to get home to Edinburgh tomorrow."

The woman looked surprised. "It's a bit far to travel for just one
night. Hardly worth coming all that way. And the expense. You should
have booked for a few days."

"Yes. If I come again, I'll do that, but I'm here on business and under
orders to get back as soon as I can."

"Oh! What business is that?"

"Sorry. I can't say. Official business."

The woman frowned. "Well. Try to enjoy your short time on our
lovely wee island."

"I will. Thank you."

"So, whom is it you're meeting with?"

"Sorry..."

"Of course. Sorry for asking. Will you be going to the Abbey?"

"Yes. It's what Iona's famous for, isn't it?"

"Aye. Well, yes it is, I suppose. But there's more to our isle than the
Abbey. We have an iron-age fort, the old marble quarry and, of course,
a rugged coast and white sandy beaches. St Columba's Bay is a little
beaut. If you have time, you must visit." Mairi nodded and thanked
her for the recommendations, but doubted she'd have time to do any
sightseeing. The local woman left her alone for the rest of the journey.
Mairi was grateful the interrogation had finished. She peered out at
the lovely scenery as the bus meandered through the winding roads,
its verges home to purple heathers.

***

Suzanna took a seat opposite the young woman, who looked nervous as a goldfinch on a bird feeder in cat territory. "You have been arrested on suspicion of murder." Suzanna opened the interview. They'd let the masseuse and her minder stew in the cells for an hour before taking them to separate interview rooms.

The woman's eyes opened wide. "I no commit murder. I only give massage. You must let me go."

"You'll not be going anywhere until I'm satisfied that you had no involvement in George White's murder. First, you must answer my questions, young lady."

"Georgie is dead?" Then she realized the *daughter* who had called her boss must be this woman. "Why would I want to kill Georgie? He good customer."

"I don't know why, yet. But what I know is you or someone you know could have let themselves into his home and murdered him. You need to convince me that you didn't kill Mr White. First off, where were you around 8 am on Tuesday, 3rd March?"

"Ha! I was in my bed, of course. I never rise until after 9 o'clock because I work late hours."

"Is there anyone who can verify where you were?"

"Verify! What is this word?"

Suzanna couldn't make out which of the Eastern European countries the woman called home. "Verify is like confirm, prove or support what you told me."

"Oh! Okay. Yes. I live with two other girls. They will confirm."

"So, let's start again. What is your full name? I assume it's not Zena."

The woman seemed to accept that she would need to cooperate if she were to get out of the station. "My name is Elizabete Jansons. I from Latvia."

"And the names of the girls you live with?"

Suzanna wrote them in her book. "We'll need to see your passport."

"I don't have passport. They keep it in office safe."

"Let's not pretend that you had gone to Mr White's house to give him a massage. We all know why you were there. But I'm not interested in what service you provide. My task is to find his murderer... Tell me, Elizabete, when was the last time you called on Mr White?"

"Each month I go to his house. It was regular booking. Last time, about three weeks ago. My phone has record when he last call. If you give me, I will show."

Suzanna gave the nod to Owen, who left the room. "What service did George like, Elizabete? Something special?"

"Switch off your recorder and I will tell you." Suzanna complied. "He liked to spank me before we had sex. He could not stand to do it, so sometimes I sit on his lap after he give me rosy cheeks. Other times I give blowjob."

Owen returned with the woman's phone. Suzanna confirmed with her eyes and he gave Elizabete her phone. She unlocked it and called up her calendar, thumbing through the dates. "Ah! Here it is. February thirteen, 6 pm." She showed Owen the phone, who took it from her.

"Thank you, Elizabete," Suzanna said as Owen started interrogating the phone, making a note of its number. "We will, with your permission, check your phone records."

"No. No permission. You no right to check."

"Perhaps you would prefer me to charge you with possession of a firearm – the pepper spray you carry. I can get a search warrant to check your phone records and to search your home. In which case, we will hold you in custody until the search is completed. Elizabete frowned, then gave her permission.

"Do you hold the key to George White's house or is it held at the office?"

"I have one key, but another is kept in the office. My minder Andrei

175

– the man you arrested – had it with him today."

"Many people could access that key, then?"

"Perhaps. I not know. I never see this key."

"And your key. Where do you keep this?"

"I have box under my bed. It is for cash. I keep cashbox key with me."

"Could anyone else have borrowed your key to the house?"

"No. I see broken box if they take key."

"Okay. So, we must check with your office. I need its location so we can visit."

"It is secret location. I must not tell you."

"Unless you tell me I cannot let you go." Suzanna waited, looking at Elizabete, wishing her to reply, but she just look down at the table tight-lipped.

Chapter 31

"So, Sergei, where is your home? Russia?" Rab asked. He and Zahir had joined their captive in Interview Room 2. The man had been slouched in his chair, arms folded, looking belligerent. But on hearing the question, he sat up and leaned forward, looking like a nun accused of being a stripper.

"I not Russian. My country is Bulgaria and my name is Andrei, not Sergei. I not mafia." He sat back, stony-faced, confrontational.

"And what might your family name be, Andrei?"

"I am Andrei Georgiev Draganov."

"Ah! So, your father is Georgi Draganov?"

"You know Bulgarian names, Mr policeman. You clever man."

"So, that's why George White was known to your company as Georgie."

"It not my company. They pay me to look after women. Make sure they not hurt."

"So, you're their minder?"

"Yes, minder. Good name. I look out for them. Keep them safe."

"Today, you entered the home of a man, uninvited. You used a key to enter this house. Where did you get this key?" Rab asked.

"Office give me key. Some customers cannot come to door. So, we have key."

"When did they hand you the key to George's house?" Zahir asked.

"Why you ask, Paki? I no speak with you."

Zahir rose to the bait, furious at the man's open racial discrimination. "How dare you call me Paki! I'm not from Pakistan." His accent deepened as he declared, "I'm Scottish."

"You born in this country but your parents Pakis, no?"

Zahir's face turned mahogany as the blood flushed his normally mid-brown skin. "No. My parents are Bangladeshi, not Pakistani."

Andrei twisted in his seat and looked sideways at Zahir. "Same thing. West or East. Still Paki."

Rab could see his colleague losing control. Could understand why. Worried Zahir might assault their suspect, he placed his hand on Zahir's arm and looked him in the eye. Zahir got the message and sat back in his seat, folding his arms, his face set hard, his eyes staring at Draganov, still fuming, but silent. Rab continued. "I'll repeat the question. When did the office give you the key?"

"I go to office after eating mid-day meal. Perhaps 1 pm?"

"And that's when you took the key?"

"That's what I said."

"When did you last have the key to George White's house?"

"When woman last time go to the house, I cannot say when." He shrugged his shoulders, crossed one leg over the other, resting his ankle on his other knee. Clearly, he was relaxing, becoming overconfident. He wore Nike trainers. White with a gold tick. Flashy. Expensive.

"Where were you last Tuesday between 7:30 am and 9 am, Andrei?"

"Last Tuesday. Early morning." He thought for a minute. "I go doctors. I make appointment 8:30 am. You check."

"We will Andrei. Don't doubt that. Your doctor's name and surgery, please?"

"His name Doctor Williams. Clinic is on Spittal Street." Zahir rose and exited the room without prompt.

"My colleague will check with the clinic. We must also speak with your boss in the office where the key is kept. What is the address and phone number?"

"They no like to tell people where office is. If they know, bad people might come. We no want fighting with mafia."

"Until your managers confirm what you told me about the key, you must stay here."

"You no keep me here. I do nothing wrong. You must let me go."

"I could charge you with assaulting a police officer. You pushed me to the ground when you ran from the house after my boss identified herself."

Andrei thought about his situation. "If I give you address, you no charge for assault. Okay?"

"Okay, Andrei. No assault charge." He passed him a pen and paper. Andrei wrote the address. "Where is your passport, Andrei, to prove your identity?"

"In my room. Under mattress. You take me there. I show you passport."

"Okay. Later. We'll also need to take your prints and a DNA sample to eliminate you from our murder suspects list." Andrei didn't respond, so Rab assumed that was acceptance. He stopped the recording, stood and left the room, leaving a uniformed constable to guard him. Zahir was on the phone, having difficulty getting the receptionist to confirm Andrei's presence at the clinic.

He looked annoyed as he listened to the receptionist denying him the information. "I'm not asking you to divulge medical details about Mr Draganov, only to confirm he had an appointment at 8:30 on March 3rd and that he attended that appointment. If you cannot confirm this, I need to speak to your practice manager. This is important police business. There's no reason for you to withhold this information." He waited a minute as the receptionist consulted someone in the office.

179

"My practice manager says I *may* tell you," the receptionist confirmed. "Doctor Williams saw Mr Draganov here at 8:30 am on the 3rd of March."

"Thank you," Zahir said, before slamming down the receiver.

"Hey! The phone never did you any harm, Zahir."

Zahir was red-faced. "Sorry, Sarge. That Andrei fella wound me up. Then this jobsworth woman refused to cooperate. A bit frustrated. Sorry."

"Okay. Get yourself together. I've another job for you. Check this address. Is it a registered business address or residential? Find out what you can about it. We'll need to pay it a visit later.

***

The female PC strode to DCI McLeod's office. "Ma'am. Miss Jansons wishes to speak with you."

Suzanna smiled and marched back to the interview room. "Have you changed your mind, Elizabete?"

"Yes. I tell you. You find out anyway, now you have my phone numbers." Elizabete took the offered pen and paper before writing the address of the office.

"We need your home address as well. We must speak to the women who share your house for confirmation of your whereabouts." Elizabete took a deep breath, then also wrote that address on the same paper.

"Thank you for your cooperation. We now need to take your fingerprints and a DNA sample to help eliminate you from our enquiries," Suzanna said. "We will visit your home and the company office. After this, we should be able to release you."

Elizabete slumped back into her chair and folded her arms, resigned to her short-term fate.

***

Suzanna and Rab discussed the way forward. The addresses Andrei and Elizabete had provided matched, so there was no doubt they had the right location. The Special Massage Services operation was clearly a prostitution business. Elizabete's work was not against the law, but the others involved in selling sexual services were running an illegal operation. They now had the opportunity to shut down this sex-trade business and lock up those living off it, provided Elizabete would give evidence against them. It would be worth diverting some energy from the murder investigation to achieve this, but she didn't want to delay the more important operation. Suzanna called across the office. "Caitlin. Do you have a little spare time?"

Caitlin's face brightened as if she'd been offered her favourite chocolates. "Yes, ma'am. What would you like me to do?"

***

As Caitlin took a seat in the interview room before she spoke. "Elizabete. I'm Detective Sergeant Caitlin Findlay. I'd like to ask you a few questions." Elizabete shrugged her shoulders and pursed her lips. "How long have you lived in Scotland?"

Elizabete thought back to when she arrived.

It was early morning in June last year and the sun was shining in a cloudless sky as they drove off the ferry at Hull. It had been a long crossing – over ten hours. They had slept in a small bunk room on hard, vinyl-covered beds. It was windowless, stuffy and damp. The other girl snored, waking her several times, so she had not slept well. The UK Border force glanced at their passports – EU – and let them through. Simple as that.

The car driver had driven them north for six hours, stopping twice to use the toilets and buy drinks. Elizabete had been awed by Edinburgh's avenues, lined by tall stone Georgian buildings. She was a village girl. Her parents, farmers. She hated the idea of becoming like her mother. Straw hair, tough red skin and hard hands from toiling in the fields, barns and kitchen. Elizabete wanted a better life for herself. She learned English in school and was happy to be in the UK. She would work behind a bar, serving drinks to people in a nightclub. Maybe she would meet a nice Scottish man and marry him to escape her otherwise rural fate.

The three girls had been taken to a flat in a place they had come to know as Oxgangs. A long row of flats stood on one side of the main street and many smaller blocks were scattered around the area. The flat had three bedrooms and one living room, plus a small kitchen and a bathroom. The beds were old and her mattress stained and sagging, with springs that stuck into her back when she laid on it. But it had mattered little at the start of her new adventure in Scotland. Their passports had not been returned. They were told the office would keep them safe for them and the girls had just accepted it.

"Eight months now. Last June I come to this country."

"Elizabete. Do you enjoy living here and the work you do?"

"Scotland is a good country. I like it. Scottish boys are nice to me."

"But the work?"

"I have no choice. First week I come here, they beat me and took photos of me being fucked. They said they would show my parents unless I did what they told me. I came to work in a bar, but there was no job. After Darius had sex with me, he give me money. Then another man forced me to do sex with him and he gave me more money. They said, you no work, you no eat. They sent another man to the flat. I not know him but he pay me." She paused, pondering what she had become. A single tear trickled from her right eye.

"They have the pictures and my passport. I cannot go home and I no get other work here because I have no papers. Only work I can do is what they give me. I not like this work. But what I do? They take most of money from customers. They say it is to pay rent for flat and pay for them bringing me to UK. But I ask them for record of my debt to them, so I can see how long I must work to pay this debt. I think it take ten years. I don't know what to do."

"Elizabete, if we get your passport for you, would you like to return home?"

Elizabete first laughed, then cried. Caitlin remained silent, patiently waiting for the young woman to recover. Elizabete wiped the tears from her eyes before speaking. "They no let me go home."

"They would not stop you if they were in prison."

"How they go to prison?"

"If you testify about what they've done to you and the other girls, we will charge them with assault and rape, and with living off the earnings of prostitution. What you have been doing is not illegal in Scotland, but what they have been doing *is* against the law. They would go to jail."

Elizabete sat with her arms folded, her face set stern, looking down at the table. "If you charge them, they will be let out on bail, until court case. Then they will find me and beat me to death, so I no give evidence."

"If you agree to testify, we will ensure they are remanded in custody. And we can find somewhere else for you to live, far from here. Social Services will help you register for benefits, so the government will give you money to live. After you testify in court, we will assist you to get home."

Elizabete's face softened as she realised there might be a way out, and tears flowed again. She sniffed, then blew her nose. "This is good plan. I no want sex every day with strangers. I want to go home. It would be better to be farmer's wife than prostitute. I help you."

Chapter 32

"Suzanna."

She looked up from her computer screen. "Oh! Hi Alistair. I was miles away."

"Or should we say kilometres away?" Alistair quipped. "I wonder how long it'll take the EU to force us into changing all our signs to kms?"

"I didn't realise you were anti-European Union, Alistair."

"Well. I've seen the EU gradually erode the UK's sovereignty over the years. We have to follow the European Commission's directives in almost everything nowadays. We don't get to make our own decisions, our own policies."

Suzanna responded, "While I agree with much of that, the advantages of remaining in Europe are similar to those of Scotland staying in the UK. We're better together. We're stronger united. They say divide and conquer. I reckon Russia would like to see the EU split up."

"Och. No. Russia's not our enemy anymore."

"Really! They seem to be moving closer and closer to a dictatorship again and their policies and actions are confrontational. They invaded Crimea last year, you'll recall. Which former USSR country will be next – perhaps Ukraine itself?" Suzanna countered. "Anyway, Alistair. What was it you wanted?"

"Oh! Sorry. It was just that we need a press release drafted and to warn you, they may want you to attend a briefing before the day's out."

"Okay. Thanks, Alistair. I'll get onto that soon." He turned and strolled off along the corridor. Suzanna called up a fresh Word document on her computer and started typing an update for the press. She'd just hit send on her email to the communications office when Caitlin arrived to inform her about the outcome of her talk with Elizabete. "Good work, Caitlin. I knew I could rely on you to persuade her."

"Thanks, ma'am. Do you want any further help, or should I get back to progressing the other cases?"

"No. Thanks, Caitlin. I'll take it from here."

***

Zahir knocked for a second time and pressed the bell push, letting it ring for several seconds. They could hear pop music being played loudly and two women's voices shouting. "Alright. I coming." A beautiful blonde woman, in a dress that barely covered her bottom, opened the door to Zahir. "What you want?" she said, looking confrontational.

Zahir held up his warrant card and told her his name. The woman swung the door towards him, saying, "I no talk to police."

Zahir thrust his shoe in the door, stopping it from hitting its frame. Suzanna stepped forward. "Justina," she said, remembering the name of the blonde girl that Elizabete had given Caitlin. "Elizabete sent us. She needs your help."

Blondie opened the door again. "How you know my name? Where is Elizabete?"

Zahir stepped into the opening and Justina backed up. "It would be best if we came in for a chat," he said. "You wouldn't want your neighbours hearing what we have to tell you." By now the other woman had entered the corridor, but Justina ushered her back into the living room.

"Please sit," Suzanna requested. "I have some news for you about

Elizabete." The room had two sofas and a coffee table between them, on which sat three cold coffee mugs. *Vogue, Hello, OK!* and *Heat* magazines lay haphazardly in a pile. Take-away pizza boxes lay open on the small, round, glass-topped dining table, unwanted crusts with bite-shaped tomato sauce edgings rested in the boxes' folds. The carpet looked like it hadn't been vacuumed for several days.

Suzanna and Zahir sat on one sofa and the women took the opposite one. "Before I tell you what's happened, I need to ask you both for your full names."

Blondie answered first. "Justina Gagas, from Lithuania."

"My name is Dorel Tamm. I from Estonia."

"Where were you both, between 7:30 am and 9 am on Tuesday 3rd March?"

"Here," they chorused.

"And Elizabete?"

"Yes. She here. We all work late and rise late," Justina said. "I was first up, just after eight. Later, maybe 9 o'clock, Elizabete and Dorel came from their rooms for breakfast."

"You're sure that was last Tuesday?"

"Yes. Most days the same."

Suzanna paused. "Earlier today, Elizabete was arrested in the home of a client. The man had been murdered and she had a key to the house. She is now at the police station."

Both women looked astounded. "Murdered?" Dorel questioned.

"Yes. Murdered," Zahir confirmed.

"Thank you for confirming where she was when the man was killed. We did not think she murdered him but needed to close that possibility. While we were questioning her, though, she admitted she has been providing sexual services to many clients since coming to Edinburgh."

The women became defensive, with Justina speaking for them both. "We give massages to our clients. No sex. No sex. We not prostitutes."

"Calm down, girls. Prostitution is not illegal in Scotland. Don't worry. We are not here to arrest you for prostitution." The women relaxed, slumping into the sofa.

Suzanna told them what Elizabete had shared with them about how she came to be in the UK. And that her hopes had been dashed. That she'd been beaten and raped, her passport taken away and she'd been blackmailed into becoming a sex-worker. "She said you two also had similar stories to tell."

The women looked at each other as if asking, *do we believe this woman?* Do we also tell her the truth?

"We have offered to help Elizabete if she cooperates with our enquiries. She will be protected from the people who control your lives. We will recover her passport and help her return to Latvia or stay here to work in a good job. If you wish to escape your work, we can also help you." Suzanna stopped talking and peered at the young women, one face at a time, letting her offer and the silence do its work.

They locked eyes with each other, communicating silently, then nodded before turning back to Suzanna. Justina spoke again. "Yes, we cooperate. We wish to stop this dirty work. We want proper job."

***

"Brodie. How are you?" Murray said, on seeing Mairi's boyfriend – now fiancé. "I hear you've popped the question."

"Aye. Had to be done. Didn't want to lose such a fantastic woman," Brodie replied. "Missing her already and she only left this morning!"

"Ah! You love-sick puppy. Get a grip," Owen jibed.

Brodie smiled. "You can't deny it, guys. She's one in a million."

"Aye well, suppose she is," Murray responded. "But you're welcome to her. It's enough having to put up with her at work. She's far too fiery for me."

"Aye, even your Heather's too much for you, though, eh!" Owen said.

"Talking about Heather, you know I told you she's a mite house-proud. Well, the other day I noticed her ironing the fitted sheets. I ask ya!"

"At least she's not ironing your socks."

"Ah! She does that as well."

Owen looked astounded and was about to respond when Rab interrupted. "Okay, guys. Let's prep for the raid." They ceased their friendly banter and gathered around to listen to the briefing. Minutes later, they drove up the road and stopped close to the SMS HQ. The office was a flat above an Indian takeaway in the Northeast of the city. The two-storey terraced property, its stone blackened by fumes and coal soot over its life, sat sandwiched between a hairdresser's and a cleaning company's office.

They had a search warrant for the premises but rather than break down the door, they let themselves in with a key provided by Andrei, strolled up the stairs and walked into the room unannounced and uninvited.

"Hey. Who are you? Get out. This is private residence," a man shouted as Rab entered – Nikolay, he assumed, going by the name Elizabete had given Caitlin. He must have been about six foot two inches tall, olive-skinned and muscular, with dark hair tied back in a ponytail. He carried a thin white horizontal scar across his forehead. The man advanced menacingly. But he stopped abruptly as Rab was followed by Owen, then Murray and two uniformed constables. On seeing the uniformed officers, he spun on his heels and darted into a room behind the office, slamming the door. Rab rushed forward to follow the man but found the door bolted. He turned to the woman, probably in her forties, who sat behind the only desk. "Is there a way out of that room?"

The woman had dyed asphalt black, frizzy, shoulder-length hair that framed her slender, well-balanced face – her nose straight and long, her lips full. She would have been pretty when young, but smoking had stolen her youth – her skin like elephant leather. She shrugged and smirked.

"Brodie," Rab shouted. "Outside. He's done a runner. Go catch him." Brodie and his colleague sprinted down the stairs. Rab kicked in the locked door, strode to the open window and confirmed his suspicion that the man had exited by a fire escape. The fugitive was already out of sight. He cursed himself for not having sent one of the uniformed constables around the back. He knew the DCI wouldn't openly criticise him for this basic mistake but he felt guilty nonetheless. Normally, he was proud of his professionalism but today he'd failed. Let his team down.

Rab returned to the office and held up a piece of paper in front of the woman's face – probably Maria. "We have a warrant to search these premises and confiscate your computers and records." Owen and Murray rounded Rab, approaching the desk, armed with cartons to house the files and equipment in the office. The woman hit the power button on the computer, shutting it down before the officers could interrogate it. She grinned at them. "You need it switched off to transport, no?"

***

Brodie ran out of the door onto the street, barely avoiding a collision with a passing pedestrian. The late manoeuvre made him slip and he fell to his knees. He recovered quickly, turned left and raced along the pavement. The other constable turned right, looking for an alley that might lead to the property's rear access. Brodie sped around the corner of a narrow road to his left. He saw a tall, pony-tailed man running away. He charged along the road in pursuit, the gap closing. The amber lights of a red car flashed and the man ran towards it. Opening the driver's door, *Ponytail* leapt in. The door closed, the engine fired up and it pulled away before Brodie reached it. The car, a BMW 640i, hurtled up the street, its V8 engine growing, but Brodie memorised the registration number. He stopped, pulled out his radio and called the operations centre, reporting the escaping criminal.

Chapter 33

Rab had not expected cooperation from the SMS staff. The woman would probably withhold the computer password when they switched it on again. But there were technical experts he could call on to get them into the computer if needed. "Where's the safe?"

The woman shrugged. "What safe."

"The safe where you hold the girls' passports," Owen said.

"We have no safe. Women have own passports. We not keep them."

"That's not what they tell us," Owen responded. The woman looked less confident, recognising that if the women had talked, she might be in trouble.

Owen read the woman her rights, then handcuffed her as Murray gathered together the equipment and documents for analysis.

Putting aside his self-condemnation, Rab searched the property. He found the safe in a wardrobe hidden behind clothing. It looked like those found in hotels. There was no point in attempting to open it by pressing buttons. Instead, he levered off the cap covering the keyhole, used when the batteries died. Having assessed what the key would look like, he returned to the office. "Have you found any keys, guys?"

"I think there's a few in the top right-hand drawer," Murray said. The woman's eyebrows raised involuntarily. Rab pulled out the drawer. There were several Yale-type keys, all labelled with a person's name, like the one found in Andrei's possession that had been labelled *White*.

But no safe key. He tried the other drawer. It had pencils, pens, erasers, a pencil sharpener, some *Blu Tack and* a reel of unbranded clear sticky tape. He noticed the woman smirk. But he soon wiped it off her face when he felt underneath. It was his turn to smile when he fingered the rear face of the drawer and detected sticky tape holding an object in place. He detached it and held it up as he peeled off the tape. It looked remarkably like the key he needed. The woman now looked worried.

Rab went back to the bedroom and tried the key in the safe's lock. It opened, revealing a rubber-banded pile of passports and a huge wad of twenty-pound notes. He stood back, not touching any of the contents. They'd need to prove who had handled the passports.

"Have you got all you need, guys?" Rab asked his detectives, on returning to the office.

"Aye. I reckon so," Owen responded.

"I've found a stack of passports. You two head back to base. Take the woman with you; get her prints and a DNA sample, then lock her up. I want you to focus on accessing that computer and piecing together information. I'll hang on here until the CSIs arrive." As he finished speaking, Brodie appeared in the doorway, an apologetic look on his face.

***

While Rab waited for the CSIs to arrive, he took another look around the flat. The living room was being used as the office. It contained a sofa and large TV, as well as the desk. All the furniture was old and tatty, suggesting a cheapskate landlord had rented it to them furnished or, more likely, they'd gone to the nearest second-hand furniture shop and bought up the cheapest items in the store.

There were two anaglypta-papered bedrooms with yellowed paint. Both were in use; each with a messy bed and a chrome-plated clothes stand; plus a bedside locker with drawers. He entered one bedroom. A large poster of a Mr Universe-type character – bulging muscles and oily bronze skin, with skimpy speedos – was attached with *Blu Tack* to the wall. Rab wondered about these men who must spend several hours every day in the gym weights room, bodybuilding. They were so unnatural – artificial even. His wife, Ainslie, said she found them repulsive. Rab opened the locker drawers with his gloved hands and found packets of cigarettes, women's knickers, bras, socks and a vibrator. He pressed the button and the device buzzed loudly, making his fingers tingle. On the clothes stand were jeans, jeggings, tops, sweatshirts and blouses.

In the other room, two posters adorned the walls. Another body-builder, but this time a bikini-clad woman whose muscles were larger than her breasts. The other, a red Ferrari. Hanging on the man's rail were two pairs of jeans, a few t-shirts and a couple of hoodies. In the drawers, only underpants and socks. Under the bed, a small pile of porn magazines rested. Rab picked one up and found several pages were stuck together. He guessed what the adhesive would be and placed it back where he'd found it. In the corner of the sweaty room sat a small set of weights.

It appeared the man and woman shared the flat and operated the business together. A CSI man entered the flat. "By yourself?

"Yeah. We've got a couple of the team off sick and the rest are scattered around the city already. You're lucky I was available."

Rab briefed him on what was needed, then left him to get on with his work. As he left the flat, he double-checked that he still had Andrei's door keys in his pocket.

***

The uniformed officer drove north on the City of Edinburgh Bypass, heading for Queen Margaret University. A security officer had reported seeing students selling drugs to others on the campus and the two PCs had been tasked with investigating. Her colleague, Kadie, sat silently looking out at the passing cars. "Did you see Poldark last night? That

193

Aidan Turner's dishy, isn't he?"

"I didn't know you liked historical dramas, Lynz. I've not watched it myself." Something caught Kadie's eye. "Hey. That looked like the BMW we were asked to look out for. A red 6-series. It was going fast.

Lynz accelerated and turned on her blue lights. Her colleague called in the sighting. They hurtled around the roundabout where the A1 trunk road headed eastwards and accelerated back onto the southern bypass in pursuit. Cars moved off to the left to let them pass. They travelled under the A68 junction and onto the roundabout where the A7 branched off south towards Galashiels.

"Where the hell has that BMW gone?" Lynz exclaimed. Kadie called in their progress. A car had been dispatched from Newton Grange to head north on the A7, so the PCs continued west on the bypass. Another car had joined the chase at the Fairmilehead junction, heading east. If the BMW was still on the bypass, they'd soon spot it.

As Lynz passed the police car heading towards them, she realised the BMW had given them the slip. Kadie called in again and was told to return to their original tasking. Excitement over until the next time, Lynz turned off the blue lights and slowed her car to the legal speed limit, disappointed not to have pursued the suspect longer.

***

"Ma'am," Caitlin said after knocking on the DCI's door. "Just had a report from uniform. The car seen speeding away from the SMS offices was spotted heading southeast on the southern bypass. They pursued the car, but it gave them the slip."

"Where was it seen, precisely?"

"Travelling between the A1 roundabout and the A68 turnoff. The officers who first spotted it headed west along the bypass until a car from the other direction met them. It can't have continued travelling west along that road." Suzanna called up a road map on her computer as Caitlin continued. "And a car from Newtongrange travelled up the

A7 to the bypass, but saw nothing."

"Hmm! The BMW could have turned off the A7 at Eskbank, but it could also have taken the A68." Suzanna pondered before speaking again. "Which port did you say Elizabete came through when she arrived in the UK?"

Chapter 34

Andrei's ground floor studio flat smelled stale, sweaty and musty. It had been just a short walk from the SMS office. The three-storey house, with a graffitied end wall, stood adjacent to a small park and was adjoined on its right to a garishly painted convenience store. Rab stepped into the single room, resisting his desire to open some windows and let fresh air blow through.

At one end of the room, a headboard-less double bed was squashed into the corner, the wall by its pillows grease-stained. A small locker sat next to it and, like the other flat, a cheap hanging rail for Andrei's clothes. Abutted to the bed's end, sat a worn-out, leather two-seater sofa. A Formica-topped table and two matching chairs stood against another wall, next to a kitchenette that provided the bare essentials for basic cooking. The only other space in the flat was a shower room.

In the locker drawer, Rab found a cigarette packet and a matchbook, with the name of a bar in Sofia across its front face. He foraged around a bit more but found nothing of interest, retrieved Andrei's passport, and left.

***

The wind had calmed and the sea subsequently settled. Mairi's newfound skill of riding waves wasn't put to the test on the ten-minute ferry ride across the Sound of Iona. The houses on Baile Mòr's seafront were typical for the Scottish Highlands: single-storey stone cottages with grey slate roofs, some with skylights and others with dormer windows. Some of the cottages' walls had been painted white, brightening their faces.

Mairi slung her bag over her back and walked up the hill away from where the ferry had offloaded, past the ruins of the old nunnery, its roofless walls recently restored. The low stone-wall-lined road took her towards the Abbey. On either side, sheep grazed in the fields. On the way, an art gallery invited her in to view their contemporary jewellery. She passed through a hamlet of white-painted, blue-window-framed cottages, a store selling local produce, refreshments and books. It tempted her to go in, but she needed to find Sheila White before doing anything else.

The walk to the Abbey entrance gate only took ten minutes. She had passed dozens of walkers and just a couple of cars. They only allowed islander's cars on Iona because of so few roads and distances being short. She entered the Welcome Centre and approached the ticket desk. "Excuse me. I need to speak with one of your residents. I called ahead. She showed the woman her police ID card. Could you point me in the direction of Sheila White, please?"

The lady selling tickets replied. "Sorry. I don't know Sheila. I'm a short-term volunteer. Not part of the permanent community. If you take a seat, I'll find someone to help you." Mairi sat and waited.

Ten minutes later, a sixty-something, grey-bearded man entered the room and looked around. Spotting Mairi, he walked straight to her. "Would you be DC Gordon?"

Mairi stood, held her hand forward and spoke. "Yes. That's me. And you are?"

"Archie Dunbar. Sheila's busy in the kitchen. Come with me. I'll take you to her." He led her across the road, through a small gate and along a narrow path to the Abbey. The building dominated its landscape, standing tall and broad. On a darker day, it would have seemed foreboding.

Evidently, it had grown over the years of its existence, with extension added to extension in a higgledy-piggledy manner. Mairi followed Archie around the back of the building complex and through a door into one of the lower extensions. He opened the door to a small room with a square pine table and four chairs. "Please wait in here. I'll bring Sheila to you." He turned and strode off into the building, to the sound of stainless-steel pans clattering and water spraying into a large sink. Going by the aromas of mince and onions frying and potatoes boiling, they were probably preparing supper.

Sheila came through the open door a couple of minutes later, drying her hands on the Iona Community apron hanging from her neck. An elasticated plastic hat masked most of her head, but wavy, mousy hair poked out from behind her ears. Sheila had a straight, slender nose, above thin lips. Her short jaw, merging into the fat around her neck, gave her a chin-less effect. She closed the door, then sat opposite Mairi. "They tell me you want to speak to me about my father."

"Yes. I'm sorry for your loss."

"Thank you but, actually, it was a relief to hear of his passing."

"I'm sorry you feel that way about your father. Your childhood must have been difficult?"

"Aye. A living nightmare I couldn't wake from. That's why I'm here. I'm now living a beautiful dream, instead."

"Have you ever shared with anyone what happened to you as a child?"

"Aye. After I became a Christian, I opened my heart to the vicar. It was cathartic to let it all out and, with God's help, I recovered." She paused. "I'm still recovering."

"Please tell me what happened."

Sheila shared her dark memories with Mairi, breaking down as she recalled what the monster had done to her. It was not long after her first period that he'd taken her into his study and spanked her bare bottom. He'd been punishing her physically for years, but on this day, things changed. Perhaps her father sensed her womanly aroma — the child in her waning as her body matured. He'd touched her. Stroked her private place, then spanked her some more.

The next time he disciplined her, her mother and brother were out of the house. That was the first time he'd raped her, forcing himself into her immature body, making her cry out as he took her virginity. Sheila had cried on and off all that day. She hated what he had done. Knew it was wrong, but didn't dare tell anyone. She loathed her father – the man supposed to cherish and protect her had instead abused her. The abuse continued for many years.

She left the family home as soon as she was old enough and never returned. Life had been difficult for her as a naïve young woman and other men took advantage. She'd been in her twenties when she found Christ and it had changed her life. Sheila still tried not to engage with the wider community and preferred to keep away from busy cities. She finished her recollection by saying, "life is good now, with Jesus by my side, in a community I trust.

"Sheila. Do you still loath your father?" Mairi asked.

"Not anymore. And that's not because he's dead. When I found Christ, I made the choice to forgive him. Hatred eats you up; controls you; rules your life; keeps you miserable. Forgiveness releases the tension and removes its influence. I would never have forgiven him if the Lord hadn't come into my life and forgiven me my sins."

"Your sins!" Mairi exclaimed. "Surely anything you've done must be minor in comparison with your father?"

"We all fall short of God's standards, Mairi. But God, through his son's sacrifice, has taken away my sins. Whenever I sin, I confess it to him and ask for forgiveness, and he graciously does. None of us are perfect, Mairi. We all sin. We all need forgiveness."

"Hmm. Is there anyone who might have wanted your father dead?"

"My mother, perhaps. He was awful to her. But she passed away many years ago. My brother, maybe. But I don't think father sexually abused Ed." Sheila paused, considering her answer. "Why would anyone wait until he was so old, frail and near to death before killing him, if revenge were the motive for taking his life?"

"How do you know your father was infirm? I thought you said you'd not seen him in decades?"

"True. But Ed informed me that father had carers going in daily to help him with basic needs."

"So, you're in regular contact with your brother?"

"Regular, yes. But frequent, no. He texts me, or we sometimes speak on the phone, but only two or three times a year."

"When was the last time you saw Edmond?" Mairi asked.

"About five years ago. He and Nancy had bought a house close to where he was working. Fort George. He was a Major in the Army. When Ed retired, they held a party and invited me."

"And you've not seen him since?"

"No."

Mairi pondered before continuing. "Sheila. I'd like you to think back to the dark days again when you were still at home. Did anyone else come to the house that your father took into his study? Or any other circumstance where he might have abused someone?"

"I can't think of anything or anybody. Ed and I never brought friends home. It would have been too risky." Sheila responded. "No. Wait. We had a cousin come to stay once. Christine. She would have been about fifteen. She is my mother's brother's daughter. So, her surname will be Dangerfield."

"Do you have any recollection of her being alone with your father?"

"I'm not sure. But I remember seeing her in tears on the day before she left. She returned home earlier than planned, but mum never told me why."

"Do you know where Christine and her parents lived?"

"Somewhere in England. Mum's family are all English. Near Peterborough, I suppose. That's where she caught the train from. But I'm not sure which town or village."

"Okay. I'll try to track her down. It might be important."

It had been harrowing for Mairi to hear her story. "Sheila. For the record, I need confirmation that you were on the island last Tuesday. Can anyone confirm that?"

"Aye. Archie Dunbar, for one. And Pamela Fisher. She works in the kitchen with me. Would you like me to get her for you?" Before Mairi answered, she added. "Actually, it would be better if you waited until after supper, as she'll be rather busy preparing it. In fact, I'd best get back to my work."

"Okay. That would be fine. Happy to speak after we've eaten. Oh! One last question. Have you had any contact with your father in the last year?"

"No, I've not spoken to him in years."

"Hmm! We have phone records showing him calling Iona a few times."

"Ah! Yes. He did call, but I refused to speak to him. In the end he gave up calling."

"I thought you'd forgiven him?"

"Forgiving him doesn't mean I have to like him or want to have any contact with him..."

Chapter 35

Dorel's over-tight denim jeans were cutting into her crotch. She stood and pulled the fabric of the jean's legs downwards to relieve the pressure, then sat again, still not comfortable, and picked up her mug of tea. Suzanna entered carrying a coffee, smiled and sat beside her. "How are you? Okay?"

"Yes, okay. How long I stay here?"

"It depends. We already have Andrei and Maria in custody, and Nikolay is being hunted. Is there anyone else we need to arrest to make you safe?"

"Yes. Etrit. He our minder. Perhaps you say pimp?"

"We'll need his details. A description. His full name, address and phone number. And a statement from you about his role in the organisation and his relationship to you and the other girls."

"Okay. He Etrit Berisha." Dorel gave Suzanna his phone number and address, before describing him and his influence on their lives. "He protects us when we are working. If any trouble, he comes quick."

"What sort of trouble?"

"If man is violent or if he not pay for service, we press panic button. Etrit comes and takes money, beating men sometimes."

"Have you witnessed Etrit assaulting customers?"

"Yes, many times. He very tough man. Sometimes he beats me and other girls. If man refuse to pay, he takes all his cash."

"What if the man has no cash?"

"He take him to ATM. Make him take out cash. More money than fee; as fine, he says. If no money in bank, he beat the man."

"Has he ever raped you, Dorel?"

"Yes. When first I come, he and Nikolay rape me and beat me." Her eyes shined as they moistened. She looked down, rubbed her eyes, then looked up again. "He say I must do as told. When Etrit like sex, he comes to house. Sometimes he rapes me, sometimes other girls."

"How do you feel when he rapes you?"

"First time he came alone, I scream and fight him, but he beat me and forced himself into me. After time, they made me take many customers. Now I treat him like any other customer but one who does not pay. What's one more fuck? It no matter – unless he violent."

"Have you seen him raping the other girls?"

"Most times he close bedroom door when he do it. I hear noises and voices but no see. But one time I see him rape Justina."

"Can you remember the date and time this happened?"

"Three weeks ago. Yes. I remember. He very bad to her."

"I'll send one of my constables to note all these details. Once we have your statement written and signed and we have Berisha under arrest, it will be safe for you to go. We have your passport. When forensic services have completed their work, we can return this to you. Then you will be free to leave the country or stay and get another job if you wish."

"Yes, I like to stay. Edinburgh nice city. My home is not in city and there is no work there."

"I'll get Social Services to help you with any paperwork required to apply for work. Is there anything else I should know?"

"No. I am happy that you rescue us from bad work. You nice lady. And your policeman, Zahir. He nice man. Very handsome – like young Omar Sharif." Suzanna smiled, glad to hear their efforts were appreciated.

THE KEY TO MURDER

"I'm surprised you know Omar Sharif. He's an old man now and hasn't been in any films for many years."

"I saw old film once. Lawrence of Arabia. Very good film. He also in Funny Girl and Doctor Zhivago, yes?"

"Yes, you're right. And many more." She left Dorel thinking about Omar Sharif and went to speak with Justina. The other girl confirmed everything Dorel had said.

***

"Zahir," Suzanna said, entering the main office. "The girls we just brought in think you're wonderful." Zahir blushed. "Miss Tamm said you look like a young Omar Sharif."

Zahir looked like he'd just seen a live chicken jump out of a KFC box. He'd seen the film star in a movie when he was young, but not since. He imagined his own face beside an old poster of the now ancient movie star, but could not see the resemblance.

Suzanna continued. "She informed me their controller is a man named Etrit Berisha. Here's his address and phone number. We need to get him picked up ASAP."

"Etrit Berisha. I've heard that name before... Don't know where, though. I'll go, ma'am, and take uniform with me."

"Best take two officers with you. She says he's a violent man. Regularly rapes and beats the girls and assaults any man who doesn't pay or if they hurt the girls. He's a hard man."

"Will do."

***

The letterbox of the yellowing UPVC front door was missing, its hole ventilated the hallway. He rattled the door knocker and pressed the bell push, but no tune or bell sounded. After waiting for a response, Zahir sent a uniform constable around back in case he slipped out the backdoor, before thumping on the door. Crouching, he shouted through the letterbox hole. "Etrit Berisha. Police. We need to speak to you. Open the door." He stayed crouching, listening. The flat was silent.

He turned to the uniformed officer behind him. "Stay here, please." He followed the other officer to the rear of the property. "Any sign of him?"

"No. It's all quiet. I had a look through the windows but there's no sign of him. Perhaps he's out?"

"Yeah. Probably is. No point wasting your time here. I'll hang around for a while in case he returns. You two head off."

"Okay, pal. If you need us, just call. We'll stay local unless redeployed."

"Great. See you later."

Zahir returned to his car, then moved it to a place where he could see anyone entering or leaving the property. He WhatsApped the team to let them know what he was doing, then Googled Etrit Berisha. "I knew it," he said when the results displayed. "Albanian professional footballer. He was the goalie for their national team in the European Championships. Plays for Lazio Roma. Obviously not the same person, but at least he now knew why the name had been familiar.

As he looked up, he noticed a man stroll along the street towards the door he'd recently stood outside. It might be him. Zahir wasn't sure because they had no picture of the man. But he met the description. Under the man's coat, his upper body seemed heavily muscled. Tattoos adorned his thick neck. The man stood about six feet tall, his dark hair cropped short. He was the type of person you wouldn't want to meet in a dark alley. Zahir watched him slow as he approached the door.

As the man entered the building, Zahir called the uniformed cops who said they'd stay local but found they'd been called away. He requested help but was informed it would be twenty minutes for assistance to arrive. He'd have to wait it out. Shortly after making that decision, the door opened and the man emerged, closed the door behind him and walked off in the direction that he'd come from.

Zahir slipped quietly out of his car and nonchalantly wandered up the street, his phone to his ear. As he followed, Zahir called in again, this time as an urgent call for assistance. They despatched a car and said it should be with him in a few minutes. The man turned right, disappearing from view. Zahir sped up to close the gap, not wishing to lose sight of him. When he turned the corner, he was relieved to see the man hadn't disappeared. Zahir relaxed into a steady pace again, matching that of his prey, but, yet again, the man turned a corner.

Zahir quickened his pace, but when he turned into the road, he could not see the man anywhere. He rushed to the next junction, assuming that was where the man would have gone. As he turned the corner, he came face to face with him.

"Why you follow me?" the man said.

Zahir backed off out of reach and pulled out his police warrant card. It was definitely Berisha. "Police," he said. "DC Usmani. We need you to come in for questioning."

"Piss off. I no come to police station." He turned and walked away. Zahir followed.

"Etrit Berisha. Stop. You are under arrest on suspicion of rape."

Etrit turned back. In his hand, a knife, its five-inch blade glinting. "I gut you like a pig, policeman."

Zahir drew his extendable baton and prepared to defend himself. Etrit stepped towards him, his knife hand forward. Instead of pulling back, Zahir surprised the man by closing the gap. He struck the man's wrist. A crack sounded as the baton struck bone and Etrit cried out, the knife dropping from his hand. Zahir moved in, grabbed his opponent's arm, stepped back again and dragged him forward. Etrit stumbled and fell to the ground, screaming as his already fractured forearm struck the ground. Taking advantage of the man's pain, Zahir spun around his body, taking the injured arm up his back, the man's scream intensifying. He grabbed Etrit's other arm and twisted that into line before cuffing him.

"Not so tough after all, Berisha. Your days of beating women are over. He knelt one knee onto his captive's back and dug it in to increase his discomfort. A police car rounded the corner, its lights flashing and siren sounding, pulling up next to Zahir. He didn't recognise the officers, so identified himself and showed his card.

"Lock him up for the night, lads. The charge is suspicion of rape and attempted murder of a police officer."

As they dragged him off the pavement, Berisha spat, "I no attack you. You assault me."

"Just shut it, Berisha. You're nothing but a cowardly woman beating rapist." With a gloved hand, he picked up the knife that Berisha had dropped, placed it into an evidence bag, then handed it to the officers. "Add carrying a concealed weapon to the other charges." They took the bagged knife and marched Berisha to their car.

Chapter 36

"Hi, Mum. How are you?" Suzanna said after picking up her mobile phone. She had just put the kettle on, so moved away from the noise of its heating.

"Good, thanks, Suzanna. And you?"

"Busy as ever. In the middle of a murder case. Long days and pressure from on high. The press braying for updates. The usual." Suzanna sensed her mum hadn't just called for a chat but had a specific reason for phoning.

"Listen. Your dad and I were thinking, it's been a while since we saw you. You rarely have time to come and see us. So, we thought we might come up to Edinburgh for a weekend soon."

"Excellent. Good to hear it. It's been too long. Have you any dates in mind?"

"Well, we wondered about this coming weekend, but I guess that wouldn't be a good time, being as how you'll be submersed in the murder investigation."

Suzanna considered her mother's term for being deeply involved. Quite fitting, actually. If she didn't come up for air occasionally, she'd drown in the intensity of the case. "Yes. You're probably right. How about the week after?"

"We're booked to go to your sister's that weekend... Thinking about it, if you could get a couple of days off during the week, we could drive up to Edinburgh on the Monday, from Charlotte's. How does that sound?"

"That's not a bad idea. At least one of my DIs should be back at work by then and I'm due some days off because I had to cut short my skiing holiday to take over the murder case."

"Oh! Lovely. We can start looking for a guesthouse nearby."

"There's no need, Mum. My spare bedroom is big enough for the two of you and now that I've remodelled my kitchen-lounge-diner into one space, the apartment is quite spacious."

"Even better. We haven't seen your flat since you had that work done – how long ago was that?"

"Eighteen months!" How time had flown, Suzanna thought as she listened for her mother's response.

"Right. I'll put it in our diary."

Suzanna heard her mother turn away from the phone and shout. "Robert, we're going to stay with Suzanna on the Monday, after we leave Charlotte's." She spoke into the phone again. "How was your shortened skiing holiday? Did you still enjoy it? You went with that new man of yours, didn't you?"

"Yes, I had a superb, if rather brief, time on the slopes. Perhaps you'll get to meet James when you come up?"

"Yes. I'd like that. I wish you and Callum hadn't split up. He's such a lovely man."

Suzanna pursed her lips as she listened to her mother praising her soon-to-be ex-husband. "Mum, please don't talk about Callum again. You know he betrayed me. He's history now. I don't want to talk about my past. I need to focus on the future, not look backwards. He's never going to be part of my life again. Please accept that."

"Sorry, sweetheart. I didn't mean to upset you. I'll try not to speak of him again."

"Thank you. I'd appreciate that."

"Did you hear that Charlotte's pregnant again? What wonderful news! Don't you agree?"

"Yes, Mum. It's brilliant. I can't wait to have another niece or nephew."

"I just wish you'd start a family. It would have been marvellous to have more grandchildren and they would have been so beautiful given yours and Callum's good looks – sorry, sweetheart; I didn't mean to mention him again. Perhaps James might wish to start a family?"

"Mum. I'm 45 years old. It's rather late to become a mother – too risky. Besides, I like my way of life."

Suzanna could picture her mother's face, her lips puckered and her head shaking, at her desire to have more grandchildren being rejected by her overly independent daughter.

"You'll regret it when you get older, you know. When your dad and I have passed on. With no children of your own, there'll be no grandchildren to watch grow up, to smile at their antics, to see their cute faces, to wipe away their tears and to spoil them when their parents aren't around."

"I'll just have to make the most of being an aunt, Mum. As I said, it's too late now."

"We'll see you on the 23rd then," her mother said, before hanging up.

After ending the call, she WhatsApped James. 'Parents planning to visit 23rd/24th. They want to meet you. Hope you'll be around xxx.'

Her phone pinged a minute later. 'Should be in the city.' He'd added a smiley face.

She placed her phone down and re-boiled the kettle, put coffee grounds in the cafetiere and switched on the radio. The hour had just passed. TV news time. Prime Minister David Cameron had declared the UK would hold an in-out referendum on the UK's membership of the EU if his party won the next General Election. Scottish National

Party leader and First Minister, Nicola Sturgeon, had said that if the UK voted to leave the EU against Scotland's will, it would create conditions for a fresh referendum on Scotland's independence.

The news worried Suzanna. The prospect of the UK leaving the EU would undoubtedly result in reduced immigration from the EU to fill the UK's vacancies for lower-income jobs that many in the UK weren't prepared to do. And it would remove the rights of UK citizens to live and work in Europe, perhaps require visas to holiday on the continent, and might be the catalyst that fragmented the EU.

Looking back at history, states uniting like the USA, the UK, India, Europe and Australia, brought stability, strength, higher standards and greater economic activity. The idea of any reversal to unification would be a backward step. If the UK left Europe and Scotland subsequently left the UK, it would be disastrous, she thought, especially if Scotland then joined the EU. Imagine a customs border between Scotland and England. Scots from Gretna Green would need their passport to go shopping in Carlisle. English tourists may need visas to visit Edinburgh. There would be no right for Scots to work in England, or for English people, like her, to work and live in Scotland. Suzanna turned the radio off and put on relaxing music, not wishing to consider it further. If there were a referendum, she'd have to hope the UK would vote to stay in the EU.

She couldn't be bothered to cook, so put a ready meal into the microwave to heat, while she finished her coffee. Her eyes closed, calmed by the music. She let her mind drift. They had raided the massage services office and tomorrow they would interview the two people arrested. Although a distraction from the murder investigation, Suzanna was pleased to have uncovered an illegal business trafficking and controlling young women. Mairi would, by now, have interviewed White's daughter. They were awaiting feedback from foreign police forces on CCC's non-British workers. What else should they be doing?

Despite the favoured line of revenge for previous actions, she wondered whether there were any other motives. Perhaps a line of enquiry they hadn't yet pursued? She meditated, letting her mind go where it wished, drifting.

The brother. Albert. They'd never spoken to him. Perhaps there'd been mutual hatred – a family feud? Could Albert have visited his brother that morning? No one had asked that question. If nothing else, he might help them build their picture of the character of George White. The microwave pinged, interrupting her thoughts. She sent herself an email as a reminder to look into Albert White.

As she finished her dinner, her mobile buzzed, then rang. She answered, "Suzanna McLeod."

"Evening ma'am. Sergeant Treliving here. Thought you'd want to know that our boys in Hull picked up Nikolay Petrov as he tried to board the ferry to Holland. He'll arrive here sometime tonight."

"Excellent news, Sarge. Thanks for letting me know. Please also inform Rab Sinclair."

Chapter 37

"Thanks for sharing with me earlier, Sheila," Mairi whispered. "I'm amazed that you have forgiven your father for what he did to you. It's no wonder you didn't want to take his calls. Just hearing his voice would have brought back terrible memories."

Mairi's attention was drawn to the senior pastor, who stood to pray. "Father God. Thank you for another day on this beautiful island. Thank you for the privilege of living each day in your wonderful creation, to see the trees bend in the wind, the flowers sway in the breeze, the sea eagles soar overhead and the sheep in our fields growing to provide us with this glorious meal. Thank you for all your provision. Lord, we are grateful that we have so much and conscious that some do not. I pray a blessing on this food, in Jesus' name. Amen."

They chorused amen and immediately started serving the food – the shepherd's pie emitting tummy-rumble-inducing aromas. They sat at long tables, Sheila and Archie her closest fellow diners. "Is it mission accomplished, Constable Gordon?" Archie asked.

"Mairi, please." She said before answering his question. "Sheila has been most helpful, so I'll return tomorrow feeling the journey has been worthwhile. I just need confirmation of her whereabouts on Tuesday, 3rd March, for the record."

"Och! I can confirm that for you. Sheila's not been off the island in months."

"But did you actually see her here on the morning of the 3rd?"

"Yes, yes. Definitely."

"Great. Thank you, Archie. Have you been on Iona long?" Mairi placed some more pie in her mouth, enjoying the rich flavours.

"Not as long as some," he replied. "Five years, now. Five and a half, I suppose. But who's counting? I lost my wife a few years back. Breast cancer. One of the ways Satan tries to spoil God's creation. He'll have his comeuppance when Christ returns. There'll be no more suffering then. Can't wait. Well, I *can* wait, of course. But I'd prefer not to."

Archie took a bite of his individual pie. "It's a vegetarian pie," Archie said after swallowing, responding to Mairi's quizzical look. "I became a vegetarian some years back. The way I see it, God created the world, put humans on it, and they ate the fruits and nuts of the trees instead of killing the animals. So, that's an example I want to follow. And when the end of these times arrives and Jesus returns, we'll go back to that utopia – the lion will lie down with the lamb, the bible says. So, why wait?" Mairi and Sheila chuckled at his logic.

After supper, Sheila offered to find Pamela Fisher, but Mairi said she was satisfied with just one verification. No need to trouble Pamela. "I believe you will inherit half of your father's estate."

"I suppose I will. Can't think who else would get his money. But I don't need the money. This is my home now."

"What will you do with it, then?"

"Probably pay it into the community's funds, to help pay for God's work."

As the meal came to an end, the senior pastor stood again and spoke. "Ladies and gents, brothers and sisters, I know that most of you have come to spend time with us because you have already given your life to Jesus and you wanted to immerse yourself for a while in a Christian community. But I just feel it in my spirit that at least one person has not yet reached that point in their lives. So, I will finish with a special prayer. I'd ask you all to close your eyes and if you wish, you can repeat this prayer with me in your heart."

Mairi had never attended church, except as a bridesmaid and for her grandfather's funeral, but even she knew the protocol. He started praying. "Lord Jesus, I call on your name. Father God, be with us tonight. Holy Spirit, join with our souls, bring us rest. I am sorry for the sins I've committed. I have fallen short of your standards. Lord Jesus, thank you for dying on the cross, so my sins might be forgiven. I renounce my sins to you now. I repent of my evil ways and seek your forgiveness. Lord, come into my life. Guide my actions and thoughts. In your name, I ask... Amen."

The hall had gone silent, apart from the pastor's words. When he stopped speaking, there was a stillness over the place. A calm like Mairi had never felt before. She'd listened to his words and although she hadn't repeated them, she had felt them in her heart. On opening her eyes, Sheila was grinning at her. "What?" she asked.

"Oh! Nothing, Mairi. I just felt that the prayer was for you and it will have brought you peace. I hope it has." Sheila gave her a leaflet to take home with her. "I'll pray for you Mairi. Every week now until I hear from you again. God bless you."

Mairi didn't comment on the leaflet – just folded it and popped it into her handbag – or respond to Sheila's assumption. She thanked her for all she'd shared, wished her well, then retired for the night. She had to rise early to get the first ferry to Mull if she was to catch the train she'd booked.

But in her room, she lay on the bed, unable to sleep, the prayer running around in her head. What if Sheila was right? We all fall short of God's standards, she said. We all need forgiveness. It will release

THE KEY TO MURDER

you from past grudges if you forgive the person who sinned against you.

She thought back to the teenage boy who'd tried to force himself into her when the petting had gone too far. Hamish Nicholson. As she lay there, she did something she'd never done since becoming an adult. She prayed. Prayed that God would forgive her for all she'd done wrong, and she forgave Hamish Nicholson for trying to rape her. Afterwards, she slipped into a restoring sleep.

***

The frumpy middle-aged woman ambled along the broad suburban street in the Ravelston area of Edinburgh, her hands in the pockets of her pale coloured quilted coat, her head covered by a woollen hat, her head down, unnoticed by passers-by. Anonymous. She'd just finished her work in the area, so was dropping off her leaflet. Perhaps the man would need her services?

He lived in a chalet bungalow. A walled garden to the front and a lawned area at the rear. A nearly new black Porsche sports car sat on the driveway, leading to the attached garage. He'd not get to enjoy that posh car for much longer. She'd make sure of that. The woman posted her leaflet and walked away – the bait slipped onto the hook and cast into his pond.

Tuesday 10th March

Chapter 38

As Mairi rode the ferry back to Oban, stood in the centre, absorbing the swell as she'd learned on the way to Mull, a thought occurred to her. If she stayed upright, flexible and positive in life, she could ride the ups and downs of living and survive. More than survive, would succeed. Would Thrive. She'd try not to forget this inspiration.

On the train to Edinburgh, Mairi reflected on her discussion with the DCI about starting a family. Now that she and Brodie were engaged, she guessed her father and Brodie's would start asking when they could expect the sound of tiny feet, and the mothers and aunts to ask when they should start knitting baby clothes. She shuddered at the thought of continual hints, but as she considered the idea more, her mind gradually turned. What is the point of marrying if it's not to create a family? Otherwise, they could have just continued living together. Maybe a baby wouldn't be such a bad thing...

The train sped along the northern shore of Loch Awe, the landscape across the lake much flatter than it had been beside Loch Lomond the previous day. As the train came towards the loch's end, Mairi spied high mountains ahead and to her right the ruins of Kilchurn Castle across the water, the lakeshore surrounding it on three sides.

As they closed on Glasgow, Gare Loch appeared distantly on their right. Mairi knew the loch was home to the Royal Navy's submarine base, but from the train, Faslane wasn't visible. A man entered the carriage, shortly after stopping at Gare Loch Head station. He staggered down the aisle, holding onto the seat-top handles.

The man plonked himself into a vacant seat in the next row, across the table from a young woman whose head was lowered, apparently engrossed in her book and headphones in her ears. He spoke to the woman opposite, but she didn't respond. He raised his voice and reached across to her, pulling the earphone by its lead from her ear. "I said, the weather's crap today. Do you not agree?"

She looked up at him and said, "Aye. It's not so grand," before replacing her earphones and returning to her book.

He leaned over again and pulled the earphone leads. "Are you heading to Glasgae, lassie?"

She glared at him. "Look. Where I'm heading, is none of your business and I've no wish to engage in conversation with you. Just leave me alone." She replaced her earphones, but he leant across and pulled them again.

"No need to be rude," the ragged-bearded man said. He stood and moved around the table. "Budge up, lassie. I'll sit next to you so we can get to know each other."

The young woman fumed. "Get away from me, you stinking drunkard."

Mairi had been watching the interaction, hoping things would settle down. She stood and stepped towards the man. "You heard the young lady. Return to your seat and leave her be, or I'll have you arrested for being drunk and disorderly."

"What's it to you? Perhaps I should sit by you instead," he slobbered, swaying as the train rocked. He reached for Mairi. "Come here, lassie. Give me a cuddle."

Mairi grabbed his outstretched hand, twisted it, causing him to swivel, rammed it up his back, then grabbed her handcuffs from her bag. He squealed like a piglet as he fell forward onto the floor, unable to retain his balance. Mairi let him go, followed him to the ground, then secured both wrists with the cuffs, before calling for assistance at the next rail station.

The Transport Police removed him from the train at Helensburgh. As Mairi retook her seat, the young woman spoke. "Thanks for that. I'm sure the creep would have groped me if I'd let him sit beside me. And he stank of whisky and cigarettes – disgusting."

"Glad to help. Just doing my job." She smiled. The train settled back into peace as it recommenced its journey to Glasgow. Only an hour left until she would change trains for Edinburgh.

***

"Right, Nikolay." Rab opened. "Thank you for returning from Hull to speak with us." Rab smiled. Nikolay sneered. "So, why were you in such a hurry to leave the UK?"

Nikolay sat with his arms folded, face sternly set. He said nothing.

"I don't need you to answer that question, anyway. Despite your denial of a safe in the property that you ran from, we found and opened your safe and discovered its contents: fourteen passports, including that of your partner, Maria Angalova." Nikolay looked like he was about to deny any relationship with Maria, but kept his lips sealed.

"It was good planning not to lock your passport in the safe with the others. Enabled you to make a quick exit. Just a shame for you that we caught you before boarding the ferry." Rab gloated. He wanted to wind the man up, to get him annoyed in the hope that he would break his silence. He detested men like Nikolay, who abused women and lived off the profits of their slavery.

"The other thirteen passports belong to young women from various Eastern European countries. Three of those women have already given evidence that you brought them into the UK and forced them to work as prostitutes. There's little point you denying it." Nikolay shrugged.

"You will be charged with living off the earnings of prostitution and with rape and assault. But what I'm interested in right now is why you murdered George White?"

Nikolay sat upright, his mouth initially open. "Murder! I no murder no one. Who is this man you say I murder?"

"He is the customer known as Georgie to the woman you sent to provide sexual services."

"Ah! Georgie." He paused. "I no kill Georgie. He good customer. Pays cash each time. No problem. Why I kill this man?" He tilted his head and pursed his lips, expressing doubt at the officer's ridiculous accusation.

"You see, Nikolay, the murderer entered George White's home with a key. And your company holds a key to this house. Yesterday, you gave this key to Andrei Draganov."

"Yes, we keep key. Andrei take key to get into house if any problems with the girl. Andrei protector. But we no kill good customer. Stupid idea, policeman."

"Your prints and DNA are now being processed," Rab said, automatically looking down at Nikolay's tarantula-like hairy hands. "If we find a match with evidence taken at George White's house, we will have means and opportunity and will add murder to the list of charges. If you killed the man, we *will* find your reason for doing so." Rab paused. "If Andrei did not kill George White and you say you have no reason, who else could have taken the key? Tell me Nikolay. Perhaps we can drop the murder charge?"

"You barking up wrong tree, policeman. Only Maria and me have access to that key – always one of us is in flat, but we not have reason to kill the man... When this murder happen?"

"On the morning of Tuesday, 3rd March. Where were you that morning?"

"It depends."

"On what?"

"What time Tuesday morning? I not stay one place all morning."

"Around 8 am. Where were you then?"

"Having breakfast. I go out at 9 am. I get shopping from store. Food for noon meal and evening time."

"Can anyone confirm you were in the flat between 7:30 am and 9 am on March 3rd?"

"Maria, of course. She in flat same time. She go in bathroom, after I take shower."

"Okay. We will check with Maria. And where did you go shopping?"

"Convenience store on next street, near Andrei's flat."

"Name of store and street, please?"

"Sign say Convenience Store. Open early 'til late."

Rab sent Nikolay back to the cells while he checked out his alibi. He doubted he *had* killed George White. As he'd said, what motive could he have? But he'd not write off the possibility until he'd checked the facts. Some people are good liars and there might be a hidden motive.

***

Maria looked dishevelled. She reeked of cheap perfume and sweat, but no one was at their best after a night in the cells. Suzanna sat opposite the woman and introduced herself before questioning her. "Please confirm your name?"

"Maria Angalova."

"That is Maria Elena Angalova; correct? And you are a Bulgarian citizen?"

"Yes. That is my name. I Bulgarian. It is true."

"Tell me, Maria, where were you last Tuesday between 7:30 am and 9 am?"

Maria thought for a while. "One week ago. Same place as most Tuesdays. In my flat. I take my shower near 8 am each day after big man, Nikolay, finished."

"And was Nikolay there that day?"

"Yes, yes. He no go anywhere. He told me bathroom free. Why you ask this?"

"Because around that time on that day, a man was murdered. A man whose house key you hold. A man whose home was not broken into but entered using a key."

"Oh! So, you think *we* kill this man?"

"Perhaps Mr White owed you money, so you went to his home and threatened him, but still he would not pay, so you murdered him?"

"How I do that when I in the shower? Tell me that."

"You say you were showering, but why should I believe the word of a woman who tricks girls to come to the UK for work, then forces them to become prostitutes? Why should we believe the word of a woman who denies having a safe and holding the passports of the girls working for you? We found all their passports within the safe, located in your flat. We have evidence to charge you with trafficking and living off prostitution. You will go to jail for these offences before being deported back to Bulgaria."

Maria stared at Suzanna, grim-faced, her arms folded, supporting her substantial breasts. "If you say so, maybe it will be true. But only if jury agree."

Suzanna continued, "So far, three of your girls have given evidence against you and Nikolay. You *will* go to prison. Be assured."

Maria slumped back into the chair, her face sagging. "I say nothing more. You get me solicitor."

Chapter 39

"Petrov's and Angalova's alibis are not sound as there's no independent corroboration," Rab said in discussion with his boss. "And they had the key, which they say was under their control at all times. Apart from the person they gave it to, Andrei Draganov. But if they or Andrei had killed George White, they would hardly have sent Elizabete and Andrei to his home yesterday, would they?"

"Agreed," Suzanna said. "And there's no obvious motive. I still think this is a revenge killing linked back to Butler and Cargrove. One of the women he assaulted, most likely."

"But *thirty years* after he abused them seems far-fetched," Owen interjected. "Why would anyone wait that long to avenge their treatment?"

"Maybe the killer had lost track of White and came across him purely by chance, triggering the hatred she'd harboured," Caitlin offered.

"Aye, that's possible, I'd say," Murray agreed.

"There have been numerous cases lately of women making accusations of rape or sexual abuse that happened to them twenty or more years before. Perhaps this is similar, but instead of making an accusation, someone took matters into their own hands?" Suzanna concluded. There were more nodding heads around the room. "Okay. We still need to keep following the Butler and Cargrove line, but the other possibility remains the care company link. How are we doing on the enquiries made to foreign police forces, Rab?"

"I've had responses from all police forces, except the Polish. But of those who replied to our requests, only the Romanians had anything of interest. So, we need a chat with Gabriela Albescu again."

"Anything back on Edmond White's children?"

Owen responded, "I took a call from Dumfries and Galloway Constabulary earlier today. They've spoken with his daughter, Linda Strider. She said she'd not seen her grandfather in ten years. Apparently, she and her dad didn't get on with his father. They stopped visiting him after their grandma died. When she was young, they used to visit occasionally, but she was always glad to leave because he was so bossy. They asked her if he'd ever interfered with her and she'd said no. On the day George White died, she'd been at work – she's a primary school teacher."

"Thanks, Owen. And the son?" Suzanna prompted. No one volunteered any feedback. "Rab, get that chased, please."

"Sure... Another one for you, please," Rab said, looking at Owen. The DC nodded and spun his chair to his desk to start work. "By the way, ma'am, I found out that Nancy White is Edmond's second wife. He split with his first wife, Claire, seven years back. When he and Nancy brought their house in Ardersier, the deposit was small and the mortgage large. Not a good position to be in just two years off retirement!"

"Yeah. But why all the credit card debt and continual overdrawing? We need to look closer at Edmond White. Has he got regular unusual outgoings, or does he just have expensive habits?"

"The hotel he stayed in when he came to Edinburgh wasn't pricey, so it doesn't seem that he has delusions of grandeur. But I'll look deeper."

"One last thing," Suzanna added. "I want Albert White interviewed. Where was he on the morning of the murder? Was there bad blood between them? Does Albert have any children? Have they had contact with George in recent years?" Rab made a note of this new requirement.

"Ma'am," Zahir said. "I interviewed Etrit Berisha this morning. He's the man I arrested yesterday. He wouldn't answer any questions, just said no comment. And he's asked for a solicitor. I'm not confident we'll get anything out of him. But we have plenty of evidence to charge him with various offences."

"Okay. Give me your report and the list of evidence and I'll get it in front of the Procurator Fiscal later today. If there's nothing else, I'll leave you to it then, guys," Suzanna said as she rose.

***

Gabriela was heating her client's lunch in the microwave when her phone rang. "Yes?" she said.

"Hello, Gabriela. Sergeant Sinclair here."

"Oh! Hello again, Sergeant. How can I help you?"

"I must speak with you again and collect a sample of your DNA and your fingerprints to eliminate you from our enquiries. You'll need to come into the station to do that."

The microwave pinged. "Just a minute, Sergeant. There is something I must do for my client." She put the phone down, took the meal from the microwave, placed it on a tray and took it through to the elderly man in the next room. "Sorry, Sergeant," she said on her return to the kitchen, "but duty called. You say I must come to police station. Which one? There are many in Edinburgh."

"The nearest to your patch would be the one in Haymarket. It's in Torphichen Place. Or you could come to the headquarters on Fettes Avenue if that would be convenient?"

"I have one more client to visit. After, I can come to Fettes Avenue. My flat is in East Pilton."

"Okay, that's great. What time would you expect to finish work?"

"Thirty minutes after three. I will come to your station 4 pm."

Rab thanked her, then informed the desk sergeant to expect her, before notifying his boss. When he returned to the office, Owen called out. "Hey, Sarge, the Polish police have responded. Maja Basinski *does* have a record."

"Bring her in for a chat and to take her DNA and prints, please, Owen?"

"Sure thing."

***

"Come this way, Gabriela," Rab said after getting the call from the desk sergeant. He led her into the CID zone and invited her to sit in Interview Room 1, where he already had a DNA sample collection kit and fingerprinting facilities. As he took her prints and scraped her cuticles, he chatted. "How long have you been in Edinburgh, Gabriela?"

"Three years. A little more."

"Do you not have a husband in Romania?"

"No. No husband. I left my country to come here for work. I from poor family. Maybe one day I find a husband. Perhaps Scottish man?"

He took a swab from her mouth and placed it inside a tube, writing her name and date on the label, before attaching it. "Thank you for the sample, Gabriela. Now I must ask you some questions. We have spoken with the Romanian Police." Her face dropped and her skin paled. "They sent us details of your criminal record. You were convicted of theft in 2011. Gabriela, you should have declared this record when applying for work. People with a criminal record are not allowed to work with vulnerable people in the UK."

"Oh my God! What will I do? You have done terrible thing asking questions of my country's police. Now I will lose my job and my mother will face many problems. I steal, but only because we very poor and my mama very ill. She in much pain. I could not let her suffer, but we had no money for medicines. That is why I come to your country, to work and send money home. I never steal from client. I would never

227

do such a thing. They are like my mother. They need my help."

"I am sorry for you, Gabriela. It is unfortunate. But there is nothing I can do. I must inform your employer. It is the law."

Gabriela burst into tears, bent forward, placed her head in her open hands and sobbed. Rab left, saying he would return in a minute. When he did, he had a cup of tea for her. He felt compassion for the woman, but powerless to do anything other than what the law required of him.

As the sobbing quietened, she took a mouthful of the now warm tea. "Gabriela. I've had a report from a client that you threatened to leave him in bed all morning if he misbehaved. Please tell me why you said this to the man."

She thought back to the occasion, about three months before. "It was Mr Condon. He was being difficult. Refusing to cooperate with me. I had to get him out of bed, help him wash, then down stairs and into his chair and give him his breakfast, in just thirty minutes. I said it to make him cooperate. He like small child. Sometimes you must tell children they will miss something if they continue to be naughty. I would never miss him off my rounds, but I had to say something to make him cooperate."

"On the morning George White was murdered, you were the last known person to see him alive. You stated you'd left at 7:30 am. Is that correct?"

"Yes, just after 7:30. I with my next client, Mr Condon, at 7:45. You can ask."

'We will,' Rab thought. He passed a photo across the table to Gabriela. "This is you, isn't it?" Gabriela took one look at the photo and burst into tears again. "This photo was taken by the cash machine where you took money from George White's account after he died. How do you explain that?"

Between sobs, she admitted to making the withdrawal. She took money out for him every week, so she had his bank card and his PIN.

"George paid me for my time when I shop for him, and he owed me for the last three weeks. When I learned he had died, I took money from bank for myself, because I think his children not pay me. They not deserve his money, anyway. They never visit him. Only £30. I could have taken more.

Rab thought about what she'd said. It was possible that she washed and dressed White, gave him toast and waited until he'd taken two bites before stabbing him, later taking money from his account. But why would she, with so little for her to gain by his death? He waited for Gabriela's crying to subside. "Did George White ever touch you?"

Gabriela looked up. "He tried to touch my breast once but I nimble. I skip around him."

"Did you not get angry when he touched you?"

"No. He just lonely old man with no wife. It no problem for me."

"Gabriela, you were the last person known to have seen George White alive. It is possible that you *were* angry with White, and in your rage you killed him."

Gabriela's mouth hung open as she absorbed the accusation. "No. I not kill George. I tell you, I not angry." She paused and Rab gave her more time to respond. "If I kill George, it would be easier to do it when he is in bed. It would make no sense for me to get him dressed, down the stairs and give him breakfast before killing him. I thought you intelligent policeman."

Rab couldn't argue with her logic but countered, "Perhaps he touched you when you gave him his breakfast. Maybe you had a knife in your hand when you served his toast and in your anger, plunged it into his heart?"

"No. No. You horrible man to say such things. I not do this. I would never hurt him. I not angry person." Tears came to her eyes and trickled down her cheeks.

Rab kept silent for a moment, considering what she had said and making a judgement on whether she told the truth. "Gabriela, it is my belief that when you left George White, he *was* alive. So, after we have checked your clothing for blood, we will release you. But I must discuss the taking of Mr White's money with my Chief Inspector. We may need to bring you in again to be formally charged with theft. As I mentioned before, we are required to inform your employer about your criminal record for theft. I think you should start looking for another job or planning your return to Romania."

She howled again, her head returning to her still damp hands. Rab left her to settle down and sent a woman PC to stay with her.

Chapter 40

Maja didn't know that the police had invited her in for more than providing elimination DNA and fingerprint samples. She had rushed to the police station to comply with their request and was keen to get on her way, tired from having put in a full day's work. The detective sergeant had chatted with her as he took the samples, which included swabbing her hands and taking scrapings from under and around her fingernails. She didn't question the reason for these extra samples. The sergeant seemed to be a nice man. Then the boss woman came into the room.

"Maja, before you leave," Suzanna said, "you could help us find Mr White's killer by telling us more about the man, so we can identify a motive for his murder. Please enlighten us about George."

Maja thought before speaking. "Enlighten? This means make light, no?"

"Sorry, Maja," Suzanna responded. "It means to shed light on or illuminate. But in this context, it means we would like you to tell us what you know about the man."

Maja frowned, not understanding why enlighten would be used this way. It was confusing. She contemplated her response before answering. "He like many old men. Thinks he still attractive to young women. He flirt with me. Tell me I'm beautiful – look at me; he must be deluded. He make suggestions."

"What sort of suggestions?"

"He ask me to give him kiss. Say older men more experienced; can give me good time. Hah! George had trouble standing. He not give anyone good time. He just dirty old man."

"Did he ever touch you inappropriately?"

"He touched my bottom, once. I just smack his hand away and tell him not do that."

"Did he try to touch you anywhere else?"

"Yes. Once he touch my breasts. When I was giving him his lunch. I had tray in my hands and he touched me. I dropped the tray on his lap. The food splashed and he complained, but I told him his own fault. He should not touch me."

"Did he touch you again after that event?"

"No, I more careful afterwards. Stay away from his hands."

"I understand you had trouble with another of your clients. You left his home in a rush and left his front door open. Why did you do that?"

After a minute's silence, Maja responded. "That was Tony. Mr Heathcote. He worse than George. He touch my cipka." Suzanna looked puzzled. "How you say? ...pussy. I was red-in-face angry. Left house quickly. I not leave door open on purpose. It was accident. I told Barbara she must find someone else to care for him. I never go there again. We had argument. But I never go back."

"I also understand you argued with Davina?"

"The office women tell you tales. Yes, I argue with Davina and Barbara. Both women are lazy. They not listen. They not bother to help. My mama was in bad health. I needed to go home for a week to care for her. They not let me go. They cruel and lazy women. My mama suffer because she not get care. When I speak with mama, I tell her sorry, but my job I will lose, then I have no money to send home. She cry and tell me it so bad for her. I cry with her but no go home."

Suzanna showed genuine concern. "I'm sorry to hear about your mother's suffering. That must have been so hard for you. Is she alright now?"

"Yes. She suffer but now okay."

"Tell me about the incident in Krakow that led to your arrest for assault."

Maja looked like she'd been slapped in the face by Suzanna's question. She sat back in her chair and folded her arms before answering. "You speak with Polish police?"

Suzanna nodded. "We had to ask questions about all women who have provided care for George White. You should have told your employers about your criminal record for assault."

"If I do that, I no have job." Her voice trailed off. "Now you find out, you tell care company, no?"

"We must inform them. It is our duty."

"Then I must return to Poland. No work. No money. No food. No Flat to live in. I do nothing wrong, but now you have broken my life."

Suzanna looked sympathetic but pressed ahead. "Maja, we need to understand why you attacked the man on a bus in Krakow."

"He another bad man. Bus was packed with many people. This man had hard *kutas.*"

Suzanna's face showed her lack of understanding. "Hard cock," Maja repeated in English. "He pressed it against my bottom. I elbow him in face and push him. He fall back in crowd to floor. Police not care what man did to me, only that I hit him. Life not fair for women."

"Maja. How was your relationship with your father when you were a child?"

"What this to do with anything? My father good man."

"Maja, you have a history of being angry with men who touched you. Why is that?"

Maja sat stern-faced, perhaps wondering why she was being asked these questions. Her face softened, then she spoke. "Boys in my school assaulted me. They cornered me and pushed me around, touching my breasts and pussy. They held me and one boy put his fingers inside me. He let the other boys smell his fingers. They all think this is great fun. I think they would all have done same. Maybe they rape me, but teacher come and they ran away. Teacher think I invite boys to be with me. But I not bad girl. So, I angry when men touch me. They should not do it."

Suzanna looked at Maja, showing empathy. "I understand." She paused. "Maja. Did George White ever threaten you? Did he say he would report you if you didn't let him touch you?"

"How you know this?" She paused. "Next time I go, he said if I care for him, I let him touch me. I tell him fuck off. He said I tell your employer you bad carer. I steal from him. He bad man. I ask Davina for change. No more George White. But she tell me I must still do work for him. There was no one else to do this. As I said, she lazy woman."

"Did you believe George White would touch the other carers? Did you want to protect them from George? Did you *hate* George White?"

"He disgusting man. Like many men, he think he has right to touch women."

"Is that why you went to his house and stabbed him in the heart," Suzanna said, her voice rising, "so he could not touch more women?"

The accusation amazed Maja. She jumped to her feet melodramatically. "No. Never. I not stab George. He horrible man, but I no kill him. You like Polish police. You not care about me, only the men. Why you betray us women?" She stood, hands on hips, staring down at Suzanna.

Suzanna responded calmly, tilting her head to the side. "Sit down, Maja. Sit down." Maja sat and folded her arms again, her face set hard. "I could understand if you wanted to rid the world of this predator. You've had many bad experiences with men. What I now need to know is where you were between 7:30 am and 9 am, last Tuesday, March 3rd?

You were not at work that day."

"It was my day off. We work shifts. I stay home in bed."

"Was anyone with you that morning?"

"What you saying? I was having sex with man? I single woman. Good Catholic. I wait for marriage."

"Can anyone confirm you were at home that morning?"

Maja relaxed a little, realising she had misunderstood the question. "My friend. I share flat with girl. She will tell you."

"Who is this friend? Was she there all the time?"

"Her name Jolanta. She left for work fifteen minutes before eight. I still in bed when she shouted '*do zobaczenia punji*' – see you later."

"Did you respond? Could Jolanta confirm you were in your bedroom?"

Maja looked at the ceiling. "She not know I was in bed," she admitted. "I asleep when she shout. I look at clock but before I shout back, the door banged."

"Maja, you will remain in custody until your DNA sample has been processed. You have a motive to kill George White, the ability to enter his home whenever you wish, and no alibi. So, we will also need to check your clothing for blood. If you cooperate, we will process things more quickly."

"Okay, I cooperate. I have done nothing wrong. The sooner you find this, the better."

"One last question," Suzanna said. "You stated that you had to continue serving George White. But there are only two carers each day for George; morning and evening?"

"Yes. I stopped going to George's house last month. Social workers say he no need help to get mid-day meal. Just dressing, and up-down stairs."

Chapter 41

As Gabriela's tears flowed, her mind travelled the *unfair* road. None of it was her fault. Fate had been unkind to her. She was born into a poor family. Why did rich people have everything but her family struggle every day to survive? It was so unfair. She had been forced by poverty to leave her home, her parents and her siblings, to earn money for the family. Unfair. She worked hard but earned little. Much of her pay was needed just to live a basic life in Scotland. So, little was left to send home. Unfair. She couldn't buy nice clothes, go to restaurants or even the cinema. She lived off supermarket basics and the nearly out-of-date discounted food. So unfair. Unfair, Unfair, Unfair...

As the tears dried, her mind began to rationalise. What would happen to her now? Perhaps they would charge her with theft. How would the UK courts punish her for taking the money? Would she be fined? How would she pay a fine, with no money and no job? Would she go to jail? Whether or not she was charged, she would lose her job. Could she find other work when they knew she had a criminal record? Who would employ her? She could do cleaning work, perhaps? No. Why would anyone let a thief into their home? Bar work? A thief allowed to handle money? Unlikely. What then? What work could she do? She wasn't well educated. She spoke basic English, but her written English was not good enough for office work. Was there any work for uneducated women with bad English? Her mind briefly flagged up sex work, but she rejected this outright. It would be better to go home and scrape a living with her family than do work that would soil her soul, destroy her dignity and commit her to hell when she died. No, no, no. "What then?" she shouted to herself.

"Are you alright?" the police officer asked.

Gabriela looked up, realising that she had vocalised her thoughts. "Sorry. Can I go now?"

"Yes. If you're ready to leave, I'll show you out."

Gabriela stood and followed the PC. As she left the station, the damp cold air added to her gloom. She walked away into an unknown grim future.

***

Suzanna was chatting with Alistair when Rab turned up. He waited until his boss gave him the nod to talk. "Thought you'd want to know that Nikolay Petrov's whereabouts on the morning of White's murder have been corroborated. He was seen at the convenience store buying groceries around 8 am, and his business partner had already vouched for his location before that."

"And Maria Angalova?" Suzanna asked.

"The duty solicitor is due in shortly, so we'll interview her again. We've been through their paper records and the computer but found nothing that would point towards a motive for killing George White. So, it looks like neither of them had anything to do with the murder."

Rab continued, "I expect by the day's end, we will be in a position to charge Angalova and Petrov with trafficking and living off the earnings of prostitution. I just wish the government would get the Human Trafficking and Exploitation Act into law. Their offence is not living off the women's earnings, it's about exploitation."

"True," Suzanna agreed. "I hear the act of parliament is due in before the year's out. We'll just have to proceed with the legislation in place. Have you contacted the other masseuses on SMS's books?"

237

"The team are dealing with that now. We've pulled in some help from uniform – female officers to accompany them on their visits. By the way, it wasn't only massages they were pretending to sell. Some of their girls were being employed as escorts.

"Okay. Interesting. Same business though, I suppose. Just a different front. Keep me posted."

"By the way. I've found out that the credit card debts of Edmond White go back to just after he met his wife, Nancy. I guess he wanted to impress her. Plus, the wedding and honeymoon cost a fortune. I'm surprised he's not found himself another job since leaving the Army to pay off his debts."

"Yes. Perhaps he's been expecting a large sum to come his way? I know he has an alibi but I wonder if he could have paid someone else to do his dirty work?"

"Don't know where he would have got the money from to pay for the killing," Rab replied.

"The murderer could be on commission, perhaps out of Edward White's inheritance?"

***

Maja's tears trickled down her face, dripping off her chin onto her lap, not sobbing, just sad. She loved Poland and would prefer to be in Krakow than Edinburgh, but economics had pushed her into moving to the UK. The wages were low, but at least she had employment and had some funds left to send home to her mama. And she had hoped she might meet a man in Scotland's cosmopolitan capital city. But instead, Maja sat on a hard bench locked in a police cell under suspicion of murder. She hadn't murdered George, of course; surely they must find out who did. The chief woman detective seemed intelligent. There was hope. But soon she would be out of work and must return home.

Why is this happening to me? Am I a bad person? Why do men think they can touch me? Why me? Do I look like a whore? The trickle turned into a torrent. She covered her face with her hands, her head falling. Despair captured her mind. Possessed it. Suicidal thoughts came to her. She would end the misery by ending her life. But there was nothing in the cell to use as a weapon. No sharp implements. No belt and nowhere to hang it, anyway. She stood and walked to the door, then crashed her head against its thick steel. She thought to headbutt the door again, but pain exploded through her head from the first strike. Maja slid to the floor, twisting as she shrank, then sat, her back against the door and howled. She couldn't even do that right.

A minute later, she heard footsteps approaching, then a banging on the door. "Move back from the door," a woman shouted. Maja rolled away from the steel, then propped herself against the cold, bland plaster of the wall. The door opened and a policewoman entered, a male colleague behind her. The woman crouched before reaching out her hand and lifting Maja's chin. "Let me look at you."

Maja let her chin rise, her eyes slowly gaining the courage to meet with those of the police officer. Blood oozed from a wound above Maja's right eyebrow, dribbling down her cheek. The policewoman turned to the man in the doorway. "Get us some tissues, please Jon and the first aid kit." He walked away and the officer locked eyes with Maja again. We'll have your eye cleaned up in a minute. Don't worry. "What happened? Did you fall?"

Maja started sobbing again, her tears mixing with the blood and running in a pink stream over her cheeks. She tried to answer through the blubbing. "Everything is lost. My life destroyed. I must end it."

She leant forward and placed her hand on Maja's arm. "It will be alright. Do not worry." Jon returned with the first aid kit and tissues. "Best call the duty doctor." She pressed a wad of tissues against Maja's forehead, stemming the flow of blood, the pressure renewing the pain. She howled even louder. "Stay still, Ms Basinski. Let me help you." She held the pad against Maja's face, talking to her gently for a few minutes until Jon returned and informed her the duty doc would call as soon as possible. "My name is Catherine. Can I call you Maja?" Maja's eyes met Catherine's silently indicating yes. Catherine cautiously peeled away the tissue pad before wiping the wound carefully with antiseptic liquid. "It's not so bad," she said, then wiped away the pink tears from Maja's face and dabbed below both eyes.

Maja's tears slowed. 'This policewoman cares about me,' she thought. Her body calmed, stilled, her mind sinking into acceptance that she must face up to her circumstances. Maybe she *could* get another job. One where they would not care that she had hit a man. Working in a nightclub, perhaps? A hotel? Cleaning bedrooms? The policewoman spoke again, encouraging her to move off the floor and sit on the bench. She complied. "We've asked a doctor to attend to look at your eye and speak with you. I'll stay with you until they arrive. Okay?" Maja tried to nod, but her head hurt. Catherine cut a strip from a medicated reel of paper tape and stuck it across the wound, pulling it together first, so the edges of the gash gently kissed. "That'll do for the moment."

Maja found her voice. "Thank you, Catherine. You are kind person." The officer sat beside Maja, wrapping an arm around her shoulders to comfort her. "Tell me about your home country, Poland."

Maja felt reassured in this woman's presence. "I am from Krakow. It is capital city in my country. My family live in small house. I have one sister and three brothers. They older. They all leave home. Have own families. Children. I only one not married. I think sometimes I will never have family." Her voice trailed off.

"Why wouldn't you have a family? You are still young, Maja. There is plenty of time."

She turned towards Catherine and smiled, their eyes meeting. "I have nieces and nephews in Poland. They are cute. Pretty. I miss them. If I go home, I will see them. I not know what I do in Poland. Not much work for me. I no have good exams and no special skills. What I do?"

"You can learn new skills. When I joined the police, I had no skills, but they trained me and now I am good at my job. You could find a job where your employer will train you?"

"Perhaps you are right. If I can find job in Krakow, it would be good to go home." Maja paused, deep in thought. "But I like Scotland. It beautiful country. And Scottish people friendly. Kind. Except my clients, George and Tony. They both dirty old men. They want to abuse me. But now I not have problem with these men. George is dead. They think I killed him, but I not do this. I was in my bed when he killed. I not like the man but not kill him."

"If you didn't murder George White, you will not be charged. DCI McLeod is good at her job and she believes in justice. She has an excellent reputation. She will find the murderer. Do not worry."

"Catherine. I hit a man in Krakow and have police record. Could I get job working in bar, in Edinburgh? Or Chambermaid? If not, I must go back to Poland."

"I'm sure you will get another job, Maja. If this were not possible, no criminal would ever work again and there would be more crime. In some bars in the city, being a strong woman would be a good thing. Men are stupid after they've drunk a few beers or knocked back some shots of whisky."

"Yes. You are right. Stupid good word. They do many stupid things and bad things. It is crime to piss in street, here in Edinburgh, yes?"

"Aha!"

"Many men piss in shop doorways or by rubbish bins when walking home. I see them do this, much."

"Yes. I know. If we see them, we arrest them and they spend a night in these cells."

Maja looked sad, remembering that she too would be spending a night, or more, in the cell where she now sat.

Chapter 42

A knock came at Suzanna's door. She looked up and saw a uniformed policewoman. "Hello, Catherine. What can I do for you?"

"Hi, ma'am. I wanted to talk to you about Maja Basinski."

"Come in. Take a seat."

Catherine sat, then told the DCI what she'd spent the last few minutes building up the courage to say. "I've just left Ms Basinski in her cell. She'd smashed her head against the cell door, split her eyebrow open and gave herself a headache. She's evidently troubled. Depressed? Perhaps even suicidal. I've done my best to talk her around and inject some positivity. The doc's with her now." She paused, gathering her thoughts. "I understand she's being held on suspicion of murder, pending results of DNA testing. From my talk with her, I doubt she murdered the man. Is there any way the DNA matching work might be prioritised, so we could release her?"

Suzanna considered what she'd heard, having not been previously informed. "Thanks for bringing this to my attention, Catherine. Maja had shown no signs of being depressed, let alone suicidal. Please ask the doc to brief me after he's examined her. Regarding DNA matching, it's not a process that can be sped up, but perhaps the forensics team might be persuaded to give it a higher priority. Just a minute." Suzanna picked up her phone and speed dialled.

"Hi, Jonathon. I need a favour......"

***

Suzanna looked up and smiled as Doctor Morrison entered her office. "Hi, Isobel. How's it going?"

Isobel perched on the front of the chair she'd taken. "I can't stay long, Suzanna. Busy as ever. Your Ms Basinski has a rather large lump on her eyebrow and a deep cut. The PC, Catherine Henderson, did a good job of cleaning the gash and taping it together. She'll not need any further treatment on the eye. I've given her some paracetamol for the pain."

"What about her mental health? Should she be placed on suicide watch?"

"I don't think so. We've talked through the issues she had that were causing her such distress and Catherine had also chatted with her about her troubles. She's in a much better place now, but I would recommend releasing her as soon as you're able – assuming she's not the murderer, of course."

"Agreed. Forensics are prioritising the DNA work, so I'm hoping that will prove we can release her by the end of the day."

"Great. Look, I can't hang around chatting. Too much on. But perhaps we could meet up one evening soon."

"That would be lovely. I can't commit to anything yet, but once this case is wrapped up, I'll call you."

***

Rab replaced the phone's handset and strolled to the DCI's office. Standing in the open doorway, he spoke. "Reports are in from forensics about Basinski's and Albescu's DNA and prints."

Suzanna looked up as soon as he mentioned forensics. "What are the findings?"

"There's no match between their DNA and that found on the knife."

Suzanna had been expecting that answer but was still a little disappointed. They could do with wrapping this one up. "Anything on the prints?"

"Not really. They've both worked in White's home before – Albescu on the morning he was killed. The CSIs found the carers' prints where they'd be expected. And nothing on the knife or even the knife block."

"Better release Maja Basinski with our apologies. You'll need to charge Albescu with the theft of George White's money from the cash machine after his death. We can't ignore that. And we can't disregard the theft charge on her records in Romania. She's proven she's a thief and she won't be allowed to continue working for CCC. We'll need to inform them." Suzanna paused, her face showing thoughts circulating in her mind. "Come in for a sec and close the door." Rab stepped in, shut the door and sat opposite Suzanna, curious about what she wanted to say, confidentially.

"As I said, if Gabriela hadn't taken the money from George White's bank, I'd have been inclined not to mention her theft record to her employer. We can't do that now. But Maja Basinski's another case. Her criminal record was for elbowing a man in the face on a bus after he sexually assaulted her. As she said, that's not fair, but of course, there was no proof he'd done anything to her but many witnesses to confirm she had struck him and pushed him to the ground."

Rab could guess where this was leading. "So, you're considering keeping that quiet?"

"Yes. Her explanations for problems with clients were both satisfactory. I believe her. She seems to be a draw for men. Perhaps she comes across as vulnerable? Something in her aura, to do with her abuse at the hands of the boys at her school. I don't know, but I feel sorry for her."

"She's not done anything wrong. Nothing illegal in the UK," Rab agreed. "And she was punished for assaulting the man who'd abused her. If her story is true – and you believe her – she's owed some leniency."

"We're agreed then?"

"Aye, definitely. I'll release her, apologise for holding her and tell her that on this occasion, we will not inform her employers. One other thing, though."

"Yes." Now it was Suzanna's turn to be curious.

"Gabriela Albescu says she was paid by George to shop for him and he owed her money, which she believed she'd not get from the relatives. She withdrew the money, only £30, because she'd been entrusted with his card and PIN, and it was owed to her. Technically, it might be theft but morally, it would appear a justified withdrawal. I think we should let her off as well."

Suzanna considered his proposal, her brow furrowed. She also would like to show some mercy to Gabriela but there were complications. "Look, Rab, when the bank account is examined by his executors, they'll notice the withdrawal after White's death." Rab anticipated her rejection of his suggestion. But Suzanna continued. "Speak to the son. Explain the situation and ask whether he would wish to press charges. If he says no, we'll not charge her. Given her circumstances, if we don't charge her with theft, I'm also inclined to forget to notify CCC about her Romanian record. But this conversation goes no further than this office. Agreed?"

"Agreed. I'll get onto Edmond White straight away. I'll go outside to make the call."

Suzanna nodded and Rab strode away to follow up, looking pleased with himself.

***

Rab opened the cell door. "Ms Basinski, please follow me." He turned and strolled away, giving Maja time to catch up. "This way." He led her into Interview Room 2. "We now have the forensics results." He paused and Maja looked at him expectantly. "There was no evidence o suggest you killed George White."

245

Maja's face brightened momentarily. "Can I go now?"

"Yes, Maja. Sorry to have detained you. But I hope you'll understand why we had to hold you, given your history of reaction against men who touched you inappropriately?"

"I miss day's work. You compensate me, no?"

"I'm sorry. We don't compensate people held on suspicion of crimes. But I have good news for you." Maja looked intrigued. "I've spoken with the Chief Inspector and agreed that we will not inform your employer about your Polish criminal record. We feel that your action on the bus was justified. It would be unfair for you to be punished twice when you were just defending yourself from a sexual assault."

Maja's face brightened. "Oh my God! That is wonderful. You make me so happy. Thank you, sir, thank you."

"No need for your thanks, Maja. Now let's get you processed and released, so you can go home."

Maja emerged from the station buoyant, smiling, striding out, feeling good about the future and reassured that there were good people in the world – even the police. She called the CCC office to let them know she was available to work tomorrow. Barbara accepted Maja's explanation for being held by the police (not the full truth). But Barbara's attitude reminded Maja there were plenty of cruel people, as well as kind ones. Her buoyancy was deflated by the conversation, returning her from floating unaided in the Dead Sea to struggling to stay afloat in the rough waters off Scotland.

Chapter 43

The office was empty when Mairi arrived at Fettes Avenue, but she noticed the interview rooms' lights were on. She hung her coat on the hook and dumped her handbag before taking out her phone. The leaflet Sheila had given her caught her eye. She extracted the sheet and dumped it on the desk, not sure she'd ever read it. A text to Brodie was next, *back at Fettes, see you later.* She headed off to the toilets.

Suzanna entered the main office and noticed Mairi's handbag on her desk, then the leaflet. 'Got questions about life?' A large red question mark spread across the leaflet's front, angled at forty-five degrees. And within the dot at its base, the word Alpha. *Another* prompt about the Alpha Course, so soon after the others she'd received – weird! She picked up the leaflet and scanned it. 'Why am I here? What is the point in life? Does life matter? Is there a God? A chance to explore the Christian faith and ask questions' She replaced the leaflet on Mairi's desk as the men entered the office, chatting.

On return from the toilet, Mairi found the office crowded. "Welcome back, Mairi. We're keen to hear what Miss White had to say about her father," Suzanna said. They listened intently as Mairi reported on Sheila's abuse at her father's hand, reinforcing what they'd heard from others. He was a sexual predator. Mairi mentioned Sheila's cousin, Christine Dangerfield, another potential victim. To complete the picture, they should interview her as well.

Rab had spoken with Albert White. He'd been at a Peebles Photographic Club meeting at 9 am on the day of George's death. The drive from Edinburgh to Peebles was, at best, forty-five minutes and at that time of day, at least an hour. In theory, he could have killed his brother and returned to attend the meeting, but none of the cars spotted in the area matched his twenty-year-old Ford Focus. And none of the pedestrians recorded on CCTV were men in their eighties. Albert had one daughter who'd emigrated to Canada nearly two decades ago. Immigration confirmed she'd not been back in the UK in three years.

"Guys," Suzanna said. "We've been distracted from the murder hunt by the trafficking and prostitution racket. As important as they are, we must refocus on the main target, catching George White's killer. I'm worried this person could now have a taste for murder and take another life. We need to find them before they do. I want you all sharp tomorrow. No more distractions, okay?" They all nodded in agreement.

Suzanna was closing down her computer when her mobile rang. She saw the caller's name, so immediately answered.

***

The woman trudged up the concrete stairs, weary from the day's toil. It had been a typical day of drudgery. Hard graft, no praise, and the knowledge that the next time she visited her clients, it would be more of the same. She closed the front door behind her, hung up her coat and hat, and kicked off her shoes. She was looking forward to some supper and putting her feet up in front of the TV when her phone rang.

Her spirits brightened when she took the call. Gerard Templeton had seen her leaflet and would like her to visit his house as soon as it was convenient. His wife had recently left him and he needed some assistance to keep on top of things. She agreed to call round tomorrow evening.

Justice had failed the women he'd abused. Their post-trial expressions came to her mind. She recalled the smirk on Templeton's face, captured by the newspaper photographer after the not guilty verdict had been passed.

She imagined what she'd do to him, to avenge his serial abuse. He would wish he'd gone to jail. Her face broke into a wide grin. He'd taken the bait. Now the sport would begin.

**

Suzanna switched on the oven and pulled a large pizza from the freezer, then salad from the fridge. James was on his way and she had nothing planned — except her fall-back of a toasted sandwich. But that wouldn't do to feed her man. She set up her computer to play music from YouTube — her default cello instrumentals. One day, she'd get around to trying out one of the music streaming services.

The doorbell rang, so she checked the video display and buzzed him in. She popped the pizza into the oven, laden with extra toppings: olives, sliced red onions and capsicum, halved cherry tomatoes, with ham on one half for James and added jalapenos for herself. And loads of extra-mature cheddar cheese. A light tap came on the apartment door. She hastened through to the hall and let him in. "Hi, James."

"Hi, Gorgeous." He kissed her lightly on the lips and passed her a bottle of wine. Suzanna walked back into the living room, while James slipped off his coat and hung it in the cloak cupboard. Suzanna placed the wine on the kitchen worktop, took a corkscrew from a drawer and passed it to James with a smile.

"How's your day been?" James asked as he deployed the corkscrew, the cork gently popping as he pulled it from its bottle.

"Busy as ever, James. How was yours?"

They perched on the barstools by the breakfast bar. James poured wine into the two glasses Suzanna had taken from the cupboard. They chinked glasses, then sipped the wine. "It'll have to be the one glass tonight. I have to drive home, as I'm heading off first thing in the morning. That's the main reason I wanted us to get together tonight."

Suzanna looked at him, curious about what would come next.

"I might be gone for a while."

Suzanna's eyebrows raised in surprise. James had only just returned from a week's skiing but now planned to go off again for *a while*. "Tell me more. Where and why?"

"I received word that my father's not well. He's been diagnosed with pancreatic cancer."

Suzanna reached across and took his hand, sympathising with her eyes. "What's the prognosis?"

"The cancer's been classified as Stage 4."

"What does that mean?"

"It can't be much worse. There's nothing they can do; his condition is terminal. They don't know how much longer he has to live. I'm booked on a plane to Singapore in the morning, then on to Sidney."

"I thought your father was in New Zealand?"

"Yes. He has a place in Arrowtown, on South Island. He had been in Wellington for his tests and consultation with specialists, but he's gone home now, to see out his last days. I catch another flight from Sidney into Queenstown. It's going to take about thirty-six hours to get there."

"Wow. That's a lot of travelling. Do you have any idea how long you'll be gone?"

"No. The partners in my company have agreed they'll cover for me, for however long I need to be away. He could die within days or weeks or could hang on for months. I'll play it by ear. I'll keep in contact, to let you know how it's going."

Suzanna squeezed his hand, stood and returned to the oven to check on dinner. As she opened the door, the fan oven blasted heat and herby tomato and bread aromas into the room. She served the pizza and they loaded their plates with salad. After eating his first mouthful of the pizza, James complimented her on producing a better pizza than any of the specialist restaurants in the city – the longer time in the oven and the extra toppings making all the difference. Their conversation lulled as they ate, but Suzanna reopened the subject of James' father as the meal ended. "I'm so sorry about your father, James. Have you had a good relationship with him?"

"He was a good dad in my younger years and through my teens. He supported me through university and professional training. We always got on well, but our relationship soured for a while after he left my mother. The split was devastating for her. They'd been together for over three decades and his leaving came out of the blue. He said he'd met someone else. That's why he's in New Zealand. His lover, now wife, is a Kiwi." His eyes focused beyond Suzanna as if something in the distance had grabbed his attention.

Then their eyes met again and he continued. "I grilled him over the reasons for leaving my mother and he explained they'd always held opposing views on many things. Their marriage had been stormy, but the friction had been well hidden from the children and suppressed when in other's company. After my younger brother left home, the glue of children dissolved and their differences magnified. Life together wasn't good. Mother forever nagged him about trivial things and he found her behaviour intolerable. Happiness became like the sun on a cloudy day – only rare glimpses shining through their mutual intolerance. Then someone else came into his life who brought him joy again."

Suzanna nodded, acknowledging, understanding. Relationships were fragile. So many marriages ended this way. Empty nesters drifting apart, looking for love elsewhere because it no longer existed at home. Time could chisel away at the bonds between two people until there was little left to keep them together.

Suzanna shared her parents' comments about marriage. "They said their life was like a walk across the Lake District fells. Periods of steep ascent, with pain and tiredness. At other times, it could be easy-going, exciting and beautiful. On those uphill sections, they felt like jumping off the fell, escaping into the lake's cool waters, but they resisted, determined to get through the challenges. The key to it, though, was communication. Talking, not bottling up their feelings."

"Your parents are wise people, Suzanna. I look forward to meeting them." James finished his glass of wine. "Thanks for supper. I'd better get back now. I have to be up at five."

"Can you not stay a *bit* longer?"

James checked his watch. He didn't want to leave but knew it was the right thing to do. "No. I really must go." They both stood. Suzanna walked him to the door, hugged him, wished him safe travels and told him to send regular updates.

She cleared the table and loaded the dishwasher, then sat on her sofa with the remains of her wine. She picked up the cloth bag, extracted the magnifying glass and peered through it at the lines on her other hand. A gipsy had once read her palm, but she couldn't remember which lines on her hand stood for life, love, fate, or health. She wondered what life had in store for her and whether it would always include James. She twizzled the glass between her fingers as she pondered. Whether or not James would always be with her, she knew life would be a little less full until his return.

Wednesday 11th March

Chapter 44

Suzanna arrived at work early, unsettled; something nagging at her. She placed her coffee on her desk and reclined her chair, staring at the ceiling for a while, noticing the astronomical plough pattern again before closing her eyes. She ran through the investigation, recalling her previous observations and their follow-ups. A thought burst into her mind.

She sat up straight, opened her eyes, then strode along the corridor to the main office. Rab was now sat at his desk and Caitlin was hanging up her coat. "Rab." He turned towards her. "Get in contact with the woman across the road, whose CCTV was inoperative. Ask her if she has a cleaner. If so, I want the name and address." She turned and marched out again. But then spun on her heels and returned to the office. Rab saw her re-enter the room, so was already looking at her in anticipation when she spoke. "Gabriela Albescu?"

"Ah! Yes. I planned to mention her, but you were too quick for me. I'll be heading out soon to give her the good news."

"The *really* good news?"

Rab nodded. Suzanna strode away again, looking happy. Before doing anything else, there was one job that just had to be done.

***

"Suzanna. What on earth are you doing stood on your desk, Alistair asked, frozen in mid-step, when passing her office doorway. He

254

admired her shapely figure as he waited for the answer, but his eyes didn't give away his thoughts, remaining fixed on her face, rather than scanning her full height.

"Flyblow, Alistair. I can't stand it any longer. There's a pattern of black spots on the ceiling that distracts my thoughts."

"Ah! That explains it. Just you take care now. We can't afford *you* to be off work with a broken leg, as well. And the bureaucracy of health and safety at work form filling is something I could do without."

"By the way, Alistair, have you heard anything about Una's likely return to work date?"

"Aye. I meant to mention it. She should be back next week. But we'll need to keep an eye on her, to make sure she doesn't go off challenging drug dealers by herself again."

"I think she'll have learned her lesson."

"Aye. In fact, she may be mentally fragile because of the stabbing. Maybe lost confidence in herself?"

"Anything on Angus' recovery?"

"He should be in next Monday as well but confined to office-based work initially. His leg will still be in plaster. At least you'll have a full deck of cards to play with again, even if a couple might be a little bent."

***

Murray rang the bell, stood back and waited for a response, the rain dripping off his coat. A woman dressed in grey jogging bottoms and a baggy sweatshirt opened the door. She was probably in her fifties, Murray reckoned. Might have been good looking in her younger days but was now overweight and unkempt. "Maureen Stevens?" he asked.

"Aye. I'm Maureen. And who are you?"

Murray held up his police warrant card. "DC Docherty. Can I have a word?"

"Aye, you'd best come in, constable." She turned and headed back towards her living room. "Put wood in hole, lad."

Murray complied, closing the door behind him, before hanging his coat on a peg by the door, rather than have it dripping everywhere. The flat smelled unventilated, the air stale. She'd already sat in a chair at her small dining table, its surface scratched from decades of wear and marked by rings from hot drinks. "Take the weight off your feet, constable," she said, indicating a second chair opposite her. He pulled out the offered chair, its legs squeaking across the vinyl floor. "Good weather for slugs, eh? It never seems to stop raining in Edinburgh, does it?"

"Funny you should say that. It seems that way. The city's reputed for being wet. But I heard the other day that Edinburgh's rainfall is well below Scotland's average. And, even more surprisingly, the rainfall is far below that of New York and Rome. Amazing, eh?" Murray sat and withdrew his notepad, before re-engaging with Maureen. "I need to speak with you about your time at Butler & Cargrove?"

"Why on earth would you want to talk about a place that I worked at three decades ago?"

"I'll get to that. For the record, please confirm your full name."

"It's Maureen Patricia Stevens."

"Maureen. I understand you worked at Butler and Cargrove for approximately two years, leaving in 1985."

"Aye, that's right."

"During your time there, did you notice anything about the behaviour of other employees, inappropriate conduct, perhaps?"

She didn't answer at once. "The manager was a bit of a creep. Some of the other girls said he would *accidentally* touch them – you know, their breast and bottoms."

"Can you remember which of your colleagues had mentioned this?"

"Most of them."

"But not you?"

"No, he never troubled me. I don't know why. Maybe he didn't fancy me?"

"Why did you leave in 1985, Maureen?"

"I got an offer of a better job, closer to home."

Murray nodded, accepting the logic of it. "Do you have any children, Maureen?"

She looked puzzled at this new line of questioning. "Aye, but I never see them. Don't even know where they live or even if they're alive."

"Why's that?"."

"After my husband left me, I had a breakdown. Lost my job. Lost my home, then the Social took away the kids. They got adopted. I couldn't cope with them."

"I'm sad to hear that, Maureen. Why did your husband leave you?"

"We just fell out. Couldn't stand living together. Argued all the time. He walked out on me, leaving me with the kids and no support."

"Maureen. I'd like to take you back to March 1985 – the 31st to be precise. You were seen that day leaving work long after all others in your department had left. Shortly after Mr White. You looked a mess and you'd obviously been crying. Why was that?"

"You're asking me about something that happened thirty years ago. I don't remember. Why would I?"

"Because it was evidently an emotional event. One that you'd probably remember." Murray could see the cogs of her mind churning. He wondered whether she was trying to remember the event or whether she might be trying to make up circumstances to hide the real reason.

She paused again. "That might be the day when I fell ill. Something I ate, I suppose. Had to run to the ladies before I left work. I remember throwing up in the toilet. Some of it missed the loo and when I got up, I slipped and fell, bruising my knees. That's why I'd have been crying."

"I see. Thanks for the explanation. What was the name of your next employer after you left Butler and Cargrove?"

"It was a small firm. In the Shandon area. The Brewery."

"The one on Slateford Road?"

"Aye, that's the one."

"One final question: where were you between 7:30 am and 9 am on March 3rd?"

"Tuesday, last week... On my way to, and then at, my client's house on Belford Road. I get the bus from around the corner, then walk. I start at 8 o'clock, as the client's leaving for work. They don't want to give me a key."

Murray completed his note taking. "Thanks for your cooperation, Ms Stevens. I think I have enough for the moment. I'll let myself out." He took his coat from the hook and walked away into the drizzle.

When Murray had moved from uniformed PC to detective constable, he had been excited by the prospect of tracking down criminals and ensuring they were locked up for many years. But he was beginning to regret his decision. The team had a good reputation for convicting criminals. But the work was mainly tedious research and evidence gathering. He missed the buzz of being on the streets at night with colleagues, the adrenaline tearing through his veins as he tackled violent offenders, cuffed them and bundled them into police vehicles – taken off the street for a while. He missed the satisfaction of protecting the innocent from abuse and being hugged by old ladies, grateful when he'd reassured them after a burglary. He missed the bumpy ride of emotions; the drug that made life thrilling, worthwhile. Perhaps he'd ask for a transfer back to uniform?

As he fastened his seatbelt, he imagined what Emily would say if he went back on the beat. She'd not like him being back on shift work, having to sleep alone many nights and regularly seeing his face bruised and cut after fights with drunken thugs. He started his car and drove off, uncertain what to do.

***

Rab drove to the end of Craig Lockhart Terrace and parked. According to the schedule, she'd soon emerge from the central door, seen easily from his car. No need to stand around in the cold rain. The retirement apartments' architecture suggested it had been built in the 1990s. They were still fresh and the grounds well cared for. He remembered his grandparents had bought a similar apartment a few years back – advertised as for over 55s, but rarely occupied by anyone so young.

He'd been amazed that they'd paid so much for their one-bedroom flat, with a single living room and a small kitchen. They could have bought a three-bed semi with a driveway, garage and gardens for the same money – what a rip-off! But they seemed happy where they were. He guessed it was not about the money, so much as the lifestyle that was important to them. Their bodies had become too fragile to maintain a garden and they didn't need spare bedrooms, because all their close family lived nearby, so could visit without overnighting. Their neighbours would be of their own age group. A quiet place, with no kids kicking balls against their front wall, no dogs barking, no drunks singing slurred songs as they staggered past on their way home. It was a place where they could feel safe.

The door opened, and Gabriela emerged. Rab went to meet her and invited her back to his car for a quick chat. He'd hung a zesty lemon air freshener from the mirror to cover any remaining stench in the car's seats – a little too zesty. She looked worried. "Gabriela. I wanted to inform you in person, as I was the one who interviewed you the other day. We've now had the forensics."

Gabriela looked curious but still concerned. Rab continued. "We now believe you were not involved in the murder of George White. I'm sorry for the worry this may have caused you." Gabriela's brow stayed crinkled; her eyebrows squashed together.

"When you tell company about theft? How long I have my job?" She asked.

"My boss, DCI McLeod, and I discussed this matter at length. Had

259

you not taken money from George's bank after his death, meaning that we would need to charge you with theft, it would have been easier for us to not mention your criminal record in Romania."

Gabriela's eyes welled up, anticipating bad news. "We believed what you told us about poverty and desperation driving the theft in Romania, and you were punished for that crime. We would not wish to see you punished twice." Gabriela's features softened a little. "We also believe you were entitled to the money you took from Mr White's account. So, I spoke with George White's son yesterday and explained what had happened. He would have been notified about the withdrawal by his solicitor. He agreed *not* to press charges." Rab smiled as he broke the news.

It took a few seconds for it to sink in, then Gabriela's face smiled tentatively. "So, you no charge me with theft?"

"No Gabriela. No charge."

"But still you tell care company. I lose my job."

"Gabriela. Given the circumstances, my boss and I will be forgetful. We will not inform your employer about the Romanian theft. You will not lose your job." He smiled more brightly as he watched Gabriela beam back. She leapt forward, grabbed his head and planted a kiss on his cheek.

"You lovely policeman. Not like Romanian police. You make me very happy. Thank you, sir." She pulled away, opened the door and virtually skipped along the path, off to her next client.

Rab was sure they'd made the right decision. He just hoped the Chief Super never heard about what they'd done.

Chapter 45

"Nice place, the Old Ferry Boat inn," the taxi driver said, after Mairi had climbed in at the railway station and she'd pulled away into Huntingdon's traffic. "Right on the banks of the River Ouse. Nice food as well."

"Good to know. I'll probably only be there for an hour or so. Can I order a return taxi with you?" Mairi liked having a woman driver and an E-Class Mercedes.

"I'll check my calendar when we get there, luv, but it should be fine. A flying visit then!"

"Yes. A business trip. A quick chat with someone, then back to Edinburgh."

"What business you in, luv?"

"Let's just say it's official, government work."

The driver tapped the side of her nose. "Hush, hush stuff, eh! Mum's the word."

A quietness fell in the cab now the driver had hit a dead end on her questions. Mairi looked out at the flat Cambridgeshire countryside, the sky mostly blue, scattered with fluffy clouds like melting snow on thinning ice. Trees lined the road on both sides and green fields lay beyond – like lush grass. But no cows or sheep grazed these fields. She wondered what this land's produce would be.

They travelled out through Hartford and bypassed Wyton, reaching

St Ives a few minutes later. She'd heard the town was quaint, but she saw nothing of it from the A1123 as they passed through its outskirts.

There were fewer trees this side of St Ives and Mairi noticed the greenery in the fields was not grass but root vegetable tops. She strained to see what they were but couldn't tell. They said this part of England was the most productive farming area in the country. She guessed the vegetables would be potatoes or sugar beet. One field they passed was definitely onions.

They entered Needingworth and turned right for Holywell, following the road to its end. The driver pulled up next to the thatched-roofed, white-painted building, its beer garden picnic benches empty now, waiting for the warmer months before the customers would spill out onto its riverside lawn.

"Will ninety minutes be long enough for you, luv," the driver asked as she checked her diary. "I've one other job booked and need to take a quick break."

Mairi paid her for the journey. "Yes, that should be sufficient." She exited the taxi and strolled across to the inn, ducking to get through its low door. Looking across the room, Mairi saw a woman sitting in a corner alcove seat, away from the bar. Christine looked much like her driver's licence photo – thin-faced, with a prominent chin and long nose – except she had a few more grey hairs and lines on her face. She waved to her, then turned to the hovering barmaid to order a drink and some food.

***

"Christine Robins?" Mairi enquired for confirmation before sitting. Christine nodded. "I hope you can talk freely here. I need to ask you some rather personal questions."

The policewoman seemed nice. "Yes. I understand. We should be fine. If it gets crowded, we can go outside and if it's too chilly, walk along the river. Thanks for meeting me here. I didn't want my husband or neighbours to know I'd had a caller. They might ask why?"

"I understand." She paused. "Listen, I've spoken with your cousin, Sheila White, and she mentioned you had visited their family home when you were in your teens."

"Yes. I got on well with Sheila, even though she was a couple of years younger than me. My mother saw me on the train at Peterborough. Sheila and her mum met me in Edinburgh. I remember being excited at the prospect of gallivanting around Edinburgh with my cousin. The towns around here are tiny and rather boring, it has to be said. Peterborough's a decent size, but there's little history there. I used to be keen on history in my schooldays. Studied it through to A level." Christine felt at ease talking to the detective. Like chatting with an old friend.

"Tell me about your stay with the Whites."

"It was lovely. Everything I expected. Their house was fairly central, so Sheila and I walked into the city's Old Town, with its grand cathedral and wonderful castle. It was a dream for me. And plenty of excellent shops to spend my holiday savings on."

"How did you get on with Mr White, Uncle George?"

"Oh! He seemed charming when I arrived. Handsome. Lovely smile. Eyes that seemed to look right into your soul." She paused, remembering. "But a few days into the holiday, it was spoiled."

"Why was that?"

"Sheila had a doctor's appointment. Her mother had to take her and her brother, Ed, was out with his friends. Uncle George had a day off work. He invited me into his study to look at his excellent collection of books on Edinburgh. After a while of flipping through pictures of the historic buildings, things changed."

Christine shuddered as she recalled what had happened next. "He said I'd been flirting with him – which I couldn't deny. It was that time of life when one needed to be sure that the opposite sex found one attractive. Uncle George said it was mischievous of me to do so and shameful that I wore such a short skirt. He said naughty girls must be punished, then pulled me over his lap and started spanking me lightly. It was fun at first. I knew he shouldn't be doing it, but I liked it and, as I said, I fancied him. I wasn't a virgin."

Christine paused as the memories returned. "The idea of sex with a mature man instead of a fumbling teenage boy excited me. So I didn't stop him when he lifted my skirt and pulled down my knickers. He smacked me again – still gently. He laughed. 'That's more like it, you naughty girl. Take that and that,' he said as he playfully spanked me."

She paused again. "I became excited. Tingling. But I realised it would be wrong to have sex with my uncle. And what if Ed or Sheila came home with my aunt? I said we should stop. It wasn't right. He said, 'Nonsense. You need to be punished'. He spanked me harder, then stood and forced me face-down over the arm of the sofa. He dropped his trousers and said something like, 'You know you want this, Christine. That's why you've flirted with me, came into my study and let me spank you.' I tried to get up and pleaded with him to release me but his hand on my back was holding me down. Then he raped me."

She stopped speaking, tears filling her eyes, then trickling from the corners as the memories returned. "I felt ashamed to have let him handle me, to have allowed him to betray his wife. That night, I called my mum and arranged to go home. I said I wasn't enjoying myself and wanted to leave. The next day, Mrs White put me on the train. She asked me why I was leaving early, but I lied to her as well, saying I was missing my boyfriend."

Mairi leaned across the table, placing her hand on Christine's, empathising with her. "Did you tell anyone about the rape?"

"No. I've kept it to myself. I shouldn't have let it happen. I had flirted with him. It was my fault. I don't think my mum would have believed me, anyway. She thought I was far too promiscuous."

Mairi responded gently but passionately. "Christine. It wasn't your fault. No man has the right to sex with a woman unless they also want it. It's rape. It's a criminal offence." Mairi paused. "Did you ever go to the White's home again?"

Christine shook her head. "Never."

"Have you ever seen George White since that day?"

"Just the once. I received an invitation to Edmond's wedding. It must have been ten years later. I'd got over the experience. I'd married and had a toddler and baby, so I believed I would cope with seeing him. And I love weddings. The beautiful dresses, the food and wine. The music and dancing, and lots of drunken catch-up chats with distant family and friends."

"And did you – cope?"

"Yes. Even when he cornered me near the hotel bar and whispered to me. 'Would you like to come to my room for a bit of fun?'"

"I stamped on his foot. A tiny act of revenge. And told him I was no longer a malleable fifteen-year-old and he should bugger off. He looked sad. Disappointed. As if he expected me to want to be raped again. But he said nothing more, turned and limped away. That was the last conversation I had with Uncle George."

"It's looking increasingly likely that whoever killed George White was avenging his abuse of them. We don't know whom yet, but we will find them. As an officer of the law, I have to be glad to catch his killer, but part of me thinks he brought it on himself and that his early demise is justice."

The detective's revelation surprised Christine but she agreed with her. "Yes. I suppose you're right. How many young women will have been abused over the years by that man? I don't expect we'll ever know. Someone's life must have been massively affected by him for them to seek vengeance so late in his life. Surely it couldn't have been a recent victim? At his age!"

"We keep an open mind about such matters. Is there anything else that might help us understand what happened or who might have killed him?"

The officer sat quietly as Christine's mind rolled around, digging up memories of contact with George White and conversations that mentioned him. "I noticed Sheila stayed away from him throughout the wedding and reception. She was on the table next to me and I never once noticed her even acknowledge her father, let alone converse with him or connect physically."

"That doesn't surprise me," Mairi said, saying no more, but the connection between the two women confirmed to Christine what she suspected. "Here's my card. If anything else comes to mind, please call me. However trivial the thought might be. It might be important."

Mairi's lunch arrived at the same time as Christine's, despite them having been ordered at different times. Both had ordered battered haddock and chips. The chips were lightly browned, crisp on the outside and soft inside – perfect. She squeezed lemon over the fish before biting into its tasty white flesh. As they ate, they chatted about the quaintness of the inn and the lovely riverside scenery. Despite George White having raped Christine at fifteen, she'd not let the event damage her life. She told the detective she'd had a good life with a loving family and a rewarding career as a solicitor.

Christine stared out of the pub window, watching the taxi drive away, carrying the personable policewoman, her mind unsettled by sharing with DC Gordon. But her faith in the police had been restored by the young officer. She seemed so caring, so human, so trustworthy and determined to seek justice.

Chapter 46

"Ah! Ma'am. I have the name of the cleaner you were after." Rab had noticed his boss passing through the office. "It's Maureen McIntyre. Do you want her interviewed about the CCTV power lead?"

"Yes please, Rab. If she had moved the CCTV hub, that would explain it. If not, we need another reason for it being disconnected." She paused again. "Might the neighbour have a motive? Husband or wife. Background checks, please, Rab." Suzanna continued her journey out of the main office.

"McLeod. My office," came the raised voice from the office Suzanna had just passed. Her eyebrows raised automatically as she heard the call. She about-faced and retraced her steps.

"Yes, sir."

"I've just seen the bills for DC Gordon's trip to Iona. Surely the locals could have interviewed her?"

"There are no resident police on Iona, Sir. The Highlands and Islands division visited the island to break the news to Miss White, but they failed to confirm her whereabouts on the day of her father's murder. I needed to ensure our questions were put to her by someone I trusted."

"We should be able to trust anyone in the force. Police Scotland officers all pass the same entry criteria and receive the same training. It's wasteful for us to travel into other regions when there are people closer, capable of doing the work."

"Sir, the locals had already failed us and the travel costs weren't that much."

"It all adds up, McLeod. It all adds up."

"Well, you'd best know now, before you find out, that Gordon has also travelled to Cambridgeshire to interview one of White's relatives."

"I refuse to believe you couldn't have obtained the same information from the Cambridgeshire force. Unnecessary spending again, McLeod. If this carries on, I'll have to insist that no travel takes place without my explicit approval."

"It might have been possible for us to obtain the same information by asking the local force, but I couldn't guarantee they'd respond in the same timescale. Mairi's confirmed what we suspected: White used to be a prolific sexual predator, who raped his daughter, niece and probably a number of people who worked under his control. I'm certain the murder of George White was premeditated; cold-blooded. We've learned from experience that murderers like that can get a taste for it. There's a risk of further murders if we don't catch them soon."

"Yes. Well. There's truth in what you say. But did you try to get assistance from the local force, instead of assuming their response might be slower? You can't go spending money, having your team gallivanting around the UK without ensuring the journey is necessary, not merely preferable."

"Right, sir. And should I contact you to check if it's okay, whatever day or time it might be?"

"There's no need for that yet. But I might need to introduce such measures if you continue to overspend the travel and subsistence budget. Do I make myself clear?"

"Yes, sir. Abundantly." She turned to leave.

"Oh! And another thing. I understand your team is using commercial communication systems for official business?"

Suzanna looked at him, puzzled.

"I'm told you are using something called What's App. We can't have official business conducted by insecure methods like that. You'll be using Facebook next to arrange raids." He stared at her, challenging her to respond.

"Sir. WhatsApp may be a commercial system, but so are telephones. Besides, the application uses end-to-end message encryption, so communications cannot be intercepted. I'm not sure even GCHQ can tap into the system. There's a near-zero risk of using WhatsApp and it helps us stay in contact and up to speed on progress and locations. I see no harm in that."

"I'll look into that, McLeod. If I find it's not as secure as you say, I'll ban you from using it."

Suzanna turned and marched away, faced puckered in annoyance at the man's penny-pinching attitude and interference. Everyone knew WhatsApp was secure – especially the criminals.

***

Owen banged on the flat door, pressed the bell push-button, then stood back, the uniformed female officer just behind his left shoulder. The door opened, so he stepped forward, holding up his police warrant card. "DC Crawford, Edinburgh CID. I need a word."

The girl tried to close the door, but he advanced again, his shoe inhibiting its closure. He pushed forward, his strength overcoming the girl's resistance. "No need to be afraid. I'm here to help you." The girl released the door and ran back into the flat's living room, shouting 'police'. As Owen walked into the room, three girls were stuffing items under seats and into bags, out of sight. Drugs, he guessed.

There were magazines scattered around, dirty coffee mugs on the table and empty drinks bottles on the carpeted floor – a carpet that probably hadn't been cleaned in years. A kitchenette was tucked into the room's corner, the sink overflowing with dirty dishes and the stove covered in used saucepans.

The female PC closed the outer door and followed Owen into the room. It smelled of perfume, weed, and dried baked beans. Owen spoke again. "Girls, please sit. I'm here to speak to you, not arrest you." They looked up at him, still suspicious, untrusting. "I need to know who's who?" He read out a list of names from his notepad and they all responded like children in class at the beginning of a school day.

By the end of this exercise, they had settled and perched on the edge of their seats, still tense. "I'm going to ask you all to come into the police station with us to make statements about how you came to be in Edinburgh. Who brought you here? And what work you have been doing since you arrived?" The girls looked worried.

"We have your passports. They were locked in a safe by your controllers. These people are now in custody and will soon be charged. They won't be able to rule your lives anymore."

One girl started crying and talking in her home language. Another consoled her. The female PC, Anna, spoke. "Why is she crying? We're here to help."

The third girl spoke. "She is happy. Now she can go home to parents. She says she like Prodigal Son. Parents no want her to come here. She hopes they take her back when she returns."

Anna smiled reassuringly. "I'm sure they will." Anna looked at Owen before continuing. "Please change into clothes suitable for the police station (they were dressed for work), then we can go."

Chapter 47

Murray had seen that walk before. He recognised her figure, her hair and the profile of her head. Could it be her?

The rain had stopped, so he'd stepped out of his car and walked to the corner of the narrow road in the Abbeyhill district to wait for the uniformed guys to arrive. That's when he noticed the woman walking towards him and the memory flashed into his mind. She turned and walked along the path towards a house, disappearing from sight.

The officers gathered at the door on their tasking list. Murray hoped this was the house she'd entered. He hesitated, wondering how she would react if she opened the door and saw him standing there. The uniformed PC stepped forward and knocked on the door, then stood back.

A short white woman appeared when the door opened. She wasn't elegant and beautiful like the woman he'd hoped to see. Her hair was a mess, her clothes were sloppy and she wore no makeup. Perhaps it was the next house that she'd entered. The woman spoke with a Glaswegian accent, "Whaddya want."

Murray glanced at his list of names and guessed which one she would be. "Are you Shona McDonald?"

"Aye, I am. What's it to you? I've done nothing wrong."

"Shona. We have news for you and the other women you share with. Can we come in, please?"

271

"Na. You can tell me. I'll pass it on."

He glanced down at her arms and noticed puncture marks, old and new, tracking up the veins like a line of angry bee stings. He knew what had caused them. She noticed where his eyes had flicked to and pulled her arms behind her back, out of sight. "We need to inform all of you together, and the street is not the place to do it."

"Just a minute." Shona slipped back inside, closing the door, but returned shortly after. "It's okay, you can come in, but only to speak. No searching. Right?"

"Yes. We're not here looking for anything. We need to speak with you." Shona stepped back. And walked into the room. Murray peeked at the list again. If she were here, what would be her name? He didn't see it on the list, but there was one possibility. He stepped inside, followed by the other PC.

"There are four of you living here?" Murray asked.

"Aye. It's a bit cramped. There's only two bedrooms. We're bunked up. But beggars can't be choosers, can they?"

"Are all the girls here?"

Shona shouted up the stairs. "Hey. We're waiting for ya. Come on doon." One woman emerged from the back room – the kitchen. Like Shona, she looked dishevelled and was white, about 18 or 19 years old. She wasn't the young woman Murray had glimpsed earlier. The girl sat next to Shona.

Another girl descended the stairs, followed by a second. Could it be, he hoped, as her legs came into sight? The first girl wore jeans and a hoodie, with pink fluffy slippers on her feet. She moved to the other sofa, exposing the fourth woman. Murray's eyes met hers and her mouth dropped open. "Murray!" She said.

"Anika!" Murray responded. "Or should I call you by your real name, Nakula Bal?"

She was as beautiful as Murray remembered when he'd met her last month in the restaurant, although not as smartly dressed or made up. He'd met with her when trying to identify the *Washed-up Woman*. She only stayed with him long enough to inform him South Asian escorts wouldn't wear a Sari when working. He'd given her his card and told her to contact him if she wanted out... She hadn't.

"Have you tracked me to this house? Are you here to arrest me?" Nakula asked.

"No. Nothing like that. As I told your friend," – Nakula's face suggested there was no friendship between her and Shona – "we have some news that affects you all." He told them Maria and Nikolay were in custody. They would be safe now and he wanted them to come into the police station to make statements.

"You'll need to do better than that. There's not just two of them," Nakula responded. "What about the others: Andrei, Etrit and Iqbal?"

"We also have Andrei Draganov and Etrit Berisha in custody. But we don't know this Iqbal. If you tell us where he lives and what his role is, we will arrest him, too."

"His role? He's a bastard." Shona said. "That's what he is. He beats us. He threatens us with a knife and he screws us when he fancies. But he also looks after my needs if you ken what I mean?" she said, bringing her inner arms back into view.

He frowned. Nakula looked concerned. Murray wondered what had tethered *her* to this organisation, to work as an escort, to sell her gorgeous body daily to strangers. There were no track marks on *her* arms and she wasn't dishevelled – far from it. Nakula looked the angel he'd seen before – the one who'd mesmerised him as she paraded towards his table, like a cat-walk model.

The female PC noticed Murray's lack of focus, so took the lead. "We'll need you all to come with us, so we can take statements and work out, for each of you, how we can help you get back to normal life." She turned to Shona. "We can get you a place in rehab if you like." Shona didn't respond. "We've two cars outside. Please change, if you need to, into something suitable for sitting around for a while. And you'll probably need a coat."

Shona's face crunched up, annoyed that the policewoman was speaking to them like children. She didn't need some cop to tell her she needed a coat! The three girls stood and went to their rooms to prepare for the future. Nakula remained. "Murray," she purred, her South Asian heritage subtly influencing her Scottish accent, "Is this a twist of fate or did you follow me?"

"I'd like to say that I sought you out, investigated your circumstances and planned to get you released from whatever bondage you're in, but I have to admit that seeing you here today is merely a coincidence. A surprise. This is an offshoot from another case we're working on."

Her eyes remained fixed on Murray, boring into him as she acknowledged what he'd told her. Unless she wanted to dress down and make herself look less stunning, she had no reason to change her clothes. She sat there, looking lovely (Murray lulled into inaction) until the other girls returned. Nakula stood. "I am ready to go with you."

***

Armed with two coffees, Suzanna entered the Superintendent's office, closing the door after her. "I thought you'd best know that the Chief Super's on his high horse about travel and subsistence expenditure again. He's complaining about Mairi going to Iona to interview White's daughter and to Cambridgeshire to speak with White's niece. Both, as suspected, had been abused by White – the daughter raped multiple times over several years."

"Hmm. Justice finally caught up with George White, perhaps. A pity it was not formal justice, though... Look, don't worry about Ewan's little rants about budgets. It's par for the course. He gets a lot of pressure about budgets from above. But perhaps you could give a little more consideration to such matters? Maybe there are ways of achieving the same results at less cost? If, or rather when, you move up a rank or two, you'll soon find out how much of the working day is focussed on statistics and finances."

"Okay, Alistair. Point taken," she said, reluctantly accepting his advice. "I just wish he would question my methods more tactfully, instead of playing the headmaster-pupil game all the time. It's not like I'm a rookie. He can't even be ten years older than me and certainly not a generation. I don't understand why he talks down to me like he does. He knows I get results."

"Aye. I have to agree. I'd not dream of speaking to you the way he does. But as I mentioned before, you don't have to put up with him for much longer." A knock came on the door and the Superintendent called out, "come."

Mairi peaked around the door. "I was hoping I'd find you here, ma'am."

Chapter 48

Maria was being represented by Martin Sweetman – his name a misnomer. "Mr Sweetman." Suzanna nodded to the hard-nosed, bolshie lawyer, not looking forward to the interview. Mairi sat beside her and switched on the recorder.

"Before we start. Ms Angalova was arrested on suspicion of the murder of George White, but now you appear to be questioning her on other charges. If you wish to question my client on these other matters, you will need to rescind the murder accusation and caution her on these other charges," Sweetman said.

"Thank you for the suggestion, Mr Sweetman," Suzanna said calmly, not wishing to ramp up confrontation so early in the interview. "Having carried out further investigations, we are now satisfied your client probably did not murder George White – although the possibility remains open. Based on the evidence we now have, we must consider other charges related to trafficking, coercion and living off prostitution. My colleague will now issue the formal caution relating to these matters."

After Mairi finished the formalities, Suzanna began questioning Maria. "Three women have already made statements implicating you in their trafficking from Eastern European countries, holding their passports so they cannot return home or obtain any other employment, collusion with four men who raped and beat these women and the supply of illegal drugs. What do you say to these accusations?"

"All lies."

"When asked previously, you denied holding these women's passports. Yet we accessed the safe in your flat and found the passports. If anyone is lying, it is you, Maria." Maria sat unresponsive, with folded arms and a stern face.

Sweetman interjected. "There is no proof the passports were placed into the safe by my client, nor that she had access to the safe. It was, after all, located in a cupboard in Mr Petrov's room."

Suzanna responded. "The passports of the women under Ms Angalova's control are currently being checked for prints by the forensics team. I am confident her prints will be found on those passports."

"Fingerprints on the passports would merely confirm she handled them. She would need to do this to note their details in employment records. It would not prove she had placed them in the safe," Sweetman responded.

"Prints have also been taken from the safe that Maria denied knowledge of. A safe that she evidently knew was in Petrov's bedroom. If her prints are matched with the safe, it will prove yet again that she is a liar and was involved in holding these passports to control the women working as prostitutes."

'Sweetman held a whispered discussion with his client before responding to Suzanna's accusations.' "My client has recalled she used the safe on one occasion but had forgotten its existence. She certainly did not place the passports into the safe and she denies holding them to have control over the women whom she coordinated. Women who worked as masseuses and escorts, not prostitutes."

"We are informed by the women we've interviewed, and some clients, that the women were indeed sex workers and that Ms Angalova knew their business. In fact, it was Ms Angalova that negotiated services and charges with new clients. There is no doubt Maria was fully aware and involved in the prostitution business." Silence followed the statement as Suzanna considered her next move. Like a game of chess, she must influence the responses of her opponent and open vulnerabilities in her defence.

"Look, Maria," Suzanna said, looking at her compassionately. "There is significant evidence you coordinated the work of these women, certainly enough for you to be convicted. The Procurator Fiscal has already agreed you should be charged with this offence. But, Maria, I am not convinced you were party to the trafficking of the women or complicit in the beatings and rapes. If you cooperate with me, providing evidence against the men who abused the women – and perhaps you too – I will not recommend charges against you on those offences."

Suzanna had offered Maria a choice, deny it all and perhaps become convicted of all charges, with a resulting lengthy prison sentence or give evidence against the men, to restrict the charges against her and her time in jail. She hoped Maria would take the opportunity. It would make life easier for her team and the prosecutors and speed justice.

"Your clumsy attempt to manipulate my client into a confession on the prostitution charges is pathetic, chief inspector," Sweetman said, sneering. "She will have her day in court and I will cast doubt on the evidence you have gathered. There is no hard proof my client knew of the work the women carried out behind closed doors. No recordings of conversations. Just the word of unreliable witnesses, who have turned against her so they may be dealt with more leniently."

Suzanna stood. "Fair enough, Mr Sweetman. I know you love the drama of court and the income it will generate for you. You have your day," she said, looking into Maria's eyes, "but Maria will be the one doing extra time in prison when *you fail*. She will be the person who suffers because of *your* overconfidence, pride and greed."

Sweetman responded harshly, "How dare you suggest I would take any action that wasn't in my client's best interest!"

But Maria had seen the passion in the detective's voice and felt her genuine concern for her. The solicitor seemed to be a shallow, self-interested person. It was true, she did not condone the women's abuse and had not arranged their travel to the UK. This British detective could see this. Maria turned, placed her hand on her solicitor's arm and spoke. "I wish to cooperate."

***

As she walked past the parked Porsche, she resisted the temptation to stab the soft-top roof, to plunge in a knife as he had plunged his penis into each of those seven women - to enact some early revenge for his victims. Gerard Templeton opened the door as she approached, catching her by surprise. Must have been looking out for her. Just as well she didn't slash his car roof. He shook her hand, his grip strong and his palm damp, before inviting her into the house.

The man looked much like the picture she'd seen in the papers and the glimpses of him being rushed into and out of court. About 50, she reckoned, similar to her own age. Long blond wavy hair, like a surfer's, with a sprinkling of grey throughout. He was muscular, suggesting it would have been easy for him to overpower the women. She wondered what profession he followed. How he earned his money. Mr Templeton seemed pleasant enough. If she didn't know differently, she'd never have suspected he had assaulted the seven women.

"Come in. Come in." He switched the kettle on. "Tea? Coffee?

She chose tea. He made himself a coffee, adding two spoons of sugar, she noted. They chatted as they drank. Strangely, he didn't ask her much about herself. He focussed on what he wanted her to do. After they'd finished their drinks, he showed her around his home. Unironed clothes were piled haphazardly on the dining table. A musty odour emanated from the utility room. The laundry basket desperately needed emptying and perhaps its cloth liner could do with a wash.

Although the kitchen floor may have been swept lately, it was evidently overdue a mopping. The bathroom sink had a line of scum around it and the shower glass screen was covered in dried-on soap splashes. The whole house had been neglected.

She suggested four hours in the first week if she could fit it in, to catch up on the backlog; after which she could drop back to two each week. Thursday afternoons were available if that would work for him. He said any weekday would be good. They agreed on a price and he gave her a key to let herself into the house. "So I don't get in your way, when are you normally away from the house?"

"I'm usually out by eight each weekday morning and home by six."

"If I need to get hold of you during the day, where would I find you?"

He dug a business card out of his wallet and handed it to her. "I own the *Stay Fit* gym in Murrayfield."

That would account for the Porsche and the muscles. Probably looks at himself in every mirror he passes. Poser! She left, promising to return the following day for her first two hours. On her way home, she reflected on this first visit. Templeton was not as clever as she'd thought. He'd not done any checks on her and had given her his key. He hadn't even asked for any ID or her address. Perhaps she would find some valuables to steal and sell after taking his life. The money would come in useful and no one would know the items were missing. Now she could start planning his torture and execution.

Sitting on a homebound bus, the answer came to her. She could buy some of that date-rape drug, Rohypnol, wasn't it? And stay on until his return home, slipping it into the coffee she'd pour him. Then he'd be at her mercy, as the women had been at his. She could violate him before plunging a knife into his heart as she'd done to George White. She smiled at the thought of it. Chuckled. A fellow traveller looked at her strangely, probably wondering what was going through her mind. If only they knew!

Chapter 49

The aromas of baked bread, cheese and herbs wafted ahead of them as Rab walked into the room, followed by the DCI and Superintendent Milne, their hands laden with takeaway pizzas. "Anyone hungry?" Suzanna asked. They spread them on the table and opened the lids. "Tuck in guys," she said. "It's been a long day." There were smiles all around.

Having brought in eleven women and taken statements, the team had gathered together in the main office for a debrief, at Suzanna's request. Officers from nearby stations had rounded up another seven women because the CID team didn't have the capacity.

They scoffed pizza as they talked through the day's events. Social Services had been called in to assist the women and caseworkers were now talking with them. Several wanted help with getting permission to work in the UK and some wanted to go home. Others had accepted the offer of help with their drug problems. Suzanna hoped Social Services could find rehab places for those girls. From what she'd heard, there was a severe shortage of places and occasional drug counselling was no substitution for full-time rehab. She wished the government would put more resources into drug rehabilitation, given the cost to society of drug-motivated crime and the huge expense to the taxpayer of prison places.

Murray finished a mouthful of pepperoni pizza, then mentioned the woman he'd first known as Anika but knew was called Nakula. "One of the women I brought in was the escort I'd met when we were investigating the Washed-up Woman case. She was the one who'd told me that escorts would never wear saris when working." He paused, looking for and finding acknowledgement in his colleagues' eyes. "She shared with me about how she'd ended up as an escort."

Everyone fixed their eyes on Murray, like cats waiting for the next movement of a dangling toy. "She said an old unmaintained gas boiler in their bathroom poisoned her mother with carbon monoxide while she lay in the bath. She'd fallen into a deathly sleep. Nakula's father drove buses and his wife had looked after the home. He couldn't cook or manage the house and children. Eventually, the bairns were placed into care. Farmed out to foster homes."

"At sixteen," Murray continued, "Nakula was taken from her foster family and moved into *independent living.* They dumped her in a multi-occupancy house with older girls and men who'd graduated from the care system. She got dragged into drugs and forced into prostitution to pay for the drugs. It was Iqbal who'd controlled her. It's Iqbal who's needing arrested now."

As the pizza munching ended, the superintendent spoke, addressing the whole team. "Folks. I want you to know how pleased I am with your work on this human trafficking case, in parallel with trying to track down George White's killer. Today's results will change the lives of these women; bring them the freedom they deserve. DCI McLeod has already acted on advice to arrest Iqbal Agha and we've just heard he's in custody. He gave uniform a bit of run-around. But they have him locked up. We'll let him stew tonight and question him in the morning."

Suzanna also praised the team, then instructed them to go home and be back in at eight o'clock, sharp. They looked at the watches: half-past eight!

***

Mairi arrived home at 9 pm to a dark, cold, quiet flat. It's what she had expected. She turned on the lights, pressed the button to bring on the central heating for an hour, then made a mug of decaf coffee. It was too late to drink caffeinated. The journey home had been uneventful, unlike her return from Oban. Scotland's problems with heavy drinking seemed to have worsened over the years, rather than diminished. She'd hardly ever seen daytime drunkards when visiting English towns and cities, apart from those who were homeless, but it was all too common in Scotland. She'd heard news reports that on average Scots drank 25% more alcohol than the English or Welsh. Was it the whisky, she wondered?

Then there were the drug problems. One of the worst records in Europe – with death from drug abuse three times higher than England and Wales. She pondered why that would be but couldn't come up with an answer. She rotated her ring – still an alien on her finger. It hadn't yet become normal to her and, in a way, she hoped it wouldn't. She enjoyed feeling that Brodie loved her enough to tie the knot, to commit to spending the rest of his life with her. It made her feel wanted, loved and secure.

***

At 2 am, Mairi awakened to the sound of someone crashing around in the kitchen. She leapt out of bed, swung open the door and marched along the short corridor. Brodie was staggering, his eyes blurred, bumping into doors and walls and knocking items onto the floor as he attempted to navigate the furniture. Mairi rolled her eyes. Before bed she'd been contemplating Scotland's drink problem and here was her fiancé demonstrating that same behaviour. She grabbed his arm. "You bloody idiot, Brodie. What are you doing coming home so late and in this state?" He stank of beer and whisky.

He shrugged off her arm, slurring. "I did'nae have much to drink.

I can get myself to bed. Nae bother." He collapsed, scattering more items. She dragged him into the bathroom, unbuckled his belt and tugged off his jeans, hoisted him onto the toilet and ran the cold tap, instructing him, like a child who still wet the bed, to have a pee. When he'd finished, she hoisted him up and supported his floppy legs through to the bedroom, dumped him on the bed, pulled off his sweatshirt and covered him with the quilt. "Did I really agree to marry this imbecile?" she thought out loud. She looked again at the ring and reflected on her decision.

Thursday 12th March

Chapter 50

It was another grey, overcast day as they gathered in the main office and the team's mood was similarly dull. They'd been successful in bringing traffickers to justice, but they still hadn't identified the murderer of George White. Suzanna asked Rab for an update.

"I called Maureen McIntyre, the Knowles' cleaner. She said she wouldn't know if she'd moved the CCTV hub, as she doesn't know what one looks like. But if they have one, she will have dusted it because she's diligent about her duties."

"Fair enough. They're not yet common or easily recognisable items in the home. Get CSI to check for prints in the Knowles' house, including asking for the owners' prints. I want to know who disconnected the CCTV power lead. And get them to search for the wooden floor cleaning fluid that forensics found in White's carpets."

Rab completed his notes before responding. "Background checks on the Knowles showed up nothing. No financial difficulties, no police records, except the husband still had points on his licence for speeding. I spoke with them yesterday and doubt we'll need to get a warrant for the checks on their home. I believe they will cooperate."

"Okay. Good. I want another pair of eyes on the CCTV footage from Coates Gardens. We need to look for a woman dressed like the neighbour had described," Suzanna said.

Rab turned to Murray, looking him in the eyes. Murray acknowledged the task with a nod.

"How did you get on yesterday, Mairi?" Suzanna asked.

Mairi reported her discussion with White's niece. "Everything I've heard so far points towards a victim seeking their own justice."

"I think the word is revenge, Mairi. Justice is what *we* endeavour to achieve. The type of justice you suggest is vigilantism," Suzanna corrected. "It would be chaos on our streets if that were the normal way to seek justice – anarchy!" Mairi looked like a chastened schoolgirl but she didn't respond.

Suzanna noticed the effect of her correction on Mairi and made a note to be more sensitive in the future. She recalled how Alistair had also used the word justice the previous day. "But I agree with you Mairi. Whoever killed White probably thought they were seeking justice." She hoped Mairi would be buoyed by her change of tone and was pleased to see a brightening in her eyes.

"Owen. Did you get feedback on Edmond White's son, from Grampian Police?"

"Aye. It came through this afternoon. His name is Joseph White. Lives in Stonehaven. They caught up with him at one of his client's homes – he's a plumber. Said he hadn't seen his grandfather since 2001. He said none of the family liked the man. When asked where he was the morning of the murder, he told them he was on a job. Gave them an address, name and phone number. They confirmed he'd been under their kitchen sink, in Stonehaven at 8 am on the 3rd."

"Okay. Thanks, Owen. Another person eliminated." Suzanna paused, turned and looked at the board, noting the link between Frances Greenwood and an image taken in the Coates Gardens area. "Zahir. Did you get the background checks on Greenwood?"

"Yes, ma'am. Nothing stood out. She doesn't have much wealth but is not in debt either. No criminal record." Zahir paused. "Another thing I forgot to mention: her sister's house, where we know she was located at 7 am on the morning of White's death, is a thirty-minute drive away."

"So, she could have driven straight to White's house, murdered him, then returned home," Suzanna suggested.

"In theory, yes, but Frances Greenwood doesn't possess a driving licence and doesn't own a car!"

"Oh! ... She'd never have made it there in time if she'd travelled by bus as none go direct to the Coates area. What about CCTV in Greenwood's neighbourhood?"

"The nearest public CCTV is two miles away!"

"Right. Let's take her off the board as well." Suzanna paused, staring again at the board. "Although we need to focus on the murder investigation, we still have the traffickers in custody. We need the gang interviews to be conducted by others." Sergeant Findlay was working on other cases but still sharing the same office. "Caitlin!"

Caitlin swivelled her chair, anticipating taking on some interesting work again. "Yes, ma'am. Would you like me to lead on the interviews?"

"Ahead of the game, as usual, Caitlin. Yes. There are five gang members to be processed. We've already conducted initial interviews with three of them – transcripts are in their files – so, the priority is Iqbal Agha. He's being held at Corstorphine station to keep him away from the girls we brought in. You can have Owen back to work with you on this. He's already up to speed with the details, so that should help. Recruit support from other stations as necessary. We need to get the girls' interviews completed today, if possible. And reports with the Procurator Fiscal, so we can charge their controllers tomorrow, at the latest."

"Okay," Caitlin said, smiling, pleased to be back in the big game again.

"Right, team. Let's get to it," Suzanna said as she rose and walked away.

***

Later that morning, Murray paused the video and looked away from the screen, where he'd been concentrating on the CCTV footage for too long. He blinked a few times, then stared out at the view beyond the office's windows. After resting his eyes, he refocused on the screen and restarted the video. He spotted a woman hurrying along Haymarket Terrace. She was dressed like the neighbour had described: jogging bottoms, a pale padded coat, dark, thick-rimmed glasses and a crocheted hat. He cross-checked it with footage from a bus he'd seen earlier. It was definitely the same person. His mind connected with an image from the day before. He'd seen a pale-coloured padded coat and a crocheted hat hanging next to where he'd hung his own coat. *And* the woman he'd interviewed had worn thick-rimmed, black plastic spectacles. "Sarge," Murray said, swivelling his chair towards Rab. "I think I've got something."

Rab rotated his chair and pushed it closer to Murray's computer screen. "Show me."

Murray re-ran the clip. "See this woman walking past the bus stop, just up from White's house?"

"Aye, she fits the description the neighbour gave us. What time is it?"

Murray looked at the text along the bottom of the video. "07:52."

"That would fit as well because she was seen crossing the road by the neighbour at around 07:35. But who is she?"

"I think I know, Sarge."

***

The cleaner let herself in with the key Gerard Templeton had given her the previous day. Today she would start her planning in earnest. But she needed to do some work to justify her presence. She placed the cash he'd left on the kitchen worktop into her purse.

Before using the iron, she had to scrub the black sticky marks from its face. Mr Templeton must have used the wrong temperature and burnt something. Men are so useless, she thought. She segregated the clean laundry into piles: cottons, synthetics and woollens, ready for ironing. While the iron heated, she found his radio and tuned in to BBC Radio 2 to entertain her as she worked. The iron hissed its readiness as Steve Wright chatted with his co-hosts.

Halfway through the ironing pile, she put the kettle on and wandered around the house while she waited for it to boil. She wanted to get to know this man and look for valuables she could take. All she'd heard on the news was he'd raped seven women. They'd all been date-rapes. In each case, it was the woman's word against his. They hadn't been able to prove he'd forced himself on the women. She would find out more about those cases and the evidence that had been given. And she'd find out what made him tick. What drove him to abuse women? Before she took his life, when he was incapacitated, she would confront him about his crimes; make him understand why he was about to die. She smirked as she thought about her next execution.

In his bedside locker, she found pornographic magazines. But that was no surprise. He was single, after all. There was a Patek Philippe watch in the top drawer of his chest. That would be worth taking. She'd get a fair bit for that at a pawnbroker's. In Templeton's lounge, she found a set of Apple AirPod Pro earbuds. They'd be worth taking as well.

On return to the kitchen, she made a cup of tea, dropping in a sweetener from the tube in her handbag before restarting the ironing. She'd cut out sugar because she'd been continually putting on weight and was worried about her health. A woman she knew in Nairn, who wasn't much fatter than herself, had lost much of her sight by the time her doctor had diagnosed diabetes. The woman knew she was obese but avoided going to the doctor's because she couldn't face being told to change her lifestyle. She'd bitterly regretted her decision to delay.

She debated with herself how quickly she should deal with the man. Perhaps she could stay on for a while. Earn some money. He was paying a higher rate than her other clients. She'd get to know him better. Could identify more valuables to take. Perhaps she could take his Porsche. She'd need to connect with professional car thieves, though, as she couldn't just sell it. But she had no idea how to contact such people. As she thought it through, she decided she'd have to leave the Porsche on the driveway. It was too risky to take it. Besides, she'd not driven in many years and wasn't sure she could handle the sports car. She'd probably crash it.

She pressed the sleeves of his next shirt, and the collar, before moving onto the body. Then, she spoke to the iron like she'd seen Pauline Collins do to her kitchen wall in the Shirley Valentine movie. "I wonder why Templeton raped those women? What do you think, Iron? Was it uncontrolled lust? Perhaps he got off on the power of controlling the women, like George-sodding-White? It's the same crime, isn't it, Iron? Date rape or rape of an employee. It's the same. They're not loony men, dragging strangers into woodland to rape them and maybe strangle them afterwards. The men have a relationship with the women, don't they, Iron? They have their trust. Then they abuse that trust. Bastards! These men don't know the harm they do. Don't realise that their two minutes of excitement can leave women mentally scarred for life, do they, Iron? They're bloody idiots."

She remembered back to when she'd been with Justin the first time. "Did I ever tell you about when I lost my virginity, Iron? I was in Justin's bedroom, listening to Queen. We were both Queen fans, Justin and me. He owned all their albums. He had a telly in his bedroom and a video player, so we were watching Queen sing their songs as we kissed and petted. When *Body Language* came on, there were sexy women and hints at sex. We both got more excited. When Justin put his legs between my thighs and shifted my pants aside, I knew what he was going to do, Iron. I knew I shouldn't let him, but I wanted him. I loved him and I was eager for sex. But thinking back, Iron, I think if I'd said no and told him to get off me, he'd have done it anyway. He'd have raped me. You know what I think, Iron? All men are potential rapists, even the Pope. That's what Marjorie Majors said to Shirley Valentine, isn't it, Iron? Do you remember that? It was when Shirley met up with Marjorie by accident. She got soaked when Marjorie's limo drove through a deep puddle. Marjorie took her into her hotel room and, after Shirley had dried off, they chatted. That's when she admitted she'd become a high-class hooker. Not an air hostess. A whore, she'd called herself. Like she was proud of it. I ask ya, who'd be proud of being a prostitute, Iron? You know what, that film probably started a movement. A movement of women rebelling against their boring, controlling husbands. A movement of women saying no to being trapped in unhappy marriages. A movement of women who went to Greek islands had sex with men who kissed their stretch marks and sipped wine under a beach parasol as the sun set behind the watery horizon. Then got divorced. But you know what, Iron, that Joanna Lumley playing a proud hooker was a bad thing. That scene supported the myth that women volunteer to be prostitutes. It's a lie, isn't it, Iron?"

Steve Wright wittered away as she hung the shirt onto a hanger and took another from the pile, pressing away its wrinkles. She looked forward to pressing Templeton into a confession once he was in her control...

Chapter 51

The bell rang as Rab pressed the push-button, his finger tacky when he pulled it away from the sticky device. He knocked on the flat door, stood back and waited. The door stayed closed. He thumped on the door and held the bell's button, listening to the continuous ringing within, like a distant school bell announcing the end of playtime. Still nothing. He wiped his fingertip on his trousers. "Come on, Owen. Let's go." Rab took out his phone as they walked out of the building and called his boss.

***

After Rab had briefed her, Suzanna replaced the phone handset and sat back in her chair. What did they know about the woman? She's self-employed as a cleaner. Employed by the Knowles and had another client on Belford Road. Her flat is on Durar Drive, near Drumbrae Library. She worked at Butler and Cargrove in the 1980s. Her boss was George White. She uses her maiden name, McIntyre, for the business but is still legally Stevens. Who were her other clients? How could they find out? Where would she be now? No answers came to her. There was no knowing. They'd have to wait for her return.

***

Rab and Owen had exhausted their thoughts about football teams and players, passed briefly over the difficulties of relationships with wives, discussed the weather and even touched on the promised Brexit referendum, when they spied Maureen walking up the path to her block of flats. They exited the car and followed her into the building. She'd disappeared into her flat by the time they reached her floor, so they knocked and waited. She opened the door and was surprised to see the policeman who had called the day before, along with another man. It was the second man who spoke.

"Detective Sergeant Sinclair," Rab stated, holding up his card. "You'll know DC Docherty. We need another chat with you, Mrs Stevens, or should we call you Miss McIntyre?" She automatically backed off as he advanced, allowing him to enter, evidently alarmed by the sergeant's mention of both names.

Maureen sat at her table and rested her arm on its surface. Rab and Murray stayed on their feet. "You told my colleague yesterday that between 7:30 and 8 am on Tuesday, 3ʳᵈ March, you were on your way to a client in Belford Crescent. Is that correct?"

"Aye. That's what I telt him. That's the truth."

"We have a picture of you on Haymarket, by the Magdala Crescent bus stop at 7:52 am. So, what bus did you get to be there at that time?"

"On Tuesdays, I catch the 26. It passes along Drum Brae Drive. Gets me there about ten to eight. Just enough time to reach Belford Crescent around eight."

"I'd say that was a fifteen-minute walk, not eight minutes. A long walk, in a city with so many bus routes."

"Well, you'd be right. It *is* about fifteen minutes. It does'nae matter if I start a few minutes after eight. As long as I'm there afore quarter past, 'cause that's when my clients leave for work. I have to arrive before they leave, as they won't give me a key to let myself in." She paused. "And there's no bus from here that takes me closer to Belford Road. I'd need to continue into the city and change buses. That would be no quicker and would cost me more in fares."

"A neighbour of George White's noticed you walking towards

White's door at 7:35 that morning. How would you explain that? And how do you account for the Knowles' CCTV hub being unplugged the very day of his murder?"

Maureen stalled, her mind churning. Then she smiled before answering. "The neighbour must be mistaken about the time and, in any case, I don't know what house this dead guy lived in, so I wouldn't know if I had been walking towards it. I *had* been to the Knowles' last Tuesday. If you'd asked, I'd have telt ya. The Knowles were away last weekend and were not due back until Tuesday evening, so instead of cleaning on the Monday, when I normally do, I got up early and cleaned their house before going to my job at Belford Road. It saved me a bus fare and some travelling time."

"That was *convenient*," Murray said. "So, given that it's a three-minute walk from the Knowles' house to the Magdala Crescent bus stop, you'd have left the house at about 7:49 am. Yet the neighbour saw you at 7:35."

"As I said, the neighbour's mistaken. It would have been more like 7:45. I remember stopping for a couple of minutes outside the gift shop on Haymarket Terrace, 'cause something had caught my eye."

"Let's just suppose that to be true. Why did you walk back to Haymarket, then up Magdala Crescent, when it's quicker to go along Glencairn Crescent and up Douglas Gardens to get to Belford Road?"

"Force of habit, constable. And it's the route I know."

Rab took over again. "Let's just summarise. In the 1980s you worked for George White, who was known as a sex pest and perhaps a sexual predator." Maureen crinkled at the word predator. Rab continued. "There is evidence you may have been one of his victims. Later, you get a job in the house across the street from where he lives. On the morning of his death, you were in that street and seen crossing the road towards his house around the time we know he was murdered. You had conveniently been at the house opposite that morning, able to see when the coast was clear, and the CCTV system had been unplugged. You were later caught on CCTV, confirming you had a window of fourteen minutes to enter George White's house and murder him."

"All supposition, officer."

"It will be more than supposition once we have the DNA and fingerprint evidence. Maureen Stevens, I'm arresting you on suspicion of the murder of George White on 3rd March 2015..."

***

Maureen stopped slouching, sat up and stared belligerently at the officers as they entered the interview room. Suzanna started the tape, then introduced herself and reminded her of her colleague's rank and name.

"This won't take long, Maureen. We have results from fingerprint analysis at the Knowles' residence and we now know that you did handle the CCTV hub."

"As I telt your sergeant. I dinna even know what one looks like. If it's not screwed down, I'd have lifted it to dust."

"Your prints were on the device, in positions that would not support what you said. Had you picked it up to dust, your prints would have been thumb on one side and fingers on the opposite side. What we found was a palm print on the top of the box, with your fingers facing downwards but no opposing thumbprint. On the lead and power connector, the prints of your other hand were found, confirming you had gripped the connector as would be expected had you pulled it out from its socket. Furthermore, we are confident we will find evidence to link you to the kitchen knife recovered from the Water of Leith."

Maureen went pale. "I want a lawyer." She folded her arms, sat back and squeezed her lips together as if to indicate they were now sealed shut.

As they left the room, Suzanna spoke. "Rab, get a warrant issued for a search of Maureen Stevens' home and surroundings. We need further evidence to connect her to this crime. And arrange for a solicitor."

Chapter 52

Maureen Stevens sat on the hard chair in the police interview room, having spent the night in the cells. Her hair was messily tied back in a ponytail, her skin pallid and her eyes bleary.

"Maureen," Mrs Singleton, the solicitor assigned to her, said, "you need to tell me everything. Remember, anything you tell me is entirely in confidence, so hold nothing back... Do you deny killing George White?"

"No."

"Okay. So, we're not disputing that. But why did you kill him? I need to understand. Let's start at the beginning. Tell me what he did to you that resulted in you taking his life."

Maureen stared at the table, avoiding eye contact, recalling when she'd killed him. As she'd plunged the kitchen knife into White's chest, she'd shuddered with the release. He hadn't seen her as a threat. His face had shown extreme surprise when the knife entered his chest, realising too late that the kitten he'd abused had become a tiger. That's how she'd felt: empowered; strong.

He'd subjected her to mental and physical torture all those years ago when she'd allowed him to rape her and he'd forced her to carry out other sexual acts. The abuse had wrecked her life. Had turned her into a withered flower of a woman, too scared to say no, too traumatised and under-confident to succeed in life. But the killing had transformed

298

her.

"Maureen. Please tell me how this all started," her solicitor requested again.

Maureen looked up at the solicitor, feeling sad, vulnerable, afraid. She'd never expected to be sitting in a police station charged with murder. "I was twenty at the time. It had been a prank. Lyndsey Lewis – she was one of the other girls in accounts – had shocked the rest of us. She showed around a picture she'd taken earlier when sitting on the photocopier with no pants on! I was shocked that Lyndsey was flashing a picture of her fanny. What if the men got hold of it? After the initial embarrassment, I laughed along with the others. It grew into a dare. We all had to do it. It was hilarious. The peer group pressure got to me after I'd held off for six weeks. Most of the others had done it before me. I convinced myself it was a bit of harmless silliness. After building up the courage to do it, I made sure I was last in the office. I slipped into the photocopying room, took off my knickers, sat on the copier then pressed copy."

Mrs Singleton pictured the event in her mind. What stupid things some young women get up to. It would never have occurred to her to do such a thing. But some are easily led, she supposed, especially those with low self-esteem and poor educational standards. "Go on."

"The second copy was rolling into the tray when the door opened. The boss walked in and caught me sitting there. I remember what he said. Every detail. I've relived it in my head so often."

"Maureen, relive it for me now, please," the solicitor asked. Maureen started speaking. It was like she was transported back thirty years and it was happening again.

'What are you doing?' Mr White said. 'Get off of that machine immediately.' He picked up the paper from the output tray and examined the contents. 'What's this?' he said, staring at the copies of my backside. 'You've been misusing office machinery to take pictures of your vagina!'

I flushed bright red. Daren't look him in the face. I stuffed my knickers into my bag.

'What have you got to say for yourself?' He asked.

I replied 'Sorry, Mr White. It was supposed to be a wee bit of fun. All the girls have been doing it.'

He looked at me suspiciously, then said, 'I don't believe you. This is some sort of turn-on for your boyfriend, isn't it? This is a blatant misuse of company facilities - theft. A sackable offence. Get out of here and report to HR in the morning to collect your P45.'

I was scared of losing my job. We were only just getting by on my pay. Without my wages, we'd not survive. I pleaded with him to discipline me instead of sacking me. He was quiet for a while. Then he said, "We could dock a day's wages to recover the costs and pay for the machine to be cleaned."

I told him I couldn't afford to lose any money. I'd not be able to pay my bills and feed my child?

He said, "You should have thought of that before you abused the photocopier."

I begged him to be lenient with me; to find another way to punish me. It was half a minute before he answered, probably 'cause he'd been thinking how he might take advantage of the situation. I was young, slim and quite pretty in those days. But I wasn't prepared for the answer he came up with when he spoke. "The only other option is corporal punishment. I'll settle for delivering a spanking. Bend over the copier."

I refused. Said it wasn't right. He replied sternly, "Then get out and collect your P45 tomorrow morning."

I shrank inside, worried about what would happen to me if I didn't comply and scared about what he would do to me if I did. My mind raced through the possibilities. I'd only been with the company for three months, having been made redundant from my last job and fallen pregnant. My husband was unemployed and looking after our bairn, so I was the family breadwinner. How would we pay the rent and buy the baby food and nappies if I lost my job? I turned and leaned across the copier.

I saw him grin as I turned. He stepped closer and slapped my behind. I yelped. He struck again slightly harder and I remember yelping louder. Again and again. He seemed to be enjoying himself. When I think back, he must have been drunk with power. Excited by having me under his control. He lifted my skirt, exposing my naked bottom and I pleaded with him to stop.

He said "Shut up Stevens. You deserve a good spanking." He smacked my naked cheeks. I cried with pain and embarrassment. After a few more strokes, his hand rested on my hot bottom then caressed it. As he rubbed his hand across my buttocks, he slipped a finger into me.

I cried. "Please, sir. Don't do that." My husband, Justin, was the only man who'd ever done that. It was wrong. I tried to stand upright, but he pushed me down, holding me flat against the copier. He ignored my pleas and explored me with his finger as I sobbed, then he slapped me hard again. I heard him fiddling with his clothing, recognising the sound of a belt being undone. Then he hit my buttocks with his leather belt. I squealed and again begged him to stop.

He struck me again with his belt and said, "Very well." His hand caressed my bottom again. I noticed him change position. I thought my punishment must be over. But after a moment, he pushed himself into me. He raped me.

The man hadn't even worn a condom. After he'd come, he picked up the photocopies and left, saying, "Now let that be a lesson to you."

"I sobbed, initially unable to move. When I left, Mr White was nowhere to be seen. I dabbed my eyes dry, threw the tissue into a bin, then went to the ladies to clean myself. When I left the office, my body was still shaking."

Chapter 53

Mrs Singleton was shocked by what she'd been told. "Thank you for sharing that with me, Maureen. How awful for you! Are you okay to continue?" Maureen nodded. "I need to understand fully your motive for killing George White if I'm to offer the best defence. I appreciate he raped you and it was a horrendous abuse of power. But it *was* thirty years ago. So, why now? How did the rape affect your life?"

Maureen lifted her eyes from the interview room table. She had been staring at the same spot for ages now and knew every scratch and ink mark; was familiar with the feel of the Formica having traced the marks with her finger.

"The week after he raped me, he called to me as I headed towards the office exit. He said he needed my assistance with something before leaving. Sally continued out the door, leaving me alone with him. I told him I needed to get back to my son.

He said, "This won't take long. Come with me." I reluctantly followed him into his office. He locked the door after I entered. I remember the fear that key-turning caused. I trembled because I knew something bad would happen. He told me that the punishment for last week's episode had been insufficient. That I deserved further punishment.

As she recalled the day, she shrivelled up inside. It was like her abuser was there again. Her voice trembled as she continued. "I felt faint with worry; refused to do as he told me. But he took out the photocopies again, waving them in my face and said he'd send them to my husband and post them around the factory if I didn't comply. The humiliation would have been unbearable. I'd have to leave my job and my husband would probably leave me. So, I gave in. He forced me to give him a blowjob. He gripped my hair as he satisfied himself. When he came, I nearly vomited all over him. I did later, in the toilets. Rinsed my mouth from the tap dozens of times, but the taste of him wouldn't wash away. I sobbed for ages, sitting on the toilet seat, hiding away from the world. There'd be no end to the abuse if I stayed with the company, but jobs were difficult to come by at that time." Reliving the assault triggered her tears. She sobbed again.

"Did the abuse continue?"

She spoke through her sobs. "Aye. The next week, he stopped me from leaving work and took me to his office again. He spanked me and raped me from behind again. He wasn't interested in me as a person. I was just an object for him to use for his sexual satisfaction. I started looking harder for other jobs after that."

"And did the attacks continue?"

"Aye. But I tried to leave the office early so he could'nae hold me back when the others left. It worked most of the time, but he still found ways to control me and rape me, until my final month. After I'd been offered a job with another company, I refused to stay late. I think he backed off when I started standing up to him. He must have been bluffing about using the photocopies."

"How did this affect your life after you left the company?"

Maureen gathered her thoughts before responding. "In the early years, after the abuse, I had no thoughts of revenge. I was relieved to have gotten away from him. I tried to carry on as if nothing had happened, but he'd shaken my confidence and trust in men. It affected my relationship with Justin. When Andrew was born, Justin didn't know our new baby might not have been his. We struggled through the next few years, but then the car accident happened." Maureen paused, thinking back to that time.

"Andrew had been playing up. He distracted me as I pulled out of a junction and I didn't see the approaching truck. It smashed into the side of my car. The fire and rescue guys cut the roof off to get us out. When I woke, after being out cold for days, I found Andrew had also been badly injured and lost a lot of blood. He's got a rare blood group, so they'd asked Justin to donate blood but found no match with his son. That's when it came out that Andrew wasn't related to him."

"He accused me of lying to him and deceiving him all those years. It was the crack in the dam that caused a total failure. Our relationship fell apart and he walked out. Left me to bring up our bairns, Michaela – Justin's daughter – and Andrew. He refused to pay maintenance towards Andrew's support. Life was hard. I went mental. Lost my job and had to rely on benefits."

"Go on."

"I've heard loads of people down-cry benefits claimants and I'd been one of them. So, when I became a claimant, I couldn't handle it. I hit bottom. I couldn't cope. Got into massive debt. Bailiffs were knocking on my door. I got evicted from our home and the council put me into B&B. But there were no cooking facilities and I didn't have money for restaurants, so we survived on breakfast cereals and sandwiches for months. Social Service took away my children and put them in foster care because I wasn't looking after them properly. In the end, I left the city. I hitchhiked to the Highlands and slept rough for a while until a kindly lady took me in. I spent many years living up there, away from Edinburgh, away from my past.

"So, this man wrecked your life. But why delay thirty years to extract your revenge?"

"I despised George White all my life. He'd caused my downfall. Had pushed me onto a helter-skelter to hell. But finding where he lived was not planned." Maureen went quiet again. "I returned to Edinburgh five years ago. Both my bairns had been adopted. I didn't know their names or where they lived. Not even if they were still alive. Social Services wouldn't tell me anything. Weren't allowed to, by law, they said."

"They were right. Once a child has been adopted, the birth parents don't have any further rights. How did you get to move back to Edinburgh? Who did you stay with?"

"The lady who'd given me a place to live had gotten too old and needed to go into a care home, but she had a friend in Edinburgh, who agreed to put me up until I got a job and found my own place."

"How did you come to know where George White lived?"

"I bumped into Sally from the company where I used to work. We caught up over a coffee and she mentioned Mr White. I never knew, but he'd abused her as well. Not to the extent he did with me, but he often touched her up, spoke sexual innuendoes and tried to get her to meet him after work. She'd left six months after me. She said she'd heard his wife had passed away and he was now infirm. Still living in the same house as he'd been in since he'd married. I'd been to that house. He'd tasked me with taking documents to his home when he was off work, sick. Even though he had a cold, he attempted to get me into his house. I refused, gave him the documents and walked away."

"But how did you get access to the house on the day you killed him?"

"I tried calling on him once or twice. Knocked on the door and rang the bell, but no one came. As I was leaving, I noticed a woman arrive and extract the door key from the key safe. I could hardly call when the carer was there, could I? So I left. But later I thought, to confront the man, I'd need the key safe combination."

Mrs Singleton waited for her to continue, her eyes never leaving Maureen's.

"Months later, a cleaning job came up on Coates Gardens and it turned out to be opposite White's house. So, while there cleaning, I observed the comings and goings of the carers. There was a pattern to their calls, although not entirely reliable. After a while, I found a pair of binoculars in a cupboard, whilst dusting. I used them to watch the carers enter the code. It took me a few weeks to get the complete number. It was difficult to see even with binoculars; often the carers' hands obscured the code."

"Tell me about the day you killed him."

"I finished my cleaning duties as the first carer left. So, I waited until she was out of sight, crossed the road, extracted the key and let myself in. I didn't go there to kill him, only to confront him. To make him understand the impact he'd had. To give him the chance to ask for forgiveness. But he was unrepentant."

"Talk me through every detail you can remember. It's important that I know."

"I opened the door and put the key back in its box. As I closed the door, Mr White called out. 'Is that you again, Gabriela? Have you forgotten something?' I walked into the room and said, 'Hello, Mr White.' He turned his head towards me and said, 'Who are you? You're not one of my regular carers.'

I said, 'No, Mr White. It's me, Maureen Stevens, from Butler and Cargrove. Do you remember me?'

He repeated my name slowly, 'Maureen Stevens. You used to be such a pretty girl, slim and shapely. What happened to you? Have you come to pleasure me again? I might be eighty-five, but I can still get it up.'

I was disgusted that the old guy still thought he could get me to do his bidding. 'No way, Mr White. Never again. I came to tell you I gave birth to your son after you raped me. That you wrecked my life, caused my marriage to fail, my bairns to be taken away from me, and sent me into a deep bout of mental illness.'

'A son, you say. Where is the young man? I'd like to meet him.'

That surprised me. I expected he'd deny Andrew's existence. I told him I didn't know where he was, not having seen him in twenty years, since they took him from me.

He said, 'Oh! That is a shame. So, why did you return to my home, Miss Stevens, if not to give me pleasure?'

'I just told you why: to let you know you'd destroyed my life by abusing me.'

'Abuse! What do you mean abuse? We just had some sex games, that's all. You enjoyed it as well. I remember how moist you were. Begging for it.'

I said, 'You disgust me, old man. Even now, you canna see what you did to me was wrong. You've no regrets for raping me.'

'No, no. It wasn't rape.' He said. 'You bent over willingly and let me spank you and have intercourse. Come, Miss Stevens, take off your knickers and lay over my lap. We could have some fun together.'

His words infuriated me. I strode into the kitchen and grabbed a knife from the block, then marched back into the living room and stood in front of him brandishing the knife. I said, 'If you suggest one more time that you want sex with me again, I'll cut your knob off.'

He said, 'Now, now, dear, don't be like that. Put the knife down and come here.'

Something about his tone, the words he spoke, and his facial expressions compelled me to lower the knife and step towards him. As I did, he grabbed the wrist of my hand holding the knife. Despite his age, his grip was strong. He twisted my wrist until I started losing my grip on the knife.

'That's it. Let the knife go,' he said, 'then come sit on my lap, Maureen.' His other hand reached around and rested on my buttock, pulling me toward him.

I was angered. I tore my hand away from him, then punched him in

307

the chest. The knife plunged into his chest. I remember the shock on his face. The surprise that I'd not complied but had fought back. His eyes glazed over and his head dropped.

The knife dragged as I pulled it from his chest – as if the body didn't want to let go. Blood oozed from the wound. I guess the heart had stopped pumping. His whole body slumped."

Maureen paused again. "I didn't go there to murder him. Even at the time that I stuck the knife into him, I don't recall any thoughts about killing, just pushing him away."

Mrs Singleton considered what Maureen had told her. "Maureen. You know what you did was wrong and although you say you didn't plan his death, the fact is that you killed him. And the prosecution may well infer, by your planning, that you had gone into his house with murder on your mind. It might not be possible to convince the jury that the killing wasn't premeditated. If the police have sufficient evidence to gain a conviction, you may go to prison for life."

Maureen's eyes returned to the familiar table again. She couldn't face her lawyer. Couldn't face the truth that her future now looked like it would be even worse than her past.

"I'll check through the evidence and advise you on the best course of action once I've seen that. Although I can't condone what you've done, I think I understand. I'll also ask for a psychiatric assessment. If an expert in these matters can find for temporary insanity, that might help your case. I'll return tomorrow to speak with you. The police can't question you any further without my presence, so hold on. I'll do my best for you. You might have taken the man's life, but you were also a victim and he was your abuser. I'll need your permission to see all your medical records as well." Mrs Singleton left the interview room and a female uniformed officer escorted Maureen back to the cells.

Chapter 54

Maureen sat alone in her cell. It seemed certain she'd go to jail. How long she would spend locked up was now her main concern. But at least she'd broken the spell White had held over her. Her mind returned to when Justin discovered his blood didn't match his son's. At first, he was confused. Astounded. Then understanding came to him and he'd confronted her. "Andrew's not my son, is he?" He'd cried.

She'd replied, "No, Justin. He's not. My boss raped me, but I daren't tell you or anyone else."

"I don't believe you," he'd yelled. "You went out on a hen-night around that time and stayed out all night. I remember worrying about you and having my suspicions. I bet you got drunk and slept with some man you'd met at the nightclub," he said accusingly.

"No. It's not true, Justin. I've never slept with anyone else. I *was* raped."

He'd stormed out of the hospital, refusing to accept the truth. Maureen had cried herself dry. They never made up. Never got back together. Life fell apart for her that day, after a decade of working hard at the marriage. Even though twenty years had passed, the memory still upset her. Still brought tears to her eyes when she remembered.

She'd seen Justin only once after their divorce. Their eyes had met as they walked towards each other. A new woman pushed a pram by his side. He turned and led his new family across the road to avoid her.

She remembered how her heart had contracted – the emotional pain of his rejection and avoidance.

Maureen hadn't seen her son, Andrew, since he was seven and her daughter, Michaela, was nine. Justin's new partner had refused to take the kids into her home, so when Maureen had failed as a mother, Social Services had persuaded her to let them be adopted. In her heart she wanted to say no, but she'd heard so many stories of fostered kids, forced out of their temporary families at age sixteen to fend for themselves, of children dragged into an underworld of promiscuity, drugs, crime and homelessness. So, she gave them the opportunity to stay with their new family. She was just thankful that, unusually, they remained together.

But both were gone now. Out of her life forever unless they chose to find her. It was too late for that now. If they tried to make contact, they'd find her in prison and that would be the end of those dreams. Tears came again as she imagined what she'd missed. Andrew growing through his teenage years. Becoming a man. Michaela turning into a woman. Perhaps babies? Grandchildren? Holding the little ones in her arms, inhaling that unique fresh smell of baby, the tiny fingers and toes...

She had no family to love her now. No man in her life. Her parents had disowned her years ago when she went off the rails. Her older sisters avoided her, too. They'd shut their ears to her pleas for understanding. No sympathy was shown when she told them she'd been raped. Like Justin, they accused her of making it up as an excuse for betraying her husband. The husband who had been her boyfriend at school. Had lived just a few doors along from her family home. Was like a brother to her sisters, a son to her parents. The man she'd married when just eighteen, having fallen pregnant by him.

She wiped away her tears and thought of the time she'd spent in the Highlands. There *had* been men in that period. A few boyfriends, but hardly any who wanted more from her than casual sex. There *had* been one significant relationship. Graeme shared a house with his brother in Auldearn, the first village after leaving Nairn towards Elgin. He used to come through to Nairn at the weekend for a night out. He was a rugged man, used to hard work. Strong muscles, but no six-pack-stomached Adonis. A wee belly hung over his belt. His unruly dark brown hair matched his shaggy beard, although it was splattered with grey streaks and blotches. What could be seen of his face was ruddy and wrinkled, no doubt from working outside in all weathers most of the time.

They started meeting mid-week. Maureen would go to his place because house rules banned male visitors to her lodgings. The relationship lasted several months. They would walk along Nairn's coast, its beaches lashed by wind and rain in the autumn. But she loved holding hands as they listened to the waves crash against the shore, the spray drizzling onto their faces. They'd laughed and loved. Played and planned. They'd talked about Graeme asking his brother to find somewhere else to live, so they could be together.

But life had been merciless to her again. Graeme worked offshore on an oil rig in the North Sea. He spent two weeks onshore and two weeks working on the rig. Maureen remembered hearing the news. On the way back to the mainland, a Super Puma suffered a main rotor gearbox failure and dropped out of the sky. She hadn't known at the time that her man was on that helicopter which had ditched into the sea, with all lives lost.

She thought about the future. By the time she was released from prison, any chance of a relationship would have passed. She thought about her intentions for Gerard Templeton. Her arrest had shattered her plans to seek retribution for the women he'd abused. Life was so cruel.

Friday 13th March

Chapter 55

"Good morning, Mrs Singleton, sorry to have kept you," Suzanna said on entering the interview room. "There was one further piece of evidence I had been waiting for, which I shall reveal to you and your client during this interview." Suzanna paused, allowing what she'd said to sink in and worry Maureen further. "As you know, Maureen, your fingerprints on the Knowles' CCTV hub prove you disconnected the power lead so that the system would not capture you entering White's property. We now know that the traces of wood floor cleaner found on White's carpet are a match to that used for cleaning the Knowles' parquet flooring and found impregnated in your shoes' soles. We also have the knife used to murder George White and we found his blood in your handbag. The rubber gloves used during his murder left prints on the award that had been smashed, and gloves matching those prints and having George White's blood on them were found in a bin along the road from your flat. These have since been confirmed by DNA matching, to have been worn by you. And lastly, your jogging bottoms were found to be impregnated with blood that had sprayed from George White's chest wound when you plunged the knife into his pumping heart."

Maureen looked defeated, teetering on the edge of confession. "Why don't you just tell us how it happened?"

Mrs Singleton whispered to her client. The evidence was overwhelming. She may as well tell them she'd not gone there to murder him, merely to seek his repentance. Maureen retold the story she'd shared with her solicitor. By the time she had finished, she was in tears.

"I think my client needs a break before you continue with your questions."

"Agreed. Interview adjourned. We will reconvene in one hour." Suzanna and Rab left Maureen to recover and sent a constable with cups of tea for them both.

***

"Okay. Maureen. We need to clarify some points about the demise of George White on March 3rd, 2015." Suzanna said. They'd reconvened after the requested break. "In the previous interview, you admitted to killing Mr White but not murdering him. Is there anything you'd like to add?" DCI McLeod asked.

"Like I said, I didn't murder him. But I did kill him."

"Maureen, I understand you were a victim. We've already spoken with your colleague." She referred to her notes. "You'll have known her as Sally Henderson. And she mentioned White's behaviour toward other women at the company where you worked. Because of what you've told us and your colleague's validation of Whites behaviour, I would expect the Procurator Fiscal to charge you with culpable homicide – manslaughter rather than murder."

Maureen nodded unemotional acceptance.

"However, there are one or two anomalies that I need to clear up. A company award had been taken from the trophy cabinet, broken into pieces and laid on a melamine tray. The tray was placed prominently, with the broken award, a clear sign that Mr White had not been worthy of the award. If George White's death was unplanned, why did you take the time and trouble to remove this award from its display, smash it, and show it off the way you did?"

Maureen thought before answering. To Suzanna, this delay suggested cold revenge, rather than the accidental manslaughter Stevens had suggested. "I'd gone there to confront him, you'll recall. What I forgot to mention was during the confrontation I took the award from the cabinet and waved it in his face, telling him it was an insult to the women he had abused for him to display it. I broke the award into pieces and dropped them onto the tray."

Maureen's explanation was believable, but something about the woman suggested she was lying, although doing a great job of acting innocent. "Thank you, Maureen. That clears up that query." Suzanna looked at the accused and spoke empathetically. "Given the abuse you were subjected to and its impact on your life, why did you try to hide the crime? Why not come forward and tell us what happened?"

"A general mistrust of authorities, I suppose. You'll remember my children were taken away from me and I was forever denied contact with them. If I'd called the police, I would have been arrested straight away and probably charged with murder. I did'nae want to spend the rest of my life in prison?"

"And your dumping of the knife used to stab George White in the heart was again to reduce the risk of you being put away for a crime you *hadn't* committed?"

"Exactly."

"That was exceedingly rational of you, thinking so clearly after having *accidentally* killed Mr White. Most people would have dropped the knife and run from the scene or left it in the body. Or even dialled 999 and confessed to killing him. And most people wouldn't have worn rubber gloves when they went to confront their nemesis. Nor washed the knife they'd used and dumped it in a river half a mile from the house."

Maureen sat quietly. There was no point in offering an explanation. She could tell the detective didn't believe her. It worried her.

"We found some letters at the scene and need to eliminate you as the author of any of them. If you would give me an example of your handwriting, please…" Suzanna said, pushing a pen and paper across the table.

Maureen took up the pen with her right hand and said, "What would you like me to write?"

"My name is Maureen Stevens," Suzanna paused as Maureen wrote, "I am… a bloody good liar."

Maureen stopped writing. "What do you mean? I'm no lying. What I telt you was true. It *was* an accident. Although that bastard deserved to die, I did'nae go there intent on killing him."

"You see, Maureen, whilst most of your story is believable and I would understand you wanting retribution for what he'd done to you, there's another problem with the *accidental* stabbing part of your *tale*."

Maureen pursed her lips as the detective emphasised 'tale'. Her worry level rising.

"A one-inch-wide kitchen knife in the hand of a right-handed woman stood facing the victim could not have been held horizontally and, by luck, slipped between his ribs, directly into his heart. The blade would be vertical or at most thirty degrees off vertical. There's *no way* the stabbing of Mr White was *accidental,* as you described." Suzanna barked.

Maureen slumped back into her chair, looking up towards the now standing DCI, astonished by the accusation. She hadn't thought about that and didn't know how to respond. Mrs Singleton placed a hand on her arm. When Maureen turned to her, she understood she should ride it out and say nothing.

"There's only one way the kitchen knife you used to stab Mr White entered his body, cleanly missing the ribs and taking his life instantly. This is what really happened. You entered the house, walked into the kitchen and took the knife from its block, picked up the tray and carried it into the room, using the tray to mask the knife. His morning carer confirmed the tray had not been left in the living room but returned to the kitchen before she left, as she always does.”

Suzanna continued. “You confronted Mr White, who was unrepentant. He stood up as if to grab you, but you moved away. You grabbed his Zimmer frame, opened the French windows and threw it into the garden. When you turned, he had sat again, hadn’t he Maureen? Because he didn’t possess the strength or stability to move without his walker. You held the knife in front of his face, demanding he apologise for what he’d done to you and others. When he failed to respond, you held the knife to his ribs and threatened to kill him if he did not repent. He did not grab your hand. Your wrist is not bruised. You did not push away from him with the knife in your hand and accidentally stab him. You drove the blade between his ribs into his heart, knowing exactly what you were doing. Taking the monster’s life. Is that not how it happened, Maureen?” Suzanna growled.

Maureen’s resolve crumbled. They had the evidence. And she knew she couldn’t go on denying it right through a trial. She needed to off-load, to relieve the pressure, to ease the journey, which now seemed inevitable. She ignored her solicitor, who whispered ‘you don’t need to say anything, Maureen’.

The floodgate of tears opened and she spoke: “Yes, yes. You’re right. He *was* a monster. He was the demon who wrecked my life and ruined the lives of other women. It was my duty to seek justice for myself and the others. He deserved to die. I did it. I stuck him. I killed him. But it was execution, not murder. I am the hero who slayed the beast. It was justice; justice the authorities should have taken.” She collapsed back into the chair, her chin on her chest, the tears gushing and the sobs racking her body.

THE KEY TO MURDER

318

Chapter 56

Suzanna reclined in her chair for a time of reflection on how they'd conducted the inquiry – glad that she'd cleaned the flyblow off the ceiling – and to consider whether they could have done better. What lessons should they learn? She'd need to call them all together soon to discuss it, but she wanted to have already analysed the team's performance. Suzanna worked her way through the investigative process, the leads they'd followed, the interviews they'd carried out, the evidence they'd identified. She was satisfied they'd done as well as could be expected. And, as far as they knew, Maureen Stevens had murdered no one else. She'd never know whether she'd saved anyone from a Maureen Stevens' execution... Or would she? She WhatsApped Rab with some instructions, then reclined her chair again.

Suzanna's mind returned to her viewing of the victim's body. She remembered its naked form laid out on the trolley. George White had looked innocent enough in death. She guessed he'd acted that role well in later life because some of his carers thought he was a 'nice old man.' She recalled his flaccid penis laying lifeless on his stomach. How much damage had that insignificant little thing done in its lifetime? How many women had he raped, driven by the need to keep it satisfied, propelled by the thrill of sexual excitement and power?

She pondered the causes of crime. Sexual satisfaction was certainly prevalent, as was the lust for power, control and for money, of course.

She remembered the misquoted biblical saying, 'money is the root of evil.' She searched for it on her computer and found a quote in the New Living Translation Bible. The correct version was, of course, not money itself, but 'The *love* of money is the root of all kinds of evil.'

The verse could easily be interpreted as the love of anything not belonging to you, is the root of all kinds of evil. Desiring what isn't yours to own. Other people's money, possessions, and even their bodies. Taking what is not yours affects the victim, no matter what the crime. If only everyone in the world would understand this biblical wisdom and live by it. As the thought crossed her mind, she decided it was time to follow the leads and hints she'd recently received. She Googled the course that several people had recommended to her and found one within the city. It was due to start after Easter.

Rab called out as Suzanna passed through the main office, "Ma'am. I've found something extremely interesting..."

She sat at a desk next to Rab's and gave him her full attention. "That late task you gave me turned out to be worthwhile checking out. I went through Stevens' phone records again and found that most of the calls made and received since White's murder were to numbers she regularly communicated with. But there was one new contact. I followed it through, and you'll never guess who this new contact was?"

***

Stevens had been transferred on remand to Edinburgh's Saughton Prison. Suzanna's job was done now, except for ensuring all the evidence was provided to the Procurator Fiscal's office to support the prosecution. She closed her computer, packed away her files, shut her office door, then checked her team had all departed before strolling along the corridor, the need for speed shed by the conclusion of the White case. "McLeod." The familiar male voice called out.

She rolled her eyes, turned and headed back to the chief superintendent's office, but checked her attitude before reaching it. Perhaps he was so hard on her because he could sense her lack of respect for him. She smiled as she reached his open door and spoke pleasantly, enthusiastically. "Yes, sir."

"Well done on the White case, Suzanna. Sterling job. Do take a seat."

She sat, disarmed by his use of her first name and the invitation to sit. She wondered why. What had changed? Her smile couldn't have made that much difference. And solving one more murder case wouldn't be enough to change the man's attitude towards her.

Ewan Robertson took off his large wire-framed spectacles and placed them on the desk, before relaxing into his chair. "I understand that if it hadn't been for your leadership and direction, and indeed your ability to read situations better than everyone else, this crime may still be unresolved. The criminal would still be walking the streets and perhaps an ongoing threat to others."

Suzanna glowed in the warmth of praise from a man who rarely gave it. She'd not seen this side of him. "Actually, Sir. We now believe Stevens was definitely a threat to others."

Ewan looked intrigued. " Tell me more."

"We took another look at her phone records and noticed a contact that had been created after George White's murder. When we tracked down the owner of the number, we found it to be Gerard Templeton... The serial rapist who recently escaped justice. It would seem he had a lucky escape from death."

"So, your instincts were absolutely correct. Well done, Suzanna. I wouldn't mind betting, though, that there are seven women out there who might wish you hadn't caught Stevens so quickly!" His eyebrows raised as he concluded, affirming what Suzanna had also been thinking.

Ewan continued, "I know those above me are equally impressed by your work... You'll probably have heard that I'll be retiring in a few months. Decided to cut and run before I got too set in my ways."

A bit late for that, Suzanna thought, not letting it show in her face.

"I've already done over my thirty years' service and I've not enjoyed being in this role. Tied to a desk and forever being challenged about the department's overspending. The Commissioner is totally focussed on budgets and statistics. He's lost touch with reality and I feel I've been dragged down the same route."

His frankness amazed Suzanna. Perhaps she'd have liked him if she'd worked for him before he was promoted to his current role?

"I've already put in a good word for Alistair Milne. I'm hoping he will take promotion into my post when I've gone. And I hope you'll move up into his. I'll certainly recommend it."

Suzanna was shocked. For months – no, years – he had spoken down to her, treated her like a naughty child in school. He'd focussed on not spending money where he didn't think it was needed. He'd tried to curtail necessary travel, been pedantic about process and rules, and damning about her and others' minor transgressions. And here he was, opening up to her and telling her he was recommending her for the Superintendent job. "Thank you, sir. It's good to know I have your backing for the promotion. If I get the job, I'll certainly give it everything I've got."

"Having seen how determined and hard-working you can be, I'm sure you will, Suzanna. I hope Alistair will take the promotion as well, rather than continuing to look for a move back to his hometown. Aberdeen's gain would be Edinburgh's loss. But these moves would be based on our current structure. And you'll probably have heard talk of Major Investigation Teams being formed?"

She nodded. Would this be the news she'd expected about her team being dismantled?

"I've been involved in the discussions about this restructure and argued the case for your team to stay together. My proposal is that your team becomes the region's MIT, with lower-level crimes farmed out to the local stations."

Suzanna looked at him inquisitively, keen to hear what more he had to say about the subject. "The decision has not yet been made, but there's a meeting planned for early April when it will be decided. Other proposals are on the table, so I can't guarantee it will go as we wish." He paused. "I thought you should know. From what I've heard, though, whether it's leading this team or another, there's a good chance you could be offered a role as head of an MIT."

Suzanna nodded, rolling around the information in her head. "Thank you for letting me know about the uncertain future. I guess we'll just have to wait and see what happens at the next strategy meeting."

A New Season

Epilogue

The journey out of winter's gloomy valley was now in the past. Easter had come and gone. April was nearly over and in between the rain showers, the sun shone. Flowers had leapt from the ground in search of its warmth. Evenings were extending now and dawn choruses arrived earlier. Spring had arrived like a cheery friend, brightening their days with positivity.

Her relationship with James had grown sturdier and they spent most weekends together. He'd returned from New Zealand just three weeks after he'd left in a hurry, his father having passed away shortly after his arrival. They still kept their own places, enjoying the space and freedom the arrangement provided. But spending the weekends together had become the norm. Suzanna hadn't worked a Saturday or Sunday since she'd closed the George White case. It had been good to have her weekends back and James was much happier now.

Suzanna had the car roof down as she drove through the city with James, enjoying the uncontained freedom. She parked close to the venue, closed the car roof and they walked hand in hand up the concrete path to the big red doors of the commanding stone building. One door was already open. They were welcomed by a young man who escorted them to the reception table. Name badges were provided, along with a small booklet each to take home and read, and course books to follow during the sessions.

They were led to another table, given teas and coffees, then onto a cluster of seven chairs circling a round table where three people already sat. The group leader, John, greeted Suzanna and James and introduced them to the other two guests.

She looked up at the magnificently high ceiling, then to its Gothic arched stained-glass windows. The walls were off white, rather than unpainted dull stone, like most churches of this era. Bright lights and scattered clusters of flowers brightened the room. Easy listening music played quietly in the background. A large screen dominated the hall, capturing a projection of the words *The Alpha Course. Christianity: Boring, Irrelevant and Untrue?* Scrolling at the bottom of the screen the words: *We will be starting in 11 minutes, 33 seconds. 32, 31, 30...*

Suzanna tore her eyes away from the screen, back to the people in her group. She was intrigued by what the evening might bring and looked forward to the talk and follow-on discussions. Her parents and sister had been *encouraging* her to return to the church, and life had been gently nudging her to investigate Christianity properly. Despite attending church through most of her childhood, she'd never really believed and had doubts God even existed.

Her silenced phone buzzed. She excused herself, moved away and took the call. "Good evening, ma'am. Sergeant Miller here..."

"Thanks, Sarge. Let me have the details and I'll go straight there." She noted the address and switched off the phone.

James had heard Suzanna's response. He looked disappointed as he saw her switch back into police mode and prepare to leave him. As she placed the phone back in her handbag, it rang again.

"Hello, Suzanna. Greg Lansdowne here. I need a decision..."

Reviews

If you've enjoyed this story, it would be wonderful if you could post a review on Amazon and Goodreads, to inform other potential readers and help me grow as an author.

About the Author

Harry joined the Royal Air Force, straight from school at the tender age of just 15. He spent the first half of his RAF career as an aircraft technician and the latter half as an engineering officer. Based in England, Scotland, Germany and Malta, he also travelled the World with the RAF. Harry's first taste of writing came when asked to write short pieces for the RAF Station's magazine, where he was based.

Many years later, he created and edited the RAF's magazine for sports and adventurous training, *RAF Active*. Harry's articles were written from his experiences in sports and adventurous activities, included: skiing, sailing, judo and scuba diving, to name a few. He was also published in the UK Defence Journal.

After his time in the RAF, Harry spent 6 years on voluntary service in West Bengal (anti-human trafficking work) and it was whilst in India that he made his first attempt at writing fiction. On his return to the UK, he attended a creative writing course and was inspired to write his first novel – 'The Glass'. His travels around the world have provided Harry with a huge source of knowledge and experiences for new books – yet to come – and he looks forward to sharing these.

You can connect with me on:

🌐 https://www.harrynavinski.com

🐦 https://twitter.com/HarryNavinski

📘 https://www.facebook.com/harry.navinski.9

🔗 https://www.instagram.com/harrynavinski

Subscribe to my newsletter:

✉️ https://mailchi.mp/f6237e815fa4/subscribe-to-mailing-list

Also by Harry Navinski

The Glass

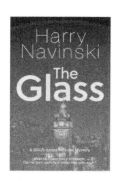

DCI Suzanna McLeod's Edinburgh-based team has a reputation to live up to. But the Chief Superintendent is a by-the-book meddler and her team members have personal problems that need her help.

Under pressure to catch armed robbers before they strike again, Suzanna's focus is challenged when her inherited magnifying glass is stolen – a cherished item that led to her becoming a detective. The young thief could never have known the impact its theft would have on him and his family.

As the chase is underway for the gunmen, Suzanna takes on the most dangerous of the criminals. But even after the case appears to be drawing to a close, something is nagging at Suzanna's gut. What could they have missed?

The Glass is the first book in the DCI Suzanna McLeod crime-fighting series. If you like fast-moving police investigations, engaging characters, action and twists along the way, you'll love Harry Navinski's fresh crime novel.

'Harry Navinski tells a tale that holds the reader's attention, with interest, drama and bonus pieces of very usual information. In many ways this book is more than a good fictional story. There are gems within.'

'I can't wait for the next book to be released.'

'loved the way this book was written.'

'enjoyed this book from beginning to end, the pace picking up as the book progressed.'

'I could easily see it made into a TV series.'

Buy *The Glass* today, to uncover the twists and turns of this exciting fresh crime-fighting series.

The Test

A dying man wants his estate to be won by merit, not gained by undeserved inheritance. He writes a Sherlock Holmes-style short crime story as a test to be taken by descendants as they turn eighteen.

In the story, consulting detective, Silvester Locke-Croft, is called in to investigate the murder of a solicitor in 1920s London, uncovering hidden evidence and revealing the incompetence of Scotland Yard's detectives. His investigation concludes with dramatic exposure of the murderer, revealing corruption and collusion along the way.

The Test precedes the revelation in *The Glass,* of DCI Suzanna McLeod's inheritance and career choice, followed up in *The Duty* – the second in this 21st Century police mystery series.

Buy *The Test* today, for an insight into 1920s London crime and Suzanna McLeod's backstory or get it as a free eBook at www.harry-navinski.com.

The Duty

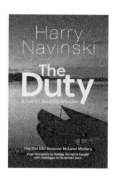

A near-naked young woman's body is found on Queensferry's riverbank. But who is she and who dumped her in the water?

A colleague is knifed but the suspect is elusive.

Edinburgh's top detective, DCI Suzanna McLeod, has a murder and a stabbing to investigate, taking her from the River Forth to the Ganges. Illegal immigration, slavery and brutality surface as she tracks down the culprits and handles her nit-picking boss, calling on all her mental and physical talents.

Suzanna is taken on a journey into her past, meeting old friends and colleagues and recalling the Test she took to win her inheritance which set her on the detective pathway. On the journey, her focus is challenged by a complex love life that makes her feel like a teenager again.

The Duty is second in the DCI Suzanna McLeod crime-fighting series. If you like fast-moving complex investigations, battles with criminals and engaging characters you'll love Harry Navinski's latest crime novel.

Buy *The Duty* today to join in the excitement of the chase in tropical Bengal.

Five Stars. *'It drew me in from the first page and didn't let go until the end and left me wanting more, a definite must read.'* Cheryl N.

For me, it was a very interesting, informative and yet suspense filled read, an eye opener to another world really, which left me desperate at the end of the book for the next one in the series. TallullahBelle.

Printed in Great Britain
by Amazon